THE NEMESIS MANIFESTO

AN EVAN RYDER NOVEL

ERIC VAN LUSTBADER

A TOM DOHERTY ASSOCIATES BOOK
NEW YORK

This is a work of fiction. All of the characters, organizations, and events portrayed in this novel are either products of the author's imagination or are used fictitiously.

THE NEMESIS MANIFESTO

A Forge Book
Published by Tom Doherty Associates
120 Broadway
New York, NY 10271

www.tor-forge.com

Forge® is a registered trademark of Macmillan Publishing Group, LLC.

ISBN 978-1-250-35674-1

Our books may be purchased in bulk for promotional, educational, or business use. Please contact your local bookseller or the Macmillan Corporate and Premium Sales Department at 1-800-221-7945, extension 5442, or by email at MacmillanSpecialMarkets@macmillan.com.

First Edition: July 2020
First Mass Market Edition: April 2021

P1

BY ERIC VAN LUSTBADER

THE EVAN RYDER NOVELS

The Nemesis Manifesto
The Kobalt Dossier (forthcoming summer 2021)

THE BRAVO SHAW NOVELS

The Testament
The Fallen
Four Dominions
The Sum of All Shadows

THE JACK McCLURE NOVELS

First Daughter
Last Snow
Blood Trust
Father Night
Beloved Enemy

THE PEARL SAGA

The Ring of Five Dragons
The Veil of a Thousand Tears
Mistress of the Pearl

THE SUNSET WARRIOR CYCLE

The Sunset Warrior
Shallows of Night
Dai-San
Beneath an Opal Moon
Dragons on the Sea of Night

THE CHINA MAROC SERIES

Jian
Shan

THE NICHOLAS LINNEAR/ NINJA CYCLE

The Ninja
The Miko
White Ninja
The Kaisho
Floating City
Second Skin
The Death and Life of Nicholas Linnear (ebook)
The Oligarch's Daughter (ebook)

THE JASON BOURNE NOVELS

The Bourne Legacy
The Bourne Betrayal
The Bourne Sanction
The Bourne Deception
The Bourne Objective
The Bourne Dominion
The Bourne Imperative
The Bourne Retribution
The Bourne Ascendancy
The Bourne Enigma
The Bourne Initiative

OTHERS

Sirens
Black Heart
Zero
French Kiss
Angel Eyes
Batman: The Last Angel
Black Blade
Dark Homecoming
Pale Saint
Art Kills
Any Minute Now

Praise for *The Nemesis Manifesto*

"[An] outstanding series launch . . . Credible action and often lyrical prose support the complex, intelligent plot. A series of twists and an extended fight sequence at the end will leave readers amazed and pleasantly exhausted. Lustbader is at the top of his game."

—*Publishers Weekly*, (starred review)

"One of the best in the business delivers a gem of a read. This one is top-notched all the way." —Steve Berry

"Lustbader is in excellent form here. *The Nemesis Manifesto* is dark, sophisticated, and compelling, and couldn't be more timely. And Evan Ryder is a keeper!"

—David Baldacci

"There are thrillers, then there are world-class, expertly plotted, thought-provoking thrillers like *The Nemesis Manifesto.* Thriller authors are probably the hardest thriller readers to please. Consider me thoroughly blown away." —Raymond Khoury, *New York Times* bestselling author of *Empire of Lies*

"Hypnotically suspenseful, rich with authentic spycraft, *The Nemesis Manifesto* by Eric Van Lustbader introduces a heroine of our times—Evan Ryder. She's deep undercover and as complex as she is exciting. . . . Lustbader weaves a spellbinding web of memorable characters, cutting-edge technology, and powerful political ambitions that could become all too real. Sit back and enjoy. You're about to read a master at the top of a very dangerous game."

—Gayle Lynds, *New York Times* bestselling author of *The Assassins*

In memory of Philip Kerr
friend and colleague, sorely missed

PROLOGUE

MOSCOW, RUSSIAN FEDERATION
OCTOBER

"I disagree."

"Of course you do."

General Boyko looked at Gorgonov skeptically. Then turned his attention to the red deer, nostrils dilated, flanks quivering, poised to run out of the clearing into the thick pine forest. Boyko's forefinger squeezed the Saiga's trigger. The resulting explosion caught the buck square in the side, lifting it off its hooves, throwing it two feet. Its eyes rolled up, its hind legs kicking still, as if it were taking its leap to safety. Blood spattered the virgin snow.

"You always disagree with me," the general said, as they both rose from their blind.

Gorgonov eyed the general's weapon; it was like Boyko to take a tactical shotgun on a deer hunt. "Not always, surely."

The two old school chums, each with a complicated past, stepped out from the cover of the pines into the killing ground.

"About this agent there can be no dissent," Boyko stated, ignoring his friend's reply.

"Ah, well." Gorgonov shrugged.

Boyko halted in his tracks, turned to his friend. "Anton Recidivich, this woman has been a lethal threat to the Federation for many years. She has stymied us at every turn, and how many of our agents she has dispatched is legion. Granted, it took me quite a while to believe a female field agent could be so effective. At first, I thought her existence was American *dezinformatsiya.* But that was absurd; who would believe such a thing? Even the Americans aren't that foolish. Then I thought she must be a front for some male black-ops assassin. But when I saw with my own eyes the results of her carnage outside St. Petersburg I became a believer. So. How could her immediate termination be a cause of contention between us?"

"You are GRU and I am SVR, for one thing," Gorgonov said. "We have different modus operandi." He picked his way toward the red deer, lying on its side, unmoving. Its eyes were glazed over. Gorgonov stared into those eyes as if trying to fathom the mystery of death. "For another, I have a better idea."

The general barked a laugh. "This is always your claim." He was a short, stocky man, bowlegged and barrel-chested. Cunning as well as strong, he had been a first-class bully in high school and college. His square face was cratered by adolescent acne scars. Possibly because of this he sported a thick Stalinesque mustache. His silver hair was brush-cut in the time-honored military fashion. His ears were simian small, set oddly low on his skull. His eyes were black, hooded, giving away nothing.

"Because I am always right." By contrast, Gorgonov had been a fencer in school—épée and sabre—and a damn fine one. He was more than a head taller than Boyko and a good deal slimmer. Being a good fencer was like being a good dancer: you needed agility, dexterity, speed, and balance. Every day, Gorgonov rose promptly at 5 A.M. for an hour of tai chi, followed by an hour of qigong. "And in this case, my dear Yuri Fyodorovich, especially so. Being a military man taught you to think in straight lines. Why else would you continue to use the same names—APT 28 and Fancy Bear—as your cyber-hacking entities? Everyone knows the GRU is behind them.

"No." Gorgonov shook out a Turkish cigarette, lit it, and took a drag deep into his lungs. The smoke shot out through his nostrils, momentarily obscuring the felled buck. "I have been thinking long and hard on the subject, Yuri. This individual requires a different approach."

"What else is there to do but terminate her?" Boyko asked testily.

"My old and dear friend, try to view the situation from a different perspective."

The general's hand swept out, slicing the air in front of him in two. "She's been a danger to us for long enough."

"But what if she wasn't a danger? What if she became an invaluable resource?"

Boyko's eyes narrowed. "Is that tobacco you're smoking or an American psychedelic?"

It was Gorgonov's turn to laugh. "Both feet planted firmly on the ground, I assure you."

"Then what the hell are you talking about?"

"You recall Lyudmila Alexeyevna Shokova."

Boyko growled. "That traitor to—"

"Come now, Yuri, whatever Shokova was or wasn't is beside the point."

"I disagree completely. She was only one of two female apparatchiks in the Politburo. Her amassing of power was extraordinary. Unprecedented, really. At every level she overstepped her authority. And then her friendship with the American field agent Evan Ryder was discovered."

Gorgonov, Stoeger 3000 shotgun held close in his armpit, gave Boyko a penetrating look. "Well, now Shokova is gone, fallen off the face of the earth so far as my networks can tell. Perhaps she's even dead, but no matter. What is of continuing interest to me is Shokova's close friendship with Evan Ryder."

The general's hand swept out again, took the cigarette from Gorgonov. Lifting it to his mouth, he sniffed the ashy end. "Why?" he said. "As you just pointed out, the sorry Shokova episode is over and done with."

Gorgonov's laughter echoed through the woods. "You see, only tobacco." He flicked away the general's notion that he was high. "But here's the thing. We can only assume that Shokova and Evan Ryder shared many things, many secrets."

"Of what use is that to us now?"

"This knowledge makes Evan Ryder even more of a threat. Who knows how much Shokova told her about the Kremlin's current and future plans."

"All right then. We terminate Ryder as quickly as possible."

"Spoken like a true officer." Gorgonov grunted. "Others have tried, all without success."

"Where they failed," Boyko stated, "we shall succeed."

"Perhaps, perhaps not." Gorgonov held up a slender forefinger. "But what if we created our own Shokova—or, in this case, Shokov?"

Boyko blinked as if Gorgonov had shone a flashlight in his face. "What are you on about?"

Gorgonov blew on his hands. "Let's go back to the dacha. I'll have my people skin and butcher the deer." He grinned. "We'll have fresh steaks for dinner, bloody, just the way you like them. And wine right from my barrel storehouse."

Overhead, birds were returning to the treetops, following the terror of the shotgun blast. Snow fell on the pines, the branches bowed beneath its weight.

▪ ▪ ▪

A murky indigo twilight had run down and murdered the ice-blue afternoon.

Gorgonov and Boyko sat at a table. Platters of venison steaks, as bloody as the host had promised, pelmeni, the ground meat dumplings slick with melted butter and redolent of bay leaf, a loaf of black pumpernickel, the ubiquitous boiled cabbage in a watery tomato sauce, a world away from the kind so familiar to southern Italians.

The men helped themselves, raking over enormous portions as they had when they were at college; in middle age their appetites had yet to diminish. For the most part, they ate silently, accompanied only by the occasional clatter of silverware against porcelain, the gurgle of Côte de Beaune poured into water glasses from the two bottles in the center of the table. Every once in a while there would be a burst, like machine-gun fire, of conversation about their respective wives and mistresses of the moment, or their off-the-books businesses, all richly lucrative.

It wasn't until they were finished with the main courses, more bottles of wine brought, along with plates of sweetmeats, including Snickers bars, a fanatical favorite of Gorgonov's, that the conversation returned to the subject matter begun in the forest.

"All right." The general sat back, hands clasped over his belly. "I have an hour or so before I have to get back to my duties. Let's hear your fairy tale." There was a smug look on his face Gorgonov didn't care for.

He rose and very deliberately poured himself two fingers of slivovitz. He drank half of it with his back turned to Boyko. Then he reached over, slid an eight-track tape into a Pioneer H-R99 relic of a player, closed his eyes, listening to the first few bars of Fleetwood Mac's "Go Your Own Way," swaying a bit to the tempo. "Do you like this song as much as I do?"

Boyko made no reply.

At length, Gorgonov returned to the table, sat opposite his guest. "The American rock group, Fleetwood Mac, was a particular favorite of Shokova's."

"Interesting," Boyko said, in a tone indicating nothing could be further from the truth.

"I've been doing a bit of research." He lifted a cardboard box stamped with the SVR insignia and labeled the Russian equivalent of Eyes Only. He patted the top of the box. "In here is everything I collected from Shokova's dacha. Well, except the eight-track player and the music tapes."

"Junk," the general said dismissively.

Gorgonov didn't bother to answer Boyko directly. "Some of what I found surprised me. Not this tape; Shokova loved American rock music. But, as it turned out, going through her papers and diaries, it seems she was a woman of great morality."

"There's no such thing as morality in today's world, let alone here inside the Federation."

"Be that as it may," Gorgonov continued. "It was Shokova's way of life."

"She was born in the wrong century and in the wrong country. She betrayed the Motherland."

A wry smile wreathed Gorgonov's face. "True enough." He produced an SVR dossier, opened it, turned it around so Boyko could see the photo that lay atop the first page.

The general's brow furrowed as he brought the file toward him. "Who's this?"

"One of the most important things I learned from my research is that Lyudmila Alexeyevna had a brother, Arkady Illyich Shokov. Arkady and his wife were killed when their children were very young."

Boyko glanced up. "Sure. She had a whole family, just like you and me. And all of them are in her SVR file."

"One would think so," Gorgonov responded. "But, no. Neither of Arkady's children were in Shokova's SVR file, nor were they in any file related to her."

Boyko's caterpillar brows knit together. "How is that possible? Your failing, surely."

"Listen, your lot didn't even have a dossier on her." Gorgonov didn't continue in this vein, though he surely could have; he had no desire to get into another pissing match with the GRU. "No, General. Lyudmila Alexeyevna made sure their records were expunged. Of that, I'm certain."

"Shokova was hiding them?"

"It would seem so."

The furrow in Boyko's brow deepened. "But why?"

"God alone knows. Of the daughter, we have no information at all." Gorgonov shrugged. "And Lyudmila Alexeyevna's nephew, Vasily Shokov, is gone. Perished resisting arrest."

"Then . . . ?"

"Ah, well, there you're looking at Vasily Shokov. *My* Vasily Shokov."

It took a moment before the lightbulb went off over Boyko's head. Gorgonov could almost see it shining.

"Okay, so this guy's one of yours."

Gorgonov nodded. "Peter Limas is a very special guy." Gorgonov took possession of the dossier. "He's a businessman in the West. He and his partner run a cyber-security company. Isn't *that* rich."

"A *businessman*?" Boyko goggled. "You're going to send a businessman in to cozy up to Evan Ryder?"

"Who better?"

"A professional *espion,* for one."

"Ryder would smell one of us at a hundred paces—as she has many times before. As you yourself said, we've continually underestimated her simply because she's a woman. We couldn't credit the damage she's caused us, we found it impossible to believe a female could be so clever, so vicious—a reaper of death to our field agents." He sighed. "No, someone *not* in the services is precisely who we need. Best of all, Limas is already embedded. He's got a legend that will never fall apart under scrutiny."

"The plan is insane. As I suspected." With a raised

hand, Boyko forestalled his friend's coming refutation. "But, all right, let's say you go ahead with this scheme, and let's say, further, that he gets close to Ryder. Then what?"

"Then he stays close to her—just like Lyudmila Alexeyevna did. He feeds Ryder actionable intel, just like Lyudmila Alexeyevna did. Only this time they'll be our intel."

"*Dezinformatsiya*."

Gorgonov nodded. "Precisely."

Boyko thought about this for some time. "Go Your Own Way" ended and "Songbird" began. Gorgonov peered at the general. It seemed that Boyko wasn't going to bring up Brady Thompson, the eight-hundred-pound bear in the room, and Gorgonov certainly wasn't.

Pushing back his chair, Boyko excused himself and went to use the facilities. Locking himself in, he took out his mobile and texted his adjutant, typing in a name, following that up with: ADD TO KILL LIST IMMEDIATELY.

He took a long, satisfying piss, rinsed his hands, and returned to the table where Gorgonov awaited him.

"So," he said, after settling back down.

Gorgonov cocked his head. "So, what?"

"So, do we want Evan Ryder dead or do we not?"

"Don't interfere with this," he said sharply.

The general spread his hands, showing that they were both open to inspection. "Now I must be off." He rose. "Thank you for your hospitality, Anton Recidivich."

"Always a pleasure, General." Gorgonov rose also. "My people have the venison on ice and packed up. It's waiting for you in your car."

"And the antlers," Boyko said. "Don't forget the antlers."

"I don't forget anything," Gorgonov replied.

▪ ▪ ▪

Unlike the Internet Research Agency in St. Petersburg, tasked by the Sovereign with spewing out both pro-Kremlin propaganda and *dezinformatsiya,* which moved around the city since being "outed" by a *New York Times Magazine* article in 2015, the home of ACT 28 and Fancy Bear was a secret so well-guarded that, outside a special operations group inside the GRU, only the Sovereign knew its precise whereabouts. Even Gorgonov didn't know its location, although to Boyko's continual annoyance he didn't seem to care.

Boyko's unit was housed in a former synagogue the GRU had "liberated" a handful of years ago. Of the original occupants, nothing remained but the faded ghost of a trial for treason that seemed to have come and gone in the blink of an eye. Of the defendants, if that was the correct term for them, nothing further was ever heard. It was as if they had never existed; efforts by their families proved fruitless, even, in the end, a bit dangerous.

The building was located on the western edge of Moscow, just inside the Ring Road, in a neighborhood of gasworks and oil refineries. Day or night, the air was murky. Often, a black snow filtered down from the factories' mammoth smokestacks, which rose like bestial fangs into the blurred sky. Ash lay on the ground, covering the patches of snow piled here and there amid the shit-brown slush in the clogged gutters. The less said about the stench the better.

Inside, though, was a different matter entirely; Boyko had seen to that. Despite being a military man through and through, Boyko enjoyed his creature comforts; he'd had his fill of being in the field as a young recruit. Under his animated direction, the military renovators had cheerfully repurposed the house of the Jewish god into a secure sanctuary from which the general's handpicked team slipped and slithered out *dezinformatsiya,* aimed squarely at America, of a far more sophisticated nature than anything the boys in St. Petersburg came up with.

His private office, though small, enjoyed the additional benefit of being within the place where the Jews had stored the holy scrolls. It still smelled of them: a pleasing combination of cloth, age, paper, and religious dust, which, in Boyko's experience, had an odor all its own, like libraries, dentists' offices, or his mother's apartment.

As he entered the building, he shook the damp gray ash off him like a dog coming out of the rain, slid off his ankle-length greatcoat, but could not rid himself of the nagging sense of unease that had accompanied him on the drive back from Gorgonov's dácha.

In the large working space, the lights were dim and indirect, the incessant hum of the anti-surveillance perimeter was like the distant buzz of honeybees. Which was appropriate because the space was a hive of electronic activity. Twenty-four workstations, twenty-four souped-up laptops, twenty-four young men hunched over the flickering blue light of their screens, sourcing code, working netbots, trolling various sites on the internet, Photoshopping photos, GIFs, and short vids. They created "news stories" from gossamer threads, as ephemeral as dreams, believable for the hours needed to get everyone riled up, start fires or fan the flames of terrorist acts, and then vanishing like soap bubbles. But these were not the only missions of Boyko's legion of online provocateurs. Take, for instance, Nemesis, his number one client. Its items took precedence over all others; rather than be ephemeral, its items were meant to reverberate over and over, fomenting the widening split in the American psyche. Nemesis's mission was Boyko's meat and potatoes, the *dezinformatsiya* the Sovereign counted on and in which Boyko specialized.

Sammy took the general's coat and accompanied him into his office, where a carafe of coffee and a bottle of iced vodka awaited him at his desk. Sammy was, of course, not his real name, which was Semyon. All of the men who worked here had been given English names the rough equivalent to their Russian names. Thus Timur was Timmy, Oleg was Ollie, Pyotr Peter, and so on. This Americanization was dreamed up by Boyko as a way to keep the men's minds focused on their target audience. He had a fistful of American newspapers flown in daily; even though they could be accessed online, he wanted his people to get the feel of the physical papers, complete with adverts and editorials and photos, some of them odd and salacious. *America,* Boyko thought contemptuously, proud to be taking part in its demise.

"Sit down, Sammy," he said to his aide-de-camp. "I've got a problem that needs solving."

Just then his personal mobile vibrated. Checking it, he saw he had been sent a clockface with no hands. Excusing himself, he went back outside the building. Every square inch of the inside was electronically monitored and secured. Switching to a burner phone, he punched in the only number in the directory. The line engaged, he heard a number of clicks, then a hollowness on the line that indicated it had been secured from any and all outside interference. He heard the voice, listened to the voice, said, "Consider it done," and pressed END. Then he removed the SIM card, crushed it against a rock with the heel of his boot.

Back inside, he returned to his desk, where Sammy waited patiently as a loyal dog for his master. Sammy, a sandy-haired man in his mid-twenties with unremarkable features and a remarkable mind, held the rank of captain in the GRU, though no ranks were ever used inside the building. Tall and somewhat gangly, Sammy folded himself into a chair across from Boyko. Unlike his boss he was uncomfortably aware that he sat in the space where the Jews had kept their holy scrolls; the thought always made his scalp itch. He fervently wished the general had chosen another place to headquarter. On the other hand, he loved the basement, which had been gutted and repurposed to house an American-style restaurant churning out hot dogs, hamburgers, French fries, and the like during the day, and at night, rib-eye and porterhouse steaks, baked potatoes, creamed spinach, and Caesar salads. Adjacent was the cinema, which screened the latest Hollywood films three nights a week. Attendance was mandatory; outwardly, no one complained, but privately Sammy felt only contempt for Hollywood's blatant pandering to the Chinese market.

"The problem?" Sammy asked.

"Solved," Boyko said, seating himself. "Earlier today, I had the germ of an idea. I'd been turning it over and over in my head, and now you and your team are going to implement it." He poured himself some coffee, laced it with vodka, took a long gulp. "As of today I'm retiring both APT 28 and Fancy Bear." It never occurred to him that the idea was Gorgonov's; in his mind, it was entirely his.

Sammy blinked. "Sir?"

Boyko beamed. "Don't look so stricken, Sammy. I'm not disbanding the unit. Far from it." He hunched forward, elbows on the desktop. "But it occurred to me that both handles have worn out their welcome."

"I thought we were happy to have the West know about us. I thought it gave us—how shall I say—a kind of arrogant edge."

"We were, and it did. Up until today." Boyko finished off his spiked coffee. "As of now, we're starting a new phase of our cyber-warfare against the United States. We began our initiative to obscure the truth, to present a confusing array of alternate truths that would appeal to fringe groups. People believe what suits their prejudices best. We have achieved that goal. But that was only phase one. I want everything purged as if it had never existed. Give me an update on the new generation of bots."

Sammy made an internal call, spoke softly for a moment, then listened. "They're almost through testing them, sir," he told Boyko.

These bots had AI brains. They could evade spam filters, CAPTCHAs, anti-malware programs, and the like.

"Excellent," Boyko replied. "How soon until they can be deployed?"

Again, Sammy communicated with the IT team. "Five hours, sir. Maybe six."

"Tell them they have three, not a moment more. Otherwise they're all purged from the unit." The general checked his watch as Sammy relayed his order over the phone. "By two this afternoon I want them deployed—an army of them," he resumed. "They're to be programmed to create several million new IP addresses from which we will rotate our outgoing *dezinfortmatsiya*."

Sammy nodded. "Yes, sir. And then what?"

"And then we're going to use the new netbot—let's call it Soul Searcher—to target Benjamin Butler," General Boyko said. "Never heard of him, right? Neither has ninety-nine percent of the GRU and the FSB. Nevertheless, he runs the blackest of black shops for the American DOD—very smart, very skilled. Being Jewish, he's also vulnerable. Keeping in mind the motto of the sheep we're targeting, 'Stupidity Is Power,' we'll tar Butler with fascist and socialist tags because our targets don't know the difference. We'll dox him as a man of loose morals, a security risk, a closet homosexual, and everything else in our malicious intent arsenal." Doxing was an internet-based term, a method of broadcasting toxic private and/or fake information about a person through social engineering.

"And why are we targeting this Benjamin Butler? So he's a Jew, but is he a Zionist?"

"Not as far as I know, but perhaps we'll make him one of those scum as well!" Boyko said jovially. "We'll create a false narrative, turn it into a conspiracy theory; our targets love nothing better than a conspiracy theory—they cleave to those like remoras to a shark." Boyko sat back, hands locked behind his head. He was going directly against Gorgonov's wishes, which was also the point. "However, Sammy, the real reason we're targeting him is that he's a good friend of Evan Ryder." Gorgonov's plan was pitiable. Boyko wanted Evan Ryder dead. Period. Dead stop. "He's the bait we're going to use to catch Ryder and kill her."

PART ONE

DECEMBER

TWO RAVENS

1

Evan Ryder hated Washington. Like Hollywood, it was ruled by greed and fear. The frenzied stench of self-perpetuation was a smog that never lifted, even on the most sublime spring day, fouling the air inside the Beltway. Despite that, chances were it was as close to home as she was ever going to get. As someone who had lost the ability to find home or those with whom she had shared it, she supposed DC's tissue-thin façade of respectability was a tonic she needed to drink from time to time, like medicine, to remind herself of mankind's essential hypocrisy and the evil that arose from it. It was this evil, this hypocrisy, and her fight against them that gave meaning to her life. As she made her way through the morning throngs on their way to jobs at various self-important bureaus, she was reminded all over again that DC was like Narcissus staring into a mirror, admiring his reflection instead of taking care of the difficult business of governing.

Nevertheless, here she was in Foggy Bottom, bucking a tide of drones—suits with thousand-yard stares, talking on their mobile phones. She moved through them like a wisp, like a ghost. Her thick black hair was tied back in a ponytail and she was clad in black pants, a cashmere sweater that matched her eyes, which were the brindled color of a gray wolf, a waist-length black leather jacket, and steel-tipped ankle boots she had had made for her in Portugal. She had a wide mouth and an athlete's body, compact, wide at the shoulders, narrow at the hips. At restaurants, sometimes, and if the diners were drunk, she would get mistaken for Emily Blunt, or, if drunker still, Katy Perry. But only sometimes. Mainly, no one paid her the slightest attention.

Benjamin Butler was the reason she was here. Butler was perhaps the only person in DC who could command her immediate attention; his briefs kept her in the field, doing what she wanted to do, what she needed to do. Evan and Butler had worked together as field agents some years ago and they had a complex, intimate history from those days. Now Butler was a director, and Evan's boss. A dyed-in-the-wool field agent, she was fine with that. Butler was one of the only two people alive whom Evan trusted; the handful of others were all dead.

Butler and Evan worked for the DOD—in a black-ops shop whose yearly budget was appropriated from one of several Pentagon slush funds, without oversight from Congress. Who Butler reported to Evan couldn't say; she knew only that whoever it was, was very high up in the DOD food chain. For that reason alone, Butler would have been feared throughout the clandestine community. Add to this his fierce personality, indomitable spirit, and uncanny ability to ferret out the bad apples, no matter how deeply embedded, and he should have been feared by everyone in the CI community. The reason he wasn't was simple: unlike any other of his colleagues, Butler trained and deployed a good number of female field agents, whereas other clandestine agencies deployed none. He was alone in understanding, as his Russian counterparts did, that females could extract intel more often than male agents, and more of it to boot. Females were considered circumspect, and could play off men's weakness for sex, love, and affection, which, most often, considering their profession, they failed to get from their wives—if they had wives, or ex-wives.

Butler, having moved from his original, inadequate quarters near the NSA, was now installed on the eighth floor of a massive white-brick residential building whose façade was slightly curved to accommodate a semi-circular drive with a porte cochere, which allowed its tenants to delude themselves into believing they were living in a Southern mansion.

True to the neighborhood's name, tendrils of fog accompanied Evan into the chandeliered lobby. Massive leather chairs and settees were ranged along the walls, below painted scenes of old-school foxhunts. Evan would have found it amusing except for the fact that everyone in the lobby was as grim-faced as gargoyles.

Stepping to the majordomo's high banc, she showed credentials identifying her as Louise Steadman, Consultant. What she consulted on wasn't enumerated and wasn't queried. She asked for Paul Roswell and, after a brief exchange on the house phone, was handed a magnetic card and directed to a bank of elevators across the marble lobby. Waving the card over the reader caused the floor buttons to light up. She pressed eight, and was whisked silently up.

"Paul Roswell" had had the entire eighth floor remade into a vast complex of rooms. The remodeling was so new she could smell the paint and corner sawdust that, here and there, had yet to be vacuumed up. The low staticky hum of electronics filled the air.

Apart from Brenda Myers, her honey-colored hair shorter and straighter than when Evan had last seen her, there were very few people in evidence. Brenda stuck out her hand for Evan to shake briefly. It was cool, dry, and hard.

"You're looking good, Evan," Brenda said as they crossed from room to room—there were no doors that Evan could see.

"Thank you. You too. Working for Ben keeps one in shape, doesn't it?" She smiled.

She liked Brenda, felt badly that they'd never had a chance to go to dinner and let their hair down. But then again, in the shadow world they both inhabited, confiding in anyone was not a good idea. As always Brenda was dressed in a pantsuit that was as stylish as it was practical. It was as if she used her style sense as an antidote to her bland, old-fashioned name. And this dichotomy brought up an echo in Evan's mind, a slippery sense that there was much more to Brenda than she showed on the surface. People went into intelligence fieldwork for any number of reasons—they were misfits, deeply unhappy, sociopaths—but most often, it was because they were running from something, possibly themselves. This last, she intuited, might be true for Brenda.

"Are you going mad yet?" Evan asked.

"Huh! Not yet. Not quite."

"Won't be long now, I imagine," Evan said. "Unless he gets you back out in the field."

"Any day now."

Brenda left her without another word at the threshold to Butler's office. Evan stepped into a large room that might once have been one of the eighth-floor apartments' master bedroom suites. It was saturated with light, but of a curious blue-green hue, as if she and Butler were submerged in a fish tank. She glanced at the window glass: bulletproof, spidery with anti-eavesdropping networks. Even though this location was well-hidden, Evan saw that he was taking no chances. She approved; but then she pretty much approved of everything Butler did.

He rose the instant she entered, coming around from behind his desk to meet her halfway across the room. He wore a dark-blue suit, a cream-colored shirt, a regimental striped tie. He was tall and stately. The year and a half since they had seen one another seemed not to have touched him at all. He still had the smooth pale skin and coffee-colored eyes of his Jewish mother, who, in her day, had been a ravishing beauty. Of his WASP lawyer father there seemed little, save for the wavy hair and the pronounced widow's peak.

When Butler smiled the sun broke out. "How was your flight, Evan?"

"I'm alive, as you can see."

Butler laughed softly. They shook hands.

"And how is Zoe?" she asked.

"Seven going on thirteen."

She nodded. "Then everything is in order."

Butler laughed again, gesturing for her to take a seat on one of the chairs in front of his desk. He folded himself into the one opposite, crossed one leg over the other.

Evan took another look around. "Like the new digs. Do we have an actual name yet?"

"Just the alphanumeric one, M171473-HG," he said.

"So still MI7." A joke of sorts. A play on the British MI6.

"Sure, but right at the moment it doesn't seem so funny."

Evan paused for a moment.

"Thank you for agreeing to come back to DC," he said.

"You know my current brief is at a critical junction."

"This takes precedence," Butler said firmly.

"Five months I've been working this brief."

Butler waved a hand. "I know. Turkey is complicated, and you've done incredible work. I'm grateful, as always. And I know there are a lot of bad memories for you here. But believe me, Evan, it was necessary that I bring you back."

There was no use in digging in her heels. All that spadework down the drain. *Well, it's not the first time,* she thought, *and it won't be the last.* It was the nature of the game. "The credentials you sent me made it easy," she said, giving in, but only somewhat.

He cocked his head, his thick black hair brilliant in the light. "You know what I mean."

Indeed, she did. "Your summons was urgent," she said now. "What's up?"

Reaching over to his desk, Butler slid a sheet of paper off it, offered it to her.

Evan made no move, eyed the paper as if it were a coiled cobra.

Butler held the sheet faceup so she could see it. "You see? No official stamps. No circulation sign-offs. This is strictly ours. One hundred percent." His forefinger ran down the list. "Six names, four agents who disappeared over the last ten months, one who came back in very bad shape, and the sixth is completely unknown to us."

"Where did you get these names?"

"The agent who returned had the original list on him. It's been scrutinized by forensics. They found nothing, not even a partial fingerprint."

"Not even our agent's?"

"That's right."

"So he didn't compile it. He never even saw it."

Butler nodded. "It's a message, a taunt. Just like the agent's return. That's my belief, anyway." He produced photos—grainy headshots from what appeared to be surveillance operations—to go with the names. "Three are ours, two MI6."

"What links them?"

Butler sighed. "As I'm sure you know, the special relationship enjoyed by us and our British cousins has been sorely tested of late. The hard truth is they no longer trust us, so getting anything out of them is like pulling teeth. But so far as I can make out, the MI6 agents were looking for the same thing ours were—a person, or organization, known only as Nemesis."

"What has Nemesis done to deserve all this scrutiny?"

"It controls an enormous network of Twitter bots that spew out the most egregious racial and gender epithets aimed at Democrats, women, Hispanics, immigrants, Muslims, and Jews."

"Surely you have IT people who can—"

"The Nemesis net is like the Hydra. Cut off a cluster of ISPs and seven others take their place. I mean, we don't even know whether Nemesis is a single person, a cadre, or a worldwide cabal. But because of our recent failures I determined that we've been going after Nemesis from the wrong direction. Hence the deployments of field agents."

Evan frowned, shook her head as she stood up. "Okay, but you have plenty of other agents to handle this kind of routine—"

"Nemesis is anything but routine. Evan, if you're worried that I'm going to be asking you to stay in DC and do work others could do—well, believe me I'm not." He took a breath, as if preparing himself for what was coming next. "Jules and Albert?"

"Two of our best."

"Were. Their throats were ripped out as if by a wild dog or a wolf or a cannibalistic madman."

"How do you know that?"

"Traces of tooth marks at the ragged edges of the wounds. We can't get any more specific than that. Forensics in this area is notoriously inaccurate."

He handed over a sheaf of photos taken by his forensics team. Evan went through them carefully, a frown deepening the line between her eyes.

"Ligature marks on their wrists and ankles."

"Yes," Butler affirmed. "They were bound."

Evan looked up at him. "I don't see any sign of blood. None at all."

"The coroner we sent out there told me that the mutilations were done elsewhere, then the bodies were drained of blood."

Evan stared at him. "*After* they were mutilated."

"Yes."

"So it's possible that their throats were torn out while they were still alive."

"That's the coroner's guarded opinion. And here's the kicker. The coroner found blood in their feet, mouths, and, in Jules's case, hair."

"Which means they were strung up by their ankles, like pigs." Evan studied the photos again. "Some form of ritual then."

"Ritual is my prime suspicion."

Evan shook her head. She was fully on board now. "Where?" she said softly. "Where were they found?"

"You'll love this. It's why I sent for you." He took back the photos. "The Caucasus Mountains, the ancient dividing line between Europe and Asia. Georgia. To be exact, inside a national park with the longest name in the world: Racha-Lechkhumi-Kvemo Svaneti Planned National Park." He gave Evan a hard stare. "The Russian Federation is virtually your backyard."

He shuffled the photos. "This is bad, Evan. As bad as it gets. These were highly skilled field agents, not a bunch of friends out for a picnic in the park. Racha, their end point, will be your starting point."

"Did you send them out together?"

"A month apart."

"But they were dumped in the same place."

"That's right," Butler said.

"And our third, the one who came back. Patrick Wilson—the Toad, as we used to call him."

Butler gave a grimace. "Seems an unfortunate nickname now. Save for being thinner and suffering from dehydration and exposure, he came back unharmed . . . physically. On the surface, at least."

"How is that?"

"Unknown. He won't see a psychologist or even a PTSD doctor, but something major is clearly wrong. Maybe you can . . . You should visit him before you head off to Georgia. He knows you. I think it would be instructive."

"And?" She rose and stepped toward the doorway. "With you there's always an 'and.'"

The ghost of a smile played across Butler's lips. "Take Brenda with you."

"You know I work better alone."

"You and Brenda have history, an excellent rapport. I'm not sending another lone agent out on this."

Butler rose as well, crossed to where she stood, still holding the paper. "The two names below our people are the MI6 agents."

Dropping her eyes, Evan looked at the list. "Have they been found?"

"Not as of today. No word from them. Nothing."

"And the sixth name?" She stared past the page to Butler's expression. "Charles Isaacs?"

"As I said, there's no info on him. None at all. He's a blank slate, a tabula rasa." His gaze turned searching. "Charles Isaacs is a legend. A manufactured identity. Must be. He's a complete enigma." He put the list aside. "One thing I have been able to determine absolutely is he's not one of ours. And I've checked with our cousins across the pond. As I said, we're not so friendly these days, but I have a few personal friends, and we still trust one another. He's not one of theirs, either. And, of course, they're intensely interested as to what happened to their two MIA agents."

"Isaacs belongs to an agency that Nemesis is out to eliminate," Evan said. "Which could mean Isaacs is an ally of ours."

"Possibly, but he could also be Russian, Interpol, or anything else, for that matter." Butler was looking more and more troubled. "As yet, we don't know Nemesis's goal, which is why we need to be extremely vigilant."

"You're sending us out on a fact-finding mission?"

"That's a Nemesis kill list, Evan, one that's destroyed the lives of three of our agents, and maybe two of theirs." He waved the sheet of paper. "This is not simply another group of netbot trolls. It's not just another terrorist organization. Nemesis is targeting Western clandestine agents. My intuition told me that you were the right one for the job. The *only* one."

Out of the corner of her eye, Evan noted Brenda standing in the doorway, silent as a shadow. How much had she heard? How much did she know?

"Go see Patrick Wilson, Evan." Butler stepped closer, gripped her arm briefly. "See if you can find out what the hell has happened to him." He nodded in Brenda's direction. "She's ready, Evan. Are you?"

2

Evan, staring out the side window of the armored black Chevy Tahoe, was reminded of her history with Butler, of their work together in the field, and of the one time they had succumbed to the pain and loss that work sometimes rained down on them, and had had frenetic, sweaty comfort sex all night long in an anonymous hotel room in Berlin. She had made such poor decisions when it came to men. But none worse than Josh, to whom she had willingly given her heart, only to have him crush it. "*I thought our love was forever,*" she had said stupidly, naïvely. Only to have him respond: "*Forever is fungible.*" He was a high-powered lawyer. "*I live in the moment and each succeeding moment changes.*" It was positively, absolutely the worst, cruelest breakup, one she never in a million years could have imagined. A breakup that even to this day, four years later, made her feel as if she had been shot through the heart.

"How bad is the Toad?" she asked, trying to bring herself back to the present. *I live in the moment and each moment changes.*

"I think that's for you to decide," Brenda said, maneuvering deftly through the traffic flow. "And by the way, thanks for that vote of confidence."

Evan ignored her gentle dig. "But you've seen him—Wilson."

"Afterward, I had nightmares for two nights running."

Evan glanced at her. "That bad."

Brenda shivered. Evan had seen Brenda on the field of battle, how fearless she was, and this made her wonder what was awaiting her in the Toad's hospital room. Then she turned back to the window, her head filled with Butler. Their shared past was why she was here, why she had acquiesced to his request to come on board when he was given his own shop. He understood her. Understood her need to stay away from DC, her desire to have no permanent home, but rather live wherever her briefs took her. And it was imperative that she work, stay occupied, although it certainly wasn't for the salary he paid her. She had long ago stashed away money—as well as other practical items—in a Cayman Islands account. More than she could ever spend in a lifetime. But then again she wasn't a spender, material things had little meaning for her. She wasn't, she reflected, much of anything. She was like a ghost, a walking, talking shell that every once in a while sprang into action, afterward retreating to her own netherworld, untouched, untouchable. That was the way she needed it, or, in any case, wanted it. She had learned over and over again that being intimate with others brought only misery, betrayal, and death.

Amid this wasted landscape there was Butler, always Butler, who lived in the shadowed margins as she did. And yet somehow he still managed to love his daughter, to be a good father. To be a complete human being. She envied him that, but she didn't understand it.

They crossed the Potomac into Virginia. For the next twenty minutes Brenda took them south by southwest, along a highway, before exiting onto a secondary road, passing by tony enclaves of large homes, guarded, set off, an all too regular sign of nervousness and paranoia. Not long after they'd passed a large shopping center, the road went from a four-lane blacktop to a two-lane rural byway. There were no signs, no markers in this part of Virginia's rolling hills, but Brenda obviously knew the way as she slowed and turned left onto an easily missable crushed stone lane.

"We're here," she said after a several bumpy minutes, pulling up before the entrance to a gated area that included a main building parking lot and heavily manicured grounds.

Brenda slid down her window, handed over a pair of ID passes. The guard checked them, peered in at her and at Evan, then nodded, handed them back.

"Spot 11," he said, handing her an official slip. "Place this on the dash before you leave the vehicle." The gates swung open, and Brenda eased the car along a wide paved drive bordered with cherry trees, bare now in their winter sleep. Ahead of them was a large, perfectly anonymous-looking structure, similar to other hospitals Evan had seen.

Brenda pulled the Tahoe into Spot 11, between a green Jaguar and a white Nissan Altima. As they got out, the chill air hit Evan's face. She followed Brenda up the gold-veined granite steps to the entrance with its seeing-eye glass doors. There was no signage, no indication whatsoever as to what the building housed.

"Butler said this used to be called St. Agnes Charity Hospital," Brenda said over her shoulder, "before it fell into disrepair and the feds bought it dirt cheap."

They passed through the sliding electronic-eye doors. Showing their credentials at the front desk, they were assigned a nurse, who arrived at speed and walked them briskly down a carpeted hallway lined with closed doors, wood panels, and abstract paintings so generic they might have been Rorschach test rejects. The light was cool and indirect. In contrast with the institutional exterior, the repurposed interior had the feel of a five-star hotel.

The Toad was waiting for them in the library and from the get-go the optics were wrong. His hair was washed and pomaded, his cheeks so clean-shaven they shone in the lamplight. He wore cognac-colored corduroys, a clean white shirt with a starched collar, and a rep tie with an impeccable knot. A black wool blazer was draped over one arm of the upholstered chair in which he reposed, one leg over the other. In his left hand he held a cut crystal glass which appeared to hold three fingers of whiskey. By his left elbow was a small oval side table on which was a cut-glass decanter with more whiskey. He smiled when they were ushered in. The nurse did not walk them over, but vanished the moment they stepped into the room.

And what a room it was. Octagonal in shape, high in ceiling, with tall windows on three sides overlooking skeletal rear gardens which, apart from several yews, were showing their winter bones. Heavy velvet curtains framed the windows. Three walls were covered in mahogany shelves filled with books of every sort. The seventh wall was taken up by the kind of enormous fireplace usually found in hunting lodges deep in the woods. The only thing missing was a mounted deer or elk head above it. Instead, there was a wall of stones on which was hung a portrait of a religious nature. Possibly St. Agnes, though whether the cowled figure holding out a hand either in supplication or in warning was female or male was difficult to discern.

Patrick Wilson watched them approach with glittering eyes. It was only when Evan and her companion neared the Toad that the illusion of normality was shattered. Wilson's eyes, once the same rich hue as his trousers, were now almost colorless. They reflected the light, making them appear depthless. And then there was his complexion, which was as pale and bloodless as moonlight, and almost as insubstantial.

Two chairs had been arranged facing him. Without waving them to sit, Wilson said, "The last time I saw you, Evan, you were a lot younger."

"I don't recall." Given the effect he had had on Brenda, Evan was determined to make this interview as straightforward and businesslike as possible.

"Ah, yes. I remember now. Forgive me, I'm feeling a little peaked these days." The Toad smelled strongly of a cheap cologne that was inadequate in masking both the alcohol on his breath and his body odor. "And looking a good deal worse."

He hadn't said a word to Brenda, hadn't looked at her, hadn't so much as acknowledged that she was even in the room with them.

"Wilson," Evan said, seating herself, "we've come to find out what happened to you and where you were when it happened."

Something akin to a shadow passed behind the Toad's eyes.

"Wilson, eh?" Those colorless eyes turned canny. "Why don't you call me Toad? Everyone else does."

"I prefer your real name," Evan said.

With that, the Toad's demeanor brightened, he bared his teeth in the semblance of a smile. This was a mistake; they looked like bits of burnt toast. They reminded Evan of photos she'd seen of prisoners released from Dachau after World War II.

"Names. What are they, really? They only mask what's underneath. The rotting self inside."

Wilson took a long draught of his whiskey, rolling it around his mouth before swallowing noisily. "Back in the day I never much cared for this stuff," he said, as if to no one in particular. "But now I've come back I've found an appreciation I never knew I had."

"And where was that, Wilson? Where did you come back from?"

Wilson twitched. "Oh, many places, Evan. Many, many places."

"Let's start with the last place. Where were you when you were damaged?"

Wilson let go a croak of a laugh the way others pass gas. Another shadow seemed to move behind his eyes. "Damaged, is it? Oh, yes, I'm damaged all right. But not in any way these quacks and cranks can figure out. I'm an enigma to them, Evan. That should be familiar to you. You're also an enigma to anyone you come in contact with. Nobody can figure *you* out."

"Just answer my questions, Wilson."

The Toad glugged more whiskey. The glass was all but empty. He reached for the decanter, Evan put a hand out to forestall him, but he batted it away. "This is *my* place," Wilson said in a steely tone. "*My* rules." His voice was full of needles as he bared his toasted teeth again. They looked loose, ready to fall out, as if he were ninety-five years old.

The Toad poured himself more whiskey. "But I shouldn't be surprised." As he placed the decanter back on the table, he threw Evan a sideways glance. "You always were afraid of the past, weren't you?"

Evan was about to tell him how wrong he was, but the image of a red-brick monstrosity rose up in her mind, clear as if she had been there yesterday. She could almost hear the ravens shriek. Then her eyes refocused, and she saw Wilson peering at her with a curious, almost avid expression.

Without knowing why, Evan felt herself withdrawing, felt herself wanting to be far away from here, as if she couldn't bear to be in the presence of this person one moment longer. She had to steel herself, had to remind herself that she was here for a purpose. She'd never cut and run from anything in her life; she wasn't about to start now, no matter the bizarre effect the Toad was having on her.

"The last place you were—the last place you can remember—was it in the country, a city, what?"

"And ravens," the Toad said. "Don't forget those fucking ravens." A muscle in one cheek began to spasm. "Where's that place, Evan? I don't remember."

3

At this time of day the church was all but deserted. The morning Mass had been given, the choir practice wasn't scheduled until 3 P.M. One or two penitents could be seen in the pews, heads bowed over clasped hands. A smattering of tourists standing in the rear. And a security detail.

"Ah, Mr. Secretary, I hoped I'd find you here," Riley Rivers said.

"You're in big trouble, meeting me like this," Brady Thompson said, waving away one of the security suits. "Get the fuck out of here."

Thompson was Secretary of Defense. Unlike with other presidents, this POTUS used Thompson, rather than the CI heads, as his sole advisor on intelligence matters. He alone had a direct pipeline to the president. He listened to others, skimmed their daily reports, but acted only on Thompson's say-so.

"I'm the newest member of our snug little cadre here in America. I have a control back in Moscow same as you."

Thompson looked to the left, at an enormous painting of the Assumption. To his right was an old-fashioned wooden pulpit straight out of *Moby Dick*. He felt a shiver run down his spine; he never felt comfortable in churches. He was a lifelong politician; politics was his religion.

"Talking directly to me is way above your pay grade." His lips barely moved, and he hadn't so much as glanced at Rivers since the other had sat down beside him. "Go," he said. "Now."

Rivers made to get up, then changed his mind, plunked his butt back onto the pew. "The thing is—the reason I sought you out, Mr. Secretary—I have an idea I think you'll like very much."

Thompson sighed. This kid was like a no-see-um you couldn't get rid of. *Might as well humor him,* he thought. "What is it?"

"OOC," Rivers said with a sly smile.

An older woman rose, threaded her way up the center aisle. Thompson waited until the church door shut behind her before he said in a harsher tone than he had intended, "What the fuck is OOC."

"The Office of Official Communications."

Thompson cocked his head. "There is no such thing."

"Not today, there isn't," Rivers told him. "But tomorrow's another day."

"Okay," Thompson said slowly. "So what is OOC, and what does it mean to me?"

Rivers told him the barest outline. "I'll need fifty million," he said in conclusion. "To start."

Thompson was on the verge of laughing. "You're out of your mind."

"Just hear me out," Rivers said.

And he did.

■ ■ ■

It was a snap for Thompson to summon the White House's director of communications. Dan Derry was a harried-looking man with thinning, sandy hair, flushed cheeks, and a mouth pursed in a perpetual expression of hauteur that reminded Thompson of the Russian Sovereign's demeanor of choice. His hands were as small as a child's, the fingers constantly in motion, drumming on the tablecloth, fiddling with a fork, tapping the bowl of a spoon against the stem of his glass, until Thompson was compelled to say, "Stop! For the love of Christ, Dan, stop." Derry withdrew his hands, held them in his lap. His right leg started to pump up and down as if he were about to jump on a bike and pedal out of town.

They were installed at a banquette at the rear of Thompson's favorite steak house, a power lunch spot on Pennsylvania Avenue. Management always had a table for him, even if he walked in at the height of the lunch or dinner hours.

The two men sat across from each other. At Thompson's suggestion they were drinking gin and tonics out of season because the place made the best gin and tonics inside the Beltway. The large menu cards lay at their respective right elbows.

"What's up with you, anyway, Dan?" Thompson said in his most solicitous voice, though he knew perfectly well what was up.

"Mr. Secretary, this damn barrage of negative press is coming so fast and furious it's all my office can do to keep the items away from POTUS." He ran a hand across his moist brow. "I'm beginning to feel like the post office on Mother's Day, except what I have to deal with twenty-four-seven is fake news. Propaganda, actually. From the Deep State."

"Condolences." Thompson shrugged, cased the room, saw a justice with his flock of clerks, a couple of representatives from opposing parties, seated on opposite sides of the room. Three members of the White House press corps huddled at one end of the bar like Roman senators in the Forum on the Ides of March. The knives were indeed out. "But what can you do except work harder?"

"We're already at the breaking point," Derry said morosely. "What I need is something to pull me out of the deep end. I'm drowning here."

Thompson picked up the menu, pretending to study it, frowning. "Get POTUS to rustle up some appropriations from Congress."

"You must be joking. What with the way the fighting on the Hill is going, I'm dreading the moment fisticuffs break out." Derry shook his head. "Plus which, even if I could get that done, to do it I would have to explain to POTUS things no one in the White House wants him to know."

This was nothing that Thompson didn't already know when he'd made the lunch date. "I think I'll have the shell steak. And a Cobb salad first," he said without looking up from the menu. "What about you?"

"Oh, please, I haven't the stomach for lunch."

"Maybe you don't have the stomach to protect POTUS from these outlandish lies." Thompson's voice was like the point of a knife.

Derry froze. "What the hell does that mean?"

"It means that if you're going to be POTUS's champion you've got to find another way."

Derry snorted. "Like what? I can't get the appropriations committee to move off the proverbial dime."

"I can think of a way," Thompson said. "A damn good way."

Derry arched one eyebrow. "Really, Mr. Secretary? Like what exactly?"

"A little operation to spread our own brand of propaganda."

Derry blew air out of his mouth. "I'm listening."

"How about I order this meal for both of us." It wasn't a question. Thompson summoned the waiter, gave their order, and when the waiter had taken away the menus, said, "What if I can get you the funding?"

Derry reacted as if the Secretary of Defense had stuck a live wire into his ear. "*Can* you?"

"It's possible."

Derry, firmly on the hook now, said, "What would make it probable?"

"You would have to be dead serious."

"Of course I'm dead serious. Jesus, man, my tit's in the fire. People in the White House want me gone. I can't have that. I *won't*."

"Good man." Thompson sipped at his gin and tonic. Patrons were drifting slowly from the bar to their tables, their conversations jocular or secretive. "You'll create a separate office of . . . well, you know . . ." he leaned forward, said in a whisper, "*counter-propaganda*."

Derry thought for a moment. "Are you involved?"

"Not at all," Thompson said. "We never had this conversation." He cocked his head. "How's your wife, by the way?"

"Betty's fine, thank you. So are Rose and Philip."

Thompson nodded. "Are you ready to move on the idea? Immediately?"

Derry nodded eagerly, with the avidity of a vulture first on the scene of a roadkill. But he would've nodded to most anything Thompson said now, seeing as how it would save him from going under for the last time.

Thompson appeared to be deep in contemplation. "Who would you get to run it—the nuts and bolts of it, I mean?"

"Well, Mr. Secretary, I'd need someone who's IT savvy, who has connections across the internet."

"As it happens," Thompson said, just as the Cobb salads arrived, "I have the very man."

4

Brenda looked from the Toad to Evan. "What ravens?"

"What ravens, she says?" Pat Wilson's smile was as crooked as his teeth. It was the first time he'd acknowledged Brenda's existence. He still hadn't looked at her though. He blinked; it was as if she were nothing more than a speck, an irritant caught in the corner of his eye. Then, all at once, he lunged toward her. As she recoiled, Evan left her seat, caught Wilson's clawed hands before he could reach her.

As Evan gently but firmly pressed him back into his chair, Wilson said in a venomous voice: "The ravens that picked me apart. *That's* what ravens."

Evan stared at the Toad, silent, while Brenda gathered her composure; no wonder she had nightmares about him. There was something seriously off about Wilson, something alien. Wherever he had been last—whatever had been done to him—had changed him significantly and most probably irrevocably. He seemed to exist in another land, unseen, unimagined.

At length, Brenda cleared her throat. "Evan, what's he talking about?"

"I've no idea."

"But you will, *Evan*." Wilson's smile cracked his face

open like the shell of a rotten egg. "It's my firm belief you will."

Evan leaned forward, elbows on knees. "Why is that, Wilson?"

"You never fail, Evan. Never, ever. Everyone knows. Everyone."

"What do the ravens mean to you?" Evan said, trying to shift the conversation away from herself. Brenda looked lost, but she couldn't help that.

"Death," Wilson said. "And another life."

"Another life?"

"The one I have now. In here. In this room. Drinking this whiskey."

"Don't you want to get out of here?" Brenda said. "Don't you want to get better?"

"I *am* better. Better than." The Toad, staring fixedly at Evan, spoke without conviction. "And, no, I'm quite content here."

"Why?" Evan said. "How can you be content here?"

Wilson said nothing for such a long time Brenda began to fidget, her hands scraping back and forth along the arms of her chair.

"Here I'm safe," he said finally.

"Safe from what?" Evan's voice had turned urgent.

"From *them*."

"The ravens?" Brenda asked.

"Of course the ravens," he spat with the same venom as before. "What else?"

"I don't understand. How did the ravens hurt you?" Evan said with grave intensity.

The Toad remained mute, but the pain behind his eyes spoke for him.

"Wilson, I need to know."

"They pecked at my brain," Wilson said, his voice suddenly silky, drifting as if on a tide of his own imagination. "As they will at yours."

■ ■ ■

"Let's stop this right here," Brenda said, moving out of her chair so that she stood between Evan and the Toad. "You've had your demented version of fun, Wilson. The time has come to stop talking in riddles and give us some straight answers."

"Listen to her!" Wilson crowed. "All cocky just like a man!" As she drew her right arm back to smack him, Evan pulled her away, stood with her in a shadowed corner, holding her gaze until she calmed down. She was clearly a talented agent, agile and quick-witted in the field, but when it came to reading people she was still raw. She had yet to learn to take the temperature of people, to control her first impulses and not allow them to get under her skin.

Leaving Brenda to consider her sins, Evan stepped back to the Toad. "You had better explain yourself, Wilson."

The Toad sighed. It wasn't one of those theatrical sighs, but one of genuine exhaustion. "It's the old bean, I'm afraid." He tapped the side of his head with a crooked forefinger. "Something rather dreadful has been done to it." His moods seemed as unpredictable as they were mercurial.

"In what way?" Evan asked.

"The ravens . . ." The glass of whiskey crashed to the floor. "Death." Wilson began to convulse.

"Wilson!" Evan gripped the agent's arms, felt spasms running up and down them as if a knot of snakes were uncoiling beneath his skin. "Pat!"

Brenda ran to the door, calling out for a doctor.

The Toad's eyes were rolling up, spittle flecked his lips, drooled down his chin. When he spoke, his voice was a dry rattle. "What . . . whatever was done to me . . . you've seen them . . ." With what appeared a supreme effort his eyes focused on Evan in a moment—possibly the last moment—of lucidity. "You'll fail, Evan. This time you'll fail. And if you don't stop, your brain will get eaten too." A gout of blood erupted from his mouth.

Then hands were peeling Evan away as a coven of doctors, nurses, and strong-armed orderlies transferred Pat Wilson to a gurney, strapped him down, and as quickly as possible rushed him out of the library.

For a long, silent moment Evan and Brenda stood looking at each other.

"What did he say," Brenda said at length, "at the end?"

Evan shook her head, then swung it away, to the view of the withered garden visible through the windows. The day had moved on; no sunlight reached the barren trees. The yews seemed made of brass. Nothing stirred, not a bird, not a breeze. Nothing at all.

■ ■ ■

Outside, they climbed silently into the Tahoe. When Evan got behind the wheel Brenda did not protest. The day was failing, the chill turned icy. The parking lot was windswept, grit whirling in ascending cones. They sat side by side. Evan did not seem inclined to go anywhere or even start the engine. It was possible that Brenda was in some form of shock.

"What the hell happened in there?" she said at last. Her teeth were chattering slightly. She turned to look at Evan. "I know he said something to you before he was carted away. What was it?"

Evan felt as if her mind and body were moving through melting ice. The hands on the wheel seemed to belong to someone else. They were frigid. There was something about those ravens.

She shrugged. "Nothing intelligible."

"I'm not so sure I believe you."

"Believe what you want. It won't change what happened."

"No, it won't." She tossed her head impatiently. "How d'you expect us to have a working relationship—"

"We don't have a working relationship," Evan said. "I work alone."

"But Butler said—"

"I know very well what Butler said." Evan hadn't meant to snap. But there it was. Pat had unnerved her—him and his bloody ravens. And now that she'd seen Pat in the flesh, seen what had been done to him, what his presence had done to Brenda, she was not about to put Brenda in harm's way. Not this time; not with what was happening here.

Brenda regarded Evan darkly. "You aren't doing yourself any favors by cutting yourself off like this, you know."

"That's not for you to say," she retorted. She felt raw, as if her insides had been scraped by a scalpel.

"Jesus, Evan," Brenda said, clearly irritated. "It's a thankless job, but someone has to."

Evan turned halfway toward the other woman. "Listen, there's nothing more for us to discuss."

"And what will we tell Butler?"

When the white Nissan Altima disintegrated, it did so in a hundredth of a second. Leaving her question blown away in the shock wave. The explosion was so powerful it shattered all the glass on the front of the former St. Agnes's façade. As for the Tahoe, the blast crumpled the entire driver's side as it lifted the SUV off its tires, flipped it over, and slammed it down onto the top of the green Jaguar parked in the space on the passenger's side.

5

Riley Rivers should have been in seventh heaven. Ever since starting his blog when he was nineteen he had dreamed of speaking to America from a national platform. But even his feverish imagination fell short of being put in charge of anything called the Office of Official Communications. What made it all the more delicious was that the propaganda emanated from various branches of the Russian secret service. His job now was to manipulate the material from those sources into salaciously tasty bits and disseminate it in the fastest way possible to the widest audience possible. Bread and circuses, as the ancient Roman Caesars dictated to help keep the rabble entertained. And wasn't that the hidden meaning of *dezinformatsiya*? To keep the other side "entertained," while you went about your deadly business unhindered.

What a world, Rivers mused now, as he stood in his new offices—a large corner suite on the third floor of a modern office building with a smart granite entrance on K Street, NW, near Nineteenth, five blocks from the White House and, coincidentally, about the same distance from MI7's new offices.

Hourly, "news" items flooded in at an even faster rate than they had before. Tweets targeting Black Lives Matter, Muslims, Jews. Items supporting what the Russians had cleverly code-named the alt-right. And today something new: the first of a number of items he would receive specifically targeting Benjamin Butler—some of the nastiest innuendoes he could recall seeing.

He rewrote this item in his inimical style. In Rivers's version, there was a certain—well, we can't come out and say spy, can we? But because we're the OOC—the Office of Official Communications—we can strongly intimate it. Benjamin Butler is a Jew, yes!, his mother was a Jew!, and he is biased toward Jews even—especially—when it isn't warranted. There was more—much more—some of it disgusted even Rivers.

This little piece of red bait, accompanied by a photo, as many of his items were, would be disseminated as only Rivers could, as an internet item. The photo was of Butler and a whole bunch of women and men, clearly prostitutes and escorts. It had been cooked up by a program known as GAN, generative adversarial network, that created what was coming to be known as "deep fakes," a combination of "deep learning" and "fake news." The process took advantage of a Google open-source program called TensorFlow, an astonishing machine learning software, to insert the head of anyone you wanted into a compromising photo or short video. The original shots, of Butler and the random unsavory folk he was apparently with, had of course been taken at different times in different places, but GAN had deftly made it seem that they were together.

Not that Rivers knew much about either GAN or TensorFlow, but through Reddit he had winkled out a kid who did, a genius and a nasty piece of work who lived for making trouble. When he found him, the kid was using GAN to make fun of POTUS. One memorable short vid was of POTUS behind a podium, addressing a rally. Someone shouts, "Raining! It's raining!" Immediately, the security detail hustles a crouching POTUS off stage. A "deep fake," but hilarious, even to Rivers. He still didn't know how the kid did it. Then again, he really didn't care. It was ridiculously easy to turn the kid from making fun of POTUS to defending him. *Money talks,* Rivers thought. *Nobody walks.*

Using both his new network and his old Reddit network, Rivers served up the item on Butler to a select cadre of ultra-left wing and white supremacist sites, and the *dezinformatsiya* was seen by millions around the world within a matter of hours.

Rivers made copies of the whole thing.

So yes, Riley Rivers should have been in seventh heaven—but he wasn't. If his life was simply to take orders from Moscow and the Secretary of Defense, everything would be going along swimmingly. But there was a shark in the water, deep down where only he could see it. This shark had him in its jaws, and its name was Isobel Lowe.

Turn your thoughts away from doubt, he told himself angrily. *Put your mind to the task at hand. Put one foot in front of the other, that is the only way to survive.*

He looked down at the street from his office window, at the pedestrians striding by, completely oblivious to how the world really worked. These denizens of the capital of the United States *thought* they knew, were convinced that they were a part of the machine. So self-deluded, Rivers thought with utter contempt.

Rivers's contempt for America and his love affair with Russia began more or less simultaneously. He'd spent his senior year abroad in London, where he fell in with a drinking crowd down from Oxford. At first, these young gentlemen treated him like a mascot. If he hadn't been American he doubted whether they would have tolerated him at all; the class system in England was still as firmly in place as it ever had been. Rivers—a born snob—found this as fascinating as it was attractive. His acid wit, which had alienated Americans left and right, combined with his encyclopedic knowledge of the American political system so ingratiated him with the rakish English gentlemen that before long he was raised into the lofty heights of being "one of them." For once, he *belonged* somewhere.

It was at an all-night drunkathon that conversation turned to the subjects of Socialism, disdain for the English upper crust, and experimental dabbling in the Russian way of life. This should have repulsed Rivers, but in fact it had the opposite effect. The disgust these gentlemen had for men's clubs, inherited stone manors in Sussex or Cheshire, regimental ties, and the strait-laced hale-fellow-well-met conventions of their parents chimed perfectly with the antipathy Rivers felt for those back home who had scorned him for his extreme politics, turned their backs on his abrasive nature, belittled him as a misfit behind his back. He wasn't handsome, he wasn't tall, he wasn't slim—that's all anyone back home cared about. Whereas these gentlemen were interested in the mind: opinions, debates, thoughtful analyses. Rivers's meat and potatoes, so to speak.

A week or two after the drunkathon, one of the gentlemen introduced him to Yuri. At least, that's what he said his name was. The door had opened into a new world—a world in which Rivers could see his future, his importance. Yuri praised his work on Reddit, assured him that the role he was offering would "make even more of a difference," would give real meaning to Rivers's life.

And so it had come to pass, slowly but surely. The Russians were fond of playing the long game. As Yuri had told him on his departure from London, "My good and loyal friend, years will pass and it will seem to you that nothing is happening, but I can assure you that behind the scenes wheels are constantly in motion, and you are a major part of that." He put a hand on Rivers's shoulder. "Patience is everything, my good and loyal friend. Patience and initiative."

There was a plan. Of course, there was a plan. Yuri loved Rivers's Reddit political site, impressed with how many members it had amassed. He communed with his superiors and they suggested one or two tweaks that impressed Rivers and which, when he returned to DC and graduated, he implemented. And so, slowly but surely, as Yuri had promised, his star began to rise above the jabbering mass of the blogosphere. Whether it was because his point of view began to resonate with a changing zeitgeist or because his posts were being favorited and repeated by the online army directed by his Russian friends was impossible to say. Most likely, he figured, it was a combination of both.

And now, finally, *this*. Yuri's advice of exercising patience and initiative seemed like the purest of prophesies. Whatever happened to him Rivers never did find out. His former handler wouldn't tell him and his new one had never heard of Yuri. Possibly not surprising since Rivers had never known his real name. But every once in a while, as now, standing in his new office, forehead pressed against the icy windowpane, Rivers could admit to himself that he missed Yuri. Yuri had been his guide through the byways and backwaters of London: beautiful girls, and boys, were Rivers's without him even asking. He was a king and—if he were to be honest with himself—a queen in the world Yuri opened for him. Yuri. His good and loyal friend. Now gone and, his missions completed, forgotten. Except by Rivers himself, who remembered him with a fondness he had never felt for anyone else.

Moments later, he left the office, locking the door behind him. As he exited the building, he was approached by a middle-aged man in a long coat and dark glasses. Rivers had been around long enough to know security when he saw it.

"Mr. Rivers." It was not a question.

Rivers nodded. There was nothing else for him to do.

"Please come this way."

The man gestured, leading Rivers across the pavement to a waiting SUV with black-out windows. It was a cherry-red Toyota Land Cruiser, which meant it wasn't government-issue. But Rivers had already figured out that this security guy was private. He had a massive body and hair down to his shoulders: also not government-issue. Besides, Rivers had the sneaking suspicion he'd seen this hulk before.

He wasn't wrong about that, as it turned out.

"Hello, Riley," a warm female voice said.

The car's interior was a whisper, in contrast to the exterior that was more of a shout.

Rivers sat down beside the willowy woman with devilish tawny eyes and an enigmatic smile.

"Always good to see you, Isobel. To what do I owe this pleasure?"

Leaning forward, Isobel Lowe gave a destination address to the driver in a voice too muted for Rivers to hear. She was dressed mostly in black: a stylish wool coat over a charcoal-gray cowl-necked sweater and a black pencil skirt. On her feet were sky-high-heel Louboutin pumps, also black. A wide leather belt cinched her waist; a thin gold chain gleamed in the valley between her breasts.

"You don't look like you're on your way to your office. Where's your veil?" he said with a short laugh that held a note of trepidation. He was afraid of Isobel Lowe, not without just cause.

She gave him a wide-eyed stare. "I'm dressed appropriately to the moment."

Rivers did not know what that meant, and he wasn't at all certain he wanted to ask, so he kept his yap shut, not the easiest thing for him to do.

"I understand you've moved up in the world," she said in that languid voice that seemed to drip honey.

"And that interests you why?" Rivers did not mean for that to come out snarky, but even he noticed the sharp edge to his words. He didn't like being picked up off the street, but truth be told Isobel frightened him deep down where he was reluctant to look.

"If I've intruded," Isobel murmured, "then I apologize."

Rivers was startled. "I've never heard you apologize before—about anything."

"Well, I imagine there's a first time for everything." Her wide lips curved in her enigmatic smile. "Speaking of which, there's a reason I'm dressed all in black. I'm happy to see you in dark clothes because we're attending a funeral."

▪ ▪ ▪

Rivers, at a loss for words, said nothing more until they arrived at the cemetery. Apparently, it was to be a graveside service, becoming more and more common in these days of human brains being relentlessly rewired by the internet. It seemed that few people had the time or the inclination for a church service, followed by a burial service anymore. Frankly, Rivers couldn't blame them.

The cemetery was in Maryland, a rather beautiful spot with old trees and an old-fashioned air of rectitude. The day was cold and clear. Here and there clouds raced across the sky. The wind was up, ruffling their hair as they stepped from the Land Cruiser.

"So who died?" he asked.

"A woman named Yana Bardina."

"Never heard of her."

They began to walk, following the lines of people, moving like ants toward a single shared goal.

"She was thirty-four." She turned to Rivers. "Aren't you thirty-four, Riley?"

His brows knit together. "What of it?"

"Shhh," she whispered. They had come upon the gravesite in far shorter time than Rivers had expected.

They stood side by side, hands clasped in front of them, heads slightly bowed, like all the others. A toddler started to fidget, then cry. His mother scooped him up and walked a distance away, doing her best to soothe him. Rivers wondered whether it was a good idea to bring children of any age to a gravesite. What did they know, or want to know, of death?

Rivers spent the next twenty minutes or so tuning out the droning of the priest or the pastor or whatever he was. Ditto, the eulogies given by the deceased's brother, aunt, and mother. The upwelling of grief was positively stifling, as if it wanted to wring the life out of the afternoon. Rivers, for the first time in his life claustrophobic in the outdoors, kept wondering what the hell he was doing here. Why had she brought him here of all places? He began to fidget just like the toddler had earlier on, until Isobel cast a basilisk look his way. His anger, which he had kept in check, began to bubble up. The damn thing finally came to an end, and he was on the verge of turning on his heel and walking away when he noticed Isobel's attention had been diverted. She was looking at a man across from them. His head was down; he seemed to be looking at the ground between his feet. A moment later, her eyes returned to the open grave. At last, the crowd broke up, the mourners making their slow, sorrowful way back to their cars and, in the family's case, limo.

"Can we go now?" he said, and hated himself for saying it, as if he were a child whining at his mother.

"Not yet."

Now the anger took him full bore. His face flushed pink and he said, "You can stay as long as you like, but as for me—"

Isobel said nothing. She didn't have to. Clamping his wrist with her slender fingers, she held him fast. She was freakishly strong, Rivers thought, as he finally stopped squirming.

"Then tell me why—?"

"Patience, Riley." She shot him another look. "You must have at least a bit of it left from your Russian masters, you man-child of the digital world."

He should have been stung by her words, but, curiously, he wasn't. She wasn't wrong to call him that; it's what he was, after all.

Once she felt him settle down, she said, "This woman moved in powerful circles inside the Beltway. She knew men in ways you could not even imagine. She gained their trust and she learned their secrets."

They were alone at the gravesite now. Even the family had departed. All the tears had been shed, all the sorrow was in the ground with the casket. The claustrophobia was lifting, but he needed to put some distance between himself and the hole in the ground. Some paces away, the gravediggers were waiting for these last two mourners to leave. Instead of turning away, Isobel moved them closer to the open grave, at the bottom of which the polished cherrywood casket was lying. As she did so, she raised her free arm, silently beckoned the workers to finish their job. Gratefully, they complied.

As they watched the grave being filled, Riley said, "What was she to you?"

"A friend." Isobel's smile had turned crooked, an expression Rivers had never seen on her before. She gestured, still holding him tight. "When Yana came it was because she was frightened. It was to tell me things, secrets that were eating her up inside. She trusted me completely."

"Why would she do that, a woman like her?"

"First, I was a woman. Second, I didn't judge her. All her trainers, all her handlers were men, and they treated her like shit. She learned, did what they asked, pleased them simply because she was used to eating shit. She didn't know any better. I tried to show her there was another way, I tried to save her."

"Save her from what?"

Isobel, abruptly lost in thought, seemed not to have heard him. The rhythmic sound of the shoveling was like the ticking of an enormous clock. "Let me tell you how Yana died. But perhaps died is the wrong term. I mean, she expired, but it wasn't from natural causes, I assure you."

"She died of an embolism," Rivers said. "Her brother said so."

"Mm, yes, she did. But it was because air was injected into her system through a hypodermic needle thrust into the crease behind her left ear."

"What? How d'you know that?"

"I was informed." The crooked smile again. The casket had disappeared beneath the freshly turned soil; the burial was almost complete.

"As I said, Yana Bardina was a precious object to some powerful men and this made her invisible," Isobel continued, "but that was deliberate, her invisibility made her perfect."

Suddenly, Rivers was listening more carefully. Somewhere in the back of his mind a warning bell had gone off. "Perfect for what?"

"For passing secrets, Riley. Government secrets to the Russians."

"Are you telling me that Yana Bardina was a Russian spy?"

"That's right," Isobel said, her smile broadening. "Just like you, Riley."

6

The interior of the Tahoe was all smoke and mirrors. For a moment Evan was seeing double; pinpoints danced maddeningly in the corners of her vision. Everything looked dull and uniform, as if she had entered a black-and-white film. The percussion had interfered with her hearing; dimly she heard the wail of sirens and, closer to, shouts of human panic.

■ ■ ■

She heard her sister, Bobbi, telling her their parents had died in a shopping center rampage: men with high-and-tight haircuts, dressed in U.S. military tactical camo, firing assault rifles. Eight dead, twenty wounded before they were brought down by mall police. They'd made no effort to hide or to surrender; they were on a suicide mission. Senseless carnage.

"*Oh, God. What are we going to do now?*" Bobbi sobbed through her tears. Their parents had been everything to them. Now, a gaping hole loomed forever. Bobbi was inconsolable, an unstable state that thrust Evan into caring for her younger sister, forced her into being the strong one, the stoic one in the bleak aftermath.

She didn't mind: she was stoic by nature, and she loved Bobbi dearly.

Evan was born on the last day of the year in the Black Hills of South Dakota. Her sister had come two years later, almost to the day. Their parents owned a sprawling horse ranch and tin and copper mines. Drive an hour or two west and you were in Wyoming. In their youth, the sisters loved to explore the nearby hidden caves system, getting lost on occasion, and forever being punished by their parents. Bobbi was abashed, but Evan was emboldened. Despite being grounded, she devised infinitely clever ways to get out of the house at night and head to what she thought of as her own Aladdin's caves. Each time she returned, Bobbi whispered to her, "*My sister, the escape artist,*" in a voice vibrating with awe and wonder.

The forbidden drew her inexorably. Despite Bobbi begging her not to go alone, she could not stop, did not want to stop. She needed to explore farther with each visit, and she did, spending nights deep inside the caves, listening to water dripping somewhere and shivering with the cold. The icy chill, the darkness—with only her flashlight for company—set every nerve-ending twanging deliriously. But even that was not enough. At some point, she decided to turn off the beam of light. She wrapped the Stygian blackness around her like a quilt, and after a time, began to softly sing, "Hello darkness, my new friend," to the first few bars of "The Sound of Silence." *This was life,* she thought. Real life, not the dull daily existence on the ranch and in school when time crawled on its hands and knees. When she would ask herself, *Is this it? Is this all there is?,* her thrilling adventures in the caves proved there was more. Much more.

Behind their home the dusty prairie rolled onward seemingly forever. But forever was shattered when their parents were killed and Evan, at eighteen, was forced into her father's boots. It was too much for her, and she didn't want it, so she eagerly took the family lawyer's advice, sold the ranch and the mines, and moved east with Bobbi, first to Chicago, where they went to college, and then, when Bobbi had graduated, to the DC area. But within the hymnal near-silence of their parents' funerals, Evan's grief was already turning to thoughts of action and revenge. This was how her mind had always worked.

While she waited in Chicago for Bobbi to finish college, Evan searched for a gym that suited her desire and needs. Here her tomboyish childhood served her in good stead. She was introduced to boxing, then Eastern martial arts. She learned how to shoot a variety of handguns, how to throw knives, both of which she loved. But what she found she loved the most was busting skulls—not literally, of course. In the ring, on the mat, in the dojo, winning was everything. She took her anger and despair at her parents' deaths out on every opponent—mostly male, though the few women she went up against were hardly spared. In her quieter hours she read anything and everything: books on history, religion, politics, philosophy, shamanism. She taught herself seven languages, aided in no small part by her eidetic memory. Also, though she could scarcely have known at the time, she was on the lighter side of the dyslexic spectrum; her mind worked at about ten times the normal human speed. Clearly, these gifts were, in large part, why she never got lost in the vast system of caves under the Black Hills.

She had always had a hankering for trouble. It drew her like a magnet, and when the sisters moved to the DC area, while Bobbi was falling in love with a lobbyist and considering how many kids she wanted with him, Evan was finding her way into the clandestine services as an administrative assistant. Had she been a man she would have raced through the hierarchy like an eel through water; she was an astonishingly quick learner; again, her eidetic memory was her best friend.

She chose "the hard road," as Bobbi called it, stoically

and patiently enduring ridicule, skepticism, sexism, and finally, resentment all the way up the slippery slope.

"*Why d'you do it?*" Bobbi asked, after the fourth time Evan was overlooked for a promotion that a man with half her intelligence and skills was offered.

"*I won't let the fuckers win,*" Evan told her. "*Not this time; not with me.*"

"*Either you're a damn fool or a courageous lioness,*" Bobbi said. "*Either way I love you,*" and embraced her.

And so she persevered and, in the end, succeeded, as an intel collator, then a coordinator, where finally she found a superior who, after eighteen months of her slogging away, agreed with her assessment that she was wasted in these desk jobs. After five months—something of a record—at a training facility deep in the Virginia woods, she became a field agent. Then, and not a moment sooner, her various bosses, her instructors claimed they'd never seen her like, certainly never in a female. Each one claimed to have discovered her first. Each one claimed to have encouraged her from day one. Each one was a liar.

Nevertheless, and defying all odds, she became well-regarded inside the American intelligence community, then grudgingly in demand. Everyone wanted her. Which was why, after two years of being inundated with briefs from both the DOD and CIA, she went off on her own, where she could take the briefs she wanted. She rejected most. She had had no permanent boss, just the way she liked it, until she joined Ben's shop. She had no life, no joy either, but that was another matter.

■ ■ ■

Something was pulling her, pressuring her shoulder so insistently she grew annoyed. At first she thought it was Bobbi. Then her conscious mind popped back into the present, and she realized that couldn't be. It was the seat belt, no, it was Brenda's head. The violent left-to-right percussion had thrown Brenda's head against the passenger's side window, then bounced it back into Evan. She was bleeding from her hairline. Evan called her name, but she was unresponsive.

They were hanging upside down, bats in a cave. Her fingers felt like frozen sausages as she fumbled at the clips of Brenda's seat belt, cradled her gently as she slipped into her arms, right side up. Evan had no time to assess her own condition. She had a fiercely thundering headache, and both her shoulders ached as if she had been mountain climbing for half a day.

She was still trying to piece together what had happened when outside figures, peering in, jerked open the driver's side door. She saw then how far off the ground they were. Slivers of what was left of the crushed green Jaguar flashed across her vision.

The figures were trying to free her, but she twisted, showing them the woman she was holding, made sure they got her out first.

"Ambulance," she managed to get out. "Concussion." To her own ears she sounded like a hearing-impaired person learning to speak. Her tongue felt as thick and rubbery as a truck tire.

It wasn't until she was certain Brenda was safely out of the Tahoe that she unbuckled her own seat belt. Strong hands grabbed her as she came loose, maneuvered her out of the vehicle. It was only as they were loading her into a second ambulance that she saw the extent of the devastation. The blast had completely disintegrated the Nissan. And as for the Tahoe, it and the Jaguar had become one twisted abstract sculpture. From some angles it was difficult to determine that they had once been vehicles.

For one moment, just after she was gently placed onto a gurney, she saw Butler's face looming over her. His expression was grim, but once he saw her staring up at him, he gave her a wan smile. He said something to her, but it was unintelligible amid the shouting, the gunning of engines, the sirens' wail.

"What?" she said or mouthed, she couldn't tell which.

He bent lower. "Lucky the Tahoe was armored."

Lucky, she thought. *Very fucking lucky.*

She was being moved again, the lights went out, and she plunged into darkness.

■ ■ ■

She is being taken through the high, iron gates of what looks like a nineteenth-century insane asylum—a red-brick monstrosity, complete with turreted towers on both ends and a steeply pitched slate roof. Oversized copper gutters and leaders guard the glowering eaves as if the roof needs protection from the inhospitable elements, or perhaps from the two ravens that cling tenaciously to the roof tiles. The architectural style is nightmarish—both Gothic and Victorian, hinting at a number of add-ons over the years. Tiny windows look out over the front lawn with blind eyes, black and forbidding.

■ ■ ■

She awoke with a start, an IV in her arm, which she promptly removed. A nurse popped in, responding to an alarm at her station, and rushed to her bedside. Taking up the IV, she made a grab for Evan's arm in an attempt to reinsert the needle. Evan took hold of her wrist, immobilizing her.

Before the nurse could cry out or reprimand her, Butler stuck his head in, said, "Ah, good. I see you're awake." He stepped in. "That will be all, nurse."

"But, the doctor's orders were—"

"That's all right," Butler said gently, showing her the door. "I'll take charge of her."

"Huh!" The nurse stalked out.

Butler stepped to Evan's bedside. "You're at MedStar Center in Clinton, Maryland. This is the closest hospital to St. Agnes with a first-rate trauma center."

"How's Brenda?"

"She'll be fine."

She remembered with vivid clarity their adversarial conversation, interrupted by—She sat up too abruptly. The room began to spin and with a firm grip Butler settled her back against the pillows.

"In a couple of minutes." Reaching down, Butler activated a motor and the upper part of the bed lifted her into a sitting position. "I have a number of questions for you first."

"About the explosion, I know."

"I have a forensics team on site, so no. I want to know what happened when you were inside St. Agnes. I want to know in detail about your interview with Patrick Wilson. I know you're up to it; I know you that well."

Evan told him word for word what had happened, excluding what Wilson had said to her at the very end. That was meant for no one but herself.

"That's it."

"Yes."

"You're sure."

When she looked at him, silent, he said, "The thing is, Patrick Wilson's dead."

Evan took a moment to absorb this, to push the ghostly image of the red-brick building to the dark recesses of her mind. "I kept pushing him even after he told me that something had been done to his mind, that the more deeply he tried to remember where he had been, what had been done to him, the more his mind would freeze up."

"It wasn't only his mind that froze up," Butler said with a sigh. "Every organ in his body shut down."

An errant chill swept through her, borne on the wings of a pair of ravens.

"Evan, what is it?"

The concern on Butler's face made her feel worse; it signified a weakness on her part. She despised all weakness and, if she were to be honest with herself, feared it as well. Weakness would get her killed. Therefore, confiding in Butler was not possible. He would start to question her effectiveness and then she'd be useless to him. She'd never get his trust back. It was important that he know he could count on her. That meant keeping her mouth shut regarding whatever the connection had been between her and the Toad. Had they been in the same place—the building of red brick? It would seem so, but for the life of her Evan couldn't remember.

This had never happened to her before—an insistent remnant of a memory floating into her consciousness like a bit of a ship sunk at sea. What had happened to her in that damn red-brick building? She thought of Lyudmila. She missed her. It was incredibly rare that she allowed herself to think such a thought, to feel that kind of emotion. But the fact was that in her present situation Lyudmila would have been the one person she could have turned to, the one person who might have helped her find out where the red-brick building was, what it was—and what was going on inside it.

"*I don't remember,*" Wilson had insisted. *Remember.* Was Evan's vision of the place, the ravens, a shard of lost memory bobbing to the surface of her consciousness, triggered by Wilson's ramblings? No answers. The whole incident was maddening. And yet somehow she knew that's where Wilson had been. In a red-brick building, with ravens.

What had been done to him there, the only one of the three agents who had gotten as far as that mysterious building, or at least the only one who had returned?

"Evan? Are you listening to me?"

"Of course."

"Did you hear . . . I asked you what Patrick said to you just before he was carted away."

"It was nothing . . . gibberish."

"That's what you told Brenda."

"She's conscious?"

"She is. And don't concern yourself, she's being well taken care of."

"I want to know what she remembers right before."

"She's already been fully debriefed."

Ignoring him, she made to swing her legs over the side of the bed, but Butler held her back with a hand on her forearm. "Doctor's orders. Plus, your own debriefing isn't over."

"As far as I'm concerned it is. I've nothing more to tell you." She took his arm away, gently but firmly, eased her legs over the side, slid down until she was standing beside him. A wave of dizziness threatened to turn her knees to jelly, but she fought it, determined not to display any hint of weakness to him.

But Butler felt her unsteadiness, helped her back onto the bed. "Calm down. You've been through a serious trauma."

"Nothing I haven't been through before."

"Each trauma is different, you know that. With each one the probability of losing a chunk of yourself rises."

The red-brick building.

Leaning forward, Butler peered into her eyes, first one then the other. "Your vision isn't yet back to normal." A small, wary smile lifted the corners of his mouth. "And for God's sake, stop treating me like the enemy. I'm your friend, Evan. Let's start from that place and go forward."

She thought about this for some time, realized that from the moment she opened her eyes and saw him she had started erecting walls—to protect herself from his inquiries. It was force of habit built up during long days and longer nights in the field. Tell no one. Tell them nothing.

A veil seemed to pass across her vision, giving way to the ghostly image of the monstrous red-brick mansion, the ravens, and what the Toad had said to her at the end: "*Whatever was done to me . . . You've seen them . . .*" He meant the ravens. This was turning into a horror story, something totally alien to her. It chilled her to the marrow.

"Evan, Brenda said Patrick said some strange things."

Evan shrugged and somewhere inside her pain flared, a fiery spike through the right side of her head. "He wasn't in his right mind when he was sent back. That was the point, the warning against sending others after him."

"So, you don't think these ravens that picked him apart were real in some way?"

"No." A breath later. "I don't know."

"And yet, according to Brenda, he said you saw the ravens."

"He must have been hallucinating."

"He asked you where this place was, where the ravens were, as though you knew it."

"He was not lucid, Benjamin," Evan said with a sense of foreboding. "Clearly."

"Really," Butler replied flatly.

To forestall him querying her any further about this, Evan said, "It occurs to me that the guard on duty will have a record of who drove the white Nissan into the parking lot. Everyone's got to show ID."

"We had the same thought," Butler said. "We have him at the office. I was about to go back to interrogate him."

Evan levered herself off the bed again, slowly and carefully. "I'm going with you."

This time, Butler did not stop her. There were many things he could have said: "You're still under observation," "You need to rest," "Your faculties are not yet back to normal." He would have said any one of these things to any of his other field agents. But this was Evan Ryder. She wasn't like any other field agent. Besides, he knew her too well to think that he could keep her away from the investigation. Once she had sunk her teeth in she'd never let go. Which was, after all, what he wanted from her, why he'd called her back from Turkey. And in any case, unless he allowed her her freedom she'd make his life miserable in so many ways.

"Clothes," she said.

"In the closet. Be my guest."

She padded across the room. Her hearing, and therefore her balance, was not quite all there yet. But she knew from grim experience that would pass in hours or at most a day. Taking her clothes from the hangers, she went into the bathroom and changed out of the hospital gown. When she emerged she found the room empty; Butler was gone.

■ ■ ■

She saw him briefly, at the end of the corridor, before he vanished into a room on the right. There was no reason to think it wasn't Brenda's. She had questions for Brenda—but only for her. She followed Butler, moving down the linoleum-covered floor, silent as a wraith.

She was at the doorway to the room now, and she stepped in. Brenda was in the bed. Butler was on the door side and a tall man with luxuriant light-brown hair, fair skin, and dark eyes was on the far side, his back to the large window that overlooked the rear of the hospital. From beyond the glass, bits of treetops, bare and arthritic, appeared to reach over his shoulders. He was dressed oddly, in perfectly tailored trousers paired with a jacket that clashed and, further, was ill-fitting. A silver pin gleamed from his lapel, but it was too small for Evan to discern its shape. Noticing the direction of the man's gaze, Butler turned and, seeing Evan in the doorway, motioned for her to step back out into the corridor, where he joined her.

"Who is that?" Evan said. "One of ours?"

"He's hers," Butler replied. "Brenda and Peter Limas have been seeing each other for six months, more or less."

"Has he been properly vetted?"

Butler snorted. "What d'you think?" He gestured. "We should get back to the office." He headed down the corridor to the bank of elevators, Evan following.

She had wanted to speak with Brenda alone, without even Butler present. Was the car bomb meant for her or for Brenda? The white Nissan was already parked when they arrived, which meant that rather than being followed to St. Agnes, someone knew their destination. So far as she was aware, only she, Brenda, and Butler knew where they were going, and why. That, by definition, made Butler a driver, though the idea of it seemed inconceivable. This was the essential danger of forming attachments in the clandestine world. Those attachments tended to blind you to reality. That Butler could want either her or Brenda—or both, for that matter—killed did not make sense. That didn't, however, preclude it being the truth. And until she had some solid proof one way or another, her security-conscious mind prevented her from giving away anything at all. Just another troubling aspect to the situation in which she was now enmeshed.

7

Donald Beacum was waiting for them, locked in a windowless room. It was painted a bilious shade of green, carefully selected by a trained psychologist. There was nothing on the walls to relieve the awful color. Overhead, a set of fluorescent tubes buzzed, pitched to be as annoying to the ears as possible. Beacum still wore the uniform Evan had seen him in earlier in the day. Now scimitars of sweat stained the fabric under his armpits. By his right hand was a half-empty paper cup of coffee and a Twix bar, as yet unopened. He looked up as they entered, his eyes, washed of color, holding an expression that was a mixture of hope and despair. His expression was slack. He had the shocked look of someone who had just witnessed a life-changing disaster.

He sat on one side of a metal table that was bolted to the unfinished concrete floor. The chair he sat on was similarly bolted. The two chairs on the other side of the table were not.

They sat down opposite him without introducing themselves. Evan slapped the file Butler had given her onto the table with such force that Beacum winced. His eyes grew wider when he saw the file. Sweat sprang out on his forehead and upper lip.

"Am I under arrest or something?" Beacum asked in

a none-too-steady voice. He could not take his eyes off the file, which he assumed was filled with incriminating facts about him.

Neither of them answered him. Instead, Evan said, "Who drove the white Nissan you let into the parking lot?" Best to point the finger right away, keep the subject off balance.

"I . . ." Beacum swallowed hard. "She had proper ID—"

"*She?*" Butler leaned forward so quickly and violently that Beacum reared back in response.

"Yeah, it was a wom—"

"What did she look like?" Evan snapped.

"She was—"

"Come on. You saw her up close."

"Okay, okay. Christ, give me a minute to breathe." He worried his lower lip. "She was hot. A real looker, you know?"

Of course Evan knew. The hot girl always got through. "Age."

"Maybe—I don't know, twenty-five, thirty? She was young, anyway."

"Color of her hair."

"Blond. A nice blond."

"Nice?" Butler interjected.

"Like a model. You know."

Evan and Butler shared a look before Butler went on: "Eyes."

"She . . . she was wearing a pair of those aviator sunglasses. I made her take them off, like the regs say. By the book. Strictly." His gaze turned purely hopeful. "Her eyes were blue. Piercing blue."

"And her name?" Butler asked in a softer, more civil tone.

Beacum's eyes darted from Evan to him. "Her . . . her name was . . . I think it was Karen Park."

"You *think*?" Butler again.

"Yeah, well . . ." He wiped his upper lip. "I mean, you have the call sheet, so you must—"

Evan opened the file, scanned the first pages on the vetting of Peter Limas. British national, educated in Cambridge, worked for his father in the elder's steelworks until forming Rubicon Solutions, his own cyber company with proprietary software known as Tether that could identify the flow of ill-gotten gains across international borders. Brought it to the States seven years ago. Unmarried, no children. A success all around. Played golf and tennis. Unattached to either political party. No improper affiliations. That's all there was to the file. Bland as a slice of white bread. "There's no such person as Karen Park," Evan said, as if reading it out from the file. She didn't know this, but it stood to reason. And she was right.

"We checked," Butler said. "We checked, Beacum, and there is no Karen Park in any government personnel list, let alone authorized to gain access to St. Agnes."

Evan: "The ID was a fake."

Butler: "But I'm guessing you already knew that."

Beacum: "What? No. N . . . no, I didn't. I mean, how would I?"

Evan: "You knew the driver."

Butler: "You two are working together."

Beacum jumped as if jabbed with a hot poker: "Why would you say that?!"

Evan: "It stands to reason."

Beacum spluttering: "But that's crazy! I mean, I never saw her before in my life!"

Butler: "So what happened to the driver of the white Nissan? The woman?"

Beacum, overwhelmed: "How should I know?"

Evan: "Because you were on the gate."

Butler: "Did she just walk out?"

Beacum: "I don't—"

Evan: "Or did you plant a car ready for her to drive out?"

Beacum's mouth worked soundlessly for a moment. Then, "My job is to check the comings. I don't pay attention to the goings. She could have—"

"Right." Evan, turning to Butler: "What d'you think? Do we have a conspiracy here?"

Beacum, almost wailing now: "A *what*?"

Butler, bending over the table: "I think we do."

Beacum, coming apart at the seams: "Oh, God, oh, God!"

Evan, rising, went around the table to stand behind the guard. "A conspiracy," she said in a stage whisper, so close to Beacum that the man flinched away.

"I had nothing to do with this!" Beacum wailed.

"Terrorism." Butler left that dreadful word to hang in the air like a noose before he went on. "Two of my people—one of them still in the hospital in critical condition—were maimed when the white Nissan exploded in an act of terrorism aimed at two federal agents." Butler stared coldly into Beacum's face. "At best you'll be charged with negligence. You may still be charged with treason and negligent homicide if the patient in ICU dies." When he was certain his words—a combination of lies and the truth—had sunk in completely, he softened his tone: "Donald, Donald, Donald, you need to prove to us that you weren't part of this act of terrorism."

"But . . ." Beacum swirled his tongue over his dry lips. "How can I do that?"

"You need to help us," Evan said from behind him.

Relief flooded across his wan face. "Of course, I—"

"I mean, *really* help us, Donald." Evan's hand clamped down on the guard's shoulder. "Whatever. It. Takes."

Beacum winced again, hunching his head into his shoulders like a frightened turtle. "I . . ." The look of relief had been transitory. His face was slick with sweat. "I . . . I can do . . . that."

"Whatever we ask," Evan said in his ear.

He bit his lower lip, then nodded. "What . . . whatever you ask." He swallowed. "Of course, of course I will. I love my country."

"And what country would that be?" Evan said.

"What? What country?" Beacum's eyes were as large as beacons. "The United States, of course. What other?"

The tension in the small room was thick as a London fog. The air was close, smelled foul with an almost fecal mixture of sweat and abject fear.

Evan continued to hammer away. "So, you're telling us that you have no idea how the driver left."

Beacum stared, wide-eyed and unseeing, down at the tabletop. Then, despair winning out over his moment of hope, he shook his head from side to side.

Butler drew out a sheet of paper with a female face drawn on it by one of his sketch artists. He turned it so that it faced Beacum. "This is the woman?"

The guard nodded, grateful to be asked a question to which he knew the answer. "It's how I described her to the sketch artist when you first brought me in."

"Look at it again, Beacum. Make sure. Make absolutely sure."

Taking the sheet up with trembling hands, he examined the sketch, screwing up his face. Then he looked up at them. "That's my memory of her." He licked his lips, added: "I'm pretty good with faces. Really I am."

Evan took the sketch out of his hands, crossed to the door.

Butler, startled, said, "Where are you going?"

"I'll be in touch," Evan said, heading out the door.

8

Evan arrived back at St. Agnes, showed her ID, but was obliged to park the car she had taken from Butler's pool on the grass verge outside the gates. The entire parking lot, centered on the area of the blast, was completely sealed off. Apart from herself, no one was being let in. Or out. St. Agnes was in lockdown; armed guards had seen to that. Butler's forensics team swarmed all over the parking lot. She avoided the black site as she crossed to the entry stairs.

The front doors' shattered glass had been removed and what was left of the doors stood open. She passed into the lobby, where she was met by more feds and EMS personnel, still sorting out the mess. She had to show her ID again, to the feds, before she was allowed through.

She passed the sketch of the woman driver around, but no one had seen anyone who looked like her. She took the elevator up to the first floor, eyeballing her fellow riders, and got out. While interrogating Beacum, it occurred to her that maybe the driver didn't leave either by foot or by car. Maybe she was still somewhere in the facility, posing as a doctor, nurse, or member of the support staff. Stopping at the nurses' central station, she showed the face around again. Still nothing. But she did discover that there was a volunteer program in place—more highly vetted than at area hospitals. Still, that would be the soft spot, the easiest place for an outsider to blend in while hiding out until the initial clamor died down.

After checking all the rooms on the first floor, she continued upward, methodically searching every nook and cranny. On the third floor, she saw a volunteer whose face, from a distance, looked like the face in the sketch. She followed her into a patient's room, turned her around. She was in her fifties; too old to be the person she was looking for. With each floor it was the same, the methodology unchanging.

In the end, Evan found her in the sixth-floor surgeons' lounge, adjacent to the OR area. She was dressed in pale-green scrubs, which was clever, cleverer than a volunteer's outfit. She sat at her leisure on a sofa, legs stretched out, feet on the coffee table, watching a film on her mobile phone. No longer a blonde, she was now wearing a dark Brenda-cut wig that Evan, herself an expert at disguise, could not mistake for the real thing. That proved premeditation: she had meant to stay inside the facility until the coast was clear. A well-thought-out plan, coordinated, masterminded not by her, not by a guard, but by someone with a chess player's mind. But it was her shoes that gave her completely away; they were expensive pumps, nothing a surgeon would wear to work, let alone in the OR.

When she saw Evan approach, she smiled, stood up without saying a word, and went with her willingly, even passively, head slightly bowed, as if in defeat. As Evan took her over the threshold to the corridor, she slammed an elbow into Evan's throat, whirled, and delivered a vicious blow to her kidneys. Then she took off, galloping down the corridor like a crazed racehorse fleeing a stable fire. She was fleet and nimble, even in those pumps, as if she had practiced running in them.

"Hold on!" Evan called after her. "Stop now and I'll

guarantee your safety. If you put up a fight it won't end well for you."

Ignoring Evan, the driver reached the door to the fire stairs, hauled it open, and disappeared before Evan had recovered sufficiently to go after her. But a moment later she did, silent and deadly, a predator on the hunt, a force of nature.

The stairwell rang to the pace of the driver's heels, like a bell sounding an alarm of fire or invasion. Looking down, seeing her midway between the fourth- and third-floor landings, and realizing she was never going to catch up with her, Evan ripped a fire extinguisher off the wall, aimed, and hurled it down. It struck the stair just in front of the driver, chipping off enough of a chunk that she stumbled and fell, her forward momentum tossing her head over heels onto the third-floor landing.

"Stop!" Evan called even as she was already off and running. "This is your last warning. I'll guarantee your safety if you come with me now."

Halfway down, Evan leapt over the side. Using the handrail to swing her legs inward through a controlled fall, she fetched up on the fourth-floor landing. But the maneuver cost her; she was assailed by a bout of vertigo so intense her knees buckled momentarily. By that time, the driver had righted herself. Her wig had come askew and, reaching up, she tore it off, revealing natural dark hair, pinned tight to her scalp. Shaking off the immediate effects of the tumble, she resumed her rapid descent.

But now Evan was only half a floor behind her, gaining with every stride. The woman bypassed the ground-level door and hurled herself into the basement, Evan mere yards behind her. St. Agnes was apparently going through a maintenance renovation—the basement was a spider's web of steel and reinforced plastic scaffolds into which the pursued vanished, slivers of her appearing here and there as if through a densely wooded forest.

Climbing onto the scaffolding, Evan was able to speed along at a good clip, unimpeded by the stacks of cans, crates, electrical tools, and hard hats strewn across the concrete floor. Soon enough, she spied her quarry right below her, weaving through the worker's paraphernalia.

Evan looked ahead, visualized the course the driver would have to take in order to navigate the obstacles. Ahead of her now, Evan waited, counting off the seconds, then leapt down onto her. They both crashed to the floor, rolled into a pile of paint cans and folded tarps. Evan was on top of her, but she produced a scalpel, wielding it expertly. The point sliced through Evan's jacket, shredding fabric. Evan grabbed her wrist, twisted hard, forced her to drop the weapon. She drove a balled fist into Evan's ribs with surprising strength, dislodging Evan, then dove after the scalpel. Evan stopped her, but she slammed the edge of her hand against the side of Evan's head.

Blackness engulfed her, a dreadful nausea washed over her as the vertigo returned in full force. The ground tilted, she could not tell which way was up, which way was down. The point of the scalpel now hovered above the left side of her chest, above the place her heart beat at a highly accelerated pace. Adrenaline pumped into her bloodstream, firing both nerves and muscles.

As the scalpel drove downward, she blocked the driver's forearm with hers, used the flat plane of the stiffened fingertips of her other hand to bruise the soft flesh just beneath the woman's breastbone. An immediate exhalation came from her open mouth, and Evan once again tried to wrest the scalpel from her. She would not let go, even when Evan slammed the back of her fist into the floor. The second time, though, did it. Her fingers flew open and the scalpel went skittering away, vanishing beneath a wooden pallet holding stacks of crates.

She hit Evan again in the side of the head and, clearly seeing the effect now, tried for a third strike. Evan, the world swimming around her, just managed to roll away, but the sideways motion caused her breath to catch in her throat as the nausea returned full bore, infecting every cell of her body. Her hands shook as she struggled to her knees. As the driver rose to a crouch and came at her, Evan extended her right leg, swung it in an arc, sweeping her off her feet. But Evan's balance was way off, and she tipped over onto her side. From this position she could see blood from a wound at the driver's hairline seeping into one eye. She must have hit her head on the corner of the pallet when she fell.

Snarling, she leapt up, turned, and ran. Evan crawled to where cans of varnish were stacked. Gaining her feet, rocking like a drunkard for a second or two, every movement seeming executed in slo-mo, she took aim, hurled a can at her quarry's back. It struck her squarely between her shoulder blades. She pitched forward, caught herself with her palms against the floor, then drew her legs under her and continued on.

For a moment, the basement faded from Evan's vision, the walls seemed to implode, and she found herself on an icy path. Birch and pine trees on either side, laden with snow. Western sunlight slanted across her, elasticizing her shadow to a giant's height. A bitter wind struck her face an unkind blow. She was looking up at the towers of the huge red-brick monstrosity. Two ravens regarded her with a terrible intensity, opened their mouths, as they lifted off into the late cyan afternoon.

Then, in the next heartbeat, she was back in the basement of St. Agnes, returned to the here and now. She saw the driver desperately fiddling with a door lock, saw her wrench the door open and, with an ungainly gait, go through it. Gritting her teeth against the pounding in her head, Evan sprinted after her. Her breath came hot and fast. She nearly ran into a vertical strut of a section of scaffolding, had to duck beneath a horizontal brace in order to keep to the shortest route.

Curiously, the door was not in one of the basement's

main walls, but rather it was an entrance to a large vertical structure rising up through the basement's ceiling.

The elevator shaft.

Evan pushed the door open, went in low. But the driver was waiting for her, and kicked the side of her head. That was the third blow in the same place, and Evan went down, blinding lights flaring behind her eyes. She felt herself being dragged to what seemed to be a plinth anchoring a central housing, then her head and torso lifted onto the plinth. She could hear the ticktock workings of the mechanism driving the elevators. Her eyes were slits, her head felt like it had been torn off. She blinked, then blinked again.

She found herself staring up into the angled shadows of the elevator shaft. They moved, these shadows, shifted as if alive. The elevator was descending. Maybe it was on the third floor, maybe the second—in her current state it was difficult to tell. A sharp pain at the back of her neck broke through her disorientation, warned her that when the elevator car reached the basement her head would be crushed. But wouldn't the fail-safe mechanism stop the elevator from crushing anyone underneath it? Still, she tried to move, get up, but was punched in the solar plexus for her efforts. The elevator was closer now, moving inexorably toward her. She could smell the oil, grease, hot metal. It was oddly akin to the stench of fresh blood and burst viscera. The driver backed away, kicked Evan to keep her in place. She was saying something, gloating no doubt, but her words fell victim to the grinding of the gears, the squeal of wheels, the soft clank of the chains and metal cables singing as the tension moved them along. Then it came to her: the driver was telling Evan that there was no exit, she had disabled the fail-safe mechanism.

The backs of Evan's hands were against the concrete floor, her fingers feeling for something, anything she could use. But there was no loose nail, no discarded screw. She reached for the driver's ankle and the driver kicked her leg up in reflex, her shoe coming loose in the process.

The elevator car was passing through the ground-floor station on the last leg of its lethal journey.

Evan made a grab for the shoe that dangled tantalizingly, like a prize, found the low sharply tapered heel, curled her fingers around it, and pulled. The shoe came fully off the driver's foot and, as the car continued down, Evan drove the end of the heel into the inside of the driver's thigh as forcefully as she could, managing to puncture flesh. Evan heard her cry out as her hands grabbed at her thigh. Evan had tried for the femoral artery, a lethal puncture, but either she had moved or Evan was off slightly with her aim. Blood seeped from her wound. She grabbed the shoe, released it from her leg, and with an animal cry, drove it toward Evan's eye. But Evan had risen up, and now she flipped the driver over, reversed their positions. The bottom of the elevator car traveled the last two feet. The driver's scream was abruptly cut short as the heavy metal bottom ground down onto her with the sickening sound of her pelvis being crushed like an eggshell.

■ ■ ■

For a time there was no sound, nothing at all apart from her blood creeping from the top of the plinth down to the floor, filling the cracks and tiny indentations of the unfinished concrete, smoothing it in a dark, spreading layer, a lake reflecting nothing, only a darkness that would never end.

Evan sat with her back against the plinth, her only company a dead adversary she had meant to interrogate, but had been forced to kill. Her legs were drawn up. Elbows on knees, she held her aching head, which seemed about to explode. Gradually, as the adrenaline was used up, leached out of her system, she sunk into herself, went into prana breathing. She did this unconsciously, a self-protecting mechanism. In this way, in the utter quictude of her mind, she regained control of herself, bit by bit reclaiming it from the pain, vertigo, nausea that the blows to the side of her head had caused.

It occurred to her that Butler had been right in insisting that she take more time to recover. The explosion had done her more harm than she had at first believed. The other side of the coin, however, was that, compromised or not, she was no good lying in bed, no good being idle. She was not cut out for rest, or for resolution. How could you have a final accounting of your life when major parts of it had been ripped from you? When the people you loved most in the world were gone? So she kept running and fighting. Running and fighting.

She rose, finally, staggered, the need to orient herself while leaning against the elevator cage overwhelming. Her nostrils flared. Hot metal and fresh blood. She closed her eyes for a moment, saw a pair of ravens etched coal-black against a pure azure sky. Another intense wave of vertigo and, with a gasp, she opened her eyes, breathed deeply as she trained her gaze on a distant section of crisscrossed metalwork. Gradually, her head stopped spinning.

At length, she looked down, to take a full inventory of the physical toll to her body. And there, around the dead driver's neck, shining silver, flecked with blood, was a necklace of delicately wrought interlocking rings at the center of which was attached a pair of silver corvids, facing each other, curved beaks melding one into the other.

Ravens.

9

In a New York minute Riley Rivers's world had been turned upside down. One minute he was riding high, at the top of his game, king of the propaganda mountain, the next he was sliding down the rubble on his ass.

At the cemetery, the day had grown ever brighter, until it was positively blinding. The sky a piercing blue possible only in winter. Now, hours later, the aggressive winter twilight had descended all too early.

He was sitting opposite her in a serpent-green fabric alcove at Q by Peter Chang in Bethesda, one of her favorite restaurants, one he'd never been to but must remember to frequent from now on. He had been her unwilling recruit for over a year now. Day and night, he was aware of her looming presence. Now and again, she asked him to pass on bits of intel to his Russian masters—*dezinformatsiya,* he was quite sure, but, really, the less he knew about the intel the better. Always he felt her boot on his neck, pressing, always pressing to squeeze more of him, and he helpless to refuse her because of what she could reveal about him, being a Russian asset.

They looked out on large round tables for eight or more. Above, an airy space that rose into a kind of atrium, filled with enormous square lanterns. Even though it was fairly early, the place was packed. He picked out faces he knew from the ranks of influencers and tastemakers, Pentagon officials and heads of private security firms, all more important than senators or representatives.

"Peter Chang used to be the head chef at the Chinese Embassy," Isobel said, as drinks were set down in front of them, but Rivers was hardly interested.

"I've still got lots to do tonight," he replied, a weak and futile attempt to maintain what was left of his dignity.

"I'll just bet you do," Isobel said with a smirk.

The truth was he'd been waiting for her to demand something big from him . . . and now, he felt sure, here it was. Slightly sick to his stomach, he said, "Okay, Isobel, what is it you want this time?"

"Huh, well . . ." She took a sip of her drink, set it down slowly and carefully in front of her. "I would better say what you want from me."

He was intent on ignoring the headache forming behind his right eye. "Meaning?"

"Don't be dense, Riley. You're smarter than that."

She placed both her hands on the table, fingers spread like some kind of sea creature, an anemone, he thought, or a sea star. Something poisonous, anyway.

"I took you to Yana's funeral and burial so you could more vividly picture yourself in the same tragic state when your usefulness to the Russians comes to an end."

"But I've been most useful to them," he blurted out stupidly.

That smile again, sharp as a scimitar. He felt as if he were in a sinking ship. *Christ,* he thought, the headache picking up hideous energy from his anxiety, which, he realized now, had seeded itself inside him while he was standing graveside, and now gripped him with the tenacity of a tropical vine.

"Well, that's your perspective, Riley. But there are other perspectives to consider, perspectives more important, more far-reaching than yours." She sighed. "It's a sad fact that Yana's usefulness to the Russians came to an end. Sad for her and for her family, not for her handlers, because there's another sap who'll take her place; there always is. Saps are a dime a dozen, for the Russians."

She paused to let that remark sink in fully, before continuing. "As for Yana, maybe the FBI had come sniffing around, maybe she allowed her fear to overrun her instinct and she made a mistake, or maybe the pressure of a double life was too much of a burden to bear any longer." She shrugged. "No matter the reason, a decision was made in FSB, was executed here in DC, and that was the end of the wasted life of Yana Bardina." She took another sip of her drink. "I'm sure she had other plans for her life, other dreams. Just like you, Riley. *Exactly* like you, in fact."

Taking up the menu but not opening it, she continued: "I say wasted because I could have saved Yana, if only she'd let me. If only she'd agreed to the terms of the bargain I laid out for her. But . . ." Her smile vanished. "'I'm in too deep,' she told me. 'I can't . . . I won't . . . It's too much. If I go any deeper I'll be buried.' And in the end she really was buried, Riley. As you saw with your own eyes.

"And so we come to you." Her gaze pierced the space between them. "I'm particularly interested in the origin of these attacks on Benjamin Butler. I want you to get to the bottom of it. I want to know who's doing the targeting."

"Why are you so interested in this particularly?" Rivers asked. "I mean, what's so special about Benjamin Butler?"

Isobel's face darkened. "Don't fuck me around, Riley. Bad things happen to people all the time in this town."

She smiled sweetly before opening the menu. "Now. What d'you feel like having?" But she wasn't interested in what he felt like having. Before he could answer, she plowed on: "Why don't I order for both of us." It wasn't a question.

■ ■ ■

The Peking duck was delicious, as was everything else Isobel ordered for them. One thing you could say in her favor: she had impeccable taste in just about everything. For some reason, perhaps the simple hominess of the act, eating settled him down somewhat. *Maybe, after switching horses, this ride wouldn't be so bad after all,* he thought. Because surely she'd want to know everything his control ordered him to do, everything he then did. Yana Bardina couldn't handle being in so deep, but he, Riley Rivers, was made of sterner stuff; he could handle anything and everything the Russians—or she—threw at him.

"So," she said, setting down her chopsticks and patting her lips free of grease, "now we get down to the nub of the matter."

A tiny butterfly was born in his stomach and, rising, began to flutter its wings.

"The bargain," Rivers said. "The terms of the bargain."

"Correct."

She sat back, regarded him so coolly and with such concentration that he felt like a horse being considered for sale. Or a servant.

"First," she began, "I want to know everything your control gives you on Benjamin Butler. Specifically, I want to know why he's being targeted. Second, I want to know everything your control gives you the moment you receive it."

The shock showed on Rivers's face. "Everything?"

"You'd make a lousy poker player, Riley." She covered her mouth with her napkin as a small, ladylike burp burbled up.

"I don't think I can—"

"Of course you can," she said. "Of course you will. Do you want to end up like Yana, or perhaps worse, in federal custody, branded a traitor? What other choice do you have?"

"Well, I—"

"Shut up and listen. Third, go about your business exactly as if this day never happened."

Riley wiped the sweat off his face. "And?"

The scimitar smile had returned, cutting into his sense of relief. "And nothing. That's it, Riley. That's all."

He closed his eyes for a moment. His hands were trembling. "I can do that," he said, when he opened his eyes.

"You *will* do that," she told him.

Jesus, he thought, resisting the urge to again close his eyes, behind which explosive pain was now hammering. "And in return?"

"In return, I will protect you from any and all depredations and machinations cooked up against you by the Russians. I will extract you from any dangerous situation before it becomes lethal."

"How do I know you can do that?"

"Because I'm telling you I can."

"I'm to take it on faith then."

Isobel laughed, not unkindly. "Listen, bucko, this new world we're living in is built on faith. Whether we like it or not." As she called for the check, her mobile rang. "I myself do not like it, Riley, but it is what it is. Get on board or get run over."

10

"According to her Canadian passport, her identity was Anna Alta," Evan said into her mobile. "What her real name is, is anyone's guess."

"We'll pick up that and her driver's license when we collect the body," Butler said, a mosquito buzzing her ear. "Any idea who manufactured the passport?"

"It's good," Evan said, studying it. "But not that good, so it can't be Israeli. Theirs are perfect." She held the passport open, its leaves bent back, checking the stitching. "It's Russian."

Butler grunted. "Mobile?"

"Not that I found," Evan said, turning Anna Alta's phone over in her hand. She'd wiped the blood off it, made sure it still worked. She should have reported it to Butler, but she was in a bloody frame of mind and not inclined to disclose much of anything.

"No matter. We'll do everything we can to ID her."

"I did find something, though," she said haltingly. She stared down at the silver raven pendant in the palm of her hand and described it to him in detail.

Butler exhaled loudly. "Ravens. So Wilson was perhaps more lucid than we thought."

"Apparently. Look, Ben, this woman's death is on me," Evan said truthfully. "I wanted to interrogate her."

For a time, Butler was silent. She sat on the edge of a bed in the ER of the hospital where she had once again wound up—and where Brenda still lay, recovering. She had been treated for the fresh wounds inflicted during her encounter with Anna Alta, or whoever she really was, and was now waiting for a prescription for antibiotics to protect her against infection.

"About this Anna," Butler said now. "What's your sense of her? Not Canadian, was she?"

"No. I'd make her as Eastern European."

"Russian?"

"Possibly."

"With the president's intended détente with the Sovereign, that would cause all manner of diplomatic complications."

That's a polite way of saying it would throw a major wrench into the president's initiative, she thought. Which would please many in the American clandestine services who were, to a man, adamantly opposed to treating Russia as anything but the enemy.

At that moment, she heard a little girl's high, trilling voice.

"Zoe just came from dance class," Butler said. "She's dying to talk to you." She heard the muffled sounds of Butler passing his mobile into his daughter's little hand.

"Hi, Evvy!" Zoe piped up. No one called Evan "Evvy" except Zoe.

She laughed. "Hi yourself. How's your dancing coming?"

"I'm learning to be a ballerina!"

Zoe sounded so much more grown up than the last time they had spoken a year ago. "You must tell me when your next recital is and I'll try my best to come to it."

"Oh, that would be super! But it's not until March." She took a breath. "So when am I going to see you?"

"Soon, honey. Soon as I can work out a date with your dad. Okay?"

"I miss you."

"I miss you, too. Now let me talk to your father."

The mobile was dutifully passed back to Butler. "She does miss you. God knows why."

"You know why."

Silence for a time. They both knew why. Zoe loved her. Improbably, she'd become a mother figure.

"Where are you now?" Butler said, wrenching Evan back to work.

"Getting mended. How's Brenda?"

He paused a moment, which was unlike him. "Her injuries are more serious than yours."

"How bad?"

"She's a strong girl."

"That's not an answer."

"You'll bounce back in no time. It's possible she will, too."

Just then, she spotted Peter Limas, Brenda's boyfriend, passing the ER room on his way to the parking lot. She glanced at her watch: 6:30. Limas had been with Brenda all day. That was devotion.

Evan made a quick decision. "Okay. I'll keep clear for now." She slid off the bed; no time to wait for the antibiotics. "But keep me informed on her progress."

"Of course. Go back to the hotel. Eat. Sleep. We'll reconvene in the morning."

She disconnected, went into the corridor, and followed Limas out into the parking lot. He was heading toward a Tesla S P85D, a cool quarter of a million bucks even without the special metallic electric-blue paint job, which seemed just about right. Evan hurried to her own borrowed car, fired the ignition just as Limas pulled out.

▪ ▪ ▪

"Okay," Donald Beacum said after Evan had left. "I can go now, right?"

Butler, studying a file his assistant Cecile had brought him, made no reply. At length, he looked up at Beacum. "You went to Yemen two years ago. Tell me about that."

The guard shrugged. "Not much to tell. My wife is Yemeni. She took me to see her family."

"Did you get along with them?" Butler asked in a conversational tone as if they were friends chewing the fat over a cup of coffee.

"What?"

"Did you like them?"

"Sure. They were fine, I guess." He shrugged again. "Nothing special."

"And how about Jaden?"

"Jaden?" Beacum repeated stupidly.

"Your wife's younger brother."

Had Beacum gone a bit pale? "What about him?"

"Was he special?"

"I don't—"

"Yes, you do. You took a trip with him."

"What?"

"While your wife stayed with the rest of her family."

"Jaden and I went fishing."

"Where?"

"Alaska."

"From Yemen?"

Beacum's expression turned sour.

"You thought we'd never find out." He tapped a page filled with close typewritten paragraphs. "I'll admit it took us all this time. I admit someone made a mistake. You were inadequately vetted."

"You people! You hear Middle East and right away you think terrorist! Fuck you! My wife's family aren't terrorists. They're law-abiding citizens."

"You're right, Beacum, they are." Butler leaned forward. "Except for Jaden. He's jihadi."

Beacum looked around, licked his lips. "I want to leave. Now. I want to leave. You have no right."

Butler stood. "It's you who have no right. Jaden took you to Syria to one of three jihadi training camps. Was it Al Noor? Dayr az Zawr? Or maybe it was Abu Kamal." He went around behind his subject as Evan had done. "No matter. The point is you were radicalized. Isn't that right, Beacum?"

"I was never in Syria. Please. I was never radicalized." He shook his head. "No, no, no, no."

Taking a fistful of plastic ties from his suit jacket pocket, Butler bound Beacum's wrists and ankles to the chair.

Beacum looked on wildly. "What are you doing?"

Butler stood up. "One way or the other you're going to tell me the truth."

"I *have* told you the truth."

"You are not connected in any way with the car bomb that went off today."

"No, I . . . I don't know anything about it."

"But, see, here's the problem, Beacum. I think you do. I think you know a great deal about it."

"You're dead wrong," he said, becoming more and more agitated. "You're confusing me with someone else."

"Mm, we'll see. It won't be long now."

"What, what d'you mean?"

Butler glanced up at the CCTV camera in the upper right-hand corner and nodded.

"What's happening?" Beacum cried. "What are you doing?"

The door opened and a dark-skinned man of obvious Arabic descent stepped in. He wore a sidearm and carried one of those enormous bottles of water used in watercoolers. It was full to the brim.

"This is Abdur Rashid," Butler said. "He's an ex-Marine." Abdur Rashid set the bottle down on the corner of the table nearest Beacum. "He served two tours of duty in Iraq, one in Syria." He returned to his position behind the guard. "He saw his best buddy's legs blown off by an IED. He saw his captain beheaded. He has rage issues. Understandably."

"I don't—" Beacum's eyes nearly bugged out of his head. "I don't want him anywhere near me."

"Why not? If, as you say, you're nothing more than a law-abiding citizen, you have nothing to fear."

So saying, Butler grabbed Beacum's head in one hand, pried his jaws open with the other. Abdur Rashid unplugged the massive bottle, picked it up, tipped the opening into the guard's gaping mouth. He sputtered and choked, the water spilling out of his mouth, down the front of him and onto the floor.

"Swallow, Beacum," Butler said gently. "Swallow."

The water went down, lots of it. Then Abdur Rashid tipped the bottle back up. The idea wasn't to drown him, or nearly drown him. That wouldn't be good for anyone. While Beacum coughed and groaned, Butler went around to stand beside Abdur Rashid, who had placed the bottle back on the table.

Butler sat, thumbing idly through the file Cecile had brought in. Abdur Rashid preferred to stand, arms crossed over his muscular chest while he stared fixedly at the subject.

"Twenty minutes?" Butler said in Arabic without looking up.

"Twenty minutes," Abdur Rashid affirmed in the same language. And then: "He understands."

"Uh huh," Butler replied, unsurprised.

Twenty minutes later, almost to the second, Beacum gasped, said, "Please untie me. I have to take a piss."

No one answered him. Butler didn't even glance up.

Some minutes went by while Beacum began to squirm in the chair. "No, really. I've got to pee real bad." Still no response. "Hey, my bladder feels like it's going to explode." And then, a moment later, "If you don't . . . I mean, I'll have to pee in my pants. Right here."

That roused Butler. He went over to Abdur Rashid,

who unsnapped the safety strap on his holster, handed him his .45 handgun. Taking it, Butler sat on the edge of the table directly in front of Beacum.

"Here's the thing," he said, again in that mild, conversational tone. "I'm not going to untie you or give you permission to urinate until you tell me the truth."

Something seemed to come over Beacum, a certain hardness in his expression, a darkness behind his eyes. "Permission? I don't need your stinking permission. I'll pee right here, right now. There's nothing you can do about it."

"Really? Is that what you believe?" Butler aimed the .45 at his groin. "I see one drop of urine, and I will shoot your dick off." Leaning forward, he put his face close to Beacum's. "Am I clear?"

Something odd happened then. Beacum burst into tears. "I told them," he wailed between sobs. "I told them I wasn't cut out for this."

11

"Why did you lie to her?" Brenda asked. "My injuries aren't bad at all."

"For the time being I want to keep her away from you," Butler replied.

They were seated in Butler's office, at right angles from each other, Butler on a chair, Brenda on the sofa. In front of them was a low table on which sat a carafe of strong coffee, half-filled mugs, and small plates with roast beef sandwiches, half-eaten, a glass beaker of oatmeal chocolate-chip cookies. On the other side of the closed door, Zoe sat, swinging her legs, eating one of the clutch of cookies her father had given her. Cecile was keeping an eye on her.

"But why lie at all?" Apart from a patch of four stitches on the right side of her forehead, a bit of bruising here and there, she looked remarkably fit. "Why don't you want her to talk with me?"

Butler took up his mug and frowned, sipped at his coffee meditatively. "I'm taking a major risk in asking Evan to go where our other agents died."

"I don't get it. She's a hunter, an infiltrator, a killer. She'll go anywhere and survive. You've got to know that. But the lies—"

"Lies are what she expects, Brenda. Lies are what she

feeds on, she feels most comfortable when she's around them." He put down the mug. "So she can figure them out."

"But—"

"I have no doubt that she's lying to me—possibly to you, as well." Butler eyed his protégé. He'd prefer to be having the conversation with Evan directly, but the world wasn't perfect, not by a long shot. "I think what Patrick said to her at the end was not only intelligible but important. Something that meant something to her."

"Why would she keep that from you?"

"That's precisely what you're going to find out."

"The sooner the better," Brenda replied.

Butler nodded. "I agree. But first, I want you to tail Donald Beacum." He handed Brenda a receiver. "He's being fitted with a wire now."

"So you were right about him."

"I knew it from the moment I first spoke to him. I could smell the fear on him."

"Not defiance? Not sullen resentment?"

"He stank of it. That's how I knew I could break him."

"Clever." Brenda did not try to hide her admiration.

"See where he goes, who he speaks with," Butler continued. "He's promised to make contact with his handler, but he says he's got to be circumspect, and I believe him. I believe everything he tells me now."

"If the people he's mixed up with know he's been in custody . . ."

"That's right. They may be suspicious of him. That's where you come in. Intervene. As forcefully as the situation requires."

Brenda nodded.

"The doctors have cleared you," Butler said, "so . . ."

"Got it."

Then Butler made a sound between his lips. "I hate mugs," he said, abruptly changing subjects. "Don't you hate mugs? They're an aberration. Plus, no matter what you do with them they're aesthetically ugly." He called Cecile on the intercom. Several moments later, Zoe came in holding a pair of porcelain cups and saucers. "Thank you, *ma petite*." Butler smiled as his daughter placed them on the table, one in front of each of them. "I won't be much longer."

"That's all right." Zoe grinned. She wore pale-blue leg warmers, white tights, and a blue hoodie, zipped up the front. Her ponytail was tied back with a purple scrunchie. It was Cecile, not Butler himself, who had picked her up from dance class. "Cecile is teaching me how to play poker."

Butler rolled his eyes as his daughter closed the door behind her. "Poker! And she'll be good at it, too." He poured them both fresh coffee, spooned a great deal of sugar into his cup. "Growing up too fast." Shaking his head, he added: "Everything's happening too fast these days."

He lifted his head, a sad smile on his lips, a melancholy cast to his eyes. "You're like Zoe, you know, growing into very adult situations so quickly it's dizzying."

Brenda, leaning forward, put her hands together, her head down. "Was it really necessary to bring Evan into this? She's not really one of us, and as you've said often enough she never will be."

"Yes. I understand your reservations, but she is the one we need. I'm more sure of that than before. Our target has retaliated close to home now, Brenda, which I hadn't expected. This was as decisive and direct as the killing of our agents. If the SUV hadn't been armored you and Evan would likely have been killed. I've gone after them and now, not content with ultimately killing all three of my agents, they've struck back."

"And we don't even know who their leader is," Brenda said bitterly.

"No. We know him only as Nemesis," Butler agreed.

"A shadow cast over the world. We know only these things about him: he lives in both the real world and the cyber-world, he's made probing hacks into at least three major nuclear-generating plants around the country, that we know of, as well as our national power grid, and the NYSE and Nasdaq trading platforms. No one's talking about it, though, and they won't. Too scary.

"Anyway, all of this means the head of Nemesis is very smart and very clever, two different traits. He's super tech-savvy or someone at his right hand is. He's exceptionally well-organized, he's got a highly trained, disciplined international network; he's a murderer, he's out to disrupt the world order, he gets pleasure in torturing human beings. Nemesis is the most dangerous adversary I've ever come up against, and I've been pitted against the best or, if you prefer, the worst. Nemesis is on an entirely different level.

"He's a clear and present danger about whom we know precious little. But, believe me, if anyone can find and destroy him it's Evan."

■ ■ ■

A premature darkness had fallen over the city like a veil, winter murdering the abbreviated afternoon. Across the Potomac, the lights of DC shone—the spotlit monuments and monolithic buildings, and, above, the winking lights of jet planes gliding through the grayness that passed for night over big cities.

Evan kept two car lengths behind Limas, moving in and out of lanes, though she doubted Limas would be looking to see if he was being tailed. As she drove she considered Butler's position vis-à-vis Brenda. It seemed odd to her that he would want to keep the two of them separate, that he didn't want them comparing notes.

Evan continued to follow Limas's electric-blue Tesla S for just over twenty minutes, whereupon he turned into the parking lot of the Federal Case Steak House. Evan followed, waited until Limas had pulled into a spot, gotten out, and entered the restaurant before she, too, parked.

Inside, it was dim and swanky. To the left was a long, S-curved bar, three-deep with suits all clamoring for their bourbon rocks or vodka martini. To the right a line of lipstick-red banquettes cozied in along the wall. Ahead of her was the maître d's podium, behind which stood an impossibly thin brunette, whose beautiful face was marred by a permanent smirk. Evan ignored her, went in search of Peter Limas.

Federal Case was one of those places—a high-end steak house featuring world-class beef—to which businessmen and divorce and tax lawyers of a certain wealth gravitated with unerring and uncanny accuracy. Federal Case was not a politician's hangout, either unknown to or ignored by the federal bureaucracy and the judiciary, who were, in any event, owing to their lower net worth, hardly welcome.

But Federal Case was definitely a haven for Peter Limas and his techie pals, riding as high as they were. The four cardinal rules of the tech world, Evan knew, were 1. Keep your gaze fixed on the horizon ahead, 2. Never look back, 3. Keep moving, 4. Protect your profits from everyone, especially the ex-wife and the taxman.

Peter Limas certainly looked the part. Evan spotted him in the last booth. He was sitting alone, speaking into his mobile as if whoever was on the other end was sitting across from him. No doubt he would be doing the same thing even if he was sitting in a cubicle in the men's room, Evan thought, as she slid onto the banquette opposite him.

He took no notice of Evan, so rapt was he in the business conference that was transpiring through the ether from cell tower to cell tower, all corners of the world available all the time.

But Evan, forearms on the table, did notice: that the silver pin she had briefly observed from a distance at the hospital before Butler had hustled her out of Brenda's room, was of two facing ravens, the tips of their beaks touching.

▪ ▪ ▪

When Butler was abruptly summoned to the Secretary of Defense's office, he asked Cecile to take Zoe home, give her some dinner, and wait with her until Butler could get there. He was expecting the worst. Then he let that expectation go. Conjuring up anticipatory scenarios was not only a waste of time, it was counterproductive. Therefore, as he sat in the anteroom of Thompson's offices, he relaxed, willing his mind to go blank, trusting that in that empty space would form both his tactics and his strategy. He had seen the wretched news item targeting himself. It was trash, but it was out there in the brave new world filled with similar trash. That was where the country was at these days. Sometimes, he regretted ever returning. He might have been far better off staying in Berlin. But his rabbi—the most unconventional rabbi imaginable—had made him an offer he couldn't refuse. Besides which, he'd never have been able to run his own intelligence shop in Germany. And taking Zoe to another foreign country, without her mother, was out of the question.

After twenty minutes of waiting, the better to put him in his place, an adjutant escorted him into the secretary's inner sanctum. Brady Thompson's office was approximately the size of a ball field. What he did with all that space—scrimmages, pickup basketball games—was anyone's guess.

He sat behind a desk as imposing as a judge's banc. It was at the far end, obliging Butler to walk the length of the office over a plush carpet of presidential blue. Behind Thompson, to his right, was an American flag on a gilded pole, and to his left the flag of the District of Columbia. Several straight-backed wooden chairs were aligned in front of the desk with such precision they might have been part of a jury box.

In fact, now Butler thought of it, Thompson's office had about it the air of a judge's chambers: airless, intimidating, vaguely frightening, like the entrance to a traveling carnival's House of Horrors. And it seemed as if Thompson himself had inculcated this atmosphere. As he looked up from whatever he was pretending to read, he seemed mightily pleased with himself. King of the castle. Lord of his domain.

What a dick, Butler thought as he sat without being asked to. At this act of insolence, Thompson frowned deeply. His tanned leathery face was reminiscent of any number of cowboy actors out of the forties and fifties. He was lean, with big, heavily veined hands, and a face as furrowed as a plot of land ready to be seeded.

He rose, crossed to the darkened window that looked out over the perfectly manicured spotlit grounds. He stood there, hands clasped behind his back. "When I was a young lad, my father would take me hunting. We'd overnight in a log cabin he had built when he was a young man. He was proud of that cabin. As would anyone." Though Thompson stared straight out the window it was clear he was speaking directly to Butler. "At night I'd lie in bed, listen to the crickets chirping, the hoot of a horned owl, the occasional howl of a wolf or a coyote. None of those sounds bothered me; I loved them, felt close to them. But there was another sound, closer to my ears, that disturbed me greatly. It was the sound of massed powder-post beetles eating away at the logs. From the inside out.

"Many was the time I'd beg my father to have the cabin tented and sprayed. It was the only way to save it, you see. But my father refused. From his point of view, the powder-post beetles were part of nature. He wasn't going to kill them.

"Well, one summer we went up there, only to discover that the damn thing had fallen down. It was nothing more than a pile of sawdust. Those fucking beetles." Thompson shook his head. "I loved that cabin. It was like my own little kingdom. But it was rotten. It was being destroyed from the inside."

He turned to face Butler. "But I could hear the destruction, inch by rotten inch."

He returned to his chair but didn't sit down, stared at Butler with his hands wrapped around its back as if it were someone's throat, someone who was destroying his current kingdom from the inside.

"Like Gary Cooper, I'm a straight shooter, so I'll get right to the nails and hammer." He leaned forward slightly. The chair creaked beneath the pressure. His eyes looked like poached raisins, at once small and swollen. "I was adamantly against your appointment, and I'll tell you why. First, you've spent too much time overseas. Second, you're a Jew."

"My time overseas was in service to this country, sir," Butler said automatically to stop himself from commenting on how utterly appalled he was. "And yes, I am half Jewish. So what."

"Third, you're an insolent son of a bitch," Thompson plowed on like a steamroller. "And, fourth, it seems mighty suspicious to me you hiring female agents. What the fuck is that all about? They your own private harem?"

Butler had to keep an iron control not to leap at Thompson and batter that smug expression off his face. "Everyone dismisses the idea of female agents, Mr. Secretary—clearly yourself included. That's what makes them so effective in the field."

Thompson bit his cheek, making a godawful sucking sound, as if that would bury Butler's rejoinder. "I know General Aristides is your rabbi," he said, the nasty edge to his voice like a razor slashing the air between them. "Those DOD people are a fucking red-flag danger; they have their hands in so many pies it's like trying to figure out who owns a shell corporation. So you have juice behind you, there's no denying that. But . . ." He held up the news item that Rivers's OOC had disseminated and which had been picked up by countless outlets around the country. "This here is a leak, Butler. A leak of monstrous proportions. Someone's eating at my kingdom from the inside. Rabbi or no rabbi, I intend to find out all there is to know about you. I'm going to be *strongly suggesting* to my good friend Senator Willis—you know Senator Willis now, don't you?, head of the Senate Intelligence Committee?—that he immediately launch a closed-door investigation of each point made in this leak. And I'm here to tell you that I'll be as good as chairing this investigation, and I assure you it will unearth the truth, even if that truth proves inconvenient to your rabbi."

He placed the news item on his desk midway between him and Butler. "Your days are numbered here, Butler. Frankly, I'd prefer it if you packed your bags today and flew back to Berlin. Or even better, Israel. You'd be more comfortable among your kind, I have no doubt." He shrugged. "Though I know you won't comply. It may not happen today, tomorrow, or even next week, but rest assured as soon as Congress reconvenes in the new year it *will* happen. That's a promise from me to you."

Smug as the president himself, he sat back, hands over his belly, fingers intertwining, basking in the tongue-lashing he had just delivered to someone his inferior in every way he could be inferior. As if he were an uppity plantation slave foolhardy enough to step out of line.

Butler, having absorbed these personal and religious blows, and not for the first time, smiled his most gracious smile and rose. "Thank you for the update, Mr. Secretary." Pretended he was smiling at Zoe. "But to be honest you haven't told me anything my own intelligence network hadn't already informed me of."

Thompson's frown deepened. Clearly, he didn't like that, just as he didn't care for Butler dismissing himself before he had done so in his own time and manner. "I don't like your tone, Butler."

"You don't have to like it, Mr. Secretary. I do my job and I do it better than anyone else." His smile widened. "You see, my set of balls are brass."

With that, he turned on his heel and made his long, humiliating exit. Once in his car, as his driver navigated their departure from federal grounds, he sat back, took a deep breath. His heart was beating like a trip-hammer and his gorge had risen into his throat. His left hand, where it lay on the armrest, was trembling. He wished it was merely from the rush of adrenaline that had flooded his system the moment Thompson started his abominable harangue, but the truth was that he was frightened. He had not come back from overseas to take this job to be harassed and intimidated. His rabbi had assured him this would not happen. He had had no illusions when he had taken the position. As Evan had pointed out, DC was still a snake pit crawling with the worst poisonous vipers, but he had been guaranteed an endless supply of antivenin.

Now this.

Leaning forward, he said, "Mitchell, I need to go to McLean."

"Yes, sir." Mitchell was ex-Special Forces with two tours in Iraq in his quiver. He was also utterly dedicated to Butler.

Moments later, they were crossing the bridge into Virginia.

■ ■ ■

So far as Butler was concerned the Pentagon was a place he was happy to visit rarely and only in times of extreme duress. This was one of those times, and as he showed his ID to the first of many guards at the many security checkpoints, he felt the claustrophobia of the federal government closing in on him like a locked cell.

General Ryan Aristides's office was in one of the inner rings, as befitted his rank and standing. What division he worked for and what it was he did precisely, Butler had no idea. Nor did he feel the need to know. What had, however, been abundantly clear to him when the two of them had been put together was that they both had a fierce and abiding interest in Russia, the Sovereign, and, in particular, the Sovereign's plans for the continuing infiltration and subversion of the American way of life.

It took a full ten minutes from the moment Mitchell drove Butler through the first checkpoint until General Aristides's adjutant guided him into the inner office. These checkpoints, delays, long walks down corridors confusing as those on an aircraft carrier, were no doubt intended to intimidate the visitor, though they had no effect on Butler other than to increase his impatience.

When he was at last ushered into the general's office, Aristides was behind his desk, squinting at a sheaf of papers and muttering to himself. He was one of those no-neck behemoths who had almost certainly been made fun of at school until his fists came out to silence his tormentors. He had the hunched shoulders, beetling brow, and heavy blue jowls of a college lineman running to fat.

After several seconds, he glanced up to notice Butler standing behind an upholstered chair that, Butler knew from past experience, was not nearly as comfortable as it appeared at first glance.

"Benjamin," he said in his deep gravelly voice, "I was about to leave for the night, but I heard you were coming." He gestured with his pen hand. "Take a pew." Squinting at him. "You look like you could stand to get off your feet."

Something about the oddly shaped room, and its complete battleship grayness, caused a wave of dizziness to sweep over Butler. He dug his fingers into the back of the chair. Or perhaps it was because he could not remember the last time he'd had anything to eat. "I'd prefer to stand," he said, determined not to give in to any weakness.

The general shrugged. "Suit yourself. You always do." Putting down his pen, he laced his fingers together. "I've already got your dailies, what's so urgent that you needed to see me in person?"

"Brady Thompson," he began.

The general's thick eyebrows seemed to close in on themselves. "That prick. What shitstorm is he brewing now?"

"I suppose you haven't looked at your online news updates lately."

The general shot him a look before swiveling to his left. Unlike other people in the federal government, his monitor was on a side table, not directly in front of him. "The Cyclops," as he called it, was, in his opinion, an unsecure gateway to lies, disinformation, and junk, none of which he wanted clogging up his brain. The walls and security gates that protected him also, it seemed, cut him off from the incessant electronic din of the outside world.

Still, out of deference to Butler, he scanned through his dailies. "Oh, shit," he muttered, and then as he read further, "Oh, fuck."

Butler told him then about Thompson's blatantly expressed hatred of him, based on the premise that he was not merely a mongrel Jew, but also both a Washington outsider and an insolent son of a bitch.

"Well, he's right about that last part," Aristides said astutely, "but also you frighten the crap out of him, on any number of levels, including the fact that you operate out of the usual chain of command. You get results, so he hasn't been able to move against you. Until now."

"He's going to pressure Willis to order a closed-door Senate Intelligence Committee investigation, which he himself will ride herd on. He's coming after me and, by extension, you."

Aristides sat back. "I didn't sign up for this level of shit." He ran a hand across his forehead. "I have assets to protect."

Butler felt his stomach plummet. "And I'm not one of them?"

"You're different, Benjamin." He swiveled away from The Cyclops. "You knew that the day you walked in here."

"You had to have your arm twisted, I understand."

The general made a face. "Figuratively speaking, yes. I was skeptical."

"Even after you'd read my CV?"

"Well . . ."

"It was an outsider issue, General. So much time spent overseas, away from America. Let's call a spade a spade. But it did me a world of good. I have a broader perspective on issues than anyone in this administration."

"And, as I said," Aristides hurried on, leapfrogging over Butler's comment, "you've come through time and time again."

"I'm a valuable asset to you."

At this, the general clammed up. He looked exceedingly unhappy.

"And yet you won't defend me."

"Look, Benjamin, you have to understand. Right now Thompson's star is in the ascendant. Going up against him is not the smart play."

"For you."

General Aristides stared at Butler as if he was made of granite.

"I see." Butler nodded. "Get back to me when you've grown a pair, General." Then he turned on his heel and got the hell out of there before the sick feeling in the pit of his stomach overwhelmed him.

■ ■ ■

"Mitchell, you know where."

"Yes, sir." Mitchell made the necessary recalculations in his head, then turned off the car's GPS, a redesign Butler had had installed privately, outside the government's purview. And thank God for that; this particular address must never show up on the GPS. Back across the river into DC they went, but not before, having heard his boss's stomach rumbling, Mitchell stopped at a diner, ducked in, and brought Butler back his favorite, a Greek salad with extra dolma. Butler thanked him, but the dolma tasted like sand and the greens stuck in his throat as if he had swallowed a pine cone.

Mitchell took them through a maze of streets, continuing to check his side and rearview mirrors every thirty seconds to see if they were being followed. Only when he had reassured himself that they were clean did he head for the highway. But even then, he took a confusingly circuitous route to their destination.

Butler stared out the window. He was breaking protocol, but there was good reason—more than good reason. He made the briefest of texts—just the numeral 2 and a time ten minutes from now—using the latest of the burner phones that arrived in the mail every five days like clockwork. At this moment, he was leaving nothing to chance. Just because Brady Thompson was a racist pig did not mean that he would make the mistake of underestimating him. Thompson had given him—and, by extension, General Aristides, his rabbi—a very deliberate shot across the bow. Thank God he didn't know the identity of Butler's *real* rabbi, and he was making damn sure he never would. Now more than ever, it was absolutely vital that Butler's security be airtight. He had just gone to their own private DEFCON 2, the last preparations to defend against disaster.

12

Butler's car arrived on the end of Tracy Place precisely ten minutes from the moment he had sent the text. As soon as it appeared, a figure wearing sunglasses, wrapped in a thick winter coat, designer scarf around her head, stepped smartly out of the mansion's back door. Mitchell unlocked the car doors and the figure slipped into the backseat beside Butler. The soundproof partition slid up, sealing them off from the front. Mitchell relocked the doors and drove off at a leisurely pace.

"Not too far," Isobel said. "I've got a pressing engagement."

"I know. We're only going around the block," Butler replied.

Isobel took off the sunglasses, slipped the scarf down to her neck. "So," Isobel Lowe said, "I think I know what has your knickers in a twist."

Butler gave her a wry smile, and told her about the cyber-story, being summoned to Brady Thompson's office, and the hell Thompson had promised to rain down on him.

"Yes, I saw the story," Isobel said. "Thompson. That cocksucker. I assume you went to see Ryan." She meant General Aristides.

"For all the good it did me. He whiffed."

"Yeah. I doubt he's prepared to go full tilt with Thompson and POTUS."

"So you needed to know ASAP."

"I certainly do." To Butler's great surprise, Isobel produced one of her wickedest smiles. "Don't give the threat another thought. On the inside, that is. On the outside, give Thompson every indication that he's scared the bejeezus out of you. He'll like that so much he'll feel comfortable going forward."

"But that's just what I don't want."

"Au contraire, darling, that's just what we do want." She took Butler's hand. "I want him distracted while I figure out what to do. Trust me."

"Our partnership is built on trust." Their partnership had been a decade in the making, a secret he held back even from Evan. He and Isobel had met in Israel. He'd been a field agent then, before he and Evan worked together. She was ostensibly a tourist but in fact was with Mossad. They were after the same target: an SVR agent posing as a businessman in Haifa. After some fireworks that came close to bursting into violence, they had formed a détente of sorts. This was all before Isobel came back to the States. But they had stayed in touch and, after she became disenchanted with the current Israeli government and quit Mossad, had decided to clandestinely work together. Her distrust and hatred of Russia never wavered, however, aligning with Butler's own antipathy. Now she worked for one of those Silicon Valley companies that had amassed more personal data on more people worldwide than the NSA and the DOD combined.

Isobel squeezed his hand. "These are some crazy lives we've chosen for ourselves."

"I think my life chose me," Butler said.

"Yes, I suppose you're right."

"Unlike you. You love your work."

Isobel chuckled. "Come on, Ben. So do you."

"Maybe. But I hate the people I have to report to."

Time to return the subject to the here and now. "Listen, Izzy, Evan Ryder is about to pay you a visit."

"You know this will happen now?"

"Yes. If we suspect Roger Hollis of using his and Peter's company as a spy network, you can be sure, hanging around Peter, she will, too."

"You think a great deal of this woman," Isobel said. "I've heard the stories, but figured, like all such gossip, they were exaggerated."

"Usually, yes," Butler said in all seriousness. "With Evan they're all true, and then some."

Pulling out her mobile, she punched in Hollis's number. "Roger. Tonight's game will be starting an hour earlier." She nodded as he agreed, then she cut the connection. "Done," she said to Butler.

He nodded. "And, listen, as we discussed, the visit isn't likely to be a friendly one."

"Leave it to me." She patted his hand. "Perhaps this will work. Your plan of throwing Peter and Brenda together was a good one, but these things have a more or less fifty-fifty success rate."

"That's why I asked Evan to come back here. We have struck out badly against Nemesis."

"You're saying you needed the A team."

Butler laughed. "I'm hoping that's the case. I need to propel her on her way."

"And who better to do that than me?"

Three people went by: a woman striding smartly, laden with shopping bags, a pair of elderly men, one with a walking stick, taking their time, deep in conversation.

Isobel gave Butler a serious look. "I went to Yana's funeral."

"I never doubted you would."

"Hollis was there."

"She really hooked him, didn't she."

Isobel nodded. "Another kind of cuckold. It's sad."

"No, it's not. It's how our life works."

Isobel kept staring out the window. A young woman with a helmet of blond hair and a nose like the prow of a ship stepped across the street, ignoring the light. "It seems odd, but I miss her."

"Who?"

"Yana."

"The first law of espionage, Izzy, don't get involved."

She turned back to give him a level gaze. "Does that include you?"

His eyes widened in surprise. "Me?"

"You and Evan."

They stopped at a red light. The street was nearly empty, just the occasional vehicle thrumming by.

I deserved that, Butler thought. *Izzy's far too savvy for me to be reminding her of security protocol. She called me on it, and rightly so.* "There's nothing between me and Evan." His voice was devoid of inflection.

Isobel, who seemed not to have heard him, leaned forward, tapped the soundproof panel. When Mitchell slid it down, she said, "When you turn the corner, pull into the curb. I'll walk the rest of the way back."

The panel slid back into place, the car turned right, pulled into the curb, and stopped. Isobel turned to Butler. "I forgive you." She placed a hand lightly on his forearm and smiled. But inside, as far as neutralizing Thompson was concerned, she was not overly optimistic.

Butler nodded. "I understand."

"Ben, our best hope is Evan. If she's as good as you say she is, if she can get to the heart of Nemesis, Thompson is going to have more on his plate than he can handle."

"Be careful, Izzy."

"And you, Ben."

She kissed him on both cheeks, and then she was gone amid the movers and shakers striding back down the street.

■ ■ ■

"I'm having dinner," Peter Limas said. "Give me one good reason why I shouldn't have you thrown out of here." He had concluded his call, presumably to his satisfaction, and had placed his mobile faceup on the table.

Evan reached for Limas's menu. "I'm starving," she said. "What's good here?"

"The steak sandwich, the Caesar salad, the shrimp cocktail."

"I'll have all three." Evan signaled for the waiter cruising past, closed the menu, held it out to Limas. "What about you?"

Limas, slightly bewildered, took the menu, stared up into the expectant face of the waiter, a large man named Paul. Clearly, he was debating whether or not to have Paul escort this interloper out of his presence. Then he shrugged. "Shrimp cocktail, Caesar salad, steak sandwich, medium-rare. For both of us, Paul."

"Very good, Mr. Limas." Paul took the menu, turned to Evan. "Perhaps a drink before dinner, ma'am?"

"Thanks, no," Evan said. "Just ice water."

Paul nodded and departed, following which a somewhat awkward silence arose, as Evan stared into Limas's face. He was a handsome man with large black eyes that looked out on the world with a kind of amused curiosity from beneath long dark lashes. He sported a small gold ring in the lobe of his left ear. A Patek Philippe watch that cost a small fortune rode his left wrist. A man, then, who was comfortable wearing his wealth on his sleeve.

"Have we met before?" Limas asked. His accent was pure British upper class.

Evan, extending a hand, wondered whether Limas had picked up on a shadow in Evan's expression, or whether his question was merely coincidence. "Vesper Lynd."

Limas laughed. "And I'm Hugo Drax," playing along with Evan's joke.

The two shook hands. His was cool and dry.

"Louise Steadman," Evan said, using the legend Butler had had his people cook up for the false IDs that got her into the country without lighting up the clandestine services computer terminals.

She showed her ID to Limas. "I'm a colleague of Brenda's."

"Ah, so that's it." Limas waggled a forefinger. "Was that you who popped her head inside her room at the hospital?"

"It was."

Limas's face darkened. "You were in the SUV with her when—"

"That's right."

"No wonder you look the worse for wear."

"You should see the other guy."

Limas's smile was wan. "Terrible thing, this."

Paul set the shrimp cocktails before them, along with a small cup of white horseradish, asked if there was anything they needed, then departed as silently as he had arrived.

Evan took a spoonful of the horseradish to add to the blood-red cocktail sauce, squeezed a hefty wedge of lemon onto the shrimp, which were the size of a Chinook salmon, took up her delicate fork. "How long have you known Brenda?"

"We've been going out for about six months."

"You seem pretty devoted for a fairly new relationship."

"Life moves at the speed of light, my friend. I'm simply going with the flow."

They ate for a time in silence, Limas at the speed of a seemingly starving man; he nearly swallowed each gigantic shrimp whole. Following this feeding frenzy he wiped his lips, said, "Is there something you wanted to ask me? And, by the way, how did you find me here?"

"The Federal Case seems to be a favorite hangout of yours."

"It is." Limas eyed her. "But how did you know about it?"

"Brenda told me," Evan said, which was of course a lie. "She was eager for us to meet." Another lie. Nevertheless, it sounded like the truth, which was all that mattered. "I'm just back from overseas." It was always best to mix in a bit of the truth to lend credence to the lies.

"I won't ask where," Limas said. "I know if you told me you'd have to kill me." This, accompanied by a weak smile at the too-oft uttered phrase.

A busboy cleared away their plates and, moments later, Paul arrived with the Caesar salad on a cart laden with a large wooden mixing bowl into which he added each ingredient separately, tossed the whole, then served two portions before rolling the cart away.

"You don't get Caesar salad like this every day, made from scratch that way," Limas said, back on solid ground. "When I was just a young lad, my aunt, God rest her soul, used to take me to this one restaurant every time she came to London. As a special treat. She taught me about real Caesar salad. How to eat steak. And also how to drink liquor." He tucked into his salad, eating as if he had an appointment in five minutes.

While she picked at her own salad, Evan considered Limas's ill-fitting jacket, and the silver pin on the lapel. The sight of the facing ravens, while the matching necklace she had taken from Anna Alta's corpse burned a hole in her pocket, put a serious dent in her appetite.

▪ ▪ ▪

"So," Limas said at length, "you never did tell me what you wanted to ask me."

Evan had been going to ask him what Brenda said about what had happened at St. Agnes, but the pin

Limas wore had changed her mind; it would be difficult to credit anything he had to say about Brenda. Instead, she said, "I was curious about the pin on your lapel—the two ravens."

For a moment, Limas appeared flummoxed, twin creases appearing on his forehead. That is, until Evan brought out the raven pendant, set it on the table between them.

"Oh, that." He touched the pin on his lapel, shrugged. "No idea. This isn't my jacket. It belongs to my partner. I ripped mine on a nail early this morning as we were going through a site we're considering for new offices. After I got the call about Brenda he lent me his jacket so I'd look presentable at the hospital." Touching the pendant, his frown deepened. "Do the ravens have a particular meaning?"

"I was going to ask you that." Evan swept the pendant off the table, pocketed it.

"Okay, well . . ." Limas glanced at his watch. Getting up, he walked a few paces away and fired up his mobile. After a short, muted conversation, he returned to the table. "I know where Roger is. I'll take you to see him."

Limas threw some bills onto the table; he'd apparently been here so often he didn't need to ask for a check.

13

Brenda's current brief was to follow Donald Beacum to his source. The hope was that Butler and Abdur Rashid had sufficiently frightened the wired-up guard to ensure he would do Butler's bidding. But just in case, Brenda was to be the goad as well as the close observer.

Beacum had left Foggy Bottom via the metro. He took the silver line west six stops to L'Enfant Plaza, where, amid passenger cross-currents pushing and shoving every which way, he leapt onto the northbound green line at the last instant. Brenda just made it aboard before the doors closed. As the train sped up, she picked her way slowly toward where Beacum stood, swaying slightly as he held onto a vertical pole, staring blankly at the tunnel rushing by outside the window, deep in that kind of netherworld akin to daydreaming passengers of all transport fell into.

At Gallery Place, he exited. Brenda followed him up and out, watching him pass through the enormous many-roofed blue, gold, and crimson gate that marked the Seventh Street border of Chinatown. Stone foo dogs, symbols of prosperity and good fortune, sat up on either side of the street.

Past the gate, Beacum took a circuitous route through Chinatown itself. They passed restaurants with red-lacquered ducks hanging in the steamy windows, bakeries, beauty parlors, souvenir shops hawking paper-and-bamboo parasols, CDs of Chinese pop music, bootleg DVDs of the latest Hollywood films. In every shop, a garishly painted cat statue sat on its haunches, right forepaw rising and falling as if in greeting.

Brenda hung back as he slowed, checked reflections in storefront windows, then darted into one of those sketchy check-cashing places that took a cut from giving you an advance or just to cash your paycheck when you didn't have an account at a bank, or didn't want the scrutiny a bank teller would give a check from an equally sketchy source.

Following him in a moment later, she saw a bare-bones business, just a counter two-thirds of the way into the store behind which a young Chinese woman dispensed bills to a middle-aged Hispanic worker. Not even a cheap plastic chair; no one was expected to linger, and if there was a line, standing was just fine for you.

Brenda watched the Hispanic worker stuff the money in his pocket and head out the door. The furtive air left with him, leaving a smell of fried garlic and money.

"The man who just came in here," Brenda said at the counter, "where did he go?"

The Chinese woman regarded Brenda with an expression as unreadable as a mah-jongg tile. "He just walked out the door." She looked as if she had never been taught to smile. "You saw that, no?"

"Not him," Brenda said. "The other one."

"No other one," the Chinese woman replied with a hint of disdain. Her eyes looked like the coins used to put over a dead person's eyes to pay her way into the underworld. "Slow day."

Brenda sighed, brought out her fake FBI ID. She was carrying, which was illegal for her inside the United States. Not so for the FBI. Nevertheless, the Chinese woman made a move with her right hand. Brenda grabbed it, drew it up slowly. A 9mm Glock with a noise suppressor came into view.

Slowly and carefully, Brenda took it from her, ejected the magazine, cleared it of bullets, took it apart, set the pieces on the counter. Then, keeping her eyes on the woman, she came around the end of the counter. Using a plastic twist tie she pulled from a box on a shelf inside the counter, she bound the bitch's wrists behind her back.

"Sit down there." She indicated the corner.

Glaring at her, the bitch curled herself up like a cat, curved spine against the wall. Back around the counter, Brenda turned the OPEN sign on the front door around so the CLOSED side faced the street. Then she locked the door.

Behind the space at the rear of the shop was a door.

"Is this where he went?"

"Drop dead," the woman spat out.

Brenda smiled at her, blew her a kiss, then passed silently as a cloud through the door.

■ ■ ■

Unexpectedly, she found herself in a warren. How could she have imagined that such a small storefront would harbor a small village? Corridors narrow and dimly lit beckoned her on. After several minutes of trying to find her way through, she stopped still and, cocking her head, listened. The slow drip of water, the sweetish smell of earth and rot, open sacks of trash, the soft, stealthy patter of rats' paws.

Then, so soft she almost missed it, the creak of a wooden floorboard. She held her breath. Another creak, two more. She swiveled in time to catch the next creak and to let it guide her. She went down corridor after corridor. None of them went far, but instead branched off in a series of right-angle Ts. She followed the floorboard creaks until, straining all her senses, she caught the low sounds of a hushed conversation, just before she came upon a door. Pushing it open, she heard first the click-clack-click of mah-jongg tiles being played so quickly they were almost a blur. No one looked up when she walked in; old women, old hands sitting around twelve square tables, so engrossed in their games it would have taken a hand grenade explosion to break their eerie concentration. The air was stifled by body heat and exhalations.

Beyond the farthest row of tables from where Brenda stood was a beaded curtain, behind which a pair of shadowed figures moved, murmured. Picking her way around the players, she stood in front of the curtain. The wooden beads clacked softly on a breeze from a rotating fan on the other side. Leaning forward, she tried to make out the conversation. Other than the fact that it was between two males, she couldn't hear a word.

On the other hand, she did feel the knifepoint in the small of her back. Turning her head, she could just make out one of the mah-jongg players, her black hair plastered into a kind of pyramid atop her head.

"Get in there," she commanded first in Mandarin and then in Cantonese.

Brenda spoke both, but, unmoving, played dumb. All that got her, though, was a sharp poke with the tip of the blade.

"Go!" the old woman said in harsh English. "You go! Now!"

Brenda went. Through the beaded curtain that her hands parted in front of her. She found herself in a small room, windowless like the mah-jongg parlor, like all the corridors she'd come down to get here. The electric fan blew the smells of rice, fried oil, and soy sauce, fermented beyond its usefulness, undoubtedly from a restaurant somewhere above them. Across from the fan the two men sat on either side of what appeared to be a discarded card table. One of them was Donald Beacum, the other a slim man, made, it appeared, of solid muscle, with a head round and hairless as one of the beads in the curtain behind her. He had large black eyes that seemed to burn right through her. He wasn't Chinese, or Asian at all. The Bead had the swarthy skin of a desert dweller. It looked like he'd recently shaved off a full beard, which made sense, since he was here in America, where such accoutrements on a face like his was bound to garner attention. And, it was perfectly clear to Brenda that attention was the last thing this man craved.

"You're the bomb-maker," she said. *In for a dime, in for a million dollars,* she thought. Beacum looked like he was about to have a stroke.

The Bead looked blandly at her. "This prick was telling me all about you and your boss." His lips moved, searching for the thick beard that was no longer there. "He seeks asylum here. With me. Trading, you see. Information in exchange for his life." He shrugged. "Desperate times call for desperate measures. Is that what you Americans say?"

"You're not going to—" Brenda began.

"But I am," he said, "giving him asylum."

Beacum, relaxing, gave her a disdainful glare. The Bead sat a bit forward. Both his hands were under the table. One of them held a gun, but that was verifiable to Brenda only after he had shot Beacum twice in the abdomen.

"Asylum," the Bead said, "of a sort."

Beyond the beaded curtain the click-clack-click of the mah-jongg tiles being played never missed a beat. The old woman with the knife had returned to her hand. *It must have been a winning one,* Brenda thought.

Beacum, chair tipped onto its back from the force of the bullets, still sat, bleeding quickly out. There was nothing Brenda could do to save him, assuming she even wanted to, which, at the moment was highly debatable.

This man was responsible for letting the white Nissan and its driver into the restricted parking lot of St. Agnes.

The Bead's head swiveled toward her like a vulture or an owl. He smiled in the most disarmingly benign manner as he said, "Now, what can I do for you, Brenda?"

Then the gun appeared.

14

"This is quite the mansion," Evan said, and Peter Limas's head swiveled toward her.

"When you're Isobel Lowe you can buy yourself just about anything," he said in a light tone of voice.

They were mounting the stone steps of a three-story cream stone and butterscotch stucco mansion near the corner of California Street NW and Massachusetts Avenue, two or so blocks from Rock Creek Park, that might have housed the embassy of a major foreign power, but didn't. A small courtyard paved with octagonal tiles was guarded by a pair of stone urns each filled with a holly bush, ruby-colored berries set off by glossy dark-green foliage. One-foot evergreen hedges guarded the front of the building.

The man who stood in the vestibule between the outer and inner doors, black skin gleaming, looked like he could go fifteen rounds with Ruslan Chagaev before knocking the former heavyweight's block off. He nodded to Limas, said, "Good to see you again, sir." If he'd had a hat Evan was sure he'd have tipped it.

"And you," Limas said. "This is my good friend Louise Steadman. Say hello to Ms. Steadman, Mike."

"A pleasure to make your acquaintance, Ms. Steadman. Anything you require, just let me know."

"Thank you, Mike," Evan said. "I'll keep that in mind."

Mike smiled with large white teeth while holding open the wood-framed glass door for them both to enter. "This way, please. I will escort you upstairs."

"Charming fellow," Evan said, and she and Limas trailed after Mike.

Limas chuckled. "Being so powerful does have its drawbacks. A certain level of security is required."

It was the violet hour, already dark outside, and lamps were lit throughout the entry, hallways, and what rooms were visible from her current vantage point. "Tell me, just how well do you know Isobel Lowe?"

"Relax, Louise. I would never cheat on Brenda. What kind of man d'you think I am?"

"I wouldn't know."

"Right." His smile was as genuine as it was disarming. "Not yet, anyway."

"But this is her home, presumably, not her office."

"About three times a week, Roger joins a small, select group for several rounds of poker."

Mike had led them across the vestibule and up the curved staircase with its magnificently carved newel post and polished oak steps to the second floor, where a pecan wood-paneled corridor branched off to their left and right.

They went left, past several closed doors. At the end of the corridor were a pair of polished mahogany doors with brass knockers in the shape of closed fists. Mike grasped one and knocked on the door three times, then opened the door inward and stepped smartly aside, taking up position just outside.

Crossing the threshold, Evan and Limas were assaulted by a fug of blue cigar smoke. Limas shrugged off the jacket his partner had lent him, draped it over his left arm.

Seven men and one woman sat around a green baize

table, playing poker. Plain vanilla five-card draw, from what Evan could see. The shades were drawn over two windows that faced out onto California Street, Evan's unerring sense of direction informed her. There was a heavy tiger oak sideboard on which was arrayed an impressive drinks service. On the opposite wall hung a pastoral painting of French origin.

The lone woman looked up when they entered and, smiling, laid down her hand, excused herself, and rose to greet them. She wore a dark-colored Armani power suit, under which was an oyster-colored silk shirt unbuttoned enough to show off her impressive cleavage. An elegantly worked gold choker showed at her throat. An emerald ring graced the third finger of her right hand.

"Hullo, Pete," she said in a husky voice. Her attention quickly turned to Evan. "And who is this vision of loveliness?" She held out her hand. "Isobel Lowe. Welcome to my home. Any friend of Pete's is a friend of mine."

"Louise Steadman." Isobel Lowe had a grip like a man. "And thank you."

"Not at all." Isobel's smile was disarming, warm and welcoming. But there was a steel mesh behind her eyes that Evan caught in intermittent flashes. "You here to observe or to play?"

Limas glanced over her shapely shoulder. "Is he winning?"

"Roger? He's always winning. And off the same poor schmucks, too."

"Louise needs to speak with him," Limas said.

Isobel made a sound deep in her throat. "You know Roger better than that, Pete. When he's on this kind of roll he won't budge until he either cleans everyone out or is cleaned out himself. But . . ." She regarded Evan. "Ms. Steadman here could take my place at the table. She'd be sitting directly across from Roger. Maybe they could get to know each other. There's no better place to get the measure of a man than at the card table." Her right eyebrow arched. "*If* you know how to play poker, that is." The eyebrow arched higher. "Are you, Ms. Steadman? A player?"

Evan normally had no desire to play poker, but from the moment she saw that Limas had taken her to a high-stakes poker game she had formulated a plan of getting to Limas's partner as quickly as possible and, she hoped, with the most impact. She needed to be on Benjamin's chartered plane to the Caucasus Mountains tomorrow morning.

"Is that a challenge, Ms. Lowe?"

"Of a sort. And call me Isobel, all my friends do, Ms. Steadman."

"Louise," Evan said. "And to tell you the truth, Isobel, I'm always up for a challenge."

"Fair warning: this is a difficult one. No one I've ever seen here plays better than Roger Hollis."

"The more difficult the better," Evan said. All eyes were on her as she went around the table. She sat down in Isobel's seat, introduced herself while looking directly at Roger Hollis. Hollis was a round man with a large, squarish head jammed onto a squat neck. He stared back at Evan with a coolness bordering on chilling. His ice-blue eyes and long nose only added to the effect.

"Everyone starts off with fifty thousand," Isobel said, placing three piles of different colored chips in front of Evan. "This is a gentleman's game. We all assume each player can cover his or her losings. No IOUs."

Evan nodded.

"Ante is a thousand a hand." Hollis shuffled the deck without taking his eyes off Evan. "No limits on raises."

Limas took a step forward. "Now wait a moment, Rog, this isn't Texas Hold 'Em."

Isobel laid a hand on his forearm. "Roger's deal," she said, "Roger's rules. For this hand only." She said this last firmly, finally.

"One hand is all I'm going to need." Hollis dealt the cards.

"No worries, Louise," Peter said. "I'll stake you to whatever losses you incur."

"Very kind of you, Peter, but it's entirely possible I won't be needing it," Evan said, which caused Hollis to snicker under his breath.

Everyone anted up, fanned out their five cards. Play began. The player on Hollis's left bet a hundred, the next three checked, putting no further money up. Evan, frowning, checked. This brought a predatory smirk to Hollis's mouth.

For the next round—the discard—all the players were required to bet. Another hundred from everyone, including Evan, who drew two cards. Hollis drew one card and bet three hundred. Half the table threw in their hands, and when Evan bet five hundred the remaining two players dropped out, leaving only Evan and Hollis. Hollis saw her five and added five thousand to it. The pot now stood at $15,500.

Evan bet ten thousand; Hollis twelve thousand. The pot was $37,500.

"Got another raise in you, Ms. Steadman?" Hollis said with no expression on his face. "Or have we gotten too rich for your blood."

"Louise, I've got your back," Limas said.

"No, you don't, Petey." Hollis didn't bother to look over his shoulder at his partner. "This is between Ms. Steadman and me."

When Peter started to object, Evan stopped him. "He's right, Peter. This is strictly between the two of us now."

There was silence for a moment; everyone seemed to be holding their breath, even Isobel, who had seen many a game devolve into a nasty pissing match. This seemed different, somehow, the animus greater, dangerous, even.

"Well, Ms. Steadman, what'll it be? Death by folding or defeat by cards?"

Evan, who had appeared to be weighing her options, added money to the pot. "I'm all in."

"Too bad," Hollis said. "I'm raising you ten."

$55,500.

"I win." Hollis leaned forward, hands ready to scoop up the chips. "I hope you're good for it, Ms. Steadman."

"One moment." Evan dug in her pocket. "I've forgotten all about this." She drew out Anna Alta's pendant, laid it on top of the pile of chips.

The pair of ravens seemed to stare up at everyone. Isobel gestured. She could not have made people vanish more quickly had she been a sorceress wielding a magic wand.

15

"Relax," the Bead said. "I'm not going to shoot you." Proving his point, at least for the moment, he set his handgun—a Walther PPQ—on the table with the muzzle pointed at the wall. He gestured. "Now you."

Brenda hesitated, then unholstered her Glock, laid it on the table opposite the Walther.

"Good." The Bead gave a high ululating whistle, and three women pushed their way through the beaded curtain. One carried a galvanized pail of an evil-smelling liquid and a scrub brush. Without a word, two of the women dragged Beacum's corpse away while the third got down on her knees and began to clean up the blood so quickly and methodically Brenda was certain she had done it many times before.

"Make yourself comfortable." The Bead gestured toward a chair against the left wall.

Brenda hooked her shoe around a leg, drew the chair up to the table. She sat facing him, careful to keep away from the kneeling woman and her industriously circling scrub brush.

"Do you by any chance speak Pashtu?" the Bead asked. "Arabic?"

Brenda shook her head.

"Pity, we could have begun our talk immediately." He shrugged. "Ah, well, I'm a patient man."

How many bombs has this man made? Brenda wondered, tapping into the river of rage that flowed through her.

He shook a cigarette out of a battered pack, offered it to her. When she declined, he shrugged again, flipped it between his lips, lit up. He inhaled extravagantly, blew the smoke straight up at the ceiling. But the electric fan caught it, distributing it around the small room along with the sharp stench of ammonia and bleach.

They sat looking at one another through the curls of smoke. "So. Brenda," he said after a time.

"I don't know your name."

He eyed her through the veil of smoke. "Let's keep it that way for the time being."

They were alone now, the third woman having taken her bucket of pink fluid and her pink scrub brush and vanished behind the beaded curtain.

He stubbed out his cigarette in a black plastic ashtray with a gold dragon emblazoned on it, regarded her appraisingly, and in a conversational tone, said, "You look like death warmed over."

It was all Brenda could do not to leap at him, squeeze his throat with her hands.

After a moment, he went on. "I haven't looked in a mirror for some time, but I imagine we both look the worse for wear." He shook out another cigarette, apparently thought better of it, put it back.

"You killed Beacum," Brenda said. "Why wouldn't you kill me too?"

"Beacum was damaged goods—in all ways possible. Your people captured him, subjected him to torture until he cracked like a nut. So how could I trust him? Would you?"

Brenda opened her mouth to answer, but shut it again.

She had no desire to engage this monster as if they were friends chatting over coffee and croissants.

"Of course you wouldn't," he answered for her.

"So what *do* you want?" He was still staring at her. Had he even blinked? She shifted nervously. "Oh, I see."

"Oh, no." He shook his head. "You misunderstand me. My choice for intimate companionship is . . . elsewhere." When he smiled he showed his teeth, nicotine-stained and pointed. "No, Brenda. But, you're right about one thing: I do want something from you."

She barked out a laugh. "You must be joking."

"I'm perfectly serious."

She crossed her arms over her chest. "Please."

"You haven't heard what it is yet."

"Doesn't matter. I'm not interested."

"Or." He picked up the Walther. "I could kill you."

Brenda spun the Glock so the muzzle faced him. "Not if I kill you first."

"Now you see the futility of this situation. The absurdity."

Sadly, he was right. "Like a scene out of a Tarantino film."

"I don't understand the reference."

"Never mind. It simply means you're right. If we take up our guns we'll likely kill each other."

"Is that what you want, Brenda?"

"Of course not."

"Then listen to me."

"You almost killed me."

"Me?" He cocked his head, kept his bad teeth hidden. "Ah, no. I didn't make the bomb that hurt you."

Brenda shook her head. "I don't believe you."

"I don't even know who did."

"Again."

"But I do know who planted it." He lifted a forefinger. "She's dead. But I can tell you her real name."

She said nothing.

"Will you listen to me?"

"I don't see why—"

"My name is Charles."

Her expression showed how little this meant to her. "Your operational name, I assume."

"Actually." He had a smile like a shark: wide, toothy, and more than a little menacing. "Charles Isaacs."

Brenda started as if he'd hit her with a Taser. Her arms unwound, her hands on the tabletop nowhere near her Glock. "You're on the list."

"What list?"

"The Nemesis hit list. Three of our agents are dead. Two MI6 people are MIA. All of them were trying to find out intel on Nemesis. Then there's you." Her eyes narrowed. "What's your affiliation?"

"Interpol," Charles Isaacs said. "I work out of Munich. Normally." He spun the pack of cigarettes around and around. "There's nothing normal about this situation. I'm following the breadcrumbs of anti-Semitism. Jews are being targeted by the Russians and by this unknown group called Nemesis."

"What do you know about Nemesis?"

"I was hoping you could tell me."

"Jesus. How is it Beacum came here to see you?"

Charles snorted. "Beacum. Well. I believed I had bought him."

"You believed wrong."

"So it would seem."

"To disastrous effect," she said.

Charles took this body blow with admirable equanimity. "Beacum was working both sides of the fence. He was a lot cannier—and more treacherous—than he let on, or our previous intel on him indicated." He put his hands together. "So. I need your help."

"I already have a job."

"You see this weapon." He tapped the Walther. "It's

here to protect me. This isn't a game we're playing. We're both in the shadow world, fighting for truth, justice—"

"And the Interpol way?"

This time his smile was somehow less sharklike; she could even discern a bit of sadness in it. "I'm counting on the fact that you and I can help each other, Brenda."

"I'm listening."

"Yes. I believe you are. At last. The girl who set the bomb, who drove the Nissan into the parking lot at St. Agnes—her name is Marina Mevedeva. St. Petersburg born and raised. Given the legend of Canadian citizen Anna Alta. Forced into the service of—"

"The SVR."

"Ah, no," Charles said. "Worse. Far worse."

"What could be worse than the SVR?"

"She's an agent of Nemesis." Deciding to smoke again, he shook out another cigarette, gripped it between his lips, lit it. At least the smoke cut through the ammoniac stench that was making Brenda's head throb.

"What was the mission's objective?"

"We believe to kill Evan Ryder." Charles covered the Walther with his hand, put it away. "You, Brenda, were collateral damage."

"How do you know about Evan?"

"Come on, Brenda. Think."

She did, somewhat abashed. "So, again, I have to ask, what do you want from me?"

"I need your help to find the bomb-maker."

"Is that your objective in coming here?"

"It is now," Charles said. "In the field, objectives turn on a dime, according to situations, which are always fluid.

"So." Charles began again. "I must be careful here in DC—and everywhere else, especially so now that I'm on yet another kill list." He produced a death's-head grin. "You have contacts I don't in DC. Plus, you have federal credentials." He gestured. "Whereas I am a stranger in a strange land. I am asking you to be my Virgil."

Brenda's brain was working overtime, extrapolating from everything she had heard so far. What lethal spider's web had she entered? "So you want to find the bomb-maker because, with Marina Mevedeva dead, he's the next breadcrumb leading you to Nemesis, right?"

"Yes. The bomb-maker will lead us back to his control."

"If we handle him correctly." Brenda frowned. "You have to know something right off the bat. I don't condone what you did to Donald Beacum."

"We all contributed to his death."

"No. It was you, all you."

Charles took a deep drag, let the smoke out through his nostrils in a double stream. He tapped the ash off the end of the cigarette. It was already half-finished. "You mean you and Benjamin Butler and whoever else was involved in his interrogation didn't use him?"

"Of course we did, but that was different."

"Of course it was different," he said in a sardonic tone. "You broke him."

"This is wrong. Just plain wrong."

"Then you're playing in the wrong sandbox." Charles pushed her Glock toward her. "You need to grow up, Brenda. The faster the better." He blew a lungful of smoke upward. "And there's no one better than me to teach you."

"I already have a mentor, thank you very much."

Charles grunted. "You're a stubborn one. I like that; you're not a pushover."

"Call it what you want. I'm loyal."

"Loyalty I appreciate even more. Listen, Brenda, what I'm asking is only temporary. Best of all, it chimes with what I assume is your own overarching brief to rid America of Russian agents."

Brenda was silent for some time, lost in thought. An add-on part of her brief was to find out who Charles Isaacs was and what happened to him. Now that she had, now that she knew who he was and what he wanted from her she was inclined to go along with this. Weighing the pros and cons was useless here, there were too many things unknowable. Unless she moved forward. And wasn't that what Butler had trained her to do? Always move forward, occasionally sideways, never back. She was almost ready to capitulate, on the precipice of stepping onto the spider's web. The question was: who was the spider, Nemesis or Charles Isaacs?

"Why are you on the Nemesis kill list?" she asked.

"No idea," Charles said. "It's not uncommon for field agents to be on one kill list or another. If we took all of them seriously we'd do nothing at all. Full paralysis."

"Okay, I get that, but—"

"*But* . . . So. You still don't know what to think," he said, interrupting her internal debate. "I get that. Do I trust this man or do I think he's conning me. Correct?"

She nodded. "Something along those lines."

"Okay. At least now we're getting somewhere." He stubbed out his cigarette, laid the butt to rest beside the first one. "So now I will provide proof that my intentions concerning you are pure."

"How on earth will you—?"

"Your boyfriend," Charles said. "What's his name?" He snapped his fingers. "Ah, yes, Peter Limas. Well, this boyfriend of yours is a Russian agent."

Brenda nearly leapt out of her chair. "What?"

"A sleeper. A player of the long game."

"That's insane. No way is Peter . . . I mean, he has his own company, he went to Cambridge."

"A known hotbed of communism from the time of Burgess, Philby, Maclean, and the rest of the Cambridge Five."

"That was a long time ago."

"Not for Cambridge, which counts its years in centuries."

"This is all bullshit." Now Brenda was truly hot.

Charles sighed. "Would that it were so."

He produced a photo, small, slightly blurred, a shadow in one corner: a rather poor long-range surveillance shot. Nevertheless, the two men in it were visible and recognizable to her. One was certainly Peter. The other was someone she had never met, thank God, but whose face she knew almost as well as Peter's: Anton Recidivich Gorgonov. Peter and the head of the SVR were deep in conversation, that much was obvious. The rest, the implications, made no sense to her whatsoever. The earth began to tilt under her.

Charles pocketed the dreadful photo. "Listen to me, Brenda. Peter Limas is a Russian spy."

Brenda's spirit had left the building. She felt like an automaton. Her pulse was racing as if she had just run a three-minute mile. There was a throbbing behind her eyes. The thick atmosphere of the room had intensified and she felt as if she had passed through Alice's looking glass and was now in some alternate dimension ruled by the Red Queen, Anton Gorgonov.

Peter. The man who had kissed her so tenderly, whom she had sat astride, who had exploded inside her was a Russian sleeper agent.

She gagged, retched, and turning away from the table just in time, vomited the contents of her stomach and her faith in human beings onto the just-wiped floor.

16

The room had cleared. After a moment of heart-stopping silence chairs had scraped back, jackets had been lifted, and six men had vacated the premises without a word or a backward glance. The rush for the door was like a mini-stampede. Only Isobel, Limas, Hollis, and Evan remained. Isobel, breaking her stasis, crossed to the door, shut it behind them. She locked it, then gestured to Limas, who crossed to the sideboard, poured three fingers of bourbon into an Old-Fashioned glass, set it in front of Roger Hollis.

"Drink," she said. And when he failed to respond, "Now!" in a sharper tone.

Only after he did as she commanded, swallowing the liquor in two convulsive gulps, did she seat herself at the table midway between Evan and Hollis. Limas remained with his back to the sideboard. For the first time, Evan realized that in draping the jacket over his arm he had hidden the raven pin from view.

"First things first," Isobel said, still with that don't-fuck-with-me tone. "Show your cards."

Hollis and Evan turned over their cards simultaneously. Hollis had two pair: kings and tens. Evan had three queens.

"Louise wins," Isobel said.

Isobel picked up the pendant as carefully as if it were radioactive. Her gaze rested heavily on Evan. "Now the game has been settled, Louise, if I may ask, where did you get this?"

Evan, wanting more time to calibrate the sudden gushing of high emotion, said nothing.

Isobel turned the ravens around between her fingertips. "It's not yours." It was a statement, not a question.

"No," Evan said, "it isn't."

"Then who—?"

Isobel's raised hand forestalled Hollis's outburst.

"Your story must be told," Isobel said to Evan. "Here. Now."

Evan glanced first at Isobel, then at Hollis. "Otherwise what?"

Isobel sat for a moment, immobile. Then: "Pete, perhaps you should give us the room."

"He stays."

Evan's tone was one Isobel recognized as her own. She nodded. "As you wish."

Evan turned her gaze on Hollis. "Do you know what a group of ravens is called?" Evan asked.

Hollis stared blankly at her. "I can't say that I do."

"A conspiracy," Evan told him. "A conspiracy of ravens."

Hollis's smile was frigid. "Useless knowledge."

"I would say it's quite useful," Evan countered. "In this instance."

Evan kept her attention on Hollis, but Isobel was always in the periphery of her vision; it was clear who ruled this roost. "And are you also part of this conspiracy of ravens?"

"I don't believe that's any of your business," Hollis said in a tone that sent a chill through the room.

Evan took the silver pendant from Isobel's hand. "The person who this belonged to is dead."

"I'm sorry for your loss," Hollis said dryly.

"I didn't know her."

"Then what's this all about?"

"I want to know if you knew her."

"Me?" Hollis barked out a laugh. "Why on earth—?"

"I want to find out everything I can about this group she belonged to."

Hollis shrugged. "Then I'm afraid you're asking the wrong person."

Evan was trying to get a rise out of Hollis, an angry outburst that might reveal something. But Hollis was not to be goaded. "And how did this dead stranger's pendant come to be in your possession?" he said almost casually.

"How did the woman I took it from get it?"

Hollis cocked his head. "Why do you answer a question with another question?"

Evan settled herself. She had asked for this, run full speed into it, in fact. Somewhere deep inside her she heard two ravens calling—to one another or to her? There was nothing for it but to push forward. "I'm waiting for an answer."

Hollis smiled thinly. "I'm not the sharing type."

"Of course. You're far too inner directed."

Hollis's brows furrowed. "I don't like being psychoanalyzed." An edge had come into his voice again, which pleased Evan.

"And I don't like being lied to."

Hollis readied himself to stand up. "I've had enough of this."

"Not at all," Evan said. She'd gotten Hollis to open up a bit; no point in pushing her luck further. "Her name was Anna Alta. At least, that was the name on the passport she was carrying."

"Why wouldn't you think that's her real name?" Hollis seemed relieved to get off the subject of himself.

"I'm coming to that."

Hollis looked hard at Evan. "Please. Don't keep me in suspense."

"She was carrying a false passport."

"How d'you know the passport was fake?"

"I have a history with Russian counterfeiting techniques in this area. I know the signifiers."

"So this Anna Alta—" Hollis leaned back in his chair, arms crossed over his chest. "Are you saying she was Russian? How do you know? She could have been anything."

"I looked in her mouth," Evan said. "The dental work was definitely Russian."

"All right. She was Russian. So what?"

This response was interesting to Evan in and of itself. Any true civilian would have said, "What the hell were you doing looking in her mouth?" or something along those lines. Hollis hadn't batted an eye. This confirmed her initial sense that Hollis was far more than he appeared to be. The response told her two other things: first, Hollis knew who Anna Alta was, and second, he was surprised by the Russian angle. Had he perhaps known her as a member of Nemesis?

"Is Nemesis a Russian SVR initiative?" Evan said, taking a stab in the dark.

"How the hell should I know?" Hollis snapped. "What's Nemesis?"

Evan dangled the pendant at the end of its chain. "I was sure you could tell me, seeing as how you seem to be a part of the conspiracy of ravens." She motioned for Peter to lay out Hollis's jacket so the raven pin was visible, then turned to Hollis. "What's your explanation?"

Hollis spread his hands. "I saw the pin in a jewelry store window. I liked it. I bought it. End of story."

Evan had to give him marks for staying cool under pressure. He was a good improviser. Still: "You don't expect me to believe that."

"Frankly, I don't give a flying fuck what you believe. I don't know who you are and why Peter had the poor sense to bring you here." He turned his lambent eyes on Limas. "Peter, who is this girl really?"

Limas swallowed. "A friend of a friend. That's all I know."

"Well, it isn't enough. Not nearly."

Hollis started to get up again, and Evan said, "Sit down and listen."

He glared at Evan.

"You might even learn something."

He hesitated long enough to make it seem he wasn't acquiescing, that he was sitting because he wanted to sit and for no other reason.

Evan admired that, too. Whoever he was working for knew what they were doing in recruiting him. Evan fingered the ravens, as if trying to tap into their wisdom. "Earlier today the Russian agent known as Anna Alta loaded a bomb into a white Nissan and, with the help of the guard on duty, drove it through the gates of a restricted compound. Subsequently, the bomb detonated while I was in the vehicle next to it. I was with Brenda Myers." She turned her gaze on Hollis. "That's how I came to Peter. That's why he brought me to meet you when I asked him to."

Her gaze seemed to bore into Hollis. "Happily that vehicle was armored. As you see, I survived. So did Brenda. Some hours later, I returned to the site and found Anna Alta. She was in hiding. She wasn't interested in answering my questions. Instead, she ran."

"So you're a federal agent. And you killed her." Hollis spit this out with a heavyweight hostility. "That's how you got that fucking pendant."

"You're upset, angry," Evan said. "So you knew her?"

Hollis screwed up his face. "Yes. All right. She was Nemesis."

Isobel's eyes snapped toward him. "Roger, you never told me any of this."

"You *knew* about this?" Peter leapt at his partner, and

Evan was obliged to pull them apart. While Evan sought to calm Peter down, Isobel pushed a button under the table. Immediately, Mike opened the door, peered in.

"Please escort Mr. Limas out."

Mike was about to take possession of Peter, when Evan said, "Wait a moment, Mike, would you." She turned to Limas. "Peter, Hollis might not be responsible for the bomb. Let's hear them out first. What d'you say?" She stared hard at Limas, trying to get her point across. Limas was still, his fists slowly uncurled.

Thank you, she mouthed silently to him before turning back to Isobel. "I'll vouch for Peter. He gives his word he's calmed down; let him stay."

Isobel sighed, gave a nod—not to Evan but to Mike. Immediately, he turned and left.

When the door closed behind him, Evan pocketed the pendant. She leaned in, hands flat on the table. She looked from Hollis to Isobel, then back to Hollis. "Anything to say, Roger?"

Isobel continued to glower. Hollis's face was as blank as a windowless building.

"What is your conspiracy of ravens? What are you mixed up in?"

Hollis's response was to pull a pistol. It was small, a .22, easy to conceal. It didn't have a lot of stopping power, but at this close distance it didn't matter. A .22 bullet could kill Evan just as efficiently as a .45.

17

"That's not what you want, sir," Mike said darkly. Isobel had signaled him and he had reentered the room, silent as a cat.

Hollis turned his animus on him. "Don't tell me what I want, black boy."

Mike's interjection and Hollis's shocking response gave Evan the opening she needed. She upended the card table with such force the opposite edge struck Hollis, tipping him over backward. Leaping onto the canted-over table, Evan slid down toward Hollis, who was sprawled on the floor half in and half out of the chair. The .22 had skittered away, lodged under the sideboard.

"What the hell!" Hollis roared.

"Tell me what I want to know," Evan said.

"What d'you think you're doing?" Hollis shouted at Mike. "You're security for Christ's sake. Do your fucking job."

Isobel gave the smallest shake of the head. Mike made no move, one way or the other.

Hollis squirmed beneath Evan's grip. "Jesus. Who the fuck are you?"

It was Limas who answered him. "What I want to know is who the fuck *you* are."

Evan shook Hollis until his teeth clacked together. "Tell me about the ravens. Now."

Evan saw Hollis's hand moving. A miniature knife appeared on his fingertips and was thrust at her so quickly she managed only a partial escape. The blade penetrated her right cheek, missing her eye by inches. Peter waded in, slamming his fist into his partner's mouth.

"You motherfucker." Hollis's voice was guttural, half-strangled. His face worked, turning it hard and ugly.

Taking in the scene in one visual sweep, Mike aimed his drawn Beretta at the center of Peter's back. Turning on her heel and rising into a crouch, Evan whipped Hollis's jacket off the floor where it had landed when the table was overturned, hurled it so it opened like a cape or a bat's wing in front of the guard's face. While Mike was fending it off, Evan leapt to the sideboard, swept a bottle of gin off the top, swung it into Mike's temple. The glass shattered, the alcohol splattered into his eyes. Mike struck out blindly, sent Peter hard into the side wall, shoulder first.

Hollis had gotten out from under the chair and now he threw himself at Evan, struck her a savage blow on the forehead with his balled left fist. Evan staggered for a moment. Mike slammed his fist into Hollis's throat. His head snapped back, and he staggered against the wall, dazed. Then he came at Mike, his head down, in a bull-charge. Mike caught him in a headlock, twisted him around. Hollis punched him in the kidneys, and again, before Mike buried a knee in his groin.

Still, Isobel did nothing; it was as if she were paralyzed by the rapid series of events.

Evan grabbed Peter by the arm, dragged him out of the room and down the corridor toward the stairs, hoping to make a quick clean exit. But as they reached the top of the staircase, another of Isobel's muscle appeared at the bottom, larger even than Mike. He stared straight up at them with a wicked expression on his granite face, and, with the grace of a dancer, leapt up the stairs two at a time.

Evan hauled Peter left down the hallway as fast as she was able. Limas was hurt—how badly was yet to be determined—but it was all too apparent that being thrown against the wall hadn't done his focus or his ability to reason any favors. He was like a sleepy child being tugged along by a hurrying parent.

The first two doors they came to were locked, the third—on their left—opened onto a smallish storeroom without a window. That left the last door on the left. This, too, was locked, but a well-placed kick from Evan and it burst inward. She manhandled Limas inside, then turned; the muscle was nearly upon her.

Evan was in no shape to take on this moving mountain in a prolonged hand-to-hand. She ducked the muscle's first punch, came inside it instead of backpedaling. A quick jab to the ribs brought home to her the muscle's body-armor-like physique. He didn't even appear to feel the blow. Instead, he rocked Evan back on her heels, causing her to stagger against the broken doorframe. Hands as huge as the side of a pig clamped around Evan's neck. The spatulate thumbs, rough as sandpaper, dug into the hollow of Evan's throat, seeking to shatter the hyoid bone, which would lead to dysphagia—difficulty swallowing—and asphyxiation. Evan, turning herself this way and that, struggled to keep those colossal thumbs from finding their target. But it was no use, sooner rather than later that precious bone would be fractured and she'd be done for.

Her vision was starting to go. Black spots danced before her eyes, and her view of the world narrowed as if she were looking at it through the wrong end of a telescope. Then Peter was on her left side. He pulled the miniature knife out of her cheek, plunged it all the way into the muscle's right shoulder. A roar like a bear caught in a trap, and the thumbs came off as the muscle's hands flew to the wound. Evan ripped off a piece of the splintered wood from the doorframe, and slammed it into the side of the muscle's head.

Turning, Evan saw that Limas had opened the window as wide as it would go. They were in an immaculate, modest-sized guest bedroom at the back of the house, but Evan had no time to appreciate its tasteful furnishings. Joining Limas at the open window, she could see the back alley with its lines of trash bins and the windowless walls of the building across the narrow way. To their left a drainpipe led down to the ground. Beside it was a nasty-looking hackberry tree, its raised bark looking like drooling candlewax.

Evan swung out onto the drainpipe. Reaching out, she grabbed hold of one of the upper hackberry branches, transferred her weight onto the sturdier support.

"Come on, Peter," she called. "Get a move on."

After a moment's hesitation, Limas slid his hands, then his arms around the metal, hugged the drainpipe as he stepped off the windowsill. Almost immediately, a bracket snapped, then another gave way, and the drainpipe started to come away from the building. Limas was bug-eyed, clearly terrified.

Swinging around, Evan wrapped her legs around the trunk of the tree. She could feel the scaliness of the bark as she pressed her knees against it. Reaching out with her upper body, she caught Limas by the elbows, then, as he let go of the drainpipe, the armpits. For a moment, Limas swung precariously over the line of metal trash bins; any of the handles would pierce his back if he fell. Then Evan had him more firmly in her grasp. Her muscles cried out in agony, strained to their limit. Halfway down, Limas's shirt snagged on a branch and ripped. Blood oozed and then stopped as, together, they climbed down through the bare branches of the hackberry to the stinking pavement below.

▪ ▪ ▪

"What the hell happened up there?" Butler said when he arrived, private ambulance and medical team in tow.

When Evan told him, he said, "I ought to shitcan you."

Evan grinned. "You knew I'd do it, didn't you?"

"I knew you'd run down anything and everything, yes."

"Well, it was worth it. Roger Hollis confirmed that Anna Alta was a member of Nemesis. The question I now have to answer is if she had a Russian-made legend, and I'm sure she herself was Russian, should we assume Nemesis is Russian?"

"Unknown as yet, but I'll get to the bottom of it," Butler said. "It's more urgent than ever that you find out what happened in Georgia."

"About Hollis—"

"He'll be taken care of," Butler assured her.

"And Isobel. She claimed she knew nothing of Hollis's involvement in Nemesis, but it would be best to keep her under surveillance too."

"I know all about Isobel," Butler said. It was at this point that he considered revealing Isobel's role as a stringer—a very powerful stringer—for MI7. On the verge of telling Evan he drew back, realizing that this impulse stemmed from his personal relationship. Security dictated that he keep the intel he gave his people compartmentalized.

He switched gears. "I'll have a doctor on board the flight. He can stitch up your cheek. We'll need a nurse, as well."

"Not for me. A doctor is enough—"

"I'm thinking of Peter Limas."

"Why? He's going to the hospital."

"No," Butler said. "He's going with you."

"You can't be serious."

"I've got everything the two of you will need," Butler

said, as if Evan hadn't spoken, "including passports for your new identities, which will be delivered to you at the plane. There's also this." He handed her a mobile phone. "It's linked directly into my mobile via a scrambled VPN network. Call me as needed."

Butler looked down at Limas, who was sitting on the back edge of the ambulance, being checked by members of the medical team. One of them was shining a penlight into one eye, then the other. Evan had a sterile pad over the wound in her cheek. It was only temporary, the doctor had told her, until the wound could be cleaned and stitched. On the other hand, her body felt as if it were coming apart.

Evan did not want to take the phone. "You know that's not how I work."

"This is a case of a different stripe, on every level."

"I don't care," Evan said stubbornly.

Butler clicked his tongue against the roof of his mouth, a sure sign that he was vexed. Then he bent over her, lowering his voice. "Listen to me, Evan. There's something I need to tell you, something I deliberately didn't tell Brenda. There was a seventh name on the Nemesis kill list. I redacted it before she saw it and before I showed you."

Despite her aches and pains, Evan's mind was working overtime. "Not Peter Limas?"

Butler nodded. "Limas goes with you," he said, in a tone of voice Evan knew all too well. "I—we—need to find out who he really is and why he's on that list. Why he has a business partner who wears a raven pin."

"So sweat him," Evan said. "We have people who are good at that."

Butler took the shot, shook his head. "That's just what I won't do; too many questions he may not answer or will lie about. Same goes for Hollis. For the moment, I want him in place. He'll be closely monitored, believe me. As for Limas, his girlfriend's been injured, his partner has proven completely unreliable. He needs a real friend now. You've developed a rapport with him, forged in battle, so to speak, and you of all people know how strong that sort of tie is. String him along. Play it right and he'll open up to you. The situation's a perfect setup." He pressed the mobile into her hand. "He's got nowhere else to turn, but to you."

▪ ▪ ▪

The moment Evan and Limas left with their escorts, Butler pulled out his latest burner phone, pressed a speed-dial number. When Isobel answered, he said, "Are you okay?"

"Right as rain."

"You're not alone."

"Correct."

"Everything went well on this end."

"Capital."

End of conversation. Butler cracked open the burner, slipped out the SIM card, ground it underfoot. On the way back to HQ he slid down the window and threw the burner into the Potomac.

▪ ▪ ▪

Three hours later, Evan, Peter Limas, a doctor, and a nurse were wheels up over the Atlantic, on their way to Malpensa Airport in Milan, on the first leg of their long, lonely trip to RLK Svaneti National Park in the Caucasus Mountains of Georgia.

Evan, her face stiff from Novocain and seven stitches, sat drinking her third bottle of water, rehydrating. Across from her, Peter Limas was slumped in his seat, knocked out from a powerful sedative the nurse had administered before the doctor reset the dislocated shoulder. He gave Evan a seven-day supply of a powerful antibiotic for herself, along with two syringes full of a painkiller for Evan to use on Peter after they landed, and a vial of anti-inflammatory tablets for Peter to take every four hours.

"That's all I can do," the doctor said. "The rest is up to you."

Evan, exhausted, having never felt more alone, closed her eyes and, within moments, plunged into a deep sleep.

▪ ▪ ▪

The red-brick building looms up before her, backgrounded by a sky white from the blinding sun. Where is the red-brick monstrosity? How did she come to be here? She cannot move. When she opens her mouth, she emits only silent breath. The glowering eaves, the ravens, and the turrets fill her field of vision. Has she passed out? Is she in the grip of a waking nightmare? She tries to sit up, tries to take several deep breaths. She wants to call for the doctor. Where is the plane?

She stops so abruptly that the woman says, "Are you all right?" When she doesn't respond, the woman frowns. "You haven't been here before. I mean, it's not in the file they showed me, but then, as they said, there are any number of things that didn't make it to the file, didn't even get to the redacted stage."

Evan blinks. She hears the ravens calling to each other. Or to her?

"I'm fine," she tells the woman as she is brought through the enormous front door of the red-brick building, but her voice seems to come from far away.

Then the door shuts behind her with the sound of a coffin lid closing.

PART TWO

THE FIRST TRIBE

18

Anton Recidivich Gorgonov was in the VIP room of the Ikon nightclub in the Arbat district of Moscow when he was given the news. It was a particularly inconvenient time, being Daniella's twenty-fourth birthday. He knew that his mistress had been looking forward to this evening for six months, maybe more. Now, because of the news he'd received, it was ruined. Ordering one of his bodyguards to take Daniella home—because with what had just hit the fan, God alone knew when he'd be able to return to his apartment—he kissed her brusquely on the lips, ignored the tears springing from her eyes, and hurried out into the street dominated by velvet ropes, long queues of impatient scions of leading oligarchs, and bouncers with billiard-ball skulls.

Snow lay in the gutters like the huddled masses around church fronts. An icy wind off the river made for hunched shoulders and thick scarves pulled up around the ears. Inside the Lincoln Navigator, however, it was toasty. *Say what you will about the Americans,* Gorgonov thought, *they know how to heat and cool their living spaces, even the temporary ones.*

Christmas had come and gone like the thief in the night it was. How he despised this time of year! When his wife expected more of him, when gifts had to be bought and presented, when Lolita was sullen and resentful for being pulled away from her friends, and his mother-in-law came to stay for the Russian Orthodox holiday.

Which was why a "work emergency" always came up, so that he could be with Daniella, free of family constraints and strife. Only this time there really was an emergency, and his very exacting plans with Daniella were in the toilet.

He stared out the blackened windows of the SUV as it sped across the city to the safe house where the alarm had been raised. No one inside the car spoke; no one dared.

Heading south, they crossed the Moskva, the city lights liquefied on its surface, like the tearstains on Daniella's cheeks as he left her. The SUV came to a stop at the head of Tolmachevsky Lane, where before the glorious Revolution the court translators were housed. It seemed like an apt place for the main SVR safe house.

Gorgonov reemerged into winter along with two of his heavily armed men. Their boots crunched softly through the snow; Gorgonov's eyelashes felt heavy with it. His men went first, guns drawn as they entered the building, past the concierge's closed and locked door, cautiously ascending the stairs to the top floor. The hallway was deserted. It smelled of boiled cabbage and melted candle wax. From a floor below, a baby cried, a radio came on, the Sovereign's voice penetrating the floors.

Inside the safe house, he found a mess—chairs smashed, the table overturned, a blackened crater in the center of the mattress where a small fire had once bloomed. A lone bottle of curdled milk stood uncertain guard inside the refrigerator. The cupboards were still stocked with whatever his men had originally laid in. His two men were in the bathroom, sitting, legs splayed, backs against the red porcelain of the tub. Lined up like proper soldiers as they were executed. One bullet to the forehead of each. Blood had congealed on the tile floor.

Gorgonov glanced out the window. It had begun to snow again, the sky low, a gunmetal gray. The snow made everything look forlorn—more forlorn than it already was. But perhaps that was simply his mood, he thought, as he turned away and stepped out of the apartment.

He cursed aloud. From the way his men had been lined up and executed the operation smacked of a GRU hit. It smacked most of all of provocation—a shot across the bow. He had warned General Boyko—he could never think of him as Yuri Fyodorovich, no matter how long they had known each other—not to interfere with his plans for Evan Ryder, but the head of GRU had gone and done just that: he was doing whatever it took to distract Gorgonov from concentrating on Evan. Evan was a difficult enough target without Gorgonov having to divert his energies elsewhere. That Boyko had pulled this off was enough to make Gorgonov want to torch the entire building. But, with an effort, he restrained himself, in part because he did not want his bodyguards with him to see how vexed he was, but mostly because he had a better idea, one that would get under Boyko's skin, make him want to scratch an itch he couldn't reach. If it was a war Boyko wanted it'd be a war he'd get.

■ ■ ■

As for the aforementioned Boyko, he was contentedly ensconced in his apartment in Tverskoi; having cajoled his wife to spend the season with her family in St. Petersburg. Of course, work prevented him from joining her—what a pity! But, he assured her, he would somehow survive.

Now, on this icy winter's eve he was sitting in his den, outstretched legs crossed at the ankles, sipping an iced vodka, watching his cache of Leni Riefenstahl films. Somewhere in the secret heart of the apartment, where neither his wife nor his cleaning lady would ever find it, was a lockbox chock-full of Nazi paraphernalia. Long ago, at school in St. Petersburg, he had come to the conclusion that there was very little difference between fascism and communism, being two paths to the same goal: to keep the masses under control. What he admired most about Hitler was that, up until his hubris had revealed his inner madness, he had kept the masses in complete thrall. That was the endgame, after all—the Sovereign had proven that. In this day and age, however, when the Russian Federation was teetering on the brink of economic disaster, when formerly posh neighborhoods like Rublyovka were now ghost towns because their former residents—oligarchs all—had fled Russia in order to keep intact the fortunes they had extorted out of the economy, there had to be a different endgame that would make Russia great again.

Boyko had to admit that there were times—like now—when, overwhelmed by Russian melancholy, he envied those wealthy sonsofbitches. They had the right idea. Having wrung all the money they could out of Mother Russia, they felt no compunction about abandoning her to the predations of its Sovereign and his small coterie of Politburo insiders, of which the general was sadly not a member. Lyudmila Shokova, the last person Boyko knew personally who was part of that coterie, was MIA. Maybe dead. Served her right, too, cozying up to the American agent Evan Ryder. But still, how Boyko ached to be within that inner circle, to bathe in the unique light of the Sovereign's trust. *Shokova had betrayed that trust, and spoiled it for all of us,* Boyko thought bitterly.

He tried to concentrate on Riefenstahl's images of super-men and -women, so exquisite they verged on the pornographic, but it was no use. His mind, now restless with envy, would not allow it. With a grunt, he rose and, refilling his glass, stepped to the window that overlooked Samotechnaya Street, under which the Neglinnaya River flowed through a hidden tunnel.

Snow was falling from a sky livid with the northern lights of oil and gas refineries, the insistent glow of government buildings built on a colossal scale the better to intimidate the citizenry, who hurried by them, faces averted, hearts beating jackrabbit fast. If the Americans were expert at heating and cooling their buildings, the Russians were expert at using theirs to crush the souls of the populace. Never mind the great unwashed all loved their Sovereign—but then they had no choice, Boyko thought gloomily. The Russian people were not good with choices. Change was not part of their DNA; they much preferred the status quo, even with all its deprivations. The country had been built on deprivations, both before and after the glorious Revolution. Was the Sovereign that much different than the tsars? Boyko thought not; anyone who believed otherwise was fooling themselves.

The snow was piling up, the sounds of car tires turning it to slush were a constant rhythm now, like the ticking of his grandfather's ship's clock. He had been a fleet admiral, much decorated, venerated by his colleagues and those who had come immediately thereafter. But, like all war heroes, he was forgotten now, a relic of Russia's past constantly remade by drone-like apparatchiks under the Sovereign's thumb.

He drained half of his vodka, glanced back over his shoulder at the large box, wrapped in gold foil, tied with a crimson ribbon. He'd bought an ermine coat for Raisa, a surprise that would surely rock her back on her heels. She had asked to come over earlier but he had wanted some time alone. He'd been surrounded by people, light, noise, rushing, high energy for close to eighteen hours, and he needed a brief respite. Now he found himself missing her acutely. He glanced at his watch, then down at the street. She'd be here within minutes. He allowed his mind to move a half hour into the future. In the two years since she had become his mistress, he'd never given her anything close to the ermine. She'd squeal just seeing the box. Then, tearing off the wrapping, she'd open it, plunge her hands into the impossibly soft fur and her eyes would get big around. He'd fetch the caviar out of the refrigerator, pop the cork on a bottle of Agrapart "Venus" Blanc de Blancs he had on ice. They'd drink the Champagne down, and the all-night festivities would be underway.

Outside, the car he had sent for her turned onto Samotechnaya Street, slowed as it approached his apartment. He could feel himself getting hard just at her proximity. The curbside rear door opened and Raisa emerged, elegantly dressed, as ever. At least what one could see of her apparel, her Zac Posen opera coat and her Louboutin pumps. He'd made sure when he bought the coat for her that it was short enough to show off her long model's legs. Underneath, however, he knew she wore nothing but Agent Provocateur bustier, panties, and garter belt that held up her old-school nylons. He was so excited thinking about this he almost raised his hand to wave, but it wouldn't do to let her see him standing at the window, waiting for her like a lovesick schoolboy.

He was about to step back when he saw her stumble over the curb. One more step and she toppled to her knees. Her Zac Posen opened and he saw the blood. The raw wound in her abdomen was enormous, as if she had been shot at close range with both barrels of a Saiga tactical shotgun.

He screamed her name, but of course she couldn't hear him through the double-paned window. Then, as she collapsed onto her stomach, like a marionette whose strings had been cut, he wondered whether she could hear anything at all.

19

The taxi let Riley Rivers off outside Isobel's mansion. It was a clear day. The bright sunshine, brittle as ice, was exhausted, without warmth. Puffballs of clouds dotted the sky as if it were a painting. California Street was, as usual, quiet at this time of day.

Mounting the steps, he pressed the buzzer. When there was no response, he buzzed again repeatedly until, after an unconscionably long time, the door opened inward, but just a crack. He was surprised to see Mike looking the worse for wear. He was savvy enough not to mention it, though.

"Mr. Rivers," Mike said shortly. He moved with uncharacteristic stiffness.

Rivers stepped into the entryway, took off his coat.

"Ms. Lowe will be with you presently."

"She's upstairs, yes? I know the way," Rivers said, which wasn't the smartest thing to say, given that Mike took hold of his biceps in a grip that was just short of being painful.

"Please stay just where you are, Mr. Rivers, there's a good boy."

Rivers looked at him as if he'd lost his mind. He wondered what the hell was going on, but was now certain he'd learn nothing from Mike, who acted as if he didn't know Rivers at all.

Ten minutes later, Mike must have received a signal in his earbud. He lifted an arm, pointing. "Library."

Rivers, feeling more and more shaky, as if he were stepping out into quicksand, stepped down the hallway to the right of the staircase. More muscle, highly refined, more than was Isobel's wont, watched him from the far end. When he reached it, the muscle frisked him, much to his surprise and chagrin. Only then did he open the heavy mahogany door.

Across the threshold, Rivers saw Isobel perched on the arm of one of two matching chairs, legs crossed at the knee, smoking a long, thin cigarette. The chairs were covered in tobacco leather you could get lost in even if you had the legs of a runway model.

He went toward her as if magnetized. "Isobel, I—"

"Not a fucking word." Cigarette in one corner of her mouth, one eye half-closed against the blue smoke, she held out a hand. She knew what was required of her in her double—sometimes triple!—life. It was vital that she exhibit an unmistakable change in demeanor; Rivers needed to feel an added pressure because Ben was feeling added pressure. But there was another reason: Ben had warned her that Evan Ryder was coming, warned her further that the visit could get rough. But she'd had no way of knowing how formidable Ryder would turn out to be. In any case, Ryder was on her way to whatever destination her brief dictated; everything now revolved around Isobel keeping her marks on a tight leash. Any break in their routines might very well alert their higher-ups that they had been compromised. The way to do that with Rivers was to keep him scuttling—so busy he had no time to think. Hollis was her mark, as was Rivers. The little twerp was easily manipulated and thus neutralized. But Hollis—Hollis had put something over on her with this Nemesis business. It was all she could do not to strangle him. She hated him with a fire that would never be extinguished until he got the end he so richly deserved.

"Just give me what you have." Her voice sounded strange—rough and uneven.

Rivers handed over the packet of the day's *dezinformatsiya*. She opened it and began to read as she drew on her cigarette. She took short, quick, agitated puffs. Halfway through her reading, she said, "Sit down, Riley," without looking up.

He sank into the enormous chair facing her. He held his hands together between his knees.

"Pour yourself a drink," she said, still not looking up. "You look like a penitent schoolboy."

He rose, crossed to the sideboard against the left-hand wall, fixed himself a generous portion of bourbon and water from the array of bottles and the stainless-steel pitcher. He noticed with chagrin that his hand trembled slightly as he lifted the water jug. He bit down on his lower lip, took a nice long slug of the bourbon.

Reading through the last page, Isobel closed the folder, set it down on the cushion of the chair upon which she perched. Only then did she finally look up at him. "There's nothing here about who is spearheading the attacks against Benjamin Butler." Her eyes glittered like knife blades. "Didn't I ask you to find out? Did you not hear me? Are you stupid?" She tilted her head, and before Rivers could respond, added, "Or maybe you're simply incompetent."

Rivers swallowed hard. "I'm still digging."

"Well, dig faster." Her fingernails clicked like an impatient insect. "I want to know who or what is behind the online attacks. I want to know who's pulling the strings."

"Besides you, you mean." It was a feeble joke, and he cursed himself silently. His voice sounded weak, watery.

Isobel produced the ghost of a smile, but it wasn't a happy one. "Yes, Riley. Besides me."

"Whoever it is, is well-hidden. It's like going through a maze that leads nowhere."

She drew on the last of her cigarette, nodded. "Finish your drink."

Rivers did as he was told.

"From this moment on you're on the clock, Riley. You have twenty-four hours to find out who's targeting Butler."

"Isobel . . ." Sweat broke out on his hairline. He spread his hands. "Have a heart."

"I can't give you what I don't have," she said so softly he had to strain to hear. "My heart was incinerated long ago, Riley. Now there's only fire and ice inside me. You don't want to come up against either, believe me."

During this discourse, she had become more animated. A fierce energy poured off her like a furnace going full-blast.

"I'll do my best. You know I will, Isobel."

Uncrossing her legs, she stood up. "I don't want your best, Riley," she said emphatically. "I want it done." Her hand swept out, making him cringe. "Work your contacts. Squeeze them hard. Call in favors. Promise them the moon. Whatever it takes. Find out who's behind this campaign against Benjamin Butler."

"Right. Absolutely." Rivers's head nodded as stupidly as a bobblehead in the back of an off-road vehicle. "Whatever it takes," he parroted.

▪ ▪ ▪

When she was sure Riley Rivers had vacated the premises, Isobel returned to the entry staircase, ascended to the second floor. Before heading to her bedroom, she looked the other way down the hall and winced to see the damage to the guest room doorframe, which was worse than she had first thought. Ben owed her one—a big one.

Her own bedroom, at the other end of the hall, was

large and light, beautifully furnished in boot-leather tans and sky blues. To the right was a king-size bed, to the left a love seat, an armoire, a chest of drawers, and a closet door. Windows along the wall straight ahead brought in western light. Every single item was aligned perfectly; the room was immaculate.

Roger Hollis was standing, gazing out of the window, smoking idly, his pose relaxed, as if he owned the room and whatever was in it. The windows overlooked a pair of pencil pine trees, beyond which was the street, a hurrying figure now, a car starting up, driving slowly away.

He stubbed his cigarette out in the crystal ashtray on the windowsill, turned back into the room. She stared with a kind of abstract fascination at the bruises and swelling on his face and neck.

"Now what?" he asked. The pain, along with the swelling, lent him a disfigured look, like a reflection in a fun house mirror.

She snorted, crossed the room to where he was standing. Her hand was a blur as she struck him across the face. So hard his head snapped around.

"What the—"

Isobel's gaze was like a second blow. "What the fuck, Roger? Nemesis?"

"What of it?" Hollis said sullenly. He was about to raise a hand to his cheek where she had struck him, but apparently thought better of it.

"Shall I spell it out for you? You work for me, that's what. I ask you to gather intel on targets and you use the Rubicon software to find it."

"You're handled by the SVR," Roger said, somewhat defensively. "I get my orders from GRU."

Isobel watched him, doing her best to keep calm. How had it taken Evan Ryder to crack this rotten egg open? No matter. Why feel jealous when, because of Ryder, she was finally getting somewhere with Hollis? "So Nemesis is a Russian initiative?"

Hollis shrugged. "I don't know who's behind it, but it's been clear to me for a while that it's needed."

"What the hell does that mean?" she snapped.

He grinned. Clearly, he felt on firmer ground. "Do you think you're the only one with a secret life?"

"That pin . . ."

"The double ravens, yes." Hollis shook out another cigarette and, without offering her one, lit up. "They're a symbol—a symbol of a new era, the start of a cleansing."

A fist gripped her heart. "Cleansing?" She shook her head. "Be clearer, Roger." But she knew; of course she knew, she just didn't want to believe it. "What kind of cleansing do you—?"

"This country needs an enema, Isobel. It needs to be cleared of all the . . . how shall I put it . . . the deadwood. The unclean bloodlines that have been befouling Ameri—"

"Ethnic cleansing." The memory of him calling Mike "black boy" came upon her with the force of a speeding train. Bad enough he was a bigot; but to learn he was . . . "That's what you mean. You're a white supremacist."

"What's the matter, Isobel?" He leered at her. "We'd all be better off, and you know it."

Isobel didn't know whether she was more appalled or furious at this creature standing before her. Him being a Russian agent she could understand. He was all about money; he went through it like water through a sieve. But he was such a good gambler he was almost never in debt. One thing you could say in his favor—now the only thing—was that he refused to embezzle from his company; its welfare and growth was of paramount importance to him. But ironically his weakness for sensual women exposed him to certain determined predators. He had been one of Yana Bardina's first conquests. He'd bought her hook, line, and sinker, fell deeply, irrevocably in love—so much so that when she asked him for favors "for my father," he didn't hesitate to comply.

Because of its sensitive work in cyber-security, Rubicon Solutions had been on the Russians' radar since it opened its doors for business. They had monitored his spending and, at the most opportune moment, when he was deepest in love, they instructed Yana to begin milking him for information—more and more. Every time he balked she threatened to leave him and, abjectly, he stood down. Hollis disgusted Yana, as did all her business paramours. In those last weeks before her murder her skin had become thinner and thinner; she was terrified that one day soon she would inadvertently bare her soul to one of them. Her friendship with Isobel, being able to confide in someone, kept staving off that moment. Unfortunately, her masters, ever vigilant, somehow got wind of her change of heart and had her eliminated.

It was through Yana that Hollis had come to Isobel's attention; so this libidinous side of him was all too familiar, even as its indiscriminate nature turned her stomach. But this—this dangerous fanatic credo of his—was anathema to her and everything she believed to the bottom of her heart. Debate was, of course, out of the question. She knew from experience that these people only dug in their heels against what they saw as antagonists. It was incumbent on her to bury her distaste for him and everything he stood for. She needed to keep Hollis close. For now.

In the meantime, Hollis moved beyond her shock; he simply didn't care. "With my company's software I could probably find out if Steadman works for the same people Myers does."

"Maybe you could, maybe you couldn't," Isobel said, still fighting to keep her rage in check. She knew she needed to get this dialogue back on track. "But do you want to risk being picked up by an NSA netbot?"

Hollis, lighting yet another cigarette from the butt of the last one, didn't seem entirely convinced. "This Steadman, if that's even her real name, knows I'm attached to Nemesis. So does my fucking partner. I don't know what got into Peter." Then his expression grew canny. "Or maybe I do. I think the fucker's been recruited by Myers, his fucking Fed girlfriend." He sucked in smoke, let it hiss out through his nostrils. "I mean, you think you know a guy. Peter was the most politically agnostic person I ever came across."

"How did you two meet, anyway?" Of course, through Ben she knew, but Hollis wasn't aware of that.

He sighed. "We met after he came down from Cambridge. He had a lot of ideas, I had the financial wherewithal. It was a good match. And hey, listen, I've kept an eye on him since we first met. We drink together, we've told each other our past histories. I trust him as a business partner. And I've never heard him utter a political opinion on any subject great or small." His bruises were turning dark and ugly, like his mood. "But now my supposedly apolitical friend brought some kind of agent in here asking about Russians and Nemesis. What the fuck. We need to find her."

Isobel stood, hands on hips. "Listen to me, Roger, going after Steadman is a distraction, a wrong turn. The last thing we need now is to go after a federal agent."

"Then fire that useless muscle of yours."

"Who, Mike? Out of the question." She swept her hand out. "And don't ask again."

"But look what that monkey did to me," he cried, indicating his bruises.

For a moment her rage sneaked through her façade. "It's you who needs to apologize to him." When he said nothing, she took a step toward him. "You *will* apologize, Roger."

He crossed his arms over his chest.

"You can be sure he'll put you in the hospital if you don't."

"You wouldn't allow that."

Isobel gave him a basilisk stare that made him blanch.

Finally, he gave the briefest of nods. Then, struggling lamely to regain some of the face he had lost, "The least I can do is inform Nemesis about this Steadman."

Isobel's eyes narrowed. "Take a moment to think that through, Roger."

"Why? It's actionable intel. Nemesis can go after this fucking female spy."

"It's also going to tell them that you're incompetent, maybe no longer of use to them. Then they get rid of you to seal the leak tight. If that's what you want, go right ahead."

A charged silence built between them. Hollis was the first to break.

"Shit, fuck." Averting his eyes from hers, he looked in the mirror over the chest of drawers. "There isn't any makeup in the world to cover the mess that cunt made of my throat."

Leaning forward, Isobel slapped him hard across the cheek. "Don't you ever—ever—use that word or the names you called Mike in my hearing again." She tossed her head. "Now forget about your bruised ego. Forget about Louise Steadman."

"And what if Peter blabs about me to his girlfriend?"

"He was seriously injured getting out of here. Who knows if he's in any condition to tell anyone anything. In any event, I have it covered. Go back to the office. Concentrate on Rubicon. You have double the work now that your partner is incapacitated."

He frowned. "And what if Peter . . . ? I mean, he's a friend as well as my business partner."

Jesus, Isobel thought. *This guy.* "We'll deal with that then, okay?"

He shook his head. "Why are you always right?"

"Because I'm the only one who takes care of you, Roger. Remember that." She gave him a steely smile lacking all warmth. "And remember, too, there will come a time when you will tell me everything I want to know about your Nemesis contact."

Hollis winced. "He's nothing. A nobody."

"As far as you've been told."

He leaned in to kiss her cheek; she tolerated it even though the touch of his lips made her skin crawl. She wondered how in hell she was ever going to get his stink out of her bedroom.

20

As soon as she had sufficiently recovered her equilibrium, Brenda called Butler, telling him about the Bead's and Peter's real identities. "Clearly, Peter was trying to infiltrate our shop through me."

"I require proof."

"Charles has a photo of Peter meeting with Gorgonov. I'll get it from him and send it to you."

"I'll have IT forensics check it for Photoshopping or any other digital manipulation. Get it to me ASAP."

"Sure thing."

"Also . . ."

"What?"

"Are you all right to continue in the field?"

The dual meaning wasn't lost on Brenda. "Perfectly," she lied.

"I don't want you distracted."

"No worries on that score."

"Okay. Don't worry about Peter," Butler told her. "Concentrate on your own brief."

On that note, they ended the call.

Having waited patiently through her conversation, Charles said, "All I know is the bomb-maker's name," Charles said. "Voron."

"An operational name, surely," Brenda said.

"Undoubtedly," Charles replied. "But a clue to his identity, nonetheless."

They were in Brenda's car, parked on a side street in NE Washington. Not a good neighborhood: run-down buildings, crumbling bodegas, boarded-up storefronts. Rubble-strewn open lots populated by makeshift tents fronted by purloined shopping carts that spoke of a scavenger, drug-addled society of the poor, the desperate, and the hopeless, dangerous when on the prowl for payment for the next high.

"A clue?" Brenda said. "How so?"

"Now I have to wonder whether the operation is Russian at all."

"What? How d'you get that? Isn't Voron a Russian word?"

"Indeed. But it's Russian for raven."

This immediately rang a bell in Brenda's mind. Wilson had been ranting about ravens. She frowned. "Does raven mean anything to you?"

"Indeed." He nodded. "We've discovered that Nemesis has its own sigil: double ravens facing each other."

Was that what Wilson was trying to say? she asked herself. *Had he been captured and tortured by members of Nemesis? Was Nemesis a Russian operation?* The raven was too much of a coincidence, but she knew she needed some direct evidence to link the two incidents.

There was something about Charles that rubbed Brenda the right way. What it was exactly she was hard put to say. Perhaps it was his plain way of speaking, as if directly from the heart. Then again he could be the world's best liar. But to be that he would have to be a sociopath, or, worse, a psychopath, and she just couldn't see either being the case. On the other hand, there was Peter. She kept coming back to how successfully Peter had lied to her. And there was this: his legend had beaten Butler's vetting process. It was the vetting process that had caused her to let her guard down.

She was so full of spiteful rage that she'd briefly entertained the notion not to tell Butler about Peter. But at the moment she couldn't even bring herself to look at the photo of Peter and Gorgonov, let alone have the people back at HQ poring over it, laughing at her humiliation. Helping Charles to bring down this cell that had almost killed her and Evan was the best way to channel her anger.

"Okay. Actually, I'm thinking this has Russian fingerprints all over it." She checked her mobile. "As it happens I know where we can start. There's a man named Nal. Russian, but definitely a man with his own ideas."

"Nal, the wild boar." Charles provided her with a sly smile. "It seems we're overrun with animals."

Nal lived in a two-story wood-shingled shoebox of a building attached to a number of others of identical size, shape, and design. The street was as undistinguished as the neighborhood. Small trees struggled, half-dead, perhaps—it was difficult to tell in the depths of winter—planted by civil engineers without a single thought of keeping them alive. Telephone poles leaning exhausted into the wind were more numerous than the trees. The block looked forlorn and forgotten.

When Charles commented on this, Brenda said, "That seems to be the way Nal likes it. I'm sure he must have enough money to live elsewhere."

"What does he do?" Charles asked as they stepped out of the car.

She laughed softly. "If you asked him he'd clam up like a Mafioso. Actually, he's into all sorts of things, most in gray areas that are at best semi-legal, at worst—well, neither of us wants to know the worst."

Brenda knocked on the front door, waited, knocked again.

He glanced at her. "Morse code?"

She nodded. "Like a 1930s speakeasy."

The door swung open. A blast of sweetly pungent

weed smoke wafted from the interior, out of which, like a genie from his lamp, appeared a small man with a halo of salt-and-pepper hair, eyes like ripe olives, and a mustache as thick as his eyebrows inhabiting his upper lip like a caterpillar.

"Hey, Brenda." He reached out a hand, the back of which was covered in dark hair. "Long time, huh?" They shook hands briefly, like two businessmen who knew each other well, but not that well. His gaze shifted. "Who's this darkening my doorstep?"

Considering Charles's swarthy complexion, he thought this hilarious, but that was Nal all over.

"My name's Charles."

"Charles what?"

"And you are Nal . . . what?"

Nal nodded. "Fair enough. I'm Muslim." He squinted. "You?"

"I'm half Muslim."

"And the other half?"

"Jewish."

Nal grunted. "Well, half is better than none. You have aversion to weed?"

"Not a bit," Charles answered.

Nal grinned, gestured as he stepped back. "You'd better come in. The neighbors will be wondering at my hospitality." He found this hilarious, as well.

He led them through a dingy entryway dominated by the steep staircase up to the second floor. They followed him to the right, down a hallway and into a surprisingly bright kitchen. There a woman, presumably his wife, was busy at the chopping block and the stovetop. She gave them a quick look over her shoulder, then bustled out the back door. Through a smeared window they could see her bending over a root and vegetable garden.

"Coffee?" Nal asked. "It's Turkish. Strong enough to put hair on even your chest, Brenda."

When they both declined he got the message. They

sat at an old-fashioned table with chrome legs and a gray Formica top with a pink boomerang pattern. The walls were painted a quaint 1950s shade of avocado green.

Nal lit a fat spliff, sucked the pot deep into his lungs, then spread his hands, which were large, square, and knobbed. *He wouldn't need a pair of brass knuckles to knock you cold in a fistfight,* Brenda thought. He offered them both a hit, but they declined that as well.

"What can I do for you?" he said, through a cloud of sweetly aromatic smoke.

"We're looking for a bomb-maker," Brenda said.

"He's probably Russian," Charles added. "He's known as Voron."

"The Raven." Nal nodded, took another toke. "I've heard of this one." His voice was thin and strangled from holding the smoke in. "Very meticulous, very excellent." The smoke emerged from between his lips in a hiss like a steam engine. "Also, very unusual. Possibly unique."

"Why is that?" Brenda asked.

"Firstly, Voron does not work for the SVR or any other faction of the Russian intelligence Kommandatura in this country."

"Who gives Voron his orders?"

Nal shrugged. "That I don't know. What I can tell you is that up until several months ago Voron was freelance. Now not." Nal grinned. "Secondly, Voron is not a man." His eyes were very large in their sockets. "Voron is a woman."

21

After several stops, in Milan, then Istanbul, the MI7 jet finally arrived at Shota Rustaveli Tbilisi International Airport, aka Tbilisi Airport. During the journey Evan had given Peter the first of his painkiller shots, and had made sure he took the anti-inflammatory tabs the doctor had prescribed. Butler had provided them with new passports and legends. They were also equipped with cold-weather clothes, including fur-lined hiking boots and toasty Canada Goose arctic anoraks for their foray into the Racha Park area.

Twilight had descended with them. By the time they took a taxi from the airport into the heart of the city the lights were on and the sky was streaked with charcoal. Tbilisi was a far different city than it had been before the Rose Revolution of 2003 ousted the post-Soviet Shevardnadze government. Evan and Limas found themselves being driven through a vibrantly painted, bustling city with good food and rosy-cheeked people with smiling faces. But Old Town was still Old Town, with its pastel-colored wooden houses, liberally sprinkled with the confetti of filigreed porches and railings. And, of course, the Kura River still placidly divided the city.

The light faded fast here and the nights were long. All through a dinner of roast chicken with sour blackberry sauce, cheese bread, and stewed wild greens at a restaurant fronting the river, there was nary a word exchanged between the two. Lights twinkled beyond the trees on the far bank, the sky was a clear navy blue. But for Evan, the image of the red-brick mansion with its towers and its ravens flickered before her, superimposing itself like a shimmering mirage over the peaceful cityscape and the snowcapped peaks toward which they were headed.

That night, she rolled off the narrow bed, its thin, sagging mattress happy to be relieved even of her weight. She turned on the light in the bathroom, through squinted eyes looked at her battered face. Her cheek was still swollen and the wound was throbbing. Peeling off the antiseptic pad, she examined the fine job the doctor had done stitching her up. He had used dissolving stitches. She thought if they left a scar it would be all right with her. Not so bad, all things considered. She swallowed an antibiotic capsule, spread antibiotic cream on the inside of a new pad, applied it to the wound.

Afterward, she stood at the window, looking out at a foreign street in a foreign land, and thought of Lyudmila. *Where are you? I know you're not dead. If you were I'd feel it in my bones. And I miss you.* All the while, she searched for familiar signs: the shadow in a doorway across from the entrance to the hotel, the anonymous dark car parked along the curb, the occasional movement of men on watch inside a cramped space. But as hard as she looked nothing of the sort was visible. Perhaps they weren't being tailed, but constant vigilance had become such an ingrained part of her life it was impossible—not to mention inadvisable—to stop. The moon presented itself as a crescent scar in the darkness. A truck rumbled by and that was all. Not a pedestrian out for a late-night stroll or walking his dog could be seen. The street was as empty as a disused warehouse. At that moment, Tbilisi seemed a lonely city. But possibly that was just her. The failure of her life—the life she had chosen (or had it chosen her? A question she had never been able to answer)—was forever with her.

She had a blank spot in her memory. From three years ago. A gap of three months during a time when she was overseas working with Butler. A gap that began soon after their mission outside St. Petersburg and ended right before Josh broke her heart. And it was during those three lost months that Bobbi had been killed. Back home in Bethesda, her sister had stepped off the curb at a busy intersection and had been struck by a hit-and-run. It had happened so fast, the scene so chaotic, that no one could provide a reliable description of the vehicle; it was dark blue, no black, it was a Chevy, no a Ford, no a GMC. Big car, though, everyone had agreed on that point, if nothing else. So an SUV. Good freaking luck finding it. But an accident? Evan thought not, especially since Butler's wife had been killed ten days earlier, in the same way, during a trip back to DC to visit her ailing father. The GRU preferred way. That damned mission she and Butler had been on outside St. Petersburg. They had taken out the deputy director of GRU as he sat feasting with his cronies and satraps at a glittering restaurant that had been cleared of all other patrons. It had been a bitch infiltrating the restaurant, but infiltration was one of Evan's specialties. And by hook and by crook they had pulled it off.

Retaliation. Both Evan's sister and Butler's wife victims of hit-and-runs within months of their returning from their mission in Russia. The GRU could have handled the two murders in different ways, but they hadn't. The Russians had sent a message: you hurt us, we hurt you back.

A terribly steep price had been paid for success. A Pyrrhic victory, if ever there was one. Another example of the quicksand of the world in which they lived. One step forward, two back, two steps forward, one back. Evan had never forgiven herself, for six months had taken herself out of the world of the clandestine agent, traveled on her own without mobile phone or laptop. Completely disconnected from the modern world. She was fed up with the shadow and modern worlds, and her place in either of them.

She had missed Bobbi desperately, wondered how her two kids were dealing. But, as with many things in the so-called normal world, she was no good with kids. Sooner or later—usually sooner—they tried her patience. Her niece and nephew were no different. She looked at their photos every morning and wept, but she didn't go back to DC to see them. She hated herself for that, just as she hated herself for having put Bobbi in harm's way, inadvertently or not. There was a photo of the two of them she kept near her, studied every night before turning off the lights and sinking into nightmare. She was nineteen, Bobbi seventeen. To ease the sadness of their first birthdays since their parents' deaths, Evan took her sister to someplace far away from everything they'd known, far from the Black Hills, the prairie, the big shouldered bustle of Chicago. She plunged into homework and came up with Sumatra for a week of sun, swimming, fresh food, massages, walks in the rain forest, and, one night, guys who had no clue how young Bobbi was. The photo had been taken by one of the resort's staff, on the beach. The sun was in their eyes and their hair was flying. Wide smiles of bliss. Behind them, the sea.

Evan came away from the window overlooking the desolate Tbilisi street. She still missed Bobbi. She took a small wooden carving from the inner pocket of her jacket, which she had thrown over a chair. They had each chosen one from a carver's street stall and had exchanged them as a remembrance of their week together, a week that had reminded them of the joys of being alive and their love for each other. Evan had given Bobbi an amulet of the shaman of healing and divination, a figure in a conical hat. In return, Bobbi had gifted her with a carving of a Sumatran mythical beast, a naga morsarang, part horse, part dragon, part lion. Evan had always thought of it as a fanciful seahorse. Its surface was shiny as glass, rubbed smooth by her fingering; it was always with her.

Behind us, the prairie, behind us the sea, Evan thought, her eyes clouded with tears. Oh, to turn back time, to have Bobbi back again. *I was supposed to protect you. I failed.*

She put the naga morsarang on the bedside table, lay back on the bed, her mind trying to work out the writing on the blank page out of time and space. Three months beyond her grasp. A black hole. A moment or forever?

It was obvious to her now that Patrick had triggered her memory, sparking flashes, images of what had happened to her. Pat had known, if only he had been able to tell her before he died. But life was never that easy. Life was hard, and getting harder by the day.

And yet perhaps Pat's death would serve a purpose; that would surely be appropriate, a fitting epitaph for the Toad. She felt herself drawing closer to the answers that had eluded her for years: where had she been during those three months? What had happened to her? Finding those answers, she was quite certain, would bring closure, retribution for what she believed to be Bobbi's murder.

Outside the night stood still and stark. An owl hooted, the lonely cry of the eternal hunter.

■ ■ ■

Morning dawned bright, clear, and cold enough to take their breath away. After a hasty but satisfying breakfast of *khinkali,* the delicious spicy mushroom dumplings that were one of Georgia's national dishes, they were directed to a store where they bought a sledgehammer, a pickax, a spade-bladed shovel, and a pair of powerful LED flashlights. Evan exchanged the equivalent of two hundred-dollars cash for a week's rental of a Range Rover with a built-in GPS, and loaded the tools in the back. They picked up a driving map at the rental agency, and were on the road by 9:30. It was 187 miles from Tbilisi to the park. In just under five hours they had arrived.

The temperature was already near zero at the entrance to the park, and as they drove higher into the Caucasus it began to drop further, precipitously, obliging Evan to turn up the Range Rover's heater to the maximum. An icy wind, bitter and inhospitable, traveled over the land, racing down from the tops of the Caucasus.

Butler had given them the GPS coordinates where the agents had been found.

A mile into the park, they pulled over and had their last stretch before they reached their destination.

"How lonely you must be," Limas said, "the life you lead."

Evan said nothing, remembering the sadness she'd felt while she'd stood at the window of their exhausted hotel. Instead, she surveyed the mountains, as if they were enemies arrayed against her. A couple of eagles could be seen, high up, and just below them what appeared to be a very large, very ugly turkey buzzard. Other than these avian predators, not a creature was stirring, not even a field mouse. And not a single raven.

"I mean, I know Brenda is lonely," Limas prattled on nervously. "Not that she's said so in so many words, but I can tell . . . so I'm assuming . . ." His voice trailed off. He glanced at Evan, then away. His breath floated away like smoke. "Christ, it's cold up here." He shivered within his thick anorak. "Bleak and lifeless."

Possibly, Evan thought, but it seemed to her there was also something impossibly majestic about the Caucasus. "Ka-kaz," she said.

"What?"

"Ka-kaz was the original name," Evan said. "Also the Hittite name for the people living on the southern shore of the Black Sea." She made a sweeping gesture. "There are centuries of history here, Limas. Greek mythology set these mountains as the place where Prometheus was bound. Jason and his Argonauts sought the Golden Fleece in Colchis—the modern Kolkhida Lowland of Georgia, which is hard by the section of the range along the Black Sea coast. And the passes through these mountains, impassible in winter but extraordinarily beautiful in spring and summer, became a major northern migration route for the ancient Fertile Crescent people of the Middle East. The peoples of this region have exhibited an extraordinary ethnic and cultural diversity since early times. Believe it or not, the Colchians were described by the Greek historian Herodotus as being black-skinned Egyptians."

"D'you really believe that?"

Evan shrugged. "To date no one's ever had reason to doubt Herodotus."

"How do you know so much about this area?" Limas asked. "Have you been here before?"

"I haven't," she said automatically. "Not to this specific region anyway." But the fact was she wasn't sure. The moment she'd caught her first glimpse of the Caucasus she'd experienced a dizzying sense of déjà vu. She thought she'd heard the flapping of wings, ravens cawing as they landed on leaded slate-roof tiles.

"Another life, maybe," Evan said, but her tone sounded defensive even to her ears.

"I'll say."

Limas was watching Evan more intently than she cared for.

Evan turned abruptly, her boot soles crunching on the icy gravel, and slid back behind the wheel. When Limas closed the passenger's side door, settled himself in the seat, Evan started the car up, put it in first gear, and drove up the steepening road. They hadn't seen another vehicle since they entered the park. Tourist season was a distant memory. The long season of death had settled over the landscape, raking it raw like talons in flesh.

"I imagine you're wondering why I brought you with me," Evan said, after a time.

"I have been wondering that."

"And I'm wondering why you agreed to come."

"I'm always up for an adventure," Limas said with a grin.

"I mean the real reason." Evan watched the rearview for a moment, then went back to scrutinizing the road, which wound above them seemingly into the heavens. The switchbacks were becoming more numerous and more acute.

"Ah, that." Limas laced his fingers for a moment, pulled them apart. "The truth is what happened back there scared the pants off me. Really, I don't know what the hell was going on with Isobel. And Roger, Jesus Christ. I mean, he's my business partner, for God's sake! Now he seems like Mr. Hyde."

"Maybe he was never Doctor Jekyll."

"Huh, yeah." Limas ducked his head. "But I mean seven years. That's not a short time to think you know someone." He sighed. "I just figured . . . I mean, after what happened to Brenda and to you—what *could* have happened . . . And then this violence over, what, a silver pendant and pin?" He shook his head. "I thought, I've been working nonstop since we opened our shop. Maybe a little ad hoc sabbatical, I mean . . . I don't know."

"Sure you do."

Limas's head swiveled in her direction. "What d'you mean?"

"The pendant, the pin. C'mon, Peter, you know perfectly well what the two ravens mean."

"The hell I do!" Limas said hotly.

Evan slowed, pulled onto the shoulder, put the car in

park, and engaged the parking brake. "Those two kissing ravens are the reason I brought you with me. You know something about them. Maybe everything." She let the silver pendant hang from its chain in the air between them. "You heard what I said to Isobel. This came from the woman who drove the car bomb onto the St. Agnes parking lot. I found her, ran her down. She forced me to kill her. She was wearing the two ravens, just like your partner, Roger Hollis."

Evan swung the pendant into his cupped palm.

Limas shook his head. "Whatever Roger might be up to he's on his own. I'm as much in the dark about it as you are."

"Really? Nemesis is a cabal of some kind. A group of conspirators that crosses international borders," Evan went on. "That's nothing new for me. I specialize in destroying conspiracies, in bringing cabals down. What Nemesis wants—what *you* want, Limas—is why you're here with me now. Why we've stopped on this deserted stretch of road in the middle of nowhere. No one will hear you scream, except maybe the eagles and hawks. They'll be more than happy to pick you apart after I throw you out of the car."

All the blood had drained from Limas's face. He looked sick to his stomach.

"I never heard of Nemesis until you brought the name up." Limas chewed his lower lip. "I know you have no reason to believe me, but I'm telling you the truth." He gestured. "Listen, I helped you out of that mess at Isobel's. I mean, that's got to count for something." He listened for an answer, some sign from Evan that wasn't forthcoming.

"Can we please come to some kind of an understanding?" he asked.

Evan's reply was as icy as the wind sweeping over the landscape. "Only when I can be sure you're not holding out on me."

■ ■ ■

"Here you are, sir." Commandant Kristov handed Gorgonov a black file folder with a red stripe slashed diagonally across the top right corner. All Confidential and Urgent communiqués were delivered to him by Kristov's hand only. Nothing appeared electronically on any SVR server. IT paranoia was a watchword Gorgonov had instituted the moment he became director of the SVR. "Direct from Turkey Forward Station."

It was late in the evening, long past dinnertime. Gorgonov had shoved some food into his mouth at his desk, though he'd have been hard-pressed to tell anyone what it was. He had more important things on his mind.

He was about to open the file when his personal mobile buzzed. Kristov raised his eyebrows, about to reach for the phone, but Gorgonov waved him off.

"It's all right. It's my daughter." Nodding, Kristov let himself out of his boss's office. Sighing, Gorgonov picked up the phone.

"Hello, my Lolushka," he said.

"How are you, Papa?" Lolita's high voice piped through the earpiece. "When are you coming home? I miss you."

"I miss you too, little one." Gorgonov was staring at the black folder with the red stripe. He needed to see what was inside immediately. "I'll be home as soon as I can."

"I want to tell you about the gymnastics tournament."

That's right. He'd forgotten all about it. He swiveled his chair to look out the window at the falling snow deepening the blanket covering Moscow like winter's ermine fur.

"How did you do?"

"First place on the balance beam, Papa!"

"How wonderful! I want to hear all about it."

"Every detail!" Lolita cried. "I won't go to sleep until after I told you." He could hear her yawn. "I promise."

"Sugarplum kisses," Gorgonov said, his usual sign-off.

He turned off the phone. He did not want to receive the inevitable call from his wife, asking why he hadn't been at the tournament. She knew why, of course; sometimes she was just into breaking his balls. One of the reasons he had a mistress, compliant and willing, no matter what he asked of her.

Tossing the mobile in a drawer of his desk, he slit open the file with a penknife and shook out the contents: printouts of chatter on the secure networks Turkey Forward Station monitored. As he read, his pulse climbed. These communiqués involved Nemesis, an organization he and his team had been monitoring, gathering intel about for the Sovereign. But more than that, one of them hinted that Boyko had a private connection to Nemesis that no one, least of all the Sovereign, knew about.

This news was so hot, he knew he needed both clarification and confirmation before he could believe it, and act on it.

■ ■ ■

"You don't look yourself," Limas said.

Evan stared out the windshield. "How's your shoulder?"

"I don't need another shot yet."

Evan nodded, seemingly satisfied.

They sat side by side in the car. Evan gripped the wheel with knuckles white with the tension of her repeated mirage. She wanted to bang the side of her head, shake loose the rest of the memory of the red-brick mansion and the two ravens.

At length, Limas said, "What is it?"

Evan ignored his question, released the brake and put the car in Drive. Checking the Range Rover's GPS, Evan saw they were less than a mile from the place where

Jules's and Albert's mutilated corpses were discovered and where they suspected the two MI6 agents might be found as well. Tension of another sort filled the Range Rover's cabin. They were fairly high up now. The sky had turned dark and ugly, but being inside the vehicle and so concentrated on what lay ahead of them, they had scarcely noticed the change.

When they arrived at their destination, however, and stepped out of the SUV, they felt the wetness in the air, along with a release of the fierce grip of the cold.

"It's going to snow," Limas said, glancing up.

"No," Evan said. "Something much worse."

They hurried over to the place, perhaps three hundred yards west of the road, where the bodies had been dumped. Due to the lack of blood in the forensic photos, Evan was certain the bodies had been killed, mutilated, and drained of blood elsewhere—where? The red-brick mansion?—before being dumped here in the desolate wastes of the park.

At first, it appeared as if the killer or killers had chosen the dumping ground at random, but closer to, it became apparent that the area must have been scouted extensively. The bodies had been laid in a shallow depression in the icy rock.

There was nothing for Evan and Limas to look at now that the corpses had been removed. Butler's forensics team—and, presumably, one from MI6—had been all over the area with a fine-tooth comb. She squatted down in the center of the depression, gathered up as much of the snowy earth the frozen ground would allow without a pickax. Doubtless, Butler had asked her to come here hoping she would spot something the forensics team had missed. But there was nothing. Nothing at all.

It was at that moment that the sky decided to open up. The hail began as a benign patter, but soon enough turned into a torrent that bounced off every hard surface like steel ball bearings. They beat a hasty retreat to the Range Rover, where they sat in silence, amid the deafening racket the hail made on the vehicle's roof.

"This looks—and sounds—biblical," Limas observed, after about ten unrelenting minutes of the hailstorm.

Visibility had been reduced to almost nil; they were hard put to make out the front end of the Range Rover's hood. They were locked in a metal cocoon. Their breath fogged up the windows.

"Louise . . ." Limas had turned toward her. "Louise, I—" He kissed her then, hard on the lips. His arms, awkward in their arctic coat, went around her, pulling her to him.

Evan straight-armed him, pushed him back against the passenger door.

"For fuck's sake, Peter."

"What?"

"Are you kidding me? Brenda's your girlfriend. She's my friend. What's the matter with you? This is how you'd never cheat on her?"

His expression was stricken. His face was darkly flushed. "You're right. I . . . I don't know . . . I just thought—"

"Well, don't—think along those lines."

He looked abruptly miserable. "I know. I'm so sorry, Louise. But you're so . . ."

A charged silence that Evan knew she had to puncture because he wouldn't.

She bristled. "I'm so what?"

"So goddamned beautiful. And then I saw you in action, I saw how you handled difficult, frightening situations, I saw how you handled men, and I thought . . ."

"What? Wonder Woman?"

He hung his head. "I . . . Well, you know, I loved Wonder Woman when I was a kid."

"Drooled over her, I bet, or—"

"Please!" he cried. "Stop!" Shaking his head. "I can't."

"No," Evan said. She didn't know whether to slap Peter or to feel sorry for him. "You can't."

■ ■ ■

The hailstorm was gone almost as quickly as it had begun. They exited the car. The air had a bruised feel to it, making everything in the immediate vicinity seem culpable. Evan's glance wandered back to the shallow depression, but immediately her attention was drawn toward the rock formation just beyond it. The hail, acting just like the ball bearings they resembled, had eaten away at the snow and the ice, which was now as heavily pockmarked as the surface of the moon.

She went around to the back of the vehicle, handed the pickax to Limas, took out the sledgehammer for herself. The ground, which had been hard and true, was now slippery and treacherous. What was left of the hail rolled under their boot soles, threatening at any moment to upend them.

"Where are we going?" Limas asked. "What have you seen?" Then he got it and hurried after her as fast as he could manage.

"There's a hollow in there," Evan said, indicating the pockmarked rock face. "Maybe even a shallow cave."

Taking up the sledge, Evan swung it down hard, and the center of the icy face exploded outward. Limas wanted to use the pickax, but Evan snatched it out of his hand.

"You're making me feel like an invalid," Limas protested.

"Relax, Bruce Banner." Evan wielded the pickax over and over, and slowly but surely the weakened wall of ice gave grudging way, making a small window through which they peered, playing the beams of their flashlights into the space.

"Two," Limas said. "I count two bodies."

Now, bum shoulder or no, Limas insisted on working beside her. Half an hour of hard labor brought them their prize: two frozen bodies. They were male, in their early thirties, clearly had been very fit when alive. Like Butler's agents, they both had ligature marks on their wrists and ankles and had been drained of blood, no doubt hung upside down while someone or some*thing* ripped their throats out. When she looked more closely Evan could just make out the semi-circular indentations made by teeth. Animal or human, it was impossible to say.

"Christ Almighty." Limas sat back on his hams and rubbed his shoulder. "Who are they?"

Evan recognized them from the photos Butler had shown her. "These are the two missing MI6 agents: Simon Fraser on the left, Ian Ridgley on the right."

"Look what's been done to them. I mean . . ." Limas rose on unsteady legs, backing away.

"Ritual murders, like the others," Evan said. "Same killer or killers."

"It's bestial, like they were attacked by a mad dog or a wolf . . ." Limas was white as the calcium rock over which he was stumbling. "How . . . how many others?"

"Two of ours. Hey, Peter, deep breaths."

Limas nodded uncertainly. Then he turned away abruptly, bent double, and vomited onto the icy ground. Evan went to him, held him as his body shuddered and spasmed.

"It's okay, Peter. Just try to take deep breaths."

When she was sure he was sufficiently recovered, she went and took out the small Leica Butler had provided, snapped as many photos from different angles, including close-ups of the faces, the feet, dark with coagulated blood, and the mutilated throats as she felt was necessary. This new, tricked-out camera was connected to the internet, and she uploaded the photos to Butler's private server.

"Looks like we did MI6 a big favor, finding their

missing people," Evan said when Limas tottered back, eyes still half-averted from the corpses. "Well, at least there's no smell."

Limas's eyes were tearing and he wiped his mouth with the back of his glove. "Sorry," he muttered. He staggered back to the Range Rover, leaving Evan with the task of returning the tools to the boot.

When that was done, Evan returned to the far edge of the depression, crawled into the shallow cave, ran the beam of her LED around every square inch, looking for something, anything the killer or killers might have left.

All she found was some dark rubble in little clumps near the bodies. It was not until she brought it out into the daylight that she saw that the rubble was actually small pieces of red brick.

22

The sun had not yet risen when Gorgonov and the Sovereign set out on horseback. Mist cloaked the lowlands outside Moscow in a mystic shawl. The horses' hooves beat the frozen ground to death, cracking ice, kicking up clods of snowy earth as the steeds thundered across the grasslands, heading for the dense pine forest to the east. The sky was streaked marble. Crows cawed and circled.

The Sovereign wore leather breeches that came up past his navel. Above the waistband he was naked, his hairless, hard-nippled chest bare to the first crescent of sun appearing over the horizon. He wore high boots, polished to a high gloss. Strapped to his right thigh was a leather holster that held his custom-made Colt .45 with crosshatched gold grips. It seemed to amuse him to be using an American manufactured sidearm.

The Sovereign had a head like a bullet, with close-cropped steel-gray hair, and the eyes of a fox that missed nothing. He was not a large man, but terrifying for all that. He had a wrestler's build, and was damn proud of it. In fact, Gorgonov knew, he had wrestled in his youth in St. Petersburg, rarely losing. He had continued that pursuit even when he joined the KGB, this prowess helping him on every rung of the government ladder he climbed with terrifying speed. People died in his wake, or went missing. No one dared question what had happened to them, or even looked very hard for the perpetrators. Certainly, they never turned their gaze toward the Sovereign himself.

Shokova and the Sovereign had been close during her time as a high-level apparatchik in the Kremlin. Maybe he even helped her rapid rise to power. Maybe he was fucking her brains out or, more likely, the other way around. In any event, the Sovereign came to trust her opinions. Which made Shokova's ultimate betrayal that much more difficult for the Sovereign to swallow. If Gorgonov were to be honest with himself, nothing had been the same since Shokova had vanished. It was only afterward, sifting through numerous clues they had all ignored before, that he had unearthed her close friendship with Evan Ryder, a betrayal that eclipsed all the others she had committed.

The horses galloped full out across the icy field, the Sovereign slightly in the lead. Gold and rose shards of light filled the morning. The horses' breath made constant puffs of steam, as if they were iron horses of old. This was not the first time Gorgonov had been asked to go riding with the Sovereign, and though it was a rarified privilege it invariably filled Gorgonov with the unpleasant sensation that at any minute the ground he was crossing would open up and swallow him whole. In the Sovereign's presence he was constantly grinding his teeth until his jaw became one giant monkey fist.

At the leading edge of the pine forest, they slowed their horses to a walk, leading their mounts through the labyrinth of trees. At length, they arrived at a clearing. Anyone else would have dismounted, but not the Sovereign. He sat, straight-backed on his saddle, peering at God knew what. Gorgonov remained a silent observer. He knew better than to speak unless spoken to.

After a time, the Sovereign jerked the reins, turning the horse around so that they both faced Gorgonov. "I'm starting to harbor doubts about our General Boyko. I don't think we have half the number of bots we should have. We need to be flooding the American internet with *dezinformatsiya*. Now that they have a comically ineffectual party in power and the opposition is in total disarray, it is our time to do anything with the government we want. And this president is nothing more than, as the Chinese say, a paper tiger. I can make him do or say virtually anything I want."

Like his mount, the Sovereign breathed out through his nostrils in twin clouds of smoke. Gorgonov had the sudden notion that although the Sovereign's horse could do no better than breathe smoke, the next time the Sovereign opened his mouth he'd be breathing dragon fire. With anyone but the Sovereign the idea would seem absurd.

"Instead, all Yuri Fyodorovich appears concerned with is bringing down that American agent." He meant Evan Ryder. Gorgonov knew that the Sovereign would never speak Ryder's name, referring to her only as *that American agent*. "In fact, to my mind he appears obsessed with her since the incident outside St. Petersburg."

It had been Boyko's hand-chosen deputy director who Ryder and Benjamin Butler had murdered in the Korovaroom restaurant near St. Petersburg. In Gorgonov's opinion the general had never been the same since.

"I don't care about that American agent, Anton Recidivich," the Sovereign was saying. "She is of no moment to me or to the Federation now that the Traitor has been erased in the revision of our past." By "the Traitor" he meant Lyudmila Shokova; he had ceased to utter her name, as well. "Do I make myself clear, Anton Recidivich?"

"As always, sir." Gorgonov was elated that his onetime school chum and friend, now his bitter enemy, had fallen from grace. At the same time he thanked his lucky stars that he had kept his own attack against Evan Ryder secret, oblique though it might be.

The Sovereign nodded. "Good. I know I can count on you, Anton Recidivich." It still astonished Gorgonov that the Sovereign's bare skin wasn't even goose-fleshed in the icy morning wind.

The Sovereign brought his mount close beside Gorgonov's; their knees were almost touching, and Gorgonov thought he could feel a fiery heat emanating from his leader.

"Now, Anton Recidivich, you have news for me about this group, yes?"

"Nemesis. Yes, sir." Gorgonov held his reins barehanded, despite his wind- and cold-reddened flesh. He resisted the urge to turn up his collar, was peeved at himself for not having done it earlier. He'd misjudged just how cold the morning would stay. The sun, struggling over the horizon, was helpless in the grip of the icy chill.

"Nemesis is a neo-Nazi organization," Gorgonov said. "My suspicion is they're an action group funded and controlled by our own RNU." He meant the Russian National Unity Party, an ultra-right-wing group, espousing neo-Nazism, anti-Semitism, Islamophobia, and Russian nationalism. It also wanted the Russian Orthodox Church to have a larger role in Russian life and government. As such, the RNU was anathema to the Sovereign and the State.

"Well, that is a surprise." The Sovereign's voice dripped contempt. "I've tolerated these criminals long enough. I want your keen eye trained on the RNU."

"That might be construed as stepping on the FSB's toes." The FSB, like the American FBI, was in charge of internal security.

"I'll handle Roskov." Alex Roskov was the head of FSB. "You do what you need to do with the RNU. It's grown at an alarming pace, and according to you, that's due to Nemesis. The two are bundled, I'm quite sure. There's a serpent at the bosom of Mother Russia, Anton Recidivich. Find that serpent and kill it."

"No matter how deeply inside Russia's bosom it resides?"

"Absolutely, yes. You have my imprimatur."

Gorgonov nodded. "At once, Sovereign."

The sky had clouded over, and there came a change in the wind—still icy, but now carrying a dampness that penetrated Gorgonov's thick coat all the way to his bones. For his part, the Sovereign seemed unaffected. Even the small silver cross that hung from a chain around his neck hugged his breastbone as if for warmth. A few moments later, the first flakes of snow began to filter down into the clearing. Both horses stamped their hooves, as if anxious to return to the warmth of the Sovereign's stable, where they would get a good brushing down and a galvanized metal bucket of oats.

The Sovereign's expression made it clear that he was deep in thought. He jerked on the reins, bringing his horse back to attention, as if it, as well as Gorgonov, needed to hear what he said next. "Attend me well, Anton Recidivich. The rise of fascism in America will tear the country apart." His eyes narrowed. "That will never happen here."

"I couldn't agree more, sir."

The Sovereign's vulpine eyes fixed on Gorgonov with terrifying intensity. "Good, good. Then get to work!"

"I will need funds, sir. Quite a lot."

"You'll have as much as you need, my friend," the Sovereign assured him. He grinned. "One day soon, when your mission is accomplished, Anton Recidivich, you and I shall go bear hunting together. How I love to kill those huge beasts! You will, too, once you get a taste of it."

With that pronouncement, the Sovereign dug his heels into the flanks of his horse. It wheeled around, taking its master back into the trees, where he vanished amid the pine needles and the snow that drifted down from a low, formless sky.

▪ ▪ ▪

Gorgonov returned to his dacha in a state of elation. His meeting with the Sovereign could not have gone better. In the matter of Boyko, the Sovereign said render therefore unto Gorgonov the things that are Gorgonov's. He had made perfectly clear to the Sovereign that only he had the means of defeating the RNU and, by extension, Nemesis, and thus his standing with the Sovereign was both cemented and, if he played his hand right, elevated. The Sovereign had called him "my friend" for the first time ever!

He basked in this glory while he took a long, hot shower, returning to his extremities the warmth in which they functioned at optimal level. Upon his arrival, he had told his chef to haul the goose he himself had shot two weeks ago out of the freezer and prepare it with figs and lingonberries for dinner. He left the rest of the menu to his chef while he went upstairs to clean his body and clear his mind, his spirit in a kind of ecstasy he hadn't experienced for many months.

He lay naked on the bed, a bearskin over him, while a fire burned in the hearth opposite the foot of the bed. Sheer white curtains stirred in the firelight as if Daniella was singing him to sleep. He drifted off missing her.

He awoke to the mouthwatering smells of the goose roasting in the oven. It was late afternoon; he realized that he hadn't slept so well, so deeply in some time. Throwing off the bearskin, he rolled out of bed and dressed for dinner in a newly pressed linen shirt, a light tunic.

Downstairs, the table had been laid using his mother's Reichenbach Dresden china with the cabbage rose motif, as he had directed. The crystal sparkled beneath the diamond light from the Swarovski chandelier. The silverware shone like his polished shoes.

Fyodr, coming from the kitchen, informed him that dinner would be served in five minutes.

"Would the Director care for an aperitif?" Fyodr asked solicitously.

Gorgonov almost said yes, but then he remembered the barrel of '71 Côte de Beaune Grand Cru red he'd opened when he'd had General Boyko to dinner and thought that wine would be a perfect companion for the richness of the golden roasted goose flesh.

Dismissing Fyodr, he went out the back door, walked the short distance through the icy nighttime air to the temperature- and humidity-controlled building he had had constructed as his vast wine store room, a passionate adjunct to the wine cellar proper in the basement of the dacha.

Inside it was cool and dim. Barrels of the wines he'd coveted most highly, and had imported especially and at great expense from the wine-growing terroirs of France, were stacked on row after row of wooden shelves. The '71 Côte de Beaune was at the far end of Row C. As he strode down the aisle he could smell the delicious effluence of the wines' slow and stately aging. There was something completely calming about being here. It was, besides the heady scents, the sense of God-like control. These barrels were under his aegis; they aged for precisely as long as he wanted them to. They were his subjects, bending their proverbial knee to his wishes.

The '71 Côte de Beaune was in a beautifully manufactured barrel in front of which he stopped. He placed his hand on the barrel head for a moment, as if he could feel the heartbeat of the delicious red wine. His mouth was already watering at the thought of savoring the velvety character, the complex mouthfeel of the Grand Cru.

But as he reached for the glass decanter, one of a dozen lined up in a special glass-fronted case, the hand on the barrel began to itch, then to burn. At once, he snatched his hand away, stared at the palm and fingers dumbly. They were starting to redden. He brought them up to his nose, sniffed, then recoiled at the acrid odor. Taking up a wooden-handled implement akin to a boathook, used to turn the barrels periodically or to move them when their time came to be brought into the dacha's wine cellar, he inserted the sharp end into the top of the barrel and tugged.

At first, nothing happened. But, then, as he put his back and shoulders into it, and began to jerk the implement backward, the top loosened all at once, so that he was just able to jump back before the liquid came pouring out.

But it wasn't just his coveted '71 Côte de Beaune Grand Cru that cascaded onto the floor. Washed out with the dark-red flood was the body of his beloved Daniella, blue eyes blackened holes, lipless mouth opened in the rictus of a dreadful scream. He had never before been witness to such an expression of pure terror.

Drowned in Grand Cru wine and muriatic acid.

23

The building was a long, low structure with a corrugated roof. It looked like nothing more than a postmodern barn or a storage facility for silage. This rural acreage in Maryland was where Nal claimed Voron, the bomb-maker, had set up her workshop. Incredibly, the voracious urban expansion that gripped most of the greater DC area had not yet reached its tentacles this far out.

Unlike the rolling hills of Virginia, the landscape here was flat and bleak, stubbly as a Marine's scalp. Once, Nal told them, the acreage had been thick with a verdant forest, but years ago it had been clear-cut in preparation for the building of yet another planned suburban community. The Great Recession had bankrupted the developer and, because more extensive testing by subsequent prospective buyers had detected water contamination from paper mills on higher ground, the land remained unsold and deserted. "It was just the ticket for a bomb-maker looking to set up shop," Nal had said, just before they left. "But be extra careful. Bomb-makers by definition are borderline crazy. From what I've heard, Voron crossed that border some time ago."

Brenda and Charles sat in the car, scanning the immediate area.

"Ready?" Charles said, after a moment.

They exited the car, keeping the doors open behind them. There was no cover between them and the building—no foliage, no outbuildings or even rusted-out vehicles to hide their silent approach. They were counting on the lack of any vehicle in the vicinity to mean that no one was inside. Nonetheless, both of them had their handguns out and at their sides, ready to use at a moment's notice. The lack of cover dictated that they come at the building from different directions, heading for different destinations, Charles to the building's rear entrance, Brenda to the front.

Charles reached the wall of the building without incident and disappeared around the back wall just as Brenda reached the front wall. The front was dominated by an enormous industrial-size opening with a steel roll-up door that was down and shut tight. Just to the left of it was a normal-size door with a four-pane window at head height. Brenda peered in, shading her eyes on either side, but the glass was so smeared and dusty she couldn't make out a thing.

The door was locked, but that proved no problem. Using a pair from a set of steel picks, she set about cajoling the tumblers to move to the rhythm she induced. Forty seconds later, she was inside.

Closing the door soundlessly behind her, she took a long look around. Daylight made its feeble way through small, filthy windows set high up in the front wall, illuminating thick columns of particles swirling like dust devils in the current of air caused by her opening and closing the door.

She found herself in a space as large as an airplane hangar. Thick steel crossbeams ran overhead, hazy with distance and the dusty air. It was frigid inside, as if the space hadn't been heated for a long time. Perhaps it never had.

There was nothing in this space, and no indication of what had once been housed here, not even a rusted screwdriver or wrench or even a particle of hay. There were two doors in the far wall directly in front of her, one more or less on each side, and it was clear from her visual of the outside that there must be another space behind the wall.

As she approached, she crossed the footprints of rodents of some kind—rats or, possibly, raccoons. She paused, listening for them—for anything, really, that seemed out of place. Evan had taught her this important lesson of spycraft when they were together in Berlin. Since then she had found the advice invaluable.

She heard nothing, however, and went on. Which door to take, the right or the left? This decision seemed to her emblematic of the majority of decisions that had to be made during the course of a lifetime. Do I go or do I stop? Do I move forward or retreat? Do I choose one person or the other? Surely, she had made the wrong choice with Limas—she no longer thought of him as Peter, just as she could no longer imagine herself holding hands with him, eating a meal with him, let alone allowing him into her bed. She shivered at the thought that she had had sex with an SVR spy, sent to weasel his way into her life. For a moment she had allowed him into her heart, but that moment was gone, washed away on the bitter tide of betrayal.

Unconsciously, she had paused again. Some animal instinct had insisted she stop while her mind was elsewhere. Furious, she berated herself. *Focus, damn you, girl! Keep your mind on the here and now!*

She found herself closer to the door on her left, so she opened it and went through into a square room with walls paneled in wide rough-hewn wooden boards. A small, scarred skylight threw a feeble handful of daylight into the space. A bare bulb hung from a length of wire from a fixture in the ceiling. A couple of old black-and-white photos in cheap black frames were nailed to one wall: in one, a young man in coveralls stood by the side of a harvester combine or some kind of large machinery, one hand on it as if it were his horse; in the other a large black dog, whose breed she didn't know, wide leather collar half-buried in the thick fur of its neck, sat with its mouth half-open, tongue out, as if it had just completed a long run. She moved closer. Neither of the photos appeared to have been taken on this property. In fact, scrutinizing the background of the first photo, Brenda didn't think it was even this country. Those mountains behind the young farmer looked like the Alps. Switzerland? Austria? She moved closer still, squinting in the gloom. Now she saw that the figure wasn't a farmer at all, or if it was, it was a farmer holding a Russian sidearm. Stepping back, she reached out to flip the wall switch to better illuminate the photos when she heard a shouted command behind her, freezing her blood.

▪ ▪ ▪

"Throats ripped out while the victims were still living. You're right, that does sound like ritual murders," Limas said.

"Or sacrificial deaths," Evan replied.

They were back in Tbilisi, at a restaurant near the Rustaveli Theater. It was crowded and smoky, but oddly cold. And loud, which was good for them; no one was going to be able to overhear their conversation in all that din. Vast quantities of lamb and the ubiquitous *khinkali* dumplings had been set before them, along with tankards of local beer.

Upon entering the restaurant they had gone straight to the bathroom, where Limas exposed his sore shoulder so Evan could administer the second shot of painkiller. Bringing up the dead had done his shoulder no good. When they emerged, they took one of the last available tables against the wall farthest from the door.

"Well, then, who the hell are we dealing with?" Limas said now. "A serial killer, a cabal of cannibals or crazed torturers, or something else altogether?"

Evan produced a small plastic evidence bag, held it in the palm of her hand.

Limas frowned. "What's that?"

"Red brick dust and rubble. I found it in the cave."

Limas shook his head. "There's nothing made of red brick in the park."

"Exactly. I'm thinking this came from the place where the agents were murdered."

Limas shrugged. "Red brick is a common building material. This could be from anywhere."

Maybe, Evan thought. *Maybe not.* Once again the mirage of the hideous red-brick mansion with its two ravens filled her mind, and for just an instant she was back there, being taken inside. She blinked. If only she could remember more, but it was as if a veil had come down over the scene, and then it had vanished entirely.

"What's going on?" Limas said. "This isn't the first time you've seemed far away."

"Nothing," Evan said. "Probably just a hangover from the explosion."

"Sure." Limas's head bobbed up and down, but something in his expression said that he didn't quite believe it. "Frankly, I think it's remarkable you've recovered so quickly. I feel bad I left Brenda still in the hospital."

"She's being well looked after," Evan said absently.

"I know. Mr. Butler assured me of that, and I trust him."

"You should. He has Brenda's best interests at heart."

Limas understood. "I said I was sorry, Louise. What more can I do?"

Evan said nothing; there was nothing to say to that. Either she could forgive Limas or she couldn't. That was up to her now.

The restaurant, ever more crowded, became cacophonous with raised conversations, shouts, hails, and laughter, the weaving of waiters holding heavily laden trays high above their heads. The clink of glasses and silverware, the usual hum elevated to that of the interior of an active beehive.

"So listen." Peter Limas cleared his throat. "Louise Steadman isn't your real name, is it?"

Instantly, Evan's attention refocused. "What gave you that idea?"

"I don't look familiar to you?"

"Should you?"

"You're Evan," Limas said. "Evan Ryder."

Limas's pronouncement was startling, but Evan said nothing, forced herself to put some more food into her mouth. She was now armed with an old but serviceable Beretta with the serial number filed off. On their return from the park, before coming to the restaurant, Evan had made several discreet inquiries in the right part of town. She had left Limas in the Range Rover while she entered a pawnshop disguised as an antiques emporium. Another discreet all-cash transaction got her the loaded Beretta and two extra magazines of ammo. The Beretta comfortingly resided under her coat, stuck in the waistband of her trousers at the small of her back.

"I know you are," Limas plowed on gamely. "You've no reason to deny it."

Evan looked up from her food. "Why would I lie to you about my name?"

"Secrecy. It's part of your job. I imagine you often use a false name."

Evan shrugged, went back to eating. "What's in a name anyway?"

"Plenty."

Evan glanced up at him. Limas had a pained look on his face.

Limas put down his knife and fork. "I have a confession to make."

It was at that moment the first bullet whizzed past the table and embedded itself in the wall. The shot came from a silenced long gun—a sniper's rifle—the report of which could not be heard over the clamor of the diners. The second came so close Evan could feel the rush of air against the back of her neck before it, too, made a neat hole in the wall. At the same time, she saw two musclemen step into the restaurant to stand on either side of the entrance. Their legs were spread at shoulder width; their hands hung loosely at their sides, fingers ever so slightly curled. They were in shooter's stance, ready for anything, and their eyes were on Evan and her companion.

"I don't believe anything you say anymore!" Evan suddenly shouted.

Limas, clearly shocked, said, "What . . . what are you doing?"

"Starting a lovers' quarrel," Evan told him in a lowered voice. Clearly, Limas had no experience with long guns, snipers, or anything in the field, for that matter. "The louder and more violent the better." *No time like the present to learn,* she thought.

She leapt up. "I know you're sleeping with her, you prick!" She grabbed a plate from the table and, with perfect aim, threw it so it sailed past his head and crashed to the floor. That got everyone's attention.

"You're crazy!" Limas shouted back, getting to his feet in such a way that his chair fell over backward. "You're a crazy woman, you know that?!"

"Crazy, am I? I'll show you crazy!" Evan picked up a fork and darted around the table, raising her hand in the air as if she was planning to bury the fork in her cheating boyfriend's head.

Limas grabbed her wrist and began shouting a string of epithets.

The two musclemen by the door left their posts and started toward the scuffle. But diners were also on their feet, rushing with glee toward the argument promising to devolve into a bloody battle of the sexes. The musclemen tried to force their way through the widening scrum, but there were too many people in their way, converging on Evan and Limas. The first to reach them tried pulling them apart. Men were tugging this way and that; in the ensuing melee an errant punch was thrown, then another. Two full-blown fistfights erupted, screams and shouts, more people joining in, while the women, standing back on the edges of the fracas, cheered Evan on in her anger at her faithless man while they craned their necks or held their mobile phones over their heads, taking blind shots.

In the widening chaos, the musclemen lost sight of their quarry, even as they made progress, shouldering their way through the tightly packed crowd. And with good reason. Evan had grabbed Limas with a whispered "*Well done. Time for us to go,*" ducking him away from a flurry of wild punches, quickly worming them both to the rear of the restaurant.

"This way." Evan hurried Limas down a dimly lit corridor that, she saw, led through the steamy kitchen, where industrial-size pots steamed and heavy frying pans burbled with hot oil ladled out from enormous metal cans, and then to the rear door. Three cooks—one older, the other two younger assistants—toiled away, rushing around as if they each had four hands. They were far too busy at their work to even glance up at Evan and Limas, let alone query them.

As the fugitives picked their way through the crowded space, two burly men passed through the rear doorway from the back alley that lived behind most restaurants, facilitating delivery and garbage pickup. They came up the short corridor and into the kitchen with weapons drawn—older Makarovs, but still more than serviceable.

Stepping forward, Evan snatched a frying pan out

of the cook's grip. Hot oil and dumplings sloshed over the rim, but that was nothing compared with what happened when it collided with the leading man's face. He screamed as the cook and his assistants ducked and scattered, plastered themselves against the huge refrigerator that took up half of the right wall.

The second man, elbowing his bent-double partner out of the way, brought his Makarov up, got off a wild shot before he had a chance to aim. That was all Evan needed. She kicked the man in the gut, snatched the lid off one of the pots, and slammed it into his face. The nose split apart, blood gushed, and Evan, stepping into the attack, wrested the Makarov out of the wounded man's hand. Reversing it, she smacked him just above the ear with the butt, then dumped an open pot of dumplings boiling in heady broth onto him. The man screamed, went down on top of his partner. The two were now squarely wedged into the narrow space between the stovetop and the cutting surface. Evan leapt over them.

Turning back, she called out to Limas. "Jump! Jump over them!"

Limas did just that, stumbling a bit as the toe of his boot caught the hunched shoulder of one of the men. His forward boot slipped on the spilled liquid and, if it wasn't for Evan, he would have gone down on top of the two writhing men.

As it was, Evan had to half-drag him out of the kitchen, down the narrow, foul-smelling corridor, and through the rear door. An old four-door Lada in a bilious shade of green was parked in the alley.

Sprinting around to the driver's side, Evan wrenched open the door, but at that moment, with a high revving sound, a motorcycle turned into the alley ahead of them, and came roaring at them. Astride the bike was a slight figure in black leather, a helmet of the same color with the reflective visor down. There was no way to tell whether the rider was male or female, let alone who it might be.

"In!" Evan shouted; Limas did as he was told. The keys were already in the ignition for a quick getaway. The engine coughed to life. "Now hold on." Limas, in the seat beside Evan, pulled the door closed, but even as he did so, Evan threw the car into gear, reversed back down the alley.

The Lada's underpowered engine was no match for the supercharged bike, which continued to hurtle at them with alarming speed. The rider produced a Makarov handgun. Pressing the accelerator to the floor, Evan popped the Lada out of the other end of the alley, turned the wheel over hard. The Lada slewed sideways to the alley. She immediately changed gears and pulled slightly forward so she had a clear view of the oncoming bike and its rider.

She was familiar with the model of Beretta she'd acquired, knew its idiosyncrasy—how it would pull just slightly to the left. Thrusting the gun out the car window, she aimed at the rider's left arm, squeezed off a shot. It hit the rider dead center of his chest. He flew back off the bike, which continued to race toward the Lada. Evan backed away from the mouth of the alley just in time. There was a scream of hot rubber meeting metal as the riderless bike sheared off the Lada's none-too-sturdy front bumper. The Lada slewed again. As for the bike, with the front tire shredded, it stutter-stepped into the blank brick wall on the alley's far side, climbing it for a fraction of a second before smashing backward onto the pavement, shattering itself in a hail of twisted metal, glass fragments, smoking bits of plastic, and smoking rubber strips. One of the pieces of metal slammed into the Lada's hood and bounced off the dent it had made. The car rocked wildly on its springs.

Limas was shaking; his face held a greenish tinge.

"If you're going to be sick," Evan said, "make sure you do it outside the car." Without waiting for a reply, she opened the door, slid out.

"What are you doing?" Limas called in a clotted, choked voice.

"Get out," Evan said. "Get out now."

As Limas staggered out of the Lada, Evan ran around the front of the car, grabbed him by the elbow and pulled him to the rear. She popped open the trunk and pointed. "Sorry. Get in."

"What?" Limas, half-stunned, looked bewildered.

Evan manhandled him into the small space, obliging Limas to curl up in a fetal ball.

"Why?" was all Limas could manage.

"Right now it's the safest place for you. Keep calm; there's plenty of fresh air coming from over the rear seat. I'll be back for you." Then she slammed the trunk.

Evan turned away. Before heading into the alley, she checked the Beretta. When the fragment of motorcycle hit the Lada, it had ricocheted into the handgun. Immediately, she had felt something give on the gun. Now she could see the crack in the barrel. Throwing the useless firearm onto the driver's seat, she picked up a three-foot length of corkscrewed metal from the wrecked cycle and headed up the alley.

Turning into it, she at once saw the rider, flat on his back, one arm flung out wide, the other bent at an acute angle, the hand beneath him. He didn't appear to be breathing, but at this distance and in the low light it was difficult to ascertain what was going on beneath the padded leather motorcycle jacket. She couldn't even tell how much blood the rider had lost.

Moving in, Evan kept one eye on the rider, the other on the far end of the alley. She wondered how long it would take for the first two musclemen to untangle themselves from the scrum, make their way outside, and perhaps come around back to see if their brethren had had better luck. Part of her knew she should get back in the Lada and get out of there as quickly as possible. But another part—the stubborn, strategic part—wanted to know who these would-be assassins were and who had sent them. She harbored a strong suspicion that fleeing the scene would only bring more of them. Also, she didn't care for being shot at or otherwise attacked. It had happened to her twice now in the space of as many days. Once was unacceptable; twice was cause for all-out war. Another reason to—

She was only six or seven paces away when the rider rose up like a phantom. His left hand came out from behind his back and fired three shots at Evan in rapid succession.

24

General Boyko was just being served a late lunch at his desk—a plate of kielbasa and boiled potatoes with thick, almost stew-like gravy—when his mobile phone buzzed. Because he was concentrating on the wording his staff had come up with for the next set of items of American *dezinformatsiya,* he ignored it. But when it buzzed again thirty seconds after it had stopped the first time he angrily picked up the call without looking at the screen.

"What?" he growled.

"Yuri . . ."

He cut the end off of a kielbasa, stabbed it with a fork, not yet reacting to the near-panic in his wife's voice. "Why are you calling me here, when I expressly forbade you to—"

"Did you send one of your people to fetch Elene?"

"No. Why would I?"

"Oh, God, oh, God!"

"Stop that and tell me—"

"Elene is missing," his wife said breathlessly.

"What!" Now the panic in her voice, as well as her words, caused him to leap up with such force his lunch plate flew off his desk, crashing to the floor. "What is that you say?"

Everyone in the large room outside his office instantly stopped what they were doing, sat still as statues.

"Yuri, I went to pick Elene up after ballet class and she wasn't there!"

"That's impossible." A terrible icy feeling rose in his guts, uncoiling like a poisonous viper. He knew that with what was going on between him and Gorgonov it was entirely possible, although he never for an instant thought that—I mean, Elene was his *daughter,* for God's sake!

"But it is, Yuri. She's gone."

Boyko found that he was holding his mobile in a death grip. He took several deep breaths, trying and failing to calm himself. Raisa's murder was still in the forefront of his mind, sending spikes of rage through him. If anything like that had happened to Elene—she was only thirteen. He ground his teeth in fury and terror. A sense of overall sickness gripped him, making the world spin around him so that he was obliged to hold onto the corner of his desk in order not to crumple to the floor.

"Yuri, Elene's *gone*!"

Then he heard her. "Gone? What do you mean *gone*?" Gone, not missing.

"The ballet mistress was very clear. Ten minutes before the end of class, someone came for Elene. That's why I thought you had—"

"Shut up! Who came for her? How could she let a stranger—?"

"He was GRU. One of your people. He showed her his official ID. That's the only reason she let Elene go, she told me. I can't tell you how upset she was when she—"

"Oh, fuck her! Who? Who came for her?"

"She couldn't remember his name. I mean, she was so upset."

Boyko snapped his fingers, mouthed *Car. Now!* to his adjutant, who immediately ran to do his bidding. "I'll go over there myself and shake it out of her."

"No, Yuri. The odd thing is he gave her a slip of paper.

An address where he said he was taking Elene. He said that's where you were."

Boyko pressed his fingers to his temples, which had begun to throb like a second heart. "The address." He scribbled it down, then disconnected his wife without another word.

▪ ▪ ▪

Boyko's armored SUV was heading southeast at speed, the way cleared by a pair of military motorcyclists, headlights flashing. The three worst neighborhoods in Moscow were clumped together like clods of shit outside the MKAD—the Ring Road that encircled the heart of Moscow like a moat. The address the kidnapper impersonating one of Boyko's own people had given his wife was in Nekrasovka, an area incorporated into the city only because of its massive waterworks. Like neighboring Kapotnya, a dung-heap all its own, very few people wanted to live in Nekrasovka, but many were forced to out of necessity because they worked at the massive water plant or because they could afford nothing better. Then there were the homeless, the drugged-up, disaffected youth, the tattooed gangs that roamed these areas, leaving misery and destruction in their wake.

But as the SUV transported the head of the GRU past the MKAD, entering terra incognita for him, these appalling facts were at the very periphery of his mind, relevant only as they pertained to Elene. His daughter was front and center in his attention. Not that he had ever spent much time with her, he brooded. He had no patience for infants or toddlers. And why should he? That was what his wife was for. He had more important things on his mind than shoveling shit off his daughter's tiny backside. And as she grew older? Frankly, he couldn't remember any of her birthdays. How was it that she was thirteen now? When did that happen? At this moment, he felt as if he had been asleep when it came to his children. Elene was the youngest of three. The two boys were off at school in St. Petersburg. He tried to summon up their faces, found only hazy bits and pieces. But, again, he felt strongly that this wasn't his job. Wasn't it enough that his wife surrounded herself with photos of them? The children were entirely her sphere of responsibility.

But now he realized, belatedly, it was true, that he felt differently about Elene. She was the youngest, yes, but she was also a girl, more vulnerable. The boys had always been able to take care of themselves. Weren't there a couple of beat-downs they had effected against those foolish enough to bully them? Yes, of course there were. His wife had been upset, naturally. But he had felt only pride in them, had rewarded them, against his wife's protests, by taking them to the GRU officers' unofficial bordello. "You're a man now," he recalled telling each one in his turn. "It's time you received a man's reward."

"We're close now," his adjutant said, from the front seat, interrupting his internal monologue.

Boyko felt an involuntary shiver run through him, and was instantly ashamed. But this was Elene, his only girl child, the apple of her mother's eye. He could see her face as clearly as if she were sitting beside him, and, with an uncomfortable start, realized that she was the apple of his eye, as well. If he were to lose her now, he would wreak such holy hell on Gorgonov he'd wish he were dead.

Death. Death by drowning. Death by acid bath.

Gripped by a dreadful anxiety, he sat forward, on the edge of the backseat. His right knee bounced up and down like a pneumatic drill. He must not think of these things, not now. Not ever. He must clear his mind for what was to come. Whatever that was.

"We're here," his adjutant said. "This is the address."

The driver signaled the escort, and they all stopped in front of what appeared to be a bombed-out tenement on an otherwise leveled block. Behind it loomed the immense bulk of the waterworks. The oldest part had been converted into low-cost housing. But as far as Boyko could see these buildings were already starting to crumble.

He emerged from the SUV. The GRU riders trotted up, handguns at the ready.

Boyko held them back. "No," he said. "I'm going in alone."

"Do you think that's the wisest option, General?" his adjutant said so softly only his commanding officer could hear. "We have no idea what's inside."

"Stay here," Boyko said, and mounted the steps. The truth was he did not want anyone to witness his reaction to what he feared was awaiting him. Up the broken stone steps he went, pushed through the front door, which long ago had had its lock shot out by God alone knew what band of reavers.

The interior was dimly lit by a rear window, half-hidden behind a metal staircase that ran up the left side of the vestibule, which was, in any event, narrow and dank, filled with a stinking miasma of rotted food, human excrement, unwashed bodies, and death.

Mechanically, he began to move farther into the vestibule, placing one foot in front of the other. He could feel his heartbeat in his throat. He had difficulty drawing breath. *Elene, where are you? Are you here? Are you alive?* He spoke to her in his mind, not daring to utter a word aloud.

He passed the staircase, where from an upper step a one-eyed cat so thin it seemed to be nothing more than a bag of bones glared down at him with a lambent yellow eye. And then, in the shadowed area under the stairs, he saw it. Big as life. An icy dagger pierced his heart, causing agony beyond description.

At that precise moment, something extraordinary happened to him that he had heard about but had never experienced. And, in fact, had doubted its existence, putting the stories down to overactive imaginations. As he stared at the wine cask, his mind seemed to leave his body. It was as if he were hovering just below the ceiling looking down at himself staring at the wine cask—the very same kind of wine cask that his men had stuffed Gorgonov's whore into. This eerie and unfamiliar dissociative state incited by his autonomous nervous system saved him from losing his mind.

Elene. Now, at the very precipice of disaster, he remembered seeing her dance: her slim form elongated on pointe. How elegant she looked! he recalled thinking. How grown up! As she spun, as her partner lifted her into the air, light as a feather, how ecstatic she looked, as she landed, his hands on her slim waist, her arms spread like a swan's wings. So beautiful he had felt a pain in his heart. The memory pulsed in front of his eyes like a video repeating over and over again. The hell with the video; he wanted to see her dance in person, see her spotlit on the company's small stage, hear the roar of approval as she and her partner finished their duet.

Not to be. He clenched his fists so hard his ragged nails bit into the flesh of his palms, drew blood. The pain felt good, deserved, as if he were already paying penance for her death.

Elene. His fragile daughter. His girl child. Drowned, her flesh being eaten away by acid, even as he stood before her, helpless, weeping as he hadn't done since he was a little boy and had broken his arm. He felt now as he had felt then. Something vital was broken. He had been sure then that it would never mend, and he was sure now this would never mend.

He couldn't leave her to rot away a moment longer.

With an animal cry, he hurled himself at the cask. With mounting horror, he saw that the end that was now on top wasn't sealed. It had been pried open, then replaced. Nevertheless, in his frantic haste, he broke half his fingernails levering the end off.

He peered in, and his heart nearly ceased to beat.

There was Elene, looking up at him with fearful eyes.

"Daddy," she said, and rose out of the otherwise empty cask, arms outstretched for him to take her home.

25

A Kevlar vest would surely save your life by stopping a bullet from getting through it, but the impact would be more than enough to knock you off your feet. And depending on where the bullet hit, you could also lose consciousness, which is what had happened to the motorcycle rider Evan had shot. It was likely that the vest was of inferior manufacture as well, because when the rider, having returned to consciousness, rose and fired at Evan, his aim was none too accurate. Evan saw his hand shaking even as she ducked and rolled. All three bullets whizzed by high and wide.

She came out of the crouch a step away from the rider, and landed a trio of powerful strikes to the left side, feeling the crack of ribs on the second and third blows. The rider grunted, offered little resistance when Evan swept the gun out of his hand.

But just as it clattered to the cobbled alley the two men who had come into the restaurant from the front burst out of the rear entrance, guns firing. Evan had no choice but to swivel, using the rider as a shield. Two bullets struck the rider's chest, making the body dance in Evan's grasp. Dropping the rider, Evan leapt at the two men. Driving the end of the corkscrewed bike fragment she had managed to hold onto through the throat of the one on the right, she twisted her torso, swept aside the second man's Makarov, giving herself enough time to withdraw the makeshift weapon and slash it sideways.

Blood spurted as the metal cracked through the skull, driving shards of bone into the man's brain. He went down like a sack of wet cement. The first man had clutched his throat, to no avail. His hands were frozen in that position as his lungs collapsed for lack of oxygen, and his heart burst under the unimaginable strain.

Retracing her steps, Evan hauled the rider up to face her, removed his helmet: a young man with black hair, a sharp nose, and a knife-slash of a mouth appeared out of the plastic wall of anonymity. His head was wet with sweat. Lifting one lid at a time, she peered into his eyes. Despite having taken three bullets to the chest, he was still alive. That vest was good for something, after all.

Hoisting him in a fireman's lift, grateful he wasn't built like the other four, Evan headed back out of the alley toward the Lada. She dumped him into the rear seat, then got Limas out of the trunk.

"Christ," Limas said as he unfolded himself. He took a couple of tentative steps on rubbery legs. "I heard more shooting." He began to move toward the mouth of the alley.

"Don't," Evan warned.

Reacting to the tone of Evan's voice, Limas halted in mid-stride, turned around to face her. "What happened?"

"The men who came after me made mistakes. Fatal mistakes," Evan said tersely.

Limas rubbed his neck, arched his back. "I feel like I've been kicked by a bull."

Evan pointed to the rider sprawled insensate on the Lada's backseat. "Imagine how he feels."

Limas peered in through the Lada's window, then immediately recoiled. "The motorcycle rider. But he's dead."

"No, he's not." Evan got behind the Lada's wheel. "Come on."

Limas eyed the now beat-up Lada uncertainly. "Wouldn't it be better to get the Range Rover?"

"In a perfect world," Evan told him. "But that sniper is still out there somewhere, and my guess is he knows that's the vehicle we came in."

Limas nodded, hurried to his seat, tried to pull the door shut. It wouldn't quite close, obliging him to hold the inside handle to keep it from swinging open on the sharp turns Evan was intent on making as they sped through the streets. For his part, Limas remained tense until they had put some distance between them and the back alley. Even then, he kept glancing over his shoulder at the unconscious rider, ignoring the pain the repeated movement caused him.

"Where are we going?" he asked at last.

"Remember the shop we stopped at before heading on to the restaurant?" Evan peered at street signs, kept changing direction. "We're going there. I need a place to hole up soon, before our guest has had it. He's taken three bullets to his Kevlar vest. Plus, I broke four of his ribs. That'd be a major trauma to anyone's system."

Ten minutes later, having taken a circuitous route, they arrived at the rear of the antiques store. The Lada's engine shut down with a shudder.

Evan turned to Limas. "Are you up to carrying our friend back there into the shop?"

With a last glance behind him, Limas nodded. "Up to now I've felt as useful as a remora on a shark's flank."

"Okay, then," Evan said, exiting the car.

Opening one of the rear doors, she reached in, slid the rider out, transferred him to Limas's waiting arms. "Take it easy, don't get dizzy. This guy doesn't need to fall on his ass after all he's gone through."

"I got this. Don't worry."

"I never worry."

She crossed the street to the battered metal back door of the antiques shop, knocked, then knocked again, more insistently this time. Several moments later, she heard footsteps approaching. The door was wrenched open, and the owner stood there with a shotgun at the ready.

"Put that thing away," Evan said, as she stepped across the threshold, Limas right behind her. "We've got an emergency."

"I'll keep it, if it's all the same to you."

Evan snatched the shotgun away from him. "It isn't." She broke the breech, unloaded the shotgun, set it against the closed door.

The owner, whose name was Amiran Kartvelishvili, stepped back, almost stumbling against an upholstered footstool so old and battered it could have belonged to a tsar. He had a dark, narrow head atop a square, broad-chested body. Short and squat as a weight lifter, he radiated a façade of unaffected indifference, no doubt erected upon years of listening to his customers' sob stories as they pawned the precious family heirlooms that Amiran made sure were worth less than they had expected or hoped. In other words, he was that particularly reprehensible subspecies of thief who stole bits of people's lives while cheating them.

They were in a storeroom of sorts, dim and packed as a djinn's cave. All manner of bric-a-brac, large, small, and in between, was tagged and set on wooden shelves, some of them so dusty it was clear they hadn't been touched in years.

Evan made way for Limas and his burden. The moment Amiran saw them his caterpillar eyebrows rose and his eyes opened wide.

Evan pointed to the rider. "You know this man," she said. It wasn't a question.

"Why would you think that?" Amiran replied, not very convincingly. He took a moment to gather himself, busying himself in preparing a narrow cot he often used when he didn't care to go home, where his shrew of a wife lorded it over him.

The moment Limas set the driver down, Evan stepped up close to Amiran and, amid a cloud of rotted food and fetid body odor, said: "It was you who recommended the restaurant we went to for lunch."

Amiran shrugged. "Was the food perhaps not to your liking?"

"The food wasn't the problem," Evan said. "The lead was."

"Lead?" Amiran's Adam's apple bobbed like a cork as he swallowed hard. "I . . . I don't know what you're talking about."

"Sure you do," she said, sticking her face right up to his and staring unblinking into his rabbity eyes.

To their right, Limas was kneeling over the rider. He'd unzipped the black leather jacket, peeled back the flaps, exposing the Kevlar vest beneath. He was now opening the rider's mouth. "He's having trouble breathing," Limas said, to no one in particular. "I think he's going to swallow his tongue."

Evan quickly stepped back from Amiran and went over to the cot. Limas moved aside to give her access. But there was nothing to do; the young man was drowning in his own blood. Evan slapped his cheek.

"Hey, don't die! Who are you? What's your name? Who do you work for?"

The rider's trembling lips opened, red bubbles formed between them instead of words. Something rattled deep in his chest, then he sighed, as if letting go of all the pain that racked his body. He went slack; his bowels gave way.

"God in heaven," Amiran cried, "what evil have you brought into my house?"

It was then that Evan saw the silver pin affixed to the lining of the rider's jacket: silver, two ravens beak to beak. She ripped it off, turned to the dealer of antiques, pawned goods, and firearms, and held it up. "You did this to yourself, Amiran. That motorcycle rider was out to kill us. So were five of his brethren. Four of them are dead."

At this news, Amiran gave a quick shuddery start. "That . . . the person you brought in is stinking up my place of business."

"I'm surprised you can tell," Evan said as an aside. Then, back on topic: "The fastest way to get rid of him and the stink is to answer my questions." Evan held up the pin. "What does this signify, Amiran? And where is yours?"

Amiran's yellow, ragged teeth were beginning to chatter. His staring eyes seemed to bulge like a frog's, looking this way and that.

"There's no escape, my friend," Evan told him. "Not from me." She shoved the pin in the dealer's face. "Tell me what I want to know or so help me I'll make sure you suffocate in the rider's shit."

"You . . . you wouldn't."

"To a lowlife like you? I wouldn't hesitate for a heartbeat."

"They'll kill me," Amiran said in a choked whisper. "You don't know—"

"But you'll tell me, won't you." Evan's tone was calm and reasonable, she even smiled, but her voice was made of steel and the smile wasn't reassuring. "With them at least you'll have a head start. For a man like you, that's something. But with me it's now or never. As long as I'm here you'll never see the sun again, or eat a decent meal, or sleep in your own bed. This will be your tomb."

"All right, all right." Amiran's tongue, thickened by terror, swiped his dry lips. Everywhere else he was as wet as if he had just stepped out of the shower; he was sweating like a crazed farm animal. "I . . . I need to sit down."

Evan's arm swung out. "Be my guest."

Amiran lowered himself shakily onto a wooden chair, its ladder back pressed against the floor-to-ceiling shelves that rose along the left-hand wall. "Where to start?" he asked himself.

"At the end—the restaurant," Evan said. "And work backward."

Amiran's eyes were bloodshot. Both hands gripped the edge of the chair seat, between his spread legs. "You're right, of course. I made the call just after you bought the Beretta," he said.

"Which turned out to be a piece of crap," Evan said. "But go on. Who did you call?"

"A man I know only as Cuervos."

"You've got to be joking."

Amiran wiped his eyes clear of sweat. "Not a bit of it. That's the truth."

Evan leaned in. "Amiran, you seem to be the sort of fellow who wouldn't know the truth if it came up and bit you on the backside."

"But . . . but I swear it," the dealer blubbered. Tears overflowed his eyes, made tracks in the dirt on his cheeks.

"What?" Limas said. "What is it?"

Evan made an animal sound, like a lioness clearing its throat. "Cuervos is Spanish for ravens."

26

"Tell me," Evan said, "what does this person who calls himself Cuervos look like?"

"I never met him." Amiran, shoulders slumped, stared down at the scuffed and dirty floor between his feet. "My only contact with him is by mobile."

"This stink is getting to me," Limas said, edging toward the back door. "I'm going to step outside for a few."

"Keep a sharp eye out," Evan said, over her shoulder.

At that moment, Amiran slid a kris out of its sheath beneath the chair seat, lunged hard and fast at Evan. Stepping inside the strike, Evan felt the curved knife blade rip through her coat. But by then she had a forearm against the dealer's throat, jamming him back into his chair, forcing his head up. Evan struck him hard just under the sternum with her free hand, and when all the breath left Amiran, she wrenched the kris away, substituting its point for her forearm.

"If you try that again . . ." And she pricked the dealer's throat, drawing both blood and an indrawn breath from Amiran. "Now," Evan said, "tell me everything you know about Cuervos."

Amiran gulped, his eyes open wide and fairly bulging from their sockets. "Please take that away," he whined. "I can't breathe."

Evan withdrew the kris, but held it at the ready in plain view.

Amiran licked his dry lips. He was sweating even more profusely. "I'm so dry my throat is closing up." He gestured. "There's some bottled water in that half-fridge over there."

Limas, the stink forgotten in the brief but frightening melee, crossed the space, bent over, and opened the door.

"One of the blue glass bottles," Amiran said vaguely. He seemed mesmerized by the curl of the kris's blade.

Limas brought the bottle over, broke the seal on the cap, held it out.

Amiran glanced up at Evan. "Is it okay?"

"Go on."

The dealer took the bottle gingerly, as if he half-expected Evan to slap it out of his grip. Then he took a swig. His eyes closed and he swallowed greedily.

"First of all," he said, "I want to make it crystal clear I'm not one of them."

"One of who?"

"I don't own a raven pin."

Evan nodded. "Okay. Good for you. Now answer my question. One of who?"

"The . . . the First Tribe."

"The First Tribe?"

"That's what they call themselves—Die Raben." Which, translated from German, meant the Ravens.

Amiran took another swig of his water, coughed softly, then continued on. "The German core of them claim to be direct descendants of Himmler, Goering, Joey the Cripp." He meant Joseph Goebbels, the Nazi Minister of Propaganda.

"That's insane," Evan said. "History records what happened to these men and their families."

"But not their illegitimate offspring."

"That's utter nonsense. Nothing more than propaganda."

"But a lie most often told becomes the truth, doesn't it?"

"Money," Evan said. "Terrorist activities cost money. A lot of it, especially on a global scale. Where is Die Raben getting their funding? And don't tell me that old wives' tale about hidden Nazi gold."

Amiran tried to laugh, but it turned into a dry, rasping cough that raised bile into his esophagus. Turning his head, he ejected it. "If I told you Nazi gold you wouldn't believe me. If I told you blood money you wouldn't believe me. So I say nothing."

"Tell me what *you* believe," she said.

Amiran shook his head. "I respectfully decline. Anyway, it doesn't matter." A small, sad smile creased his face. "Not now."

"What's that supposed to mean?" Limas had come closer. He was standing just behind Evan, peering over her shoulder.

The dealer looked at them, and smiled. "What d'you think it means?" His eyes began to cross, then they went out of focus.

Evan knocked the bottle away as Amiran tried for a third and last swallow. She grabbed the dealer by the shoulders, shook him.

"Amiran. Amiran!"

"What's happening?" Limas asked anxiously.

"He's taken poison." Evan slapped the dealer's pale cheeks. "That damn water." She slapped Amiran harder. "Listen to me. Where is Cuervos? What's his mobile number?"

But Amiran was beyond all speech. His gaze had flown inward, like a bird returning home to its ancestral nest, empty now apart from memories. All too soon they, too, were gone.

Amiran slumped in Evan's arms.

"Quick," Evan said to Limas. "Hold him up."

As Limas did so, Evan went through the dealer's

pockets until she found what she was looking for: Amiran's mobile.

"Now," she said, "let's get out of this charnel house."

■ ■ ■

"As you were saying." Evan swallowed the last bit of a tough and stringy grilled rabbit the proprietor boasted he had snared himself, set down her fork. He should have made it into a stew, she thought, but maybe even that wouldn't have helped. "You have a confession to make."

They had driven to the other side of Tbilisi and, on the outskirts of the city, had found a small inn that catered to hikers and mountain climbers. Evan drove about a mile past it, turned off the road, into a deep ditch. Despite their weariness now that the adrenaline rush was wearing off, they hiked back to the inn. It was nothing fancy, but the rooms were clean, though small. This time of year they more or less had the inn to themselves. Best of all, it didn't take much to persuade the owner to take double the rate for not logging them in.

Now they sat in the narrow strip of dining room that overlooked the mountains. A half-empty bottle of vodka sat on the table between them. Evan was nursing her second pour but Limas was already on his fourth. Clearly, the events of the last two days had unnerved him.

"Before we get to that please tell me if you found anything of interest on Amiran's mobile."

"I did," Evan said.

"You aren't going to make me beg, are you? I think the time has come, as the Walrus said, to speak of many things."

"Wrong venue," Evan replied drily. "I don't know anything about cabbages and kings."

Limas gave out a brief laugh. "I've been through quite a bit in the last two days. I should think you owe me."

"The first thing you should know about me, Peter, I don't owe anyone anything. In my world, that kind of attitude will get you killed." *And it almost had, a number of times,* she thought, but, of course, didn't say. "The second thing is, yes, I found something of great interest. Namely, Cuervos's number. By the country and city code I know he's in Obersalzberg, Germany."

"I suppose that's where you propose to head next."

"Tomorrow, if at all possible," Evan affirmed.

"Ah, well."

Evan frowned. "Meaning?"

Limas looked away for a moment, then reengaged Evan's gaze. "The confession I was about to make to you. One of the reasons I agreed to come with you is my partner, Roger," Limas said. His hair was disheveled and the points of his cheeks were cherry red, a perfect match to his red-rimmed eyes. "After the way he acted at the poker game, I don't know who he is, maybe who he ever was. I mean, I've known him for a good number of years. In England and then the States. We've gone out together, had beers, even shared a girl once—though I'm not so proud of that night. But still . . . I thought I knew him. And now . . . now we know what the raven pins mean—the First Tribe? Neo-Nazis?—Christ, I really don't know what to think."

Evan pushed her plate away; the greasy rabbit was lying in her stomach like a handful of lead shot. "Your current situation reminds me of the famous riddle posed by Martin Gardner in his book *Entertaining Mathematical Puzzles*: 'An island is inhabited by two tribes. Members of one tribe always tell the truth, members of the other always lie. A missionary meets two of these natives, one tall, the other short. "Are you a truth-teller?" he asks the taller one, whose answer the missionary recognizes as a native word meaning either yes or no, but he can't recall which. The short native speaks English, so the missionary asks him what his companion said. "He says yes," replies the short native, "but he's a liar." What tribe does each native belong to?'"

Evan spread her hands. "Things are like that for you now. You don't know who's lying and who's telling the truth. You feel like you're caught between a rock and a hard place. You don't know who to trust."

Limas nodded bleakly. "But there's another, far more important reason I'm here. I have a sister. We grew up together, but not for long." He turned his glass around and around between his hands. "I haven't seen her since we were children. And I want to. I want to very much. So I was hoping . . ." He spread his hands wide.

"We're in the Republic of Georgia, Limas, not England. You thought, what? You'd just fly on over to London and—"

Limas stared at her with his bleary eyes, a look of desperation creeping into them. "Moscow, actually, and well, to be honest I thought we both might go. I mean, that you'd help me."

Evan looked at him as if he'd lost his mind. "What? Why would I do that? Moscow? What are you even talking about?"

Limas sighed. "So, you truly don't recognize me, do you?"

"You asked me that before. Should I?"

Limas looked crestfallen. "I admit to being disappointed, I was hoping you might, but the longer I'm with you and you still say nothing . . ." He lowered his voice even though there was no one around to overhear their conversation; the lone waiter was at the other end of the room, smoking and looking out the window. "How I know who you really are—my aunt told me all about you. And she showed you a photo of me," he whispered. "Or at least she told me she did."

Evan stared at him, mute.

"It was years ago," Limas went on. He felt his cheeks with the tips of his fingers. "Yet another humiliation at having made a pass at you. And Brenda . . . I promise it won't happen again. But you don't know how I've imagined you for all this time." He laughed without amusement. "Like a real-life Wonder Woman. And then suddenly there I am with you and you're . . . larger than life. I don't know, I thought that maybe you liked me, maybe if we . . . we'd be closer." He watched Evan with a terrible trepidation. "Presumptuous of me, I'm sorry. And insane, now I think about it."

Evan chose to ignore this part of his confession. She didn't want to think about the fact that he was right, she did like him, and if it weren't for Brenda she might not have pushed him away. And besides, what he felt about her was of no interest to her compared to how he knew who she really was. And why he would be looking for his sister in Moscow.

"Your aunt?" was all she said.

"That's right," Limas replied. "My aunt Lyudmila. Lyudmila Alexeyevna Shokova."

▪ ▪ ▪

As soon as General Boyko reached his office, Timmy arrived with the latest batch of items from Nemesis. He went through them while he was still shrugging off his greatcoat. "Why is the American government harboring a Zionist terrorist in its secret services?" the first one read. It went on to accuse Benjamin Butler of the most despicable crimes, the latest in what was now a barrage of "newly unearthed facts" incriminating him. Boyko turned to the next several communiqués. It was immediately apparent that Nemesis was also stepping up its campaign to trash any American not of the Caucasian persuasion. Two items accused the black American professional athletes of being un-American. The first, for taking the knee during the playing of the national anthem at the beginning of sports events. The second, for speaking out via social media, condemning the president's stance. A third item was in defense of the president for tweeting that the American flag burning by the neo-Nazis, now called the alt-right, an amusing euphemism that Boyko had dreamed up himself, was an acceptably peaceful manner of protest. These items, which he gave off to Timmy to disseminate through the latest iteration of bot-armies, like many from Nemesis that passed through Boyko's hands, tickled his funny bone so deeply that he was forced to guffaw out loud. It was immensely amusing to him that Nemesis was his number one client.

What fools these Westerners be, he thought, returning to the much less entertaining paperwork with which he was constantly flooded. Which, in its way, served the purpose of keeping his mind away from what had almost happened to his daughter.

■ ■ ■

"My real name is Vasily, Evan. Vasily Shokov. But after my parents died, Lyudmila gave me a new identity in Russia as Vasily Mevedev so she could smuggle me out. When she came to me, Aunt Lyudmila was very circumspect," Limas said. "She was like a grand master chess champion. 'Always play the long game,' she told me once. 'No one else does; they're all too eager to get over on one another in the short term. In the end, you're the one who survives.'"

"Just like this, you want me to believe that you're Lyudmila's nephew?" Evan shook her head. "She never showed me a photo of you."

While they had been at dinner night had fallen, and though the temperature had plummeted with the death of the sun, they had mutually agreed to continue their discussion as they walked the meager grounds of the inn.

"Aunt Lyudmila said that you and she had been friends for some time. She told me she trusted you, even though you were an American. She showed me your picture, a snapshot, taken in sunlight and shadow, leaves all around. In a forest glade maybe."

Evan knew exactly which photo Limas meant; she remembered that day so clearly. She and Lyudmila had met for lunch in the Kadiköy section of Istanbul. Afterward, they had strolled into a small leafy park, away from the roiling crowds, the brutal sun. They had taken photos of each other—just one each. To keep. That was their secret, their silent acknowledgment of a friendship that transcended nationality or ideology.

"I knew it was you the moment you sat down across from me at the steak house. So mightn't she have told you about me?"

"She did say she had a niece and nephew," Evan said. "But she never showed me a photo of either of you."

He was quiet for a moment. "She told me she had. But if she actually didn't, I'm sure it was out of a sense of security. She was ultra-sensitive about both me and my sister. She made it her business to keep us out of the spotlight, off the FSB and GRU books. You see, we were very young when my parents died. A car crash on the Ring Road, a tractor-trailer. The driver was blind drunk. Aunt Lyudmila changed my sister's and my name to Mevedev, and brought us to England. But my sister was never happy in England, and she left to go back to Russia, Moscow I think, when she was twelve. I don't know how she did it, she must have been in touch with someone there. So very long ago, and I haven't seen her since.

"Lyudmila could have kept us, I suppose, brought us up. Instead, in England, she brought us to friends of hers who lived in a very big stone house in Sussex. The Limases. She wanted a different life for both of us. But she also . . . well, she saved me for a particular purpose."

"What purpose?"

"I think she foresaw a day when she would run against the grain of Russian Federation policy. She loved

Russia dearly, but she didn't believe in what had happened to it. She despised the Sovereign's Russia."

"I know very well what you mean," Evan said, recalling numerous discussions she'd had with Lyudmila over the years of their friendship.

"So while I was being brought up English, while I was excelling at school, before I went up to Cambridge, Lyudmila never let me forget my roots—that I was Russian. She'd set up a trust for me; the money came from there. But she guided everything.

"And just before she vanished, she sent me a coded message. She told me that if anything seemed out of place, if anything changed in my situation, I should go find you."

Almost unconsciously, Evan fingered the tiny wooden carving in a secret pocket of her trousers. "How did she suggest you do that?" Evan couldn't keep the skepticism out of her voice.

Either Limas didn't notice Evan's tone or chose to ignore it. He just shook his head and said, "She told me to find Evan Ryder. She told me to find you."

There was a prescient suggestion, Evan thought. And the clearest sign that Limas might just possibly be telling the truth.

"But you found me first. And when I saw you I . . ." He stopped, licked his lips. "Listen, Evan, I know you won't believe me now, but I love Brenda. I love her with all my heart. She's got a good soul, she doesn't ask me awkward questions about my work because I know I can't ask about her work. She's smart and strong and, frankly, loves sex, but . . ."

Evan's brows knit together. "But what?"

"I don't think I'm worthy of her." Said in a rasping whisper, as if pulled out of his guts. "Deep down I don't believe I'm good enough. She's so much what I've always wanted, what I was sure I'd never find, and that makes me think . . ." He took a deep, shuddering breath before continuing. "It makes me think she can't possibly love me, that for her we're just a temporary fling until the next guy comes along."

"Is that what you think of Brenda? That she's just playing you?"

Limas turned to Evan, his moonlit face so very sorrowful. "Isn't that what she does for a living, play people?"

Evan had no answer for that. How well did she know Brenda, after all? And playing people was what she did for a living, too.

Their forms passed through light and shadow, like candles flickering in a strong breeze or at the end of their lives. A dog barked far away, the sound echoing among the shanks of the mountains, a lonely, melancholy sound. They came to a shed where the proprietor kept his snares, ropes, and green saplings, stripped of bark, ready to be bent with the tough netting to snare larger game—red deer, no doubt. Evan peered in briefly, the paraphernalia silvered by the moonlight.

They had just completed their seventh circuit of the property; it was high time they got some well-earned sleep. But as Evan turned to head back to the inn, Limas caught her by the arm.

"Listen, I'm sorry it took me so long to come clean with you. I just . . . well, I didn't know where I was."

"And now you do?"

Limas gave a rueful little laugh just before they both went inside.

▪ ▪ ▪

She is inside the red-brick mansion. The air is thick with fear and desperation. There are faces, blobs of light moving back and forth. Voices come to her as if from beneath the sea. Or perhaps she is the one under the ocean. She feels herself falling through dark water, deeper and deeper. She knows she is meant to fall apart.

She doesn't fall apart, but when, heart pounding, she opened her eyes into the still darkness of her second-floor room, she found herself thinking of Pat Wilson, who had been taken apart inside the mansion, and wondering when her own moment would come.

27

"Don't move!" the voice said from behind her. "Don't even breathe!"

The voice was Charles's. She did as he ordered.

"Now," he continued, "very slowly take your hand away from that switch."

"I was just going to turn on the light."

"Exactly what Voron would expect someone coming after her would do." Charles came toward her. "That switch will trigger a blast that would kill you instantly."

Brenda felt a tentacle curling in the pit of her stomach. She gestured. "I wanted to take a closer look at those photos on the wall. You should too. That man is military, maybe a general. And the mountains are the Alps. I'm certain they're a clue to Voron's identity. I want to take them with us."

"No way," he said, his voice returned to its original alarmed tone. "Five will get you ten Voron secreted the explosives behind them. There are no other photos or wall hangings anywhere else on the premises. Those photos are bait."

"But intriguing bait nonetheless." Brenda stepped toward them, took a series of photos with her mobile, then turned back to Charles. "No sign of Voron herself, I take it."

"Just tiny bits and pieces. She's in the wind."

"Bits and pieces like what?" Brenda asked.

He beckoned. "Come take a look."

She followed him back out into the cavernous empty main space and then through the door she hadn't chosen, the one to the right, into a good-sized room.

Her mobile buzzed. It was Butler.

"Butler, I've seen the online attacks on my Twitter feed. How are you?" Brenda asked. "Is everything all right?"

"It will be soon enough," Butler said. "Give me a sit-rep."

"We're closing in on the bomb-maker. Her operational name is Voron."

"The bomb-maker is *female*?"

"Affirmative. One of my contacts confirmed this." She took a breath. "We found her lair—well, former lair, anyway. She's flown, but she left behind a couple of photos. I'm uploading them to your private server right now." Her fingertips were busy on the phone for a moment. "Okay, you've got them."

"Good. Anything further?"

"No."

"Well, I have something for you: we've confirmed that Anna Alta was a Nemesis agent."

Brenda took a breath, almost dreading to hear Butler's reply to her next question. "Butler, do you have eyes on Peter?"

"In a way. He's with Evan," Butler said. "In the Republic of Georgia."

"What?" Brenda couldn't believe her ears. "How the hell did that happen?"

"They found the two missing MI6 agents."

Focus, Brenda thought. "Dead?"

"Evan sent photos. Ritually murdered. Throats ripped out just like our agents."

"So that list really is a kill list." Brenda took a breath. "Charles is the only one on it who's still alive."

One last silence. For some reason, this one frightened Brenda. "Butler?"

She heard her director breathing. "The list I showed you was redacted. I thought under the circumstances it wasn't wise . . . But now after what you've told me . . ."

Brenda's heart was in her throat. "What circumstances?"

"The original list has seven names on it, Brenda. Peter is the seventh."

■ ■ ■

Gorgonov had been up all night in his office suite working on plans, counterplans, contingencies, exit strategies, and fail-safes all regarding his mandate from the Sovereign to tie RNU to Nemesis and to, as he had said, kill the serpent at Mother Russia's bosom. But by dawn's early light, it seemed that he was still no closer to finding the source point of Nemesis. He knew he was missing something—a vital link that would unravel the whole—and it was driving him crazy.

Disgusted, he came out from behind his enormous desk, padded barefoot over to the mini-fridge where there were always bottles of vodka and, for special occasions such as this one, champagne chilling. Popping the cork, he poured the sparkling wine into a flute, took it and the bottle over to the window, stood sipping as he looked out onto Lubyanka Square, where the wide-shouldered buildings blocked out the fragile light of the coming day. Few people braved the elements at this early hour—just a few hardy souls, bundled into anonymity, hurrying diagonally across the square, coming to relieve members of the SVR night shift.

Draining his glass, he poured himself another, and another after that, until half the bottle had been consumed. By this time, the square had begun to come to life, in the Moscow fashion. The first tourists of the day were there with their in-country guides, staring at the Lubyanka goggle-eyed with the same ersatz terror that gripped them during American spy films. Gorgonov made a face. Setting glass and bottle on a low coffee table, he threw himself on the long Italian sofa, drew a featherweight blanket over himself, and fell instantly to sleep.

He was awakened by his adjutant with a bucketful of morning extracts from SVR units around the globe and intercepts of GRU communications. The latter interested him the more. He pored over these while he was served fresh coffee and a plate filled with a pyramid of Entenmann's chocolate-glazed doughnuts, flown in daily for him. He wolfed them down, three bites each, while marking up the intercepts for follow-ups this afternoon. He had set aside this completed work, when he was handed a last-minute communiqué that his people had intercepted between General Boyko and someone by the name of Alice. But then he saw that because the paper had been smudged on its way over to him he'd read the name wrong: Boyko was corresponding with Allis. An Allis in Germany. His people had narrowed the source down to somewhere in Bavaria. And, the person who had transcribed the intercept had circled two words that had not been in Cyrillic: Die Raben.

Gorgonov fairly leapt out of his seat. His hand was shaking so much the paper fluttered like a bird's wing. *Die Raben.* The Ravens. Boyko hooked up with a German—a German in Bavaria, no less, the birthplace of Nazism. Now a hotbed of neo-Nazis. His heart rate climbed precipitously, and it was all he could do not to let out a shout.

Die Raben was Nemesis.

■ ■ ■

By then it was lunchtime. He'd been working almost continuously since yesterday morning, and he recognized that he needed a break. Donning his long, fur-collared overcoat, he strode out of his office, taking the wide marble stairs with their wrought-iron guardrails down the three flights to the street to get the cramps out of his legs.

His car was waiting for him, with his driver and daytime bodyguard at the ready, as always. But he was in a festive mood and instead of going straight to his favorite restaurant, he had his driver take him to the gymnastics center where his daughter, Lolita, took her lessons. He got out of the car and waited for her, wanting to surprise her. This he did. Breaking away from her new bodyguard, she came running over to him when she saw him.

His wife had told him that the bodyguard made Lolita more nervous than when she didn't have one. She had no idea what was going on—nor did his wife, for that matter—but it was slowly dawning on him that in the absence of facts children flooded the void with their darkest fears.

"Papa!" she cried. "What are you doing here?"

"I missed you, *lastochka*." He held out his arms and hugged her. "How would you like to come with me for lunch?"

"Really?" Her blue eyes got big around. "Yes! Oh, yes!" She clapped her hands, then, almost immediately, frowned. "But my diet. Miss Olga says I must be very careful what I put in my body."

"What Miss Olga says can wait until tomorrow. You deserve a day off." He ushered her into the backseat of the SUV, where she happily squirmed her hard little backside into the plush leather.

Arriving at the restaurant, he made sure Maks went through to the back, to hang out in the kitchen while he and Lolita were seated at his usual prime table.

At this hour the place was just half full—the restaurant did the bulk of its business at dinnertime and afterward, when DJs invaded and the tables in the center were packed up and the petals of a portable dance floor flowered open.

Now all was calm and sedate, just the way Gorgonov liked it. The room was done up like a living room, with sofas and upholstered chairs in sapphire velvet. Uniformed waiters picked their way around lamps and side tables on which drinks were arrayed. The cuisine was European, the meats prime cut, the fruits and vegetables fresh off the cooperative farm. Gorgonov ordered for both himself and his daughter, drank an ice-cold vodka gimlet, while she sipped on a Coca-Cola because, after all, this was a special occasion.

He ate slowly and meditatively, clearing his mind of the clutter built up over the last twenty-four hours of scheming, interspersed with reading a veritable blizzard of intel dailies coming in from all points, focusing on RNU and Nemesis activities. Still, he listened with one ear only to Lolita's recitation on her gymnastics class and the trials and tribulations of her best friend, whom she was trying her best to help.

For dessert, he asked for two of the pastry chef's excellent Pavlovas.

When Lolita piped up "I don't like Pavlova," he said, "You'll like this one. I guarantee it." And paid no attention to her small grimace.

When he was finished, he sat back, feeling for the moment so replete that he initiated further conversation with his daughter, finding as he did so the fondness he had felt for her when she was born.

Telling Lolita he'd be right back, he rose, went into the rear corridor, used the facilities. When he returned to his table he saw that his daughter was holding a plush bear, its coat shiny brown.

"What is this?" he said with a sense of foreboding.

"A man gave it to me."

"Man?" Gorgonov looked around. "What man? Do you see him now?"

Lolita craned her neck, then stood up on the sofa she and her father had been sitting on, turning her little body this way and that. "No, Papa. I don't see him."

She hugged the bear to her chest. "His name is Yuri, the man told me."

He held out a hand and she sat down again. He looked at the bear for a long moment. "What did this man look like?"

She shrugged. She was still hugging the bear to her. The Pavlova sat untouched in the center of her dessert plate. "Just a man."

"Was he tall or short, fat or slim?"

"He was neither tall nor short, neither fat nor slim," Lolita said maddeningly. She appeared quite uninterested in this line of questioning. She began to speak to Yuri the bear.

Gorgonov sighed before turning and beckoning his waiter over.

"Did you see who gave my daughter this bear?"

"No, sir."

"Who did? Anyone?"

"I'm sorry, sir. I can't say. I didn't see anyone deliver it, but then I was busy in the kitchen, picking up plates for diners at another table." The waiter gestured. "May I bring you more coffee, sir? Or your daughter a different dessert? A scoop of ice cream, perhaps?"

Gorgonov shook his head. "We're finished." Then, with another glance at Lolita, said, "No, wait. Bring her some ice cream. Chocolate, if you have it. Chocolate's her favorite."

"Right away, sir." The waiter scurried away, clearly relieved that he hadn't been yelled at for his inattention.

"Lol, I need to take the bear," he told his daughter. She handed it over, having heard that chocolate ice cream was coming, which was enough to mollify her for the moment. Gorgonov took the bear and stalked away. He found Maks in the kitchen.

"Did anyone come through here?" he asked him. "Anyone holding this?" He held up the bear.

"No, sir. Not a soul," Maks replied.

Gorgonov sighed. "All right. Take this bear and tear it apart. And do it carefully. I don't know what might be inside."

"Yes, sir."

Maks accepted Yuri the bear and, taking up a carving knife, slit open the seam along the animal's back. Out fell a cheap pay-as-you-go mobile phone.

Gorgonov stared at it as if it might bite him.

"Sir?" Maks was waiting for an order.

With difficulty, Gorgonov tore his gaze from the phone, which seemed to be magnetized to the instrument. "Yes, well, all right. Get some of the string they use here to sew up the birds after they're stuffed. Repair the bear and then bring it back to Lolita. Sit with her until I return. Don't let her out of your sight for even an instant."

"Yes, sir. Right away."

Scooping up the mobile, Gorgonov left the kitchen and returned to the restroom. There he entered a cubicle, locked the door, and turned on the phone. As soon as it grabbed hold of the network he saw that there was one text message waiting for him. His thumb hovered over the key for a moment before pressing it.

DOES SHE LIKE YURI? YES? NO? he read. No salutation, no signature. But then none were needed. ONLY TWO WAYS TO PROCEED. WHICH ONE?

His suspicion was confirmed. Boyko was behind this. Their feud had gotten out of hand. Bringing their children into it had been an enormous miscalculation. But now they were in it up to their necks. Boyko had begun this war by poaching Brady Thompson. Added to that, he had trashed an SVR safe house, in the process executing two of Gorgonov's men. Proceeding along either of the two paths Boyko was implying was out of the question. He was not going to back down. FUCK YOU AND YOUR FUCKING BEAR, he typed.

With a strangled growl he pressed SEND.

28

"Bad news?" Charles said as Brenda came across from the other side of the space where she had been conversing with Butler.

"Just the opposite," she said brightly. "Send me that photo of Limas and Gorgonov, would you?" She gave him her phone number.

Charles nodded. "Right away."

Taking out his mobile, he pulled up the photo. The moment it appeared on her screen, she forwarded it to Butler's private server. That done, she looked around the large space. As elsewhere in the building, murky light came through small grimy windows high on the exterior walls. A large wooden table with a scarred and burned top stood in the center of the room. Charles led her into the small space where Voron had tapped into the existing electrical wiring that had led him into the smaller room with the photographs.

She went over to the table. "This must be where she assembled the bombs."

"That's right," Charles said, following her over. "Every scar, every burn tells another story of her work. Look here." He pointed. "She's meticulous, neat, precise. No shards of metal, plastic, or wire insulation anywhere. It's the bomber's equivalent of policing your brass—gathering up the spent shells after you've fired your weapon." He grunted. "Honestly, I've never seen anything like this."

As she stared at the tabletop, Brenda fell into a kind of reverie or trance, as if trying to conjure up the afterimage of the bomber, catch a scent of her, intuit what was in her mind. It was in this altered state that she became aware of the hint of airflow caressing her cheek.

"Charles, is there a window open somewhere?"

He craned his neck to look up at them, one by one. "No. They're all closed up tight. I don't think they're meant to open at all."

"I need to calm down." She held out a hand. "I could use a smoke."

"What, now?" He regarded her quizzically for a moment. "Really?"

She waggled her outstretched fingertips, and, shrugging, he shook out a cigarette. She took it, put it between her lips, and he lit it for her. She inhaled, went over to one of the walls, blew smoke at it, watched it dissipate. She did the same thing as she moved along the wall, into the far left corner. She repeated this process along the back wall, and then, finally, the right-hand wall. Through the length of this odd ritual, Charles trailed after her with a bemused look.

When they returned to the table she smiled at him, as if to say, "No, I'm not crazy." Then she squatted down, exhaled smoke under the table. Charles squatted down on the other side of the table, just in time to see the smoke swirling down between the floorboards.

Brenda looked at him, pointed to where the smoke had disappeared, and he nodded, getting it. They both stood and, without a word, picked up the table, moved it off to one side, exposing the floor underneath. Stubbing her butt out on the tabletop, Brenda drew her sidearm while Charles squatted again, ran his fingertips over the rough-hewn boards. The nature of their surfaces made detection difficult and laborious, but after several moments he discovered a short length of clear plastic cord jammed into the crevice between two of the boards. He pulled it slowly upward until it was taut. He looked up at Brenda briefly. She was standing three or four paces away, in the classic shooter's stance: arms stiff, legs at shoulder width, both hands on her gun, aiming directly at the center of what they now saw was a trapdoor to what must be a root cellar.

They both knew, without voicing it, that Voron might well be hiding down there. Brenda's pulse quickened. Her senses sharpened; she could feel the blood flowing through her veins and arteries, the ticktock workings of her heart.

Ready? Charles mouthed.

She took a deep breath, let it out slowly. Nodded.

Charles pulled up on the cord. Slowly, firmly, with a constant motion. The trapdoor began to rise up, like a vampire's coffin lid. He paused, checked for a tripwire. Seeing no sign of one, he continued to pull on the cord. The trapdoor opened.

And the blast hit Charles full force.

The percussion threw Brenda backward, off her feet. She lay stunned, hearing only the echo of detonation filling her ear canals, an incessant pressure against her eardrums. Smoke and debris filled the air, sawdust in a carpenter's work space. Charles lay on his back, legs twisted under him. He had been lucky and unlucky all at once. The wooden trapdoor had protected him from the brunt of the blast, but as it flew apart a thick shard of wood had pierced his chest like a javelin thrown by a powerful adversary.

And as Brenda watched, half-stunned, deafened, that adversary rose up from the root cellar where, indeed, she had secreted herself when she heard their car driving up.

Voron. The bomb-maker. The Raven.

Dark-haired, light-eyed, her body small and compact, a gymnast's body, unformed, like a prepubescent girl, or, even, a young man not yet grown into whiskers. When she was only halfway into the room she swiveled her torso, even as she continued her ascent up the stairs or ladder that was hidden from Brenda's view. A basilisk stare that would have creeped out Medusa struck Brenda like a stone from David's slingshot. She felt it in the center of her chest, could swear her muscles contracted, convulsing as if with trauma.

Voron raised a Springfield Armory 1911 TRP pistol, a 10mm with a 6-inch longslide barrel that could stop a bear in its tracks. Her fingers, long and spidery thin, were wrapped around the polymer grips. Brenda watched mesmerized as the Springfield's muzzle swung toward her. The pain in her chest lurched her brain into survival mode. The autonomous nervous system, working faster than conscious thought possibly could, brought her sidearm up and fired it, all in one smooth motion.

Voron grinned; the longslide bucked, an explosion resounded a hairsbreadth from Brenda's left temple, though she felt, rather than heard it, which was even more terrifying. She screamed, fired, rolled, all at the same time.

Brenda lifted herself to her knees, keeping her eyes on Voron the whole time. The grin on Voron's face remained fixed. The bomb-maker was still staring at the spot where Brenda had lain mere seconds before. Brenda's thighs were trembling so badly she couldn't stand up. Crawling across the floorboards, she approached Voron. As she did so, the basilisk stare turned in her direction, and she shuddered. That stare was impossible to process.

Voron's face turned very white, her eyes reflected an all-encompassing pain, and that's when Brenda saw the blood. Her first shot had fractured the right clavicle, rendering Voron's gun arm useless. It flopped on the floorboards like a landed fish, the back of the hand banging and banging, seemingly of its own volition. The grin was abruptly transformed into a rictus and her entire body began to thrash just like the useless hand. Brenda's second and third shots had passed through Voron's throat to sever her spinal column, ripping apart nerves as well as muscle and bone.

As Brenda drew close to her, the bomb-maker's mouth gaped open and a torrent of blood gushed out.

"Oh, God," Brenda whispered, and crawled on, past the trapdoor and its bloody occupant to where Charles lay.

"Charles," she called with all her might, though it was only the soft, hoarse cry one emits in a dream. "Charles, wake up." She was weeping openly, past knowing or even remembering that he never would wake up.

Agonized moments later, her eyes rolled up, and she collapsed, unconscious, stretched between Charles and the devil.

29

Brenda awoke with the unholy racket of an AC/DC concert thundering through her head. For some time, she lay where she had fallen, disoriented and suffering from temporary amnesia. During this time she just concentrated on breathing and making sure that she was still alive and not inhabiting some ghostly limbo suffused with the stench of an abattoir.

Then, as was the nature of these things, in the blink of an eye everything came flooding back: the discovery of the hidden trapdoor, her giving Charles cover while he pulled the cord, the explosion catching both of them, Charles fatally, and the subsequent rise of Voron with her demonic weapon that by the grace of God had not killed Brenda herself.

Slowly, painfully, she rose onto all fours. Her head hung down, the pit of her stomach churning like the sea in a hurricane. She coughed, retched several times, brought up nothing but bitter bile, a tiny bit of her insides that lay between the mess Voron had made of Charles and she, Brenda, had made of Voron. Then, still slowly, feeling as fragile as blown glass, she looked at Charles. Immediately, she wished she hadn't. He lay sprawled, one arm outstretched, the other in front of him as if trying to ward off the inevitable. The shard of wood sticking out of his chest seemed to have penetrated through to his spine, severing it.

Up on her haunches at last, Brenda made her wobbly way over to him. Dizzy, sick at heart, she knelt beside him, took his outstretched hand as though to comfort him in his time of need, when it was in fact her own time of need. In death, she had granted him the power to comfort her. There was little doubt in her mind that he had given his life to protect her. In retrospect, neither of them should have pulled that cord. Easy enough to say now, to think that they should have stood well back while peppering the trapdoor with bullets. But that was blood under the bridge now, and the only thing to do was to go on, one step at a time.

His entire front was covered in blood, drying, darkening, stiffening, which made her deep dive to find his mobile phone particularly unpleasant. She couldn't wish away the feeling that she was plundering the dead. Still, it had to be done, and only after she had found it, pocketed it, did she break down.

"Dammit, Charles," she whispered hoarsely. "Dammit to hell." She sobbed soundlessly, head bowed, hand in his, her heart hollow and aching. At some point, she came to the realization that she was crying for herself, for allowing herself to be gulled, used by Peter, and this made her feel small and petty. But, upon further reflection, it also caused her to understand better Evan's coolness to her and to everyone else who came into her orbit. It was a form of self-protection against just what Brenda was feeling now.

All cried out at last, she slipped her hand from Charles's and turned her attention to Voron, the source of their misery. She rose, picked her way over to the trapdoor, never mind that she shambled like someone from *Night of the Living Dead.* As a matter of fact, that was precisely what she felt like: mindless, rageful, cold as a graveyard at midnight. For some time, she studied

Voron's face, which looked to her much like it had when the bomb-maker was alive; her eyes had been dead long before Brenda had shot her. Her torso had been pushed back against the side of the floorboards farthest from where Brenda had pulled the trigger. Her arms were half spread out, palms lying upward. Brenda bent down, the rush of blood to her pounding head causing chorus lines of black spots to dance before her eyes. She sucked in a breath, let it out, and picked up the bomb-maker's weapon: the Springfield 1911 TRP 10mm longslide. Brenda was familiar with its profile and workings. She emptied the gun, stashing the bullets in her pocket before jamming it between her skin and her waistband. She took out her mobile, snapped a boatload of photos of Voron from every conceivable angle, close-ups and long, establishing shots, so Butler could get a sense of the bomb-maker's corpse in situ.

Then she hunkered down in front of Voron. She wished she had a pair of latex or even leather gloves to put on, though surely the leather would be ruined five minutes after she started rummaging around the bloody corpse, but all she had were her bare hands. She began by hauling the bomb-maker all the way out of the trapdoor and laying her out on the floorboards.

Her dark hair was close-cropped, her light eyes large and staring. Soon enough they would milk over. She had a round face, almost as unformed as her body. Brenda tried to guess her age, but failed. She could be anywhere between twenty and her late thirties. Her nails were cut short, square across, except those on her thumbs, which were ragged, bitten down to the quick. Nerves, then, at least sometimes, though surely not when she was building her bombs.

Though there was even more blood across her front than on Charles's, it was still possible to tell what she was wearing: tight black jeans, a silver-gray tank top that betrayed just the barest hint of breast buds. Her shoulders were square and wide, her arms hairless, and as powerful as a gymnast's. Patting her down, searching for any personal effects she might have on her, Brenda found herself wondering what Voron had been like, what had caused her to become a bomb-maker, what her personal politics and prejudices had been. Was she someone who would listen to viewpoints other than her own, or had she been radicalized beyond any form of civilized communication? Brenda found herself feeling a certain form of sadness which, under the extreme circumstances, she knew to be inappropriate. And yet she felt sad. Another unfathomable attribute of being a human being.

She found no mobile on the woman, no ID, nothing. Turning away from the body, she descended into the root cellar on an almost vertical wooden ladder. She pulled a string hanging from the ceiling and a bare bulb came on, its sickly yellow glow illuminating, sadly, nothing much at all. Taking a tour around the circle of light, it seemed clear that Voron had beat a hasty retreat down here; there was no sign at all that she had bunked here: no blankets or bedding of any kind, no torn-open wrappers of packaged foods, no pizza boxes, no cans of soda. The root cellar was as bare as Old Mother Hubbard's cupboards.

Except . . .

At the farthest edge of the circle, in the penumbra, where the yellow light dimmed into shadow, lay a small slip of paper that, Brenda thought, had likely slipped out of Voron's pocket. Brenda stooped and picked it up, opening it as she moved back into the center of the circle where the light was bright enough to see without eyestrain.

It was a receipt from Willie's Swap'n'Shop, a pawnshop in Anacostia. The ticket was for a Springfield Armory 1911 10mm longslide, the very same 10mm that now resided at the small of her back.

▪ ▪ ▪

Copper and salt. She smells the blood. On the walls, the floor, or simply hanging in the air. Her nose is filled with it as she is rolled down a narrow corridor. Fluorescent lights above, like arrows pointed toward—where? Slipping in and out of another dreamworld, a dense forest of pines, icy, snow-bound. She is running. Above her a conspiracy of Ravens follow, yellow eyes fixed on her as she runs. With a whoosh, the shaft of an arrow passes by the side of her head, so close she ducks away, falls, regains her feet, keeps running.

Running into the snare . . .

▪ ▪ ▪

She awoke with a scream in her throat, a scream in her room: the mobile phone given to her by Butler was lit up. Its ring was like a prison Klaxon. Bleary-eyed, she rolled out of bed and answered it.

"Evan."

She needed a moment to shake free of the tide of dreams that had borne her away across the mysterious ocean of sleep, out of sight of all land. "Here, Butler."

"Got your photos."

The photos of the MI6 agents. Right. "Mmm. So, hold on . . . so one thing we now know for sure is the park is a secondary crime scene." Evan scrubbed the last of her dreams out of her eyes. "The agents were all hung upside down, throats torn out, and blooded somewhere else."

"Any idea where the primary is?"

Evan picked the plastic evidence bag with the red-brick dust she had found in the shallow cave up off the night table. "Not yet."

"Are you any closer to the killer or killers?"

"On the way to Obersalzberg."

"Decided to take in the Alpine air in the middle of it all, have we?"

"Right." She laughed. Butler was just attempting to lighten the mood.

"The jet is refueled and waiting for you at Shota Rustaveli. Is that where you are now?"

She stood by the window staring out at a child's bicycle lying on the grass of the inn's front yard, by the side of the road. It looked mournful and forlorn, the visual equivalent of a far-off train's hoot in the night.

"Not yet."

"Why not?"

"Something I need to do before we leave."

"Do you know anything about the person you're chasing in Germany?" he asked. Butler knew better than to query her on the subject of where she was and why.

"A mobile number. And his name. Cuervos, if you can credit it."

"Ravens."

"Right."

"Curiouser and curiouser," Butler observed. "And Limas?"

"He's started making noises about wanting me to go with him to Moscow to find his long-lost sister."

"Don't."

"I wouldn't worry about that." Butler had had no reaction to Limas wanting to go to Moscow, having a sister. Evan knew she was about to find out why.

"I mean it." That certain steel she knew well had entered Butler's voice. "Not only is Peter Limas in on the Nemesis kill list, but we just found out he's an SVR agent. We have a visual confirming it."

She should have felt something—anything—but betrayal was a way of life. *Does that make me less than human?* she wondered. *Or more.*

"Ben. If he's a Russian spy, then why is he on the Nemesis list?"

"I'm counting on you to get me the answer to that," Butler said.

By the gray dawn's light, Evan saw a boy of about ten emerge from the inn's front door, pick up the bike, and pedal away, a khaki knapsack on his back.

Evan said: "A visual?"

"I've just sent it to you. A photo of Limas talking with Anton Recidivich Gorgonov. From the looks of them they might be the best of friends."

Evan took the phone away from her ear, thumbed open the photo, zoomed in on the two faces. Butler was right; chatting like pals.

"It's been vetted by forensics, and verified," Butler said as if reading her mind. "It's them definitely together, all right."

"Quite a puzzle," Evan said.

"How so?"

"Limas is claiming to be Lyudmila Shokova's nephew. He says that Lyudmila spirited him out of Russia after his parents were killed, set him up with an adopted family in England."

"The Limases."

"None other."

"That can be easily verified."

"Not so easily, the way Lyudmila deep-dove her legends."

"Yes, I remember quite vividly," Butler admitted.

"He also told me that Lyudmila spent a great deal of time and energy shielding him and his sister from the FSB and GRU records department."

"Okay then, which is he? Lyudmila Shokova's nephew or a long-game SVR operative?"

"The question of the hour."

"And what if he's both?"

Traffic was sparse on the road beside the inn. At this early hour it was mostly just milk vans and vegetable wagons heading to Tbilisi from countryside farms and markets. The treetops on the far side of the road stirred in the last of the early morning haze.

Evan recalled the conundrum she had related to Peter of the tall native and the short native, one who only told the truth, the other who invariably lied. How to tell which was which? Evan had very few vulnerabilities. Up until this moment, she had never considered that Lyudmila could become a liability, but in her world of shadows and betrayals, any form of friendship could be exploited by a clever and resourceful enough enemy. Is that what had happened here? Had Gorgonov given Limas the mother of all legends—an entirely credible background that led Evan back to her friend? If so, it was a diabolical plan. But toward what end?

"Evan?"

She cleared her head of speculation. "I suppose I'd better find out what the hell his mission is," she said.

"I also want to know what, if anything, he knows about Roger Hollis's involvement in Nemesis." Butler hesitated a moment. "I know this must be difficult for you. The specter of Lyudmila coming back in such an insidious manner."

Evan did not want to comment on this, so, once again gripping the small wooden carving in her pocket, an amulet, a way home, she changed the subject. "How is Brenda?" she asked.

Butler knew her so well that he did not query her abrupt change of subject. "She's . . . Like you, she's recovered far more quickly than I'd imagined."

Evan, hearing the slight hesitation in his response, said, "I suggest that you give me all of it."

"Yes. I suppose so." Butler sighed. "I had her follow Beacum, to see if he would lead us to his control, or someone up the Nemesis food chain." He told her about Charles Isaacs. "He says he works for Interpol. He got onto Nemesis through the anti-Semitic angle."

"That tracks," Evan said. "Tell Brenda I want to speak with this Charles Isaacs as soon as."

"Right," Butler replied. "In the meantime I've got actionable intel. Through intercepts, it's becoming clear that there's a fatal feud going on between the SVR and the GRU. The latest intel is that Gorgonov and General Boyko are at each other's throats, over what we don't know, but it seems possible that Limas is the key. He's Gorgonov's agent and he's on the Nemesis kill list."

"Better he's with me than anywhere else."

"Agreed."

"Anything more?"

"No. Oh, yes, there is one other bit of news. We may have ID'd the woman who drove the car bomb into the St. Agnes parking lot. We think her real name is Marina Mevedeva."

Marina Mevedeva. Evan felt all the air rush out of her. "I knew she was Russian. And from my violent encounter with her, certainly Russian trained. Could the Russians be bankrolling Nemesis?"

"Huh. If that's true, the prime driver would be General Boyko. With its troll bot presence and its active agents on the ground, it seems logical the GRU would be behind them."

"Yes. Consider the rapid rise of neo-Nazis in America," Evan said. "Think of the destabilizing effect they're having on the country."

Butler thought of his own online antagonists. "Along with the false flag of 'fake news,' they're doing a good job of helping to polarize the country."

"What if all of it is GRU's doing?" She whistled through her teeth. "Send me a coroner's photo of the Mevedeva woman."

"Why? What is it, Evan?"

Outside it was brighter now, the air clearing. As she glanced down, Peter Limas appeared, looked up at the sky, and, breath steaming, stretched. Then he turned and, briskly rubbing his hands together, went back inside.

Evan moved back, sat down on the rumpled bed. Her head was spinning. "Peter Limas said he lost track of his sister," she said. "It's a long shot, but maybe he can ID the photo."

30

Having missed Christmas with Zoe because his hellacious work schedule had required him to rush from crisis to crisis, trying to put out the fires that seemed to pop up like a game of Whac-A-Mole, Butler determined to spend the evening with his daughter, as any father worth his salt would.

They went shopping together. While Zoe had a ball picking out presents for herself, she was also adamant about buying him presents with the money she had apparently saved from the weekly allowance Butler gave her and for doing chores around the house for which Butler also paid her.

As they went from department to department in Neiman Marcus, happy the store was open late during the Christmas holiday season, Butler could not help but be bowled over by the manner in which Zoe chose and paid for the presents for him. Most adults he knew wouldn't have expended as much thought as Zoe did on what the recipient of these presents would like. She chose a gift pack of Fruition chocolate bars, her father's favorite, the shaving cream he preferred, and a comfy-cozy-looking plaid flannel shirt on sale that Butler had admired but had not bought for himself, intent as he was on shopping for his daughter. He was careful not to amass a boatload of presents in order to compensate for him missing Christmas; that was not his modus operandi and, anyway, guilt was not an emotion he normally entertained, especially when it came to Zoe. That was not a trait he wished to pass on.

The pair started promptly at six o'clock, and now it was almost nine, and both were in need of sustenance and then home to bed.

"I didn't know shopping could make me so happy and so tired, Dad," Zoe said.

Butler took her hand as they walked out of Neiman Marcus and through the Mazza Gallerie, past the huge festive Christmas tree that no one wanted to call a Christmas tree anymore. Butler laughed. "This won't be the last time you feel that, sweetness."

Their free hands were loaded down with packages, gaily gift-wrapped in the bright red and green colors of the season. Even though both knew what was in each package, Zoe had insisted on having them wrapped, saying, "They wouldn't be presents otherwise, would they, Dad?" And Butler had to agree that they most certainly wouldn't.

"I wish it was snowing," Zoe said, her pink cheeks upturned to her father's face when they emerged onto windswept nighttime Wisconsin Avenue NW, tinsel and glitter all around them. "O Come, All Ye Faithful" flowed from pairs of outdoor speakers. "Wouldn't it be great if it snowed now?"

"I think that would be wonderful," Butler admitted. They crossed the crowded sidewalk at the front of the mall. "But so far the evening's been pretty wonderful without the snow, don't you think?"

"I think it's been perfect, Dad!" Zoe cried. "I love being with you!"

Butler bent, hugged his daughter tight, with the result that all their packages scattered onto the pavement. They both laughed as they helped Mitchell, Butler's driver/bodyguard, pick them up. He saw Zoe into the backseat of the car, then helped Mitchell pack all the boxes and bags into the trunk. As Mitchell slammed the door down, Butler caught a glimpse over his shoulder of a black four-door Ford sedan nosing out of the traffic flow and double-parking three cars behind them.

Nothing happened for a moment. Then the curbside rear door began to open.

"The Cheesecake Factory," Butler said, Zoe's favorite, as he ducked into the car. A moment later, Mitchell pulled them out into the thick traffic, slowed to a crawl. Turning in his seat, Butler peered out the rear window. Through the glare of streetlights and the beams of headlights he could just make out the Ford pulling away from the curb and following them.

"Dad," Zoe said, reactive as ever to her father's change in mood, "what's the matter?"

"Nothing, darling." He turned back around, took his daughter's hand in his. "I thought I saw someone I knew, that's all."

It was only a short drive up Wisconsin to the restaurant, but he was tense the entire way. In truth, Thompson's threats had unnerved him, even after Isobel had assured him that she had the Defense Secretary under control. It wasn't that he doubted Isobel; he never had before and he sure as hell wasn't going to start now. No, it was the fact that Thompson's aggressive action had obliged him to go to Isobel in the first place. He hadn't wanted to do it, had hated being forced to do it, and now felt weakened by it. He had let Thompson get to him—a pig like that! He was filled with self-disgust. The evening had begun so well—he was so happy to be with Zoe, so pleased to see the joy bursting from her. And now this: the black follow-on Ford had sullied his time with Zoe, made him feel as if his good feelings were just an illusion, like hearth and home. In his world there was no place for good feelings. This bedrock truth was something he and Evan shared, deep down, in the marrow of their bones.

On the seat beside him, Zoe was humming a familiar melody, and then she broke out the song in her high, clear soprano, the Christmas carol. "Good King Wenceslas looked out/On the feast of Stephen." And then Butler joined her for the next line: "When the snow lay round about/Deep and crisp and even."

When Mitchell stopped in front of The Cheesecake Factory, as Zoe was singing "Brightly shone the moon that night/Though the frost was cru-el . . ." Butler saw the black Ford slow and come to a stop near them. Perhaps for this reason, he now recalled that Wenceslas, king of tenth-century Bohemia, had been assassinated by his brother.

"Sweetie," he said when Zoe had slid out of the car after him, "how would you like to go inside with Mitchell?"

Those big blue eyes searched his face. "Okay, but you're coming, too, aren't you?"

"What a question! Of course I am." He smiled down at his daughter. "It's just that I have to take care of a little business, and, anyway, I bet it's super busy inside and you know Mitchell is so good at getting a table right away."

"Cool!" Zoe laughed and nodded. "But promise you won't be long."

Leaning over, Butler kissed the top of his daughter's head. "I promise, sweetness."

Zoe held out her hand, and Mitchell took it, at the same time giving his boss a meaningful look, which said, *If you need me . . .* Butler shook his head.

As soon as Mitchell and Zoe had disappeared into the restaurant, Butler turned to face the black Ford, its hood reflecting light from the store windows. The rear door swung open, a slim young woman with ice-blond hair in a tan business suit stepped out and stared directly at Butler. She strode toward him on thick, sensible heels.

Butler tensed, feeling for the haft of the switchblade he wore in a sheath at the small of his back.

He had pulled it halfway out when the woman in the tan suit stopped in front of him, smiled, and said, "You are Benjamin Butler, correct?"

The blade was three-quarters drawn. "Correct."

When the woman reached inside her suit jacket, Butler drew his knife out fully and kept it hidden against the palm of his hand. However, it wasn't a weapon of her own that the woman now had in her hands, merely a sheet of thick paper, neatly folded in thirds. She held it out, and when Butler took it, she said, "You've been served," with the nicest smile Butler had ever seen.

He did nothing, apart from watching the young woman walk back to the black Ford. The moment she was inside, the Ford drove slowly away. He could see now that it had a federal license plate.

He looked down at the folded sheet of paper as if surprised he had hold of it. Then, as carefully as if it were a bomb, he opened it. He had to read it through three times before the reality set in: he was summoned to appear on January third before a Senate Intelligence Committee chaired by the Secretary of Defense's good friend, Senator Willis.

Brady Thompson had made good on his threat.

▪ ▪ ▪

"Yes, they're both dead," Brenda said into her mobile, on her way to Anacostia. "The bomb-maker, Voron, and Charles Isaacs."

She listened to Butler's thin voice, too busy being exhausted to be made tense by the obvious strain in her boss's tone. "No. No idea what either of their real names are." More chatter. "Of course I checked everything. They were both professionals; they carried no hint of their true identities." Still more chatter. "No, I don't require the concussion protocol. I'm fine." The throbbing in her skull was quickly turning into the mother of all headaches. She'd have to find a pharmacy before she drove to the pawnshop. "Well, it doesn't matter that you don't believe me. I'm here in the field and you're at The Cheesecake Factory with Zoe."

Silence on the other end of the line. "Sorry." Brenda licked her chapped lips. "I'm a little overwhelmed by events." She took a breath to gather herself, right her ship's course. "Maybe your forensics team can ID the corpses from fingerprints. Who knows? Interpol may very well have them—or at least one of them—on file. Listen, I've got to go. I need to follow up a lead before it goes cold," she said, eager to get off the call. "I'll check in with you when I know more."

It was only later, after she had bought a bottle of ibuprofen, taken three with a half-bottle of Fiji water and was sitting behind the wheel with her eyes closed, replaying the conversation, that she realized something was wrong at home. For home, read Butler—for that was what Benjamin Butler had provided for her: a home more secure than any she had ever had before.

For a moment or two, she wavered in her brief, wondered if perhaps she should return to Butler, find out what was wrong, and try to help. But almost immediately she realized it was nothing more than an ego-driven idea; Butler was perfectly capable of taking care of himself.

And so she got out of the car and walked a block and a half in the dark and cold to the plate-glass front of Willie's Swap'n'Shop. The pawnshop, the only place on the block open at this hour, was sandwiched between a bodega offering an all-day breakfast and a shoe store that, judging by the display behind its squeaky-clean window, sold nothing but high-top kicks for three hundred dollars and up. A handwritten sign posted on Willie's front door said, "OPEN TILL MIDNIGHT."

A little bell made an unexpectedly homey sound as

she went in the door. A greasy-looking man in his mid-fifties with the shifty marbleized eyes of a junkie looked up from behind one of the glass cases that ringed three sides of the shop. He was polishing a bronze trophy cup with a filthy rag, both of which he put aside as Brenda sauntered toward him.

He pasted a smile on his face, an unfortunate reflex as it bared his nicotine-stained teeth.

"What can I do for you?" he said in a surprisingly high voice. A little fat guy, his hands were square, the nails black with grime. He wore an oil-stained suede vest over a T-shirt emblazoned with a grinning skull on fire that ballooned out over his stomach. Great crescent sweat stains darkened the underarms. Unmentionable smells seemed to waft up from his stiff blue jeans.

"Are you Willie?" Brenda asked, trying not to wrinkle her nose.

"Depends." His eyes narrowed. "Who wants to know?"

"This guy." Brenda whipped out the longslide from its place at the small of her back. "Mr. Springfield Armory is asking."

"Uh, so yeah, I'm Willie."

He seemed so nonchalant Brenda was briefly worried that he was going to fall asleep on her. She lay the longslide on the countertop with the muzzle facing Willie.

"You wanna hock that hunka burnin' love?" Willie asked. "I can maybe swing you a good deal."

Without taking her eyes off him, she took out the folded receipt she had found in the root cellar, spread it out on the glass facing away from her. Willie glanced down at it, then back up to her.

"Yeah? So fucking what?"

"So fucking this," Brenda said, showing him her federal ID.

"Ah, shit, fuck, and corruption." Willie passed a hand

across his forehead, leaving horizontal streaks of greasy dirt like war paint.

"Right. Selling guns without a license is a major no-no, Willie."

"I tell you right now I ain't sellin' anything illegal."

Brenda tapped the longslide. "You were going to make me an offer for Mr. Armory here."

"Hey, I was just bein' friendly."

"And you didn't ask if I had a license for it."

"I was gettin' around to that," he said sullenly.

"Like hell you were." Brenda reached across the counter, grabbed him by his vest, and, trying not to breathe in the noxious fumes, jerked him toward her. "Enough with the bullshit, Willie. What can you tell me about the woman who bought this gun?"

"Now, this isn't my chosen field of expertise, you unnerstand. My partner—"

Brenda jerked him against the edge of the counter. "You've just about worn out my patience, Willie."

"Okay, okay. A woman came in coupla days ago. Small, dark, looked like she could take care of herself though. To tell you the truth I didn't like the look of her."

"Why not?"

Willie licked his lips, made a little animal sound in the back of his throat. "She didn't look like no civilian, that's why."

"A professional, is that what you're saying?"

"Rightly so."

"Then what?"

"She asked for the longslide in particular, like she knew we had one, which we often don't."

"You got a name for her?"

"What am I, the national register?" Willie cleared his throat, which did nothing for the thickened air Brenda was breathing in. "I can tell you she wasn't buying, though. Trading, more like it. A pawn, temporary-like.

She said she'd bring it back in a coupla days. I said, 'Better not be the worse for wear.'"

"How did she react?"

Willie gave an uncomfortable laugh, like he'd just passed wind. "She like as pinned me to the wall with her eyes."

"What did she have to trade?"

"Dunno. I didn't want any part of her so I passed her on to my partner."

"And who would that be, Willie? I mean, your shop doesn't say Willie and Partner, does it?"

"It wouldn't. He's silent, you see, my partner." Willie's beady eyes seemed about to work their way out of their sockets. "Works the other side a the street, so to speak."

"The non-civilian side," Brenda said.

"Rightly so."

"And where might I find this partner of yours?"

Willie jerked his head so violently his vertebrae made a cracking sound. "He's in back."

"Does this partner have a name?"

"Dave."

Brenda sighed. "Dave what?"

"Gilly. Dave Gilly."

Brenda gathered up the longslide, pointed it at Willie. "Let's you and me take a walk on the wild side."

Willie blinked. "Say what?"

"I want to talk to Dave Gilly," she said. "I want to see what the woman gave him on loan for this weapon because for some reason it's not written on the receipt." She came around the end of the counter. "Take me to him."

She shoved him forward, down a narrow, evil-smelling corridor that led to a back room. If she had been thinking clearly, she would not have followed him down the corridor. If she hadn't been critically overextended, she would have ordered Willie to call his partner out into the showroom. If her brain wasn't still reeling from the multiple shocks of the explosion, Charles's death, and having to kill Voron to keep herself alive, she wouldn't be entering the back room just behind Willie.

As it was, she narrowly avoided death only by dint of her reflexes. A movement in the corner of her eye caused her to turn slightly to her left. As a result, the blow meant to split her skull instead struck her on the right side of her head and skidded off. The impact was hard enough to knock her off her pins, however. She slumped to the floor, the gun skittering out of her grip, across the filthy floor, and into Willie's waiting hands.

Her hearing and eyesight flickered on and off, as did a massive pain that was growing into a mountain of agony threatening to crush her. She tried to rise but her limbs were dead weights. She heard but didn't see someone say, "Get the rope." And some time later, "Truss her like a hog." And, finally, just before oblivion took her, "We're going to have us a nice old-fashioned weenie roast."

31

Peter Limas was already having breakfast in the inn's small, sun-splashed dining room when Evan came in through the front door. She sat down opposite Limas and ordered eggs, sausage, and two slices of Georgia's thick, dense black bread. While she waited for her food, she stared out the window and sipped her mug of coffee.

"Out for a morning constitutional?" Limas said with an unsuccessful attempt at a grin.

"Just checking the grounds," Evan said. "I'm looking for someone."

"Out here, in the back of beyond? Who?"

"The sniper who shot at us at the restaurant yesterday. He's unaccounted for."

Limas stiffened, craning his neck to peer out the window. "Do you really think he'll try again?"

"I killed the rest of his team," Evan replied. "I certainly would."

Evan's breakfast arrived and she dug in. The eggs and sausage were a whole lot better than the greasy dinner. She felt as if she hadn't had a decent meal since she left the States. Meanwhile, Limas had moved himself out of line with the window, preferring a solid wall, rather than a pane of glass, between him and whoever might be stalking them outside. He seemed to have lost a bit of color from his face.

"It's a good thing you didn't tell me this last night. I never would've been able to fall asleep." He squirmed a little in his chair. "As it is I can't stop thinking about those photos you showed me, how those agents were killed. MI6s, and . . . two of them were Brenda's colleagues." Now real alarm showed on Limas's face. "Is she in danger?"

"I don't think so. She isn't on the list, Peter." Evan tore a piece of black bread in half and began mopping up a broken yolk as she glanced up at Limas. She took a bite of the yolk-soaked bread, chewed, swallowed, then added, "But you are."

"What, me?" Whatever was left of Limas's color drained away. He put both hands to his head. His eyes went out of focus. "Bloody hell." Then he refocused on Evan. "Why me?"

Evan speared the last bit of sausage, popped it in her mouth, and chewed meditatively, drawing out the moment, letting Limas twist in the wind. Finally, wiping her lips, she said, "I should think that was obvious, Peter."

"Maybe to you, but—"

"Your aunt had many enemies inside Russia. They have never forgiven her for what they see as her betrayal of the Motherland." Evan poured herself more coffee from the pewter carafe. "The time has come to face facts, Peter."

"Someone knows I'm Lyudmila's nephew."

Evan drank her coffee. Eyes never wavering from Limas's face, she said nothing.

Limas sat back, arms crossed defensively across his chest, as if to protect himself against imminent attack. "But who?"

Evan put down her mug very carefully. "Now would

be the time to tell me what you really know about Nemesis."

"What? But I've told you, I don't know anything about it. I mean, until you just told me I had no idea I was on—what do you call it?"

"A kill list."

Limas shuddered. "Right." His eyes looked left, right, as if searching for an answer in the interior of the inn. "But . . . but all the other names on the list—Brenda's colleagues." He gestured. "And the British MI6 agents we found. I mean, they're all spies."

Evan continued to silently sip her coffee.

"I mean . . ." Limas's expression had gone a bit wild. "Bloody hell, why don't you say something?"

"What would you have me say?"

"*Some*thing. Anything."

"All right." Evan pushed her chair away from the table, stood up. "At this moment, you hold all the cards."

She turned and walked out of the dining room, through the front hall. A moment later, Limas heard the front door open and close.

■ ■ ■

"What does that mean, I hold all the cards?"

Limas, hurrying after Evan, caught up to her in the courtyard adjacent to the small graveled car park.

"What the hell does that mean?"

"Why ask me," Evan said, turning to face him, "when you can ask your pal Anton."

Limas's eyes opened wide. "Who?" He was already back on his heels.

"Anton Recidivich Gorgonov."

"I don't know who that is," Limas said, shaking his head.

Evan, watching him like a hawk will an adder, said, "I'll show you then." Producing her mobile, she brought up the photo of Limas getting cozy with Gorgonov, and presented it to Limas. They appeared to be doing what any good friends would be doing.

Despite the temperature, sweat broke out on Limas's forehead and upper lip. "Where did you get that?"

"I'll ask the questions, Peter." Tucking away the phone, Evan closed with Limas.

"What's the matter with you? It's obviously been Photoshopped. It's a fake."

"As it happens it's not," Evan said. "The photo has been verified."

"But I'm Lyudmila's nephew, I'm your *friend*."

"No. Lyudmila was my friend. You're Gorgonov's friend. What you were meant to be to me must now be determined." Evan took him by the elbow, waited for a gap in the traffic, and frog-marched him across the road and into the woods on the other side.

They entered the cathedral of trees and pine needles, with cones crunching underfoot. Evan took them deeper and deeper, the chill seeping through their sweaters and trousers, and into their muscles, stiffening them. She led them into and across a small, roughly semicircular clearing, the back of which was an almost solid wall of trees.

Evan positioned herself within the clearing and pushed Limas back against a rough-barked pine tree. "You're blown, Peter. Any way you slice it or dice it, the plan you and Gorgonov had for getting close to me is fucked, over. Finis." Evan gestured with her head. "You might as well call him and tell him as much."

A curious expression crossed Limas's lips, as mysterious as that of the *Mona Lisa*. It seemed as if he was almost relieved that the ruse was over.

"Huh! You've boxed me," he said in an altogether different tone of voice. Evan became aware of his lovely British upper-class accent. "If I say yes you'll grill me and, whether I end up telling you the whole truth or not, you'll kill me; I've witnessed how easily you kill another human, without a bit of compunction or remorse." He took a breath. "And if I say no, you won't believe me because I've lied to you."

"That's about the size of it."

"I'm in a no-win situation, I reckon," Limas said. "What would you do?"

"I wouldn't get myself into a no-win situation."

"What if you're in one now," Limas said with so much conviction it didn't seem to be a question. "This seems to be the real-life equivalent of the riddle of the two tribesmen you told me."

"The difference is that had a peaceable solution," Evan said. "With you there's no such thing."

"Obsessive thinking," Limas said, "often leads to taking the wrong fork in the road."

What was most curious to Evan was that now that his real identity had been blown Peter showed neither concern nor regret.

"Why are you pretending to be Lyudmila's nephew? To befriend me, that's certain. But then what? What is it Gorgonov enlisted you to get out of me?"

Limas leaned his back against the pine. The early morning birds twittered in the maze of branches above his head. "If I'm a betting man," Limas said, "I'd wager you know what a palimpsest is."

"I do," Evan said. "It's from the Greek meaning 'rubbed again.'"

"Just so." Limas nodded. "A palimpsest is a page on which the original text has been rubbed away and overlaid with a new one. However, since the rubbing out can be, and often is, incomplete, a close study of the page can reveal the original text, hidden by time and circumstance."

Evan watched Limas with a quizzical expression, wondering where this was leading. Then again, it might simply be a diversion. In her experience people under extreme duress or in fear of their lives will go off on tangents if only to delay the inevitable.

"And?"

Limas spread his hands. "And I am a living, breathing palimpsest."

"Explain yourself."

Limas held out his hand. "May I see the raven pendant you've been dangling around?"

"Why?"

"I may actually know something about Nemesis, after all."

Evan dug out the pendant, showed it to him.

"I've been thinking," Limas said, peering at the two corvids. "The raven is a powerful symbol in ancient Germanic myth. Wotan, or Odin, the god-king of Reginheim, had a pair of raven familiars named Memory and Thought. These ravens would daily bring the great god news from the nine realms."

Evan nodded. "Yes. And the upper echelons of the Third Reich—especially Hitler himself—put great store in the myths and magic of the ancient Germanic tribes. So that's likely where Nemesis got the name the First Tribe."

"But why use two separate names?"

Evan, registering the silence that comes with a cessation of morning birdsong, put a forefinger across her lips. Limas's eyes narrowed. *Don't move,* Evan mouthed. Long seconds ticked by. Limas mouthed, *What? Patience,* Evan answered him silently.

All at once, there was a sharp snap and then a great whooshing as of a strong wind getting up between the trees. But the treetops above them remained unmoving.

"Now," Evan said, heading out of the clearing into the deeper woods, Limas hot on her heels. Three hundred yards away they came upon a snare, triggered and hanging five feet above the forest floor. In it was a struggling red deer buck. As they watched, a bolt from a hunting bow struck the buck in the neck. The buck's eyes rolled in its sockets. The black lips pulled back, revealing its square ruminant teeth, the mouth gnashing and snapping in the agony of its death throes. If it could scream it would have.

32

"Goddammit. Stay here." Evan took off through the trees.

Limas was having none of it. He followed Evan's curious zigzag path as best he could, failing ultimately because the route Evan took was so unpredictable all Limas could do was stumble blindly after her.

Ahead of her, Evan saw the sniper—who, in the quiet countryside, had traded his long gun for a Russian Interloper Styx, a powerful hunting crossbow. The hunter, caught unawares by Evan's erratic headlong sprint toward him, fired even as he was driven backward in order to keep an optimal distance between him and his quarry. As a result, the bolt passed through Evan's parka, missing her side by inches.

The stalker was still backing up when another small but distinct snap sounded, and he was taken off his feet as the second snare, which Evan had driven him into, caught him. The crossbow, stuck in the webbing, was now useless, and, coming up to him, Evan wrenched it out of his hand, pulled it free of the webbing. She was glaring at the stalker through the prison the trapped man was futilely trying to tear apart as Limas came up beside her.

Limas fairly goggled. "How?" He shook his head. "How did you set this up?"

"There's a third snare back another three hundred

yards," Evan said without taking her eyes off the sniper. "To answer your question, after some judicious scouting, I borrowed what I needed from our proprietor's hunting gear in the shed I peeked into during last night's stroll."

"You were right." There was a note of awe in Limas's voice. "He did come after us."

"I gave him only one angle to shoot me," Evan said, cutting through the netting. "Where he'd have the best line of sight."

The sniper, forced onto his haunches, growled at Evan and, as he was hauled out, bared his teeth, yellowed and fanged. Limas, shocked, lurched backward as the stalker wielded a wicked hunting knife, stabbing it forward. Evan, stepping into his attack, caught his wrist and, with a violent twist, broke it.

Limas watched as Evan smashed her fist into the sniper's mouth. A set of fanged prosthetics popped out, and Evan crushed them under the heel of her boot. Then she lifted her knee into the sniper's nose, shattering it. The man went limp, his eyes turning upward.

"Bugger it." Under the increasing stress, Limas was reverting to phrases from his British upbringing. "For a moment there I had this weird notion that he was a real werewolf."

Pointing out the sniper's shaven tattooed head, Evan said, "Not enough hair."

Limas snorted in amusement. Her unconscious attempt at humor helped calm them both.

"But in a sense, he is a werewolf," she added.

"What d'you mean?"

"Think Werner Naumann, history buff."

Limas tapped his lower lip in thought. "Yes. Naumann was Goebbels's aide at the end of the war. It was his idea to create a Nazi Werewolf Unit that would attract the most skilled of the Nazi soldiers still alive, forming a fifth column, a lethal underground resistance against Allied occupation. But by that time the Nazis had no more fight left in them, and, according to historical records I've seen, the Werewolf Unit was never formed."

"Well, it's been resurrected as the First Tribe," Evan said. "Take a good look at the tattoo on the top of his head." It was the Third Reich's Imperial eagle, wings stretched, talons grappling a globe containing a swastika. "I think the First Tribe is Nemesis's name for its field personnel."

The sniper's eyelids began to flutter and Evan grabbed him by his shirtfront, hauled him to his feet. She slapped his face twice to bring him around.

"Who are you?" Evan said. "Who do you work for?"

The sniper opened his eyes, brown as mud and, grinning like a lunatic, spat in Evan's face. He wasn't even holding his broken wrist; it was as if he didn't feel the pain of it or his shattered nose.

Out of the corner of her eye Evan saw Limas girding himself for action, and she determined this was the time to deploy her ace in the hole.

Digging out her mobile, she thumbed through until she came to the photo of Marina Mevedeva that Butler had sent, the Nemesis agent who had slipped into the United States on a Canadian passport using the legend Anna Alta.

Pulling Limas closer, she said, "I want to show you something, Peter." She turned the phone so Limas could see the photo, a close-up of Marina, eyes closed, face white, laid out on the coroner's table.

"A dead woman? Why are you showing me a dead woman?"

Keeping one eye on the bloodied sniper, Evan said, "We think her name is Marina Mevedeva." Her other eye was fixed on Limas. Not even the slightest tremor of recognition.

"Well, the last name is mine, but I have no idea who this woman is."

"Peter, your sister's given name isn't Marina?"

"No. It's Illyena." Peter shook his head. "How did this woman die?"

Evan watched him closely. "Nemesis trained her and sent her out to plant the car bomb that almost killed Brenda and me." That statement was true as far as it went. "Subsequently she was killed resisting arrest." There were times when the absence of truth and truth intersected, especially in the field where exigencies dictated snap decisions.

"A martyr. Another fucking martyr who almost succeeded."

"But she didn't, Peter. Brenda and I are alive and well."

"Brenda." At once, tears streamed from Limas's eyes. At the same time, his limbs began to spasm. His legs became so weak he fell to his knees. But in the next second he was up, his face ruddy with rushing blood. Cords stuck out from the sides of his neck and his hands balled into fists.

"Good luck, fucker," Evan told the sniper as she stepped back.

Limas launched himself at the werewolf, his fists beating a rough tattoo on the man's face, neck, and torso. When the man attempted to fight back, Limas thrust his head forward. His mouth opened, snapped shut. The sniper screamed as Limas came away with part of his left ear. Limas took a step back, spat the bloody flesh onto the mat of fallen pine needles that made up the floor of the woods.

When he went after the man again, Evan grabbed him around the waist, held him back. "That's enough, Peter. That's enough now."

"It's not enough," Limas snarled. "He's a monster. He and these fucking savages almost killed Brenda. It'll never be enough. Never-fucking-never." He turned his face to Evan, his lips and teeth blood-red. "Let me at him. Please. I'm begging you." He struggled in Evan's grip.

"I know you don't owe me anything, liar that I am. But you'll understand the truth soon enough. So let me—"

Evan shook him a little, to return some sense to his traumatized mind. "Peter, if you beat him to death you'll regret it for the rest of your life. It's not a small thing to kill another human being."

"I don't care."

"Not now, perhaps. But in the days to come you will."

And then Evan let him go. The stalker had already affirmed that he wasn't going to give up anything, and Evan believed him. She had had more than her fair share of run-ins with fanatics. The main problem with them was that they weren't afraid to die. Worse, they felt that bearing pain—even excruciating pain—was the hero's way of keeping their group or cadre or sect or tribe safe and secure. They embraced martyrdom the moment they signed on; Amiran, the gun dealer, being the most recent example of how much they devalued life.

But, inevitably, as she watched Limas return to pounding the stalker over and over in savage glee, she wondered who the monster was now.

At length, Limas's attack slowed and then ceased altogether; he crouched over the raw slab of meat, sated. As for the stalker, he had ceased to care, or even breathe, some time ago.

33

At this time of the year, the Moskva River was filled with silver and gray ice. The water itself was sluggish, as murky as the Federation's politics.

"It's colder than a nun's kiss down here," Vilen Vladimirovich Aliyev complained, shivering in his greatcoat.

"One of the reasons it's one of the safest places in Moscow to meet," General Boyko said.

Aliyev grunted. "Nevertheless, Yuri, you know I dislike meeting in the open under the best of circumstances."

The two men, bundled up against the icy wind skating along the riverbanks, elbows on an iron railing, stared out at the bleak scene. Without traffic, the river and environs looked like a painting by an artist on the verge of suicide.

Aliyev was a tall, slender, saturnine man with rounded shoulders and a nose that had been broken once too often. His dark eyes, deeply set in sockets too close together, peered out at the world with inveterate suspicion from beneath a heavy brow. When put together, these features made his gloomy face look like the subject of an El Greco portrait.

"It was killing weather like this that did in Hitler's army," Aliyev said.

"I do believe the heroic Communist forces played their part," Boyko retorted.

Aliyev was the district head of the RNU, the radical splinter group that had its own agenda separate from that of the Sovereign. Over the past nineteen or so month's the RNU had greatly increased its power, helped immeasurably by the deepening poverty and privations brought on by the Sovereign's insistence on growing and modernizing the army for forays into Ukraine, Syria, and beyond.

The two men had met five years ago, when the RNU was so inconsequential it hardly came up in Boyko's circles. Boyko and his family had been on vacation at a resort fronting the Black Sea. Out smoking cigars on the terrace late one night Aliyev had mentioned his admiration of the superb manner with which the Nazis had run Germany, and what a shame it was that they had been led down the garden path by a syphilitic madman. Six weeks later, back in Moscow, Boyko had invited Aliyev to dinner at an out-of-the-way restaurant he often favored when he didn't want to be seen or even noticed. Afterward, as they enjoyed one of the General's vintage brandies in the apartment Boyko kept for his assignations with his parade of mistresses, he had brought out his carefully curated Nazi memorabilia as proudly as if they were his prized pupils. He'd never before showed his treasures to anyone else, but he trusted Aliyev to both understand and appreciate the Third Reich as he did. And he hadn't been wrong. From these poisoned roots a solid alliance had grown, slowly but surely bearing its poisoned fruit.

"Our plan is progressing even better than I had anticipated," Boyko said. His cheeks were pink and plush as a child's unicorn toy. "Our alliance with Nemesis has advanced our mission in bringing strength and hope for the future to America's neo-Nazis."

Breaking out a pair of cigars, he offered one to Aliyev,

bit off the end of his, lit them both with a large gunmetal lighter with a wind shield. He took a couple of preliminary puffs to make sure the cigar was well-lit, then continued: "Our false Facebook and Twitter accounts have also helped create and incite the far-left radicals, Antifa, into domestic terrorist designation by the administration, the FBI, and Homeland Security." He shook his head. "It's astonishing to me how easily these American radical groups are led by feeding them news stories they want to hear, that further their own causes." He laughed. "What a joke."

"It doesn't matter whether they're on the right or the left?" Aliyev asked, through a stream of aromatic blue smoke that was hijacked by the icy wind onto the river.

"Not in the least." Boyko guffawed. "When it comes to American radicals, their particular affiliations are irrelevant; they're all prone to falling into the traps our bots are spewing out.

"Here, let me show you my current favorite meme my people have come up with." Drawing out his mobile, he thumbed through his photo files until he came to the one he sought. Bringing it up to fill the screen, he showed it to Aliyev: a cartoon of a vaguely Jewish-looking figure with "Antifa" scrawled on his back. He was busy caulking a brick wall with swastikas. The meaning was direct and clear: it wasn't the neo-Nazis who were scrawling the symbol of the Third Reich around America's cities, but members of Antifa.

Aliyev nodded as he exhaled more smoke. "Quite brilliant, Yuri. I'm impressed."

"And at the same time the antagonism building against us by the American press has been the biggest boon to your cadre."

"True enough." Aliyev nodded. "As we know, deprivation breeds discontent, discontent curdles into resentment, which, under the right conditions, foments rebellion. This process is now being felt by the Russian people, and, as a result, the RNU grows by leaps and bounds."

Boyko, saying nothing more, pulled on his cigar meditatively. Above them, the weakened sun lost its struggle to break through the clouds.

"So," Aliyev said, after some time in the silence, "what can I do for you?"

Boyko barked a laugh. "You know me too well, Vilen Vladimirovich."

Aliyev grunted. "Well enough, anyway."

"You're not wrong." Boyko stared straight out at the chunks of ice, slowly colliding with one another. "I've got a problem," he said.

"Hmm. I assume since you've come to me, this problem isn't small."

"Well said." Taking the cigar butt out of his mouth, he examined the ash end as if reading tea leaves. "I need something done and I can't be involved."

Aliyev blew smoke out of his mouth, making puffs of humid mist. "So. You need a solution, Yuri. What kind?"

"A final solution," Boyko said without hesitation.

34

They brought the fresh-killed buck to the proprietor, partly as recompense for Evan taking three of his snares, partly because Evan didn't want to leave it hanging in midair. Though he looked askance at the bolt in the buck's neck, the proprietor seemed happy enough to declare lunch was on him, plus dinner and another night's stay, if that suited them. Lunch did, but as for the rest, what they needed from him, and what he promised to provide, was a lift to Tbilisi Airport where Butler's jet awaited them. It was too dangerous to go back for the Lada, which already might have been spotted.

The proprietor brought them a multi-course feast, and though they had had breakfast not so long ago, they found their hunger close to the surface. Limas, particularly, ate like a bear just out of hibernation. In fact, everything about him echoed that aspect. He seemed a wholly different man than the one Evan had led, half-willingly, into the dense woods across the road.

It bothered Evan that she felt nothing for the dead sniper, but it bothered her more that Limas didn't, either. "So now I've seen how eagerly you kill another human, without a bit of compunction or remorse."

Limas lifted his head. "I suppose I deserve that."

"About being a palimpsest," Evan prompted.

"Right." Limas nodded. "The truth and nothing but the truth: I was born into secrecy. I recall my mother only hazily and my father not at all—unless you count the two or three photos Aunt Lyudmila showed me of her brother. But he was much younger then, before he was stationed in Parechgadem, a place I never heard of and couldn't find on any map."

"Probably a secret SVR or GRU base," Evan said, though the name set off a bell tolling far back in the recesses of her mind. She frowned, for a moment distracted. "Possibly an internal name only."

Limas nodded dismissively. "I never knew much about my father's life, nor my grandfather's. I asked Aunt Lyudmila once but she wouldn't say, and with Aunt Lyudmila I had learned never to ask a question twice."

That certainly jibed with the Lyudmila Shokova Evan knew.

"Anyway," Limas went on, "I didn't lie to you about Aunt Lyudmila. Every word I said about her bringing me to England, setting me up with the Limas family, my going up to Cambridge was true. Actually, I was so advanced in my studies that I was accepted at King's College two years early. As you can imagine I received a good deal of ribbing for being so young. Until I showed off my rowing and fencing." He took a ragged breath, and his face seemed to change, become drawn and pale. "But . . ."

"But you left out the rest."

Limas nodded, but seemed reluctant to continue. A middle-aged woman, red-faced and overweight, toddled in and sat down at a small, round table. She ordered tea and cream cakes, just as if they were in Devon. The proprietor didn't bat an eye, let alone say, "This isn't an English teahouse, madam."

"So, in any event, what I had told you was the beginning of the palimpsest, the part of my life that became all but erased by what was written afterward."

"I feel Anton Gorgonov lurking around the next bend in your road."

Limas let a wry smile curl his lips, but it was wiped away soon enough. "I have no doubt that you're well-acquainted with Cambridge's reputation as a hotbed of recruitment of a specific sort."

"Better to call a spy a spy, Peter."

Limas's head bobbed up and down. "I suppose so, yes."

Evan tensed, hearing the roar of motorcycles drawing up into the inn's car park. Limas caught her look and fell silent. He followed Evan's gaze as two burly bikers stomped into the dining room in leather boots and heavy, fur-collared jackets. They chose a table in the rear corner.

"Evan—?" Limas said under his breath.

Evan shook her head, silencing him. The proprietor bustled out of the kitchen, carrying a tray with the heavy woman's order. After he set her up, he went over to the bikers, greeted them jovially, slapped them both on their broad backs. He told them a joke and they laughed uproariously, stamping their feet. They ordered, and then became engrossed in low conversation. They seemed uninterested in anyone else in the dining room.

"Continue," Evan said.

"So, you're right, Gorgonov was just around the corner—a very dark corner, indeed. Like some of my colleagues I was befriended by a dapper young man, thin as a pencil, ever so British in his pinstriped three-piece suit and a brolly so tightly rolled it seemed more of a walking stick. It was very expensive, that brolly, and later I discovered why: the bottom two-thirds served as a sheath for a very useful stiletto hidden inside."

The proprietor brought out steins of ale, set them in front of the bikers. He told them another joke, at which they laughed even harder.

"Of course, this dapper Brit wasn't from the Foreign

Office, as MI6 is often euphemistically called among the everything-difficult-or-secret-must-be-a-euphemism. He was an outrider for the KGB, as the SVR was called then, a recruiter on foreign shores, in a fecund garden, a tough weeder, a delicate picker of the most fragrant flowers. His instincts were impeccable." Limas laughed without a trace of humor. "Apart from me, of course."

"Meaning you weren't recruited?"

"Oh, yes. I was, indeed." Limas's eyes had turned as hard as marbles. "But my one condition was that Gorgonov be my control."

Evan frowned. "How did you know about Gorgonov at that stage?"

"Aunt Lyudmila had told me all about him. In fact, she had showed me Gorgonov's dossier. He was a junior apparatchik in the KGB at the time, but he was talented and, more important, immensely ambitious. And, even more important than that, he was connected to powerful people, which, in Russia, as you know, is everything."

"Why did she make you aware of Gorgonov?" Evan asked, although her grand chess master mind, racing ahead along with that of her friend Lyudmila, had already worked out the astonishing answer. Still, she wanted to hear it from Limas.

"She had already marked Gorgonov as a future problem—a 'major problem,' she told me."

"So you signing on as Gorgonov's asset was the price for stashing you away in England with a wealthy family that could give you the best of everything."

"The best education, anyway. That's what Aunt Lyudmila wanted for me. She knew how smart I was, what I could become given the right circumstances."

"She wanted to harness your intellect."

Limas nodded. "If you think that for a minute I resent what she asked of me, you're wrong. I owe my entire life to Aunt Lyudmila; I'd do anything for her."

Heaping platters of sausages and cabbage were set

before the bikers, who dug in with astounding gusto, like pigs at a trough. Evan could swear she heard one of them grunt.

She returned her attention to Limas. "Anything," she repeated. "Even put your life at risk, being a double agent working for Gorgonov and reporting back to her."

"That was my choice. I told her I would."

"But now that Lyudmila is gone, who do you report to? What's Lyudmila's backup plan? Knowing Lyudmila, she must have had one."

"There's the third level of the palimpsest," Limas said. "It's why she told me to seek you out if things got tough for her. And they did. Perhaps the toughest."

"So, what, I'm to be your control?"

"You are Aunt Lyudmila's backup plan. She trusted you more than anyone else, Evan."

Evan looked away, first out the window, then obliquely at the bikers, who were both on their second round of ales.

"There's one last thing." Limas hunched forward. "I suppose I should have mentioned this sooner, but with you seeming to not believe a word I'd said, I was afraid."

Limas had her full attention again. "What is it?"

"When you showed me the red-brick powder you'd found in the shallow cave with the bodies it rang a bell. But, really, I didn't put it together until I got a good long look at the pendant. Those two ravens. And then it hit me. Aunt Lyudmila told me about a place she'd been to with you. She told me not to use it as a way to prove I really am her nephew because she was uncertain whether you'd remember it." Limas spread his hands on the table. "She told me that you and she were in this place—a castle of red-brick, Victorian-looking turrets and towers and, yes, a pair of trained ravens that hung around the slate rooftop. Aunt Lyudmila went and got you out of there. It was very dangerous; she almost lost her life. You remember the deep scar in the muscle of her left shoulder?"

"I do."

"That came from the rescue mission. You were in very bad shape when she extracted you. Six weeks in a private hospital outside Moscow convalescing. She went to see you every day."

Evan felt the contents of her stomach try to rise up into her throat. She dropped her head into her hands and squeezed her eyes shut. Here was what Pat Wilson had known, here was the gap in her memory. Here was the missing splinter of time she had never been able to access. She forced herself to breathe, to open her eyes and look up at Limas.

"Yes. She was right to worry that I wouldn't remember. I didn't until just recently. But now I am beginning to remember that building, the ravens," Evan said. "Small flashes of the interior. But nothing else. I think that's where five of the six agents on that list were tortured, and four killed. The fifth subsequently died before he could tell me where this place was. Did Lyudmila tell you?"

"Yes and no," Limas said.

"Stop playing this game, Peter. It wasn't amusing to begin with, and now it's going to get you killed. If not by me right here, right now, then by your pal Anton when he eventually finds out you're a double."

"Gorgonov's not my friend."

"I've only your word for that," Evan said shortly. "And so far that hasn't meant much of anything."

Limas licked his lips. "I'm not trying to obfuscate, honest. But, really, well, what Aunt Lyudmila said was that she'd already told me where you'd been taken."

"Meaning?"

"That's just it," Limas whispered. "I don't know what she meant." He hung his head. "I didn't want to look like a fool in front of you."

"Too late." Evan rose. "Come on. It's time to go."

■ ■ ■

"Do you believe me?" Limas rubbed his hands over his thighs as if trying to wash away all his lies. "You do believe me, right?"

Evan, staring out at the passing countryside, said nothing. As promised, the proprietor, whose name was Giorgi, was driving them to Tbilisi Airport. Evan and Peter were in the backseat of his monstrous GMC, which looked more like an armored Humvee than it did a truck, its forbidding grille like the portcullis of a medieval castle. A storm was approaching fast, heading right for them, and the wind had gotten up to the point where the gusts rocked even the heavy vehicle.

Limas turned toward Evan, who was sitting directly behind Giorgi. "Listen, these people we're up against, the First Tribe, they're right spinners. Crazy as loons." And when Evan didn't reply, "I know you're angry with me."

"Angry? No," Evan replied. "It's simply that I can't trust you."

Limas made another try. "You've saved my life more than once since we've been out here in the back of beyond. I'm eternally grateful to you. I could never lie to you now. Never." He spread his hands in a form of entreaty. "Think what you want of me. I can't help that. I've said all I can say on the subject. But if there's any way I can prove myself—"

Limas broke off as he followed the direction of Evan's gaze. Directly ahead of them a barrier of concrete blocks had been set across the road. In front of the barrier, the two bikers whom Giorgi had served earlier stood, spread-legged, submachine guns at the ready. On either side of them were a half-dozen of their biker mates, all armed. As the truck approached, they aimed their submachine guns directly at the truck.

"What's going on?" Limas said.

For instead of slowing down, Giorgi stamped down on the accelerator. The GMC leapt ahead, gaining speed by the second, cleaving through the high wind that was now bending the tips of the pines and shaking the branches.

"We're heading straight for the barrier!" Limas cried.

A moment later, the bikers opened fire.

35

The instant Evan realized that Giorgi had depressed the accelerator, she lunged halfway over the seatback, stretching herself over the proprietor's shoulder, and triggered the hood latch. The oncoming wind, combined with the GMC's speed, banged the hood up so that when the fusillade came from the bikers' submachine guns the bullets struck the heavy hood instead of splitting open the windshield and peppering the interior.

That protection wouldn't last long, Evan knew. Throwing her body completely over the seatback, she opened the driver's side door, fending off Giorgi's awkward defense, and kicked the proprietor out of the truck's cab. His body was lifted into the air, then dropped to the ground somewhere on the road behind them.

Now in control, Evan turned the wheel over hard to the right, so the truck was paralleling the barrier. The truck slewed, tires squealing. It was so close to the bikers that they broke ranks, running this way and that. Evan could only see this intermittently through the driver's side window and the holes and rips in the flying hood, canted over to the right, bouncing up and down, half off and half on, like the broken wing of a wounded bird. When they were clear of the barrier, she steered the truck off the road, narrowly avoiding a drainage ditch and coming within a few inches of the pine forest. Thick lower boughs, laden with needles and frozen snow, scraped and battered the hood and needles flew through the air like tiny darts. Evan drove a bit farther in, the right side of the truck scraping some trunks. Then, all at once, the hood was ripped off, and she could see again. She skewed the truck hard to the left, now paralleling the road and passing the barrier.

The submachine-gun fire started up again, this time from behind them. Limas, lying prone on the backseat, cringed as the back window shattered, and glittering bits of safety glass covered him like hail. The truck shuddered on its shocks as a fusillade of bullets struck the rear bumper, but because of the erratic path Evan was taking none punctured the thick tires. Evan zigzagged wildly back onto the tarmac, the road ahead clear, and accelerated away toward Tbilisi, leaving both bullets and bikers behind.

PART THREE

NEMESIS

36

Arriving early at his office, Gorgonov had swept up the daily intercepts of the communiqués between Nemesis and its patron, the GRU—specifically General Boyko. These intercepts chronicled the fake news from Nemesis that Boyko's vast and chimeric bot-army would soon disseminate under the Nemesis aegis. On top was a sheaf of fake news items attacking Benjamin Butler. The smears against him, emphasizing his—nonexistent—radical Zionist sympathies, were ludicrous on the surface, until one considered how fractured America had become, how paranoid and, yes, prone to bouts of hysterical violence.

Gorgonov read these intercepts with particular interest. His path had crossed Benjamin Butler's several times when Butler was working with Evan Ryder. He had been a fine operative, one he had admired. Not quite as much as Evan, but still Butler had shown himself to be quick-witted and exceptionally agile in the field and in his wet work. After a hiatus of several years in Berlin, he had returned to Washington as the head of his own shop under the aegis of the American DOD, name as unknown as its charter, except that Gorgonov suspected he was behind the rising number of his SVR moles inside the American federal government being blown, forcing him to eliminate them before they could be arrested or turned.

His musings were interrupted by his adjutant, Kristov, reminding him of his 10 A.M. appointment at the Kremlin. Gathering up the rest of the intercepts, Gorgonov rose, swung on his leather greatcoat, and strode out of the office.

He now traveled everywhere with a contingent of six bodyguards. Climbing into his armor-plated SUV, he settled into the backseat beside Maks, the youngest and smartest of the six. Snow was threatening almost from the moment they set out, and on the exceedingly slow drive over to the Kremlin it began, not with a fluttering of flakes but rather a full-on driving curtain of white. Not that Gorgonov noticed. He was busy poring over the latest file from his people. These reports were particularly noxious and inflammatory, as they contained photos of American and British agents strung up by their ankles, their throats ripped out, and drained of blood. "AMERICAN AND BRITISH SOLDIERS KOSHERED BY THE JEW BUTCHERS!" screamed the headlines.

The weather was foul, the streets treacherous with new snow atop the old snow turned to ice during the freezing night. Several blocks from the Kremlin, traffic came to a standstill. There was an accident up ahead, his driver informed him, and the street was clogged with rush hour traffic. Gorgonov had a hard appointment with the prime minister regarding budgets, a vexing but necessary duty he had to perform twice a year. He ordered his driver to pull into the curb; he and the bodyguards would have to walk the final blocks to make his appointment.

His contingent formed a sort of flying V, the better to cut through the milling throngs. This close to the Kremlin, the sidewalks were teeming with tourists, clicking photos of the monuments, their group, and selfies, always selfies of themselves, with their mobile phones.

At some point, Maks stumbled into him, righted himself as he mumbled an apology. Seconds after that, he collapsed.

Three of the bodyguards immediately closed ranks around Gorgonov, hustling him back into his armored SUV, where the driver waited anxiously, engine purring. He put the SUV in gear, but froze when Gorgonov ordered him to wait. Gorgonov turned his head to peer out the rear window.

The remaining two bodyguards had called for an SVR ambulance, which arrived with pleasing alacrity amid screeching brakes and scattering pedestrians.

Maks was dead. There was no use taking him to the hospital, so Gorgonov gave the order for the ambulance to go directly to the SVR morgue.

"Follow them," Gorgonov told his driver.

Sergei, the bodyguard beside him in place of Maks, turned to him. "Sir, if I may, your meeting is a hard appointment—"

"Reschedule for this afternoon," Gorgonov snapped. "Right now I want to know what happened to Maks." He assumed Maks had had either a heart attack or a stroke. Though he was a young man, these things often happened, coming from out of the blue. In any case, it wouldn't do to abandon one of his chosen.

■ ■ ■

"Heart attack?" Gorgonov said hopefully as he and his bodyguards strode into the morgue and spread out. The windowless room was a chiaroscuro of blues, grays, and glaring whites.

"It certainly seems that way," the coroner replied. He was smoking one of those vile Turkish cigarettes that to Gorgonov smelled like burning trash. All the way over, as his SUV raced along after the ambulance, a carousel of pitch-black thoughts had been running through his head.

He joined the coroner, standing over Maks's corpse, laid out on the autopsy slab. "Seems? I want a definite diagnosis."

The coroner shrugged vaguely. He was a man of middle age with a body shaped like a question mark, as if he had been a miner or was a hunchback. His shock of white hair stood up in the center of his yellow-white skull, wispy as a newborn's locks. He had the look of someone who had seen so many dead bodies that they had ceased to have any meaning for him. "I would say heart attack, yes."

"I don't see how that's possible without performing an autopsy," Gorgonov stated in a tone bristling with sharpened knives.

The coroner's neck vertebrae cracked he turned his head so sharply. "Autopsy? No one ordered an autopsy."

"*I'm* ordering it, doctor."

The coroner was so astonished he neglected to pluck a bit of tobacco off his lower lip. It hung there like a sign of last night's debauchery. "But, sir, it's your own organ which has given me standing orders that in cases like this one an autopsy isn't necessary."

"Listen, doctor, this was my man—a person charged with guarding my life." Gorgonov's eyes flashed a warning, if only the coroner had been paying attention. "Is it your opinion that I should forgo the knowledge of how he died?"

The coroner's arms flailed around, spreading a trail of ash onto the cold tile floor. "Well, you know, there's probably nothing to find. Frankly, it would be a waste of time."

Gorgonov hauled off and buried his fist in the coroner's solar plexus. As the coroner grunted, jackknifing over, Gorgonov said, "Is that frank enough for you, doctor?" The only reply that came was a piteous moan, and he grabbed a handful of the coroner's hair, hauled him up to face him. "When I give you an order, that order supersedes any other orders you may have received in the past, standing or otherwise." Snatching the Turkish cigarette from the coroner's fingers, he aimed the burning end at his victim's right eye, bringing it close enough to cause the coroner to whimper like a child. "Am I making myself clear?"

The coroner licked his dry lips with the tip of a reptilian tongue. "Absolutely." His head bobbed up and down.

"Good." He released the coroner. "Now get cracking. I want answers within the hour." As the coroner turned away, Gorgonov called him back, stuck the butt of the cigarette in between his lips. "Go forth and prosper, doctor."

He stood with hands on hips, legs spread to shoulder width, watching the doctor with the intensity of an anatomy professor grading a student. At the thirteen-minute mark he called for a coffee. At the eighteen-minute mark he called for a sandwich, which, by the thirty-minute mark he had devoured completely. He was sucking on a mint to freshen his breath when the doctor called him over. It was precisely forty-six minutes after the coroner had begun the autopsy.

"All right," he said with a peculiar kind of weariness. "Your friend here did, indeed, die of a heart attack. But—" He held up a forefinger clad in a bloody latex glove. "That would not be the official cause of death."

Gorgonov took a step closer, doing his best to ignore the stink rising from the human remains like a noxious cloud. "What are those two marks? They look like the bite from a vampire."

"Oh, they're much worse than that, I assure you. At least when a vampire bites you, you retain a semblance of life, eh?" He gave a little chuckle. "Not your man."

Turning Maks's head toward them, to better see the

side of his neck, he pointed at the marks Gorgonov had noticed. "Sir, you may recall an incident four years ago. Our ambassador to Prague was strolling in Kampa Park. It was a beautiful spring day. A Sunday. And he was crossing a canal via an old stone bridge to meet a contact when he was jostled by a woman on a bicycle. He moved to get out of her way and was stabbed twice in the side of the neck. It happened so quickly, and he was of course distracted, that he didn't even feel the attack. Well, why would he; they used hatpins, the points of which were coated with a poison derived from the blue-ringed octopus. Mimics a heart attack, and is virtually undetectable because it leaves the bloodstream very quickly."

Of course Gorgonov was familiar with this particular method of assassination. He knew that the Sovereign himself had ordered the swift termination of their ambassador to Prague. The "contact" the coroner mentioned was in fact the ambassador's MI6 handler.

The coroner's weasel face configured itself into a concerned expression. "Sir, are you all right? You've suddenly gone very pale."

"I'm perfectly fine, doctor." But the truth was he felt rather queasy. Perhaps it was staring down into the Y-shaped gap in Maks's corpse, or the icy but stifling atmosphere of the windowless morgue. Or even that awful sandwich he'd wolfed down. In any event, he called for a chair, but as he turned, the coroner said: "Please don't move, sir. Stay as still as you possibly can."

"What is it?" Gorgonov snapped, having little patience for the coroner, or this place, for that matter. Which was, in itself, strange; he'd been to the morgue many times in the course of his work without feeling much of anything.

A chair had been brought by Sergei, but the coroner wouldn't allow him to move, let alone sit. Gorgonov felt a certain weakness in the backs of his knees. He put a hand on Sergei's shoulder, and in so doing saw it, glinting like a shard of glass in the fabric of his overcoat.

The coroner had been busy looking through his instruments. Now that he was back, he clucked his tongue. "Sir, sir, I told you not to move!"

"What is that thing?" A mass of ice formed in Gorgonov's belly.

But the coroner was concentrated on extracting what looked like a stainless-steel pin from the leather on the upper right arm of Gorgonov's coat. His lips were pursed and the tip of his tongue had appeared as he removed the object as if it were a grenade with the pin pulled. When he had it out, he dropped it into a kidney-shaped steel pan, which he set aside also with the greatest of care.

"Remove your overcoat, please."

No "sir," no anything. This was extremely serious. Though he was not used to taking orders, Gorgonov did as he was told, hanging the coat over Sergei's crooked arm.

"Now your suit jacket."

Again, Gorgonov did as he was told. He felt chilled beyond the effect the icy atmosphere was having on him. He thought of the darkness of the grave, of his wife dressed in black weeping not a single tear for a man she loved but didn't love her back. He thought of the son she had never bore him, the heir he had wanted so desperately. He thought of Lolita, of her charm, her grace, of her intelligence, which he never would have expected. The idea of never seeing her again was so unthinkable, so loathsome, that his guts liquefied, and he became terrified that he would soil himself in front of his men. He gasped for air, felt the icy atmosphere of the morgue close around him as if fresh earth were being shoveled over him.

"What the hell is going on, doctor?" he said in a strangled voice.

"Nothing, or everything," the coroner said. "Alpha or omega."

He was now peering intently at the cloth of Gorgonov's

shirt just below the seam that held the right sleeve to the body of the garment. "Excellent fabric. French?"

"Italian," Gorgonov said. "Doctor—"

The coroner let out a deep sigh. "Yes, yes. All is well, sir. The pin did not puncture your shirt. It didn't reach your skin."

"You mean that thing?" Gorgonov tossed his head in the direction of the pin that lay on the bottom of the kidney-shaped pan.

"Yes, indeed, sir. I am quite sure that when I do a tox screen of its tip I will find the same blue-ringed octopus venom that killed your man." He looked up at Gorgonov. "There's no doubt. You were the target of the attack. Your bodyguard did his job. He got in the way. Lucky for you, but not, unfortunately, for him."

Gorgonov let himself slowly down into the chair, where he sat for a moment, immobile, breathing deeply of the icy air that was now as sweet as the sweetest candy. Each color that before had seemed so dull, so monochromatic pulsed with an almost psychedelic incandescence. And he arose from his grave, brushing off the newly turned earth, climbed out onto the green grass of life, while his nerves twanged like Chet Atkins's guitar. He liked Chet Atkins, always had, ever since he'd been introduced to him by the boy who . . .

But never mind that; he had the present to think about, not to mention the future. *His* future. *Start at the beginning,* he told himself: Maks stumbling into him. At the time, he'd thought nothing of it, or if he had he'd put it down to the slippery sidewalk. But now he knew better. Possibly Maks had seen something out of the corner of his eye, had reacted instinctively, just as he should have.

Gorgonov stood up and, pushing away Sergei's proffered arm, made his way to the autopsy table. His knees were still on the rubbery side, but they were gaining strength with each step he took. Thus, the life he had taken for granted flowed back into him with new and enhanced meaning. He had told Boyko to fuck off, and this was the result. Perhaps it was the inevitable outcome, but part of Gorgonov had resisted the idea of the general going this far. He had crossed a line, which was the beginning and the end of it.

Everything had now changed. Boyko had tried to kill him, and what could he do in retaliation that he hadn't already done? He had gone as far as his conscience would allow him to go. Clearly Boyko had no such inhibitions. There had to be a definitive way to stop Boyko. But what?

And then, as if out of the blue, a notion popped into his head, and he thought, *Fuck me, I've been going at the problem ass-backwards. I need to start at the end, not at the beginning.*

He stood over Maks's corpse, head bowed, and whispered, "Thank you, you poor bastard." When his head came up, he signaled to Sergei. "Call Commandant Kristov. Have him set the wheels in motion for a senior officer's funeral, all the pomp and circumstance we can muster, then inform him that I wish to meet with him this evening for dinner. He'll know the place. Tomorrow morning, inform Maks's widow yourself, but not before you pick up a medal—choose one that's most appropriate to present to her when you tell her."

"Yes, sir. Right away."

"Make sure she knows that we will provide for her and the children."

"Maks had no children, sir. They were planning—"

"Oh, hell, his parents then, assuming they're still alive."

Sergei helped his boss on with his suit jacket and then his overcoat. On their way out, Gorgonov turned back to address the coroner. "I want the full report, doctor. Couriered to me directly. No copies. Get me?"

The coroner nodded. "Of course. Standard operating procedure around here." Then he picked up the kidney-shaped dish. "You're a lucky man, sir. A very lucky man."

Turning a deaf ear, Gorgonov fished out the pay-as-you-go mobile Boyko had stuffed into the bear. The general had offered two paths, neither of which Gorgonov found palatable. But there was a third path. Like the third rail or a live wire, using it was dangerous. Nevertheless, it was the one path to victory. No pain, no gain, that's what the muscle builders said. He could relate to that.

With a deeply felt shudder, he composed the terse reply: MEET TOMORROW AT DANILOV MONASTERY 9AM.

37

A brown widow spider crouched on a window ledge. The pane of glass was so grimy everything beyond it looked out of focus. The brown widow, however, was clear and present in Brenda's vision. She had returned to consciousness moments before, befuddled, muzzy-headed, needing a CliffsNotes refresher to figure out what had happened. That's where the brown widow came in.

"You fucked up," the brown widow said. "You lost concentration. You weren't paying attention."

"My bad," Brenda said.

Using two of its forelegs, the brown widow cleaned its face. "It's no joke. Look where you've wound up."

"That's just the problem," Brenda said somewhat testily. "I don't know where I am."

"Storeroom in the rear of this hellhole."

At that moment, she heard a grinding noise from across the room. A door opened and someone walked in. Brenda was crouched in the far corner beneath the only, lonely window and the ledge where the brown widow had been, as if she were a bit of flotsam washed up on a distant shore in the wake of a hurricane. The brown widow was gone. It had scurried away at the noise, or else it had never been there at all, a figment of her imagination. Her head throbbed evilly, and all of a pain-filled sudden she remembered being coldcocked as that Willie, fat fuck pawnshop owner, had led her into this back office, where his partner, the gun broker, was.

Between the door and her corner was a stack of open boxes, some cans of paint, a pile of filthy rags, a table with one chair. A laptop lay opened on the tabletop. Nothing else. The figure walked past it all and came to stand in front of her. Brenda looked up bleary-eyed. Frankly, she'd rather have seen the brown widow spider.

"You must be the so-called Dave Gilly."

The figure laughed like a hyena. "That's what Rank Willie calls me, anyway." He squatted down, giving her a better view of him. He held her ID in one hand, the longslide in the other. "So you're the so-called Brenda Myers."

If she could be any more in shock, she was now. Gilly was far younger than she had imagined, a dark-skinned teenager, by the look of him. He was young only in years; the street and its rough life had toughened him into a sad middle-age—arrogant and brittle at the same time. His flat nose and thick lips lay like an alligator-infested swamp beneath large intelligent eyes and the broad brow of a professor. But, judging by his attitude, all he was a professor of was death and destruction.

"What chew doing nosing around in Rank Willie's store? Nice young bitch like you shouldn't be waving around a 10mm longslide. This here's a mighty nasty weapon."

"You ought to know," Brenda said. "You sold it to a woman named Voron."

Gilly's forehead crinkled up. "Don't know no Voron. Know this here weapon, though."

"She was a bomb-maker, you know," Brenda said.

"Her money's as good as yours. *Better* than yours, 'cause I sold her this. I wouldn't sell you nothing. By the look of you, your money'd be Fed-marked."

"I can't argue with that," Brenda said. "I'd like some water."

"So would I," Gilly replied, "but here we are."

"Get Rank Willie to fetch us some."

"Rank Willie?" Gilly's laugh grated on her ears like razor blades. He had very large, very white teeth. "Shit, he'd likely pee in the cups."

"Can I get up then?"

"I took your shoes off, so sure. You ain't goin' nowhere."

Gilly rose with her, but she had to reach for the sill to keep herself steady. She blinked heavily several times, took a breath. Life flooded back into her in a wave so powerful it almost threw her off her feet.

"I'd like to leave now."

"Wouldn't we all," Gilly said reflectively. "But like the man say, No one here gets out alive." He cackled like a wet hen.

"I don't want any trouble." Even to herself she sounded fatuous.

"Yah? I think that's fake news." His eyes clouded with menace. "You came here lookin' for trouble." He spat. "Knees. Now."

When she didn't comply, he pressed his palm against the crown of her head, forcing her down. Leaning in, he put the long muzzle of the gun against the side of her head, grinding it in until he drew a tiny circle of blood.

"By the way," Brenda said, "I ought to tell you that the gun is empty. Do you really think I'd be stupid enough to come into Willie's with it loaded?"

The split-second he took to check was all she needed. Her left arm blurred outward, and she grabbed his testicles through his jeans, squeezing as hard as she could. At the same time she jerked her head away. He doubled over, his cry as piercing as a newborn's. She slammed her balled fist into his left ear, creating an agonizing suction that ripped a hole in his eardrum.

Clutching at her clawed fingers, he lashed the barrel of the longslide into her cheekbone. Her grip on him loosened, and she fell back. As he came at her, she kneed him as hard as she could between his legs. He screamed as he fell. She wrested the pistol away from him, crawled out from under him, sat astride him, and loaded up the gun.

"First," she said, doing her best to ignore the ringing in her ears, "you're going to show me what the woman who wanted this weapon gave you on loan. Then I want you to tell me about your connections: why Voron came to you and who else like her you've serviced."

"Fuck you," Gilly wheezed. Unrepentant.

Brenda now jammed the gun's muzzle into one of Gilly's nostrils and twisted viciously.

"Muthafuck!" Gilly's eyes opened wide. "Okay, okay." He tried to take a breath, but Brenda wasn't making it easy for him. "Inside jacket pocket. Take it. I don't want the freakin thing, anyways."

Carefully, Brenda pulled back the flap of his jacket, dipped two fingers into the narrow pocket. What she pulled out was a thin necklace with a silver pendant of two ravens, beak to beak.

"Where did she have this?"

"Where d'you think?" Gilly said sullenly. "Around her pretty little neck, which, looking back, I shoulda wrung like a chicken."

Dropping the necklace into her pocket, Brenda said, "Keep going."

Gilly hesitated long enough for her to give him another painful lesson. Blood began to leak out of his nostril. He tried to sniff it back. His eyes began to water. "So, look, everything's done electronically—orders, payments, all that shit. I never meet no one."

"Who contacts you?"

"Your guess is as good as mine. Name of Alice."

"Just Alice?"

"That's all. Alice."

"What's her voice sound like? Does she have an accent?"

"Never spoke to her. She never calls. It's all done through texts."

"Show me."

"With you sittin' on my chest?"

"Where's your mobile?"

Gilly's eyes blazed with resentment-making humiliation. "Right front pocket of my jeans, bitch."

For that, Brenda gave the gun barrel another vicious twist, this time so deep in his nose the muzzle was almost at his sinus.

"Mutha*fuck*!"

"Keep going with that trash talk," Brenda said as she dug the phone out of his pocket, "and I'll take your whole nose off."

Gilly squirmed under her. "Let me up. I'll show you the texts."

"Like hell you will." Brenda took the muzzle out of his nose. "Turn over. Cross your ankles." When he did as he was told, she pulled two coils of wire out of an open box, lashed his wrists and ankles. Only then did she rise. Looking around, she grabbed an oily rag, stuffed it into his mouth.

Pushing his mobile into her pocket, she hunted for her shoes, found them in one of the open boxes. She put them on, then snatched his laptop off the desk.

As she crossed to the rear door, she noticed that the brown widow had reappeared. "Atta girl!" it said. *Could spiders actually smile?* she wondered as she let herself out into a noxious back alley. If she never saw Gilly or Rank Willie again it would be too soon.

38

After receiving Brenda's call, Butler ordered an ambulance to pick her up outside the pawnshop. Instead of taking Brenda directly to the hospital, however, the ambulance transported her to the bomb-maker's building, where Butler met her. While the doctors and a surgeon did patchwork on her injuries, Butler toured the interior of the structure, saw both Charles and Voron. He only relinquished his scrutiny when his forensics team arrived to go over the entire property.

Now Butler and Brenda were at Midnight at the Oasis, an all-night canteen. Yellow lights blazed. The rolling doors were down against the chill, and with loops of old-school red and green lights winking, it was cheery inside. The Oasis was more of a greasy spoon, a converted gas station with an old truck, painted a lurid green, sitting out front up on cement blocks; the tires were long gone. The name of the place was painted in Day-Glo yellow on either side. A zinc bar ran along the rear wall behind which was an old neon Schlitz clock with a sweep second hand, four shelves laden with all manner of alcohol, backed by a mirrored wall.

Big Ref, the owner, ranged behind the bar, dispensing drinks and drawing a selection of eight draft beers for those in love with craft beer. The Oasis hunkered down like a border outpost a block away from the start of a sketchy part of DC, the SE quadrant. Occasionally, and most often around Christmas, New Year's, and Martin Luther King Day, pistol shots could be heard now and again peppering the night. Once a fire. And like a border outpost it was armed. Big Ref had earned his name for keeping the peace in and around the Oasis. Below the bar and within easy reach of his meaty hands, was a sawed-off shotgun, a Colt .45, and an old-school nightstick, a trophy of his former profession. The fact was Big Ref had many friends within the local police precinct. To a man, they were more than happy to let Big Ref settle ill-considered incursions into his territory any way he saw fit. "Better him than us," was a mantra often muttered inside the precinct and in patrol units.

Brenda was just about dead on her feet, as Butler astutely observed over the other's protestations. He would deliver Brenda to the hospital when they were done here, but his immediate goal was to quickly debrief her, take possession of the intel, and get it processed in the most expeditious manner possible. He began asking questions.

"The problem," he said a short time later, "is whether I'll be able to actually do anything with this treasure trove of intel you've provided." He told Brenda about being summoned to the Defense Secretary's office, and Thompson making good on his threat to get him and his agency shut down.

"Congress is in recess, as is most of the government. What's he doing working this holiday week?"

"It seems the devil never takes a holiday," Butler said. "January third I have to appear before a Senate Intelligence Committee. I tell you this because it will be a witch hunt. Thompson is clearly out for my blood, and I don't want you caught up in the shitstorm that's sure to come."

"There's no question of me leaving," Brenda said in a voice edged in steel. "I haven't gone through hell just to see everything we've worked for destroyed by this self-important dirtbag."

Butler smiled, and as the waiter passed, ordered a burger for himself and steak frites for Brenda, a carafe of coffee, and another large bottle of Badoit sparkling water—one of the reasons, along with the burger, he frequented the Oasis.

"Loyalty will get you everywhere," he said in a low voice. At this time of night the Oasis was normally inhabited only by insomniacs and wanderers who littered the darkened streets, and barflies who had already been ejected from their favorite watering hole. But these nights the place was more than half full. The number of insomniacs at the Oasis had tripled in the past two years. No one, it seemed, was sleeping well, not here in the capital, not anywhere in the country. The insomniacs clumped together in a far corner, while the alcoholics clustered along the bar, like black flies, each seeking comfort in their own kind. Like everywhere else, tribal imperatives drove these human beings at the margins.

He would have asked Brenda how she was doing after killing Voron, except that he already knew the answer; Brenda would never talk about her kills. Whatever healing or soul-searching she did had to be on her own terms, in her own time.

"And then there's Evan," Brenda said. "Your secret weapon." She gulped down more water. "Where is she, anyway? Still in Georgia?"

"She's on her way to Obersalzberg, following a lead to the center of Nemesis. Someone with the moniker of Cuervos."

"Ravens in Spanish."

Butler nodded. "That's right."

"And is Peter still with her?"

"Yes. It's still the best way we have to find out who and what he really is. Which is definitely not clear at this point."

Brenda said nothing more about Peter, turned her attention to her bloody steak, which had been put down in front of her, and to her work. "Let's get back to our business here."

Butler appreciated that focusing on the nuts and bolts of their work together was what Brenda needed now. It was what they both needed; they were alike in that way.

As Brenda took her first forkful of steak, Butler began. "Let's go over your intel again now, piece by piece, even though parts of it, like the laptop, have yet to be vetted by IT forensics."

Brenda recounted her meeting with Charles Isaacs, the field operative who claimed to be working for Interpol, the death of Donald Beacum at Charles's hands, and the reason for it. Butler had been briefed on Marina so he skipped that part, moved immediately to Nal, her Russian contact, and how he had directed them to the abandoned farm where Voron was constructing her bombs.

"Speaking of which," Butler said, putting down his half-eaten burger, "we've yet to ID Voron or the man in uniform in the photo you found on the barn wall. Somehow I doubt that we will." He pointed. "Eat your spinach, as well. For iron."

"Thank you, Daddy Dearest." Brenda meant to be sarcastic, but almost immediately realized how grateful she was to know this extraordinary man, let alone work for him. She began to eat her spinach.

Butler sipped his coffee, watched a vagabond who looked like he hadn't slept since puberty enter and order a draft beer, then pull up a chair in the insomniac section. "What we really want to know is whether Voron was under General Boyko's control."

"Like Marina." Brenda dipped a French fry into a small pool of ketchup, then chewed on it meditatively. "A Nemesis action."

"Obersalzberg. In Bavaria." Butler's thoughts had wandered back to Evan. "Spanish names, Russian connections of some sort . . . but could Nemesis be German in origin? Maybe Boyko is funding them through the GRU."

"That makes sense."

"And both Voron and Marina had a necklace with the double raven pendant."

Brenda washed down a bite of steak with some Badoit. She was already starting to feel, if not normal, at least halfway human again. "So the women are connected."

Butler took out the necklace and pendant Voron had traded for the 10mm longslide, which Brenda had turned over to him. "From the same cadre, maybe. This is certainly identical to the description Evan gave me of the pendant Marina was wearing." He gestured. "Let's see the texts Dave Gilly was receiving from this Alice."

Brenda turned on Gilly's mobile, then brought up the Messaging app. There were a number of texts from Alice, starting last September, along with a single name for each date: Lily, Rose, Tulip, Violet, Marina. The last one was Voron, three days ago. After each name was a figure, ranging from 500 for Rose to 5,000 for Voron.

"Payments," Brenda said. "So now we have a connection between Alice, Marina, and Voron." She frowned. "But how do we find out who Alice is? Do we have enough here to follow the money back?"

"Indeed we do."

At last a smile out of Brenda. "Bingo!"

Butler nodded toward Brenda's food. "Now finish your food."

Brenda's smile blossomed like a lotus in moonlight. "Every last bite."

■ ■ ■

Riley Rivers's mind was running in overdrive. He felt as if he'd had three too many triple espressos. He hadn't been a jackal among thieves for decades without developing a sixth sense for the winds of change. He had begun to sniff that change several days ago, in Brady Thompson's increasing belligerence. At first, he had put it down to Thompson taking his cue from the president himself who, increasingly, was going off message in his public speaking engagements, ad-libbing in whichever direction his mind wished to take him at that particular moment. So much so that there had been rumors in the back corridors of the White House, among its staff, that POTUS had had a series of tiny strokes the cumulative effects of which were beginning to show in his increasingly erratic behavior.

When he had reported this to his SVR controller, he was told in no uncertain terms not to report such rumors, no matter how pervasive they might become. In fact, he was to do everything in his power to protect the president's standing. In between these words, Rivers, whose snout had developed the same level of expertise as a truffle-hunter, could detect the delight at the idea that POTUS might be even more vulnerable to *kompromat* than the Russian Sovereign had believed when he began to target him some years ago. A compromised POTUS had been the dream and the goal of the Sovereign's top priority initiative for six years now. The long con, in its endgame phase, had become the short con.

And then there was the matter of the change in Isobel's behavior, the urgency in her voice, in everything she did now. Most especially her insistence on intel concerning Benjamin Butler's defamers. What was going on that he didn't know about? The questions without answers were driving him crazy.

These questions Rivers continued to ponder darkly and deeply as he stepped to the curb in front of the Foggy Bottom building that housed his Office of Official Communications. He waited, surprised that Isobel's Land Cruiser wasn't already there, engine purring like a Bengal tiger, ready to be unleashed. And then, up ahead in a break in the early morning traffic, he saw the red SUV.

He stepped off the curb so the driver could easily see him and, sure enough, the huge vehicle swerved to the right. Coming right at him.

But instead of slowing down it sped up. It took several seconds for Rivers to recognize this anomaly. Disbelief paralyzed him. Seconds ticked by before his brain came out of its shocked stasis. By then the SUV was almost upon him. He waved stupidly; didn't the driver see him, recognize him? And only then did it dawn on him that the SUV was accelerating toward him *because* the driver recognized him; the driver meant to do him harm.

Like a battering ram, the SUV bore down on him, and even as he stumbled backward, it jumped the curb, the nearside front fender clipping him, tossing him backward as if he was as light as a feather. He lay on the sidewalk, stunned and numb. Then the pain set in—a sharp stabbing that intensified with each ragged breath he took, making him weep as he cried out.

For a long time nothing happened, and, afterward, what he remembered most vividly was the passersby. They either ignored him or gawked before hurrying on to their very important appointments.

39

Evan and Limas were stopped at the airport, taken out of line, detained in a windowless room the approximate size of a broom closet. Apart from a metal table bolted to the polished concrete floor, two chairs on one side, a single chair on the other, there were no furnishings. The room smelled of old socks and fear.

A Georgian military official of indeterminate rank paged through their false passports with hands as large as paddles. He wore tight pants, had a nose like a mushroom and eyes like a pig. He stank of boiled cabbage and seemed not to have either shaved or bathed in some days. He questioned them in somnolent fashion for perhaps an hour, then abruptly left, sweeping their passports off the table and taking them with him.

For the next hour, nothing happened. Then the door was unlocked and a very different sort of man stepped smartly in. He wore a suit and tie. The scent of lemons and sage wafted in their direction, a welcome corrective. This man, younger than the hulk who had already questioned them, was the polar opposite. He smiled thinly, offered his hand and a brief but sincere apology. He did not offer his name and Evan didn't ask.

"In three hours a high-ranking member of the GRU will be arriving from Moscow. I don't know what the two of you have done to warrant such attention from the Russians and, frankly, I don't care. Whatever you've done or are suspected to have done is of less importance to me than my abiding hatred of Russians." He handed Evan and Limas their passports. "Your plane has been cleared for immediate takeoff. Two of my men are waiting outside to escort you directly onto it."

Do not pass Go, do not collect two hundred lari, Evan thought, as they left the stifling interrogation room. The diplomat—for Evan concluded that was what he must be—said not one more word, and they did not see him again, until, having boarded Butler's jet, Evan noticed him watching the plane from the departures lounge window. He did not turn away until the jet had lifted off.

▪ ▪ ▪

She picks her way through ruins all too familiar to her—as if she is coming home. These ruins are unique in that they are people rather than buildings. People Evan knew, ones she had killed and those who had been killed because of their association with her. Ruins because they appear to her as they had in the moments after their deaths—maimed, incomplete, sometimes barely human. They speak. They speak all at once, in so many languages she can't separate one from the other.

When she moves past the ruins she had made, she comes, inevitably, to the red-brick monstrosity . . .

▪ ▪ ▪

And started awake with the single caw of ravens echoing in her head.

In the tiny toilet, she slapped tepid water on her face until she was certain she was free of the dreamworld spiderweb that seemed to ensnare her every night since she had first seen the image of the red-brick mansion. She touched the sterile pad over the wound in her cheek, found the swelling greatly reduced. Then she swallowed another antibiotic capsule, washed it down with a mouthful of filtered water.

Back in her seat, she first determined that Limas was sound asleep before taking up the mobile Butler had given her and dialing an overseas number she had memorized some years ago.

She heard the hollowness of the line, the clicks and buzzes as the call was filtered through a number of electronic screens and filter gates.

"Yes?" an electronic voice sounded in her ear.

Evan spoke the three-word parole she had been given.

"Moment," the same simulacrum enunciated.

True to its word, a moment later, a real-life human voice came on the line. A familiar female voice. "Who is speaking, please?"

"Evan Ryder." Of course she knew who was speaking; Evan had been given a parole specific to her.

"I have intel for you."

"Who is speaking, please?"

"I always told you you were an amusing woman."

"How are you, Alli?"

"More to the point, how are you?" Warmth flowed from Alli Carson, through the ether, from Interpol HQ in Paris.

"Difficult to say, at the moment."

"I bet." A pause. "Charles Isaacs. We sent him to DC."

"And now he's dead."

"Who killed him?" Alli was not one to waste time on sentimentality.

"A bomb-maker named Voron."

"Voron was known to us."

"She's dead, as well."

"Did you kill her?"

"I wasn't there. Back to Charles—he's why I called."

Alli sighed. "He was sent against my recommendation, I might add. And now what I was afraid of has happened."

"I think it's time we spoke directly to each other."

Another pause. "I've got to get clearance, Evan. I'll call you back within the hour."

Evan liked Alli, but that wasn't necessary. What was necessary was that she trusted Alli, whose intel was always right on the money. Still, there was a brittleness between them. Alli hadn't approved of Evan's relationship with Lyudmila.

"You're on a secured mobile," Alli said now. "The number is blocked. Please give it to me."

Evan did.

"I'll be in touch," Alli said.

"Wait, what was Charles Isaacs supposed to—?"

But Alli had already disconnected.

▪ ▪ ▪

"Two broken ribs" . . . "Contusions . . . Lucky no organ involvement" . . . "Make and model of the SUV, check. What about a description of the driver . . . the model year, the plate number?" *Are you fucking kidding me?* Rivers thought as the drugs being pumped into his arm began their undertow. Nurses, doctors, cops, all wanting a piece of him. Swirling down. Who was the Good Samaritan who called emergency services, while everyone else kept on going because their lives were so very important . . . And lastly: *Who did this to me? Who wants me dead?*

Later, awake at last, he stared at the hospital room. It was so bright and white, like the snow globe in his bedroom when he was a child. His only company were machines beeping and ticking by his bedside like grandfather clocks gone berserk. Needles in his arm, taped against his skin. Liquid in . . . shifting uncomfortably . . . liquid out. White gum-sole shoes whispering past his open door, hushed voices rising and falling like the Chesapeake tide, a half-seen elderly gent lying on a gurney parked against the far wall of the hallway, immobile. Alive or dead? Slippery consciousness, eeling its way in and out. At one point, it occurred to him that no one would come to see him. He had no friends—only a slush fund of contacts for whom he was a machine that dispensed favor for favor, and enemies, all of whom had better things to do. Except the one who had tried to kill him. And all at once his pulse began to race. He could feel his heart pounding against his damaged rib cage, painful even through the sludge of drugs in his veins.

What if that someone came here to his room while he was helpless to finish the job? Into his mind flashed the iconic scene from *The Godfather,* where Vito Corleone is lying helpless in a hospital bed, protected only by his son Michael and the terrified Enzo, the baker's son-in-law. The Don was lucky to have Michael and not Sonny there; Michael had the foresight to ask a nurse to help him move his father in his bed from one room to another to hide him from the would-be assassin.

Rivers had no such son, nor anyone else, for that matter, to stand vigil or to move him, if there was, in fact, an assassin coming for him. And that led him to the chilling thought that it might have been Isobel who had ordered his death. Wasn't the Land Cruiser the exact color as hers? But why would she do such a thing? He still hadn't delivered the material on Benjamin Butler she had ordered him to research. Had she become impatient? Or, somehow worse still, had someone above her given the kill order? The memory of Yana Bardina's funeral to which Isobel had very deliberately taken him as a warning was still a fresh wound in his memory. Wherever the truth lay, the fact was that he'd never felt more alone.

And then, with a clickety-clack of expensive high heel pumps, that self-same Isobel entered his room.

40

"I suppose it could have been worse," Dr. Selsby said, "considering that over the past seventy-two hours you seem to have tussled with a series of cement mixers." Dr. Adam Selsby's smile had its way with Brenda. He was a robust, confident type, with a shock of blond hair and probing eyes. Because he was cleared by Fed Intel, Brenda didn't have to hide anything from him, which was a relief.

"All your tests have come back normal," Dr. Selsby went on, consulting his iPad. "EEG, EKG, MRI, the works." He looked up into Brenda's face. "But you're not out of the woods yet. I prescribe at least ten days complete rest."

They were in a hospital room on a secure floor. Only intelligence officers in or out. Thinking back to St. Agnes Brenda took that restriction with a palm full of salt.

"Your body's taken a beating, Brenda. More than it had any right to endure. And that's not even counting the psychological and emotional stress you've been under." He tucked the iPad under his arm. "Frankly, it's a wonder you don't have a concussion. And there's a distinct likelihood that within the next week or so you'll begin to experience some or all of the symptoms of PTSD. Another reason I'm ordering bed rest. You notice I said *order,* not *prescribe.* I'm absolutely serious about this. Without proper rest you could do yourself more harm than the cement mixers you encountered. Clear?"

"As glass."

That smile again, like a pod of dolphins bathing her in a particular kind of warmth. "There's a car and driver waiting for you downstairs." Pressing two vials into Brenda's hand, he added, "Vicodin and Ambien. I imagine I don't have to warn you not to abuse either." He stuck out his hand, and Brenda took it. It was cool and dry and as firm as his voice. "Go home. Rest. I wish you peace and a long life."

■ ■ ■

Brenda did, in fact, go home. She had no choice in the matter. Butler's people not only walked her to her door, they went in with her, checked the apartment for, she supposed, electronic surveillance bugs. They poked everywhere.

"Find any spooks?" she said archly, as she saw them out. They made no reply. Apparently humor was in short supply, even the grim kind.

Then they remained in front of her building, in their vehicle, smoking and chatting—about what? her underwear they'd pawed through?—for a full hour after they left her company. Clearly, they had their own orders concerning her enforced sabbatical.

It should have been a pleasure to be back in her own space, but then why was she pacing back and forth in her living room like a caged tiger? At length, she padded into the bathroom, took a long hot shower, reveling in the water sluicing over her, washing away the accumulated layers of sweat, dirt, and grime. She closed her eyes, water steaming her face, the gentle, insistent pressure like the fingers of a masseuse. When, at last, she stepped out, toweled off, she felt pink and scrubbed. But that was her surface. Beneath, the darkness of the last three days continued to swirl, enfolding her in its noxious embrace.

Nevertheless, she forced herself to get into bed, sliding between the sweet-scented sheets. The softness felt good against her skin. But she was still in pain. Turning, she saw the two vials Dr. Selsby had given her. She despised taking drugs of any sort, had been brought up to believe that she could power through any pain or sleeplessness by force of will alone. Now, however, her body hurt so much in so many places, not the least the side of her face where Dave Gilly had struck her with the barrel of the Springfield pistol, that she was sorely tempted to swallow a Vicodin or two. In the end, though, she turned away, lay on her side, and thought of Evan.

Better to think of her than Peter. She had built up a mini-storehouse of knowledge regarding Nemesis and Charles Isaacs and Voron that Evan ought to hear from an eyewitness—namely her—who could relate details no one else could. But try as she might to concentrate on that aspect of the present, her thoughts kept being borne back ceaselessly to Peter. His betrayal was a violation that cut her to the quick. He had reached down into the core of her, ripped a piece out. It was not simply that he had made a fool of her, he had insinuated himself past all her defenses, had made a mockery of all her expertise. Even worse, he had caused her instincts to fail her. Love had blinded her to his perfidy, his true self. Hard as it was to admit, what she also felt was shame—the shame of being raped, which had nothing at all to do with sex and everything to do with power, control, and abuse that didn't need to be physical. All three of these, she felt in retrospect now she knew the truth about him, Peter had wielded over her.

She wept then, feeling broken, fragile, bereft. Trembling in her bitterness, she cried herself to sleep.

It was still dark when she awoke, the anesthesia of sleep keeping the pain at bay for precisely fifteen seconds, before it inundated her all over again, making her gasp out loud, her fingers clawing the warm sheet beneath her as if it were a living body on whom she could take out her rage and sorrow.

The moment she recognized her continuing sorrow as self-pity, she sat up and, ignoring the pain, rose from her bed, went to her dresser, then her closet, and dressed in jeans, a black flannel long-sleeve top, midnight-blue sneakers. She perched on the end of her bed, bent over to tie the laces, and when she sat up the room began to spin so badly she was obliged to squeeze the comforter in a death grip.

She waited, her heart pounding, her breath coming hot and fast. Gathering her wits, she went into prana, long, deep breaths, exhaling all the way down to her pubic bone, as her martial arts sensei had taught her to do when she was anxious or under stress. She had come to a point where she was both. But knowing it, as her sensei would say, is half the battle won. Doing something about it was the second half.

Burrowing into the back of her closet, where even Butler's guys hadn't gone, she pulled up a corner of the carpet, revealing two loose floorboards. From beneath them she pulled out a dull olive-green ammo box, took from it a legend passport in the name of Amy Kendell, which not even Butler knew about, several other docs, and ten thousand dollars in cash. She put the ammo box back in its hidey-hole, replaced the floorboards and carpet. Standing up slowly, she packed an overnight bag with clothing and essential toiletries, took a black shearling car coat from the hall closet, and, checking from the living room window to make sure the car was gone, let herself out of her apartment, locking the door behind her.

Never before had she been a victim. She was determined never to be one again.

■ ■ ■

"Isobel, you look like a million bucks." Rivers's terror made his smile too wide and his voice too brittle.

"And you, you little pipsqueak, look like something I just scraped off the bottom of my shoe."

Isobel wasn't smiling. She swept off her black cape-like coat as she advanced across the linoleum floor. Rivers couldn't look at her as he winced.

"You're meant to be working for me. What are you doing getting yourself run over?"

"*Almost* run over."

"Huh." Isobel put fists on her hips. "From where I stand I can't tell the difference."

Rivers looked up, visibly hurt, hoping to curry some sympathy at least. She wore a cranberry-colored tweed suit that showed off her figure well. Her hair was pulled back in what might have been an old-fashioned chignon on some women; on her, it enhanced her glamour. Rivers eyed her up and down. Her legs seemed to go on forever.

"Me, I never did mind the male gaze," Isobel said. "I feel empowered."

"To do what?" Rivers said, screwing his courage to the wall. "Kill me?"

"Kill you?" Isobel's lips formed a perfect O. "Where in the world did you get that idea?"

"The vehicle that tried to run me down was a cherry-red Land Cruiser." He pulled himself up to a sitting position. "You own a cherry-red Land Cruiser, Isobel. I've ridden in it."

Isobel was about to show Rivers how wrong he was, to tell him that he wasn't the only one who wanted to know who had tried to run him down, when she saw just how frightened Rivers was. Far more frightened than when she had taken him to Yana Bardina's funeral. There was nothing like a scrape with death to clear the mind, she reflected. And so, for the moment she changed tack, took a stab in the dark.

"You're holding out on me, Riley."

Rivers was instantly terror-struck. "What d'you mean?" His voice had risen an octave in panic. "I was bringing you the intel you asked for—and more, I might add—when you almost killed me."

"Yes, well, we'll get to that in a minute, Riley." She came close to the bed. "There's something else, something you've been hiding since the moment I recruited you."

"I don't know—"

She scrutinized every expression that flitted across his face, no matter how momentary, no matter how shadowed. "Saving it for a rainy day, are you."

"No, I—"

"That rainy day is here, Riley. It's a fucking downpour, and either you spit it out or you're going down the drain."

"Okay, okay." Rivers, his eyes open wide, his hands trembling, licked his lips. "It's about Brady Thompson."

Isobel's eyebrows lifted. "The Secretary of Defense? What about him?"

"He's a Russian asset."

"What?"

"That's right." Rivers was both pleased and relieved that he had surprised her with actionable intel. "He's been an asset for a while."

"How did the Russians . . . ? Sex? Money? What?"

"He got in over his head with reckless banking and real estate deals. When they all fell through he had nowhere to turn. Then the Russians stepped in to bail him out, for their usual price."

"I'll bet they did." Isobel was still trying to wrap her head around the astonishing revelation that Thompson was a Russian asset. She knew the federal government was lousy with Russian moles—both she and Ben were working clandestinely, each in their own way, and together, to root them out. She had been too focused on Ben, the one person who gave her tunnel vision; she'd dropped the ball on Thompson. "I'll also wager that it was the Russians who made sure Thompson's deals fell through."

"Christ," Rivers said. "I never thought of that."

"That's why I get the big bucks," she said wryly.

He laughed without a trace of mirth.

The next thing she said was: "Do you have any proof?"

"Sadly, no."

"What about communiqués, intel, anything?"

"My control told me Thompson was off limits, totally protected. He said his political star had risen in the sky. Now it was important that he rise to the zenith and not fall prematurely." Rivers licked his lips. "By this I inferred that Thompson had been transferred to another corpus."

"Corpus?"

"That's how he put it. Thompson was originally an SVR asset, but I took that to mean that he no longer was."

Isobel's face darkened. "And you didn't make a recording of this conversation?"

Rivers spread his hands. "So I could incriminate myself one day? No, no, absolutely not."

"And you told me none of this. Idiot. You weren't thinking at all."

Rivers hung his head.

Time to move on, Isobel thought, even as she realized that she could never trust him again. She never should have trusted him in the first place. "Okay, Riley, let's have the information regarding the origin of the social media attacks on Benjamin Butler."

"Okay, well, it took some time—"

"Oh, get on with it, Riley!"

"It's a netbot called Soul Searcher."

"Run by whom, exactly?"

"It's not SVR, it's not my control. I made sure. Now, I can't be one hundred percent positive, but I strongly believe it's the GRU, the Russian military—"

"I know what the GRU is, Riley."

"Okay, well, it seems that two months ago the usual GRU netbots, APT 28 and Fancy Bear, went dark. Winked out altogether and haven't been heard from since. A couple of days later, Soul Searcher started up. Too coincidental for it to be run by anyone other than the Russians. Another thing: the Soul Searcher netbot is far more sophisticated than either of its predecessors. The Russians must have made a quantum jump in their tech. So my bet is that for whatever reason, the GRU has decided to target this Benjamin Butler. Any idea why?"

Isobel had a perfectly good idea why: because Ben was their American spy network's biggest threat. But why now specifically, so aggressively . . . it had to have something to do with his going after this Nemesis group. Of course, Isobel was not about to share these thoughts with Rivers. And she was sure she could get a lot more useful information out of him.

"Well, Ben has Jewish blood, which is what they're going after. But that can't be the answer. At least not all of it. There has to be more of a reason, something we're not aware of. Yet." She considered a moment. "Perhaps you could ask your friendly Russian control if he has any idea why GRU would target Butler?" Her voice had changed completely. It had softened, become more sympathetic. Rivers's head came up. He showed her a watery smile. *If you understand simple psychology, men are so easily manipulated. At heart, they're nothing more than little boys,* she thought as she sat down on the corner of his bed, crossed one leg over the other to give him a view.

"He isn't very accommodating in that way." Rivers had already perked up from his former desolate state. "And if I start asking about Soul Searcher he's bound to get suspicious." His brows knit together. "I assume that's why you haven't asked your control."

She closed her eyes for a moment, gathering her thoughts, deciding how to proceed now that the ground had shifted beneath her. How best to use the intel on Thompson that Riley had coughed up to protect Ben, and for more. When she opened her eyes, she stared directly into Rivers's eyes, catching him by surprise. "Riley, I know there's something else you'd like to share. Now's the time."

"There isn't—"

"If you lie to me now, Riley, you might as well kiss your career, your life goodbye."

He lifted his hands as if to ward off the blow. "Okay. But . . . In my defense, I didn't tell you what was going on with Thompson because, well, I was embarrassed that I didn't have any hard evidence. All I could have given you was my word that he was a Russian asset."

Isobel sighed deeply. "What did I tell you about holding out on me?"

"So you did try to have me killed, after all."

"Stop being so dense, Riley. Why would I try to kill you when you were supposedly about to give me what I'd asked for?"

Rivers frowned. "I must not be thinking clearly."

"You think? Look, everyone knows what car I ride around in. How difficult do you think it was to get an identical one?"

"But only one of them did a hit-and-run number on me."

"That's the first smart thing you've said since I walked in here. Did you by any chance get the license tag—or at least a part of it?"

"Everything happened so fast, and I was in shock . . . I mean, you can understand . . ." He dropped his head. "Okay, well, if it wasn't you, then who was it?"

She tapped one forefinger against her lower lip. "Clearly, whoever it was wanted you to *think* it was me."

"Then mission accomplished." Rivers shook his head, immediately regretted it, as pain broke out anew in his chest. "But d'you have any drivers in mind?"

"Huh, well, that list is a very short one. Almost no one knew that I had tasked you with finding out who was behind the disinformation about Butler."

"You mean besides you and me, someone else knew?"

Isobel didn't reply. She pulled out her mobile, punched in a speed-dial number as she crossed to the window at the far end of the room. She listened for a moment, then said, "I know it's the middle of the workday. I know you're swamped, being shorthanded. I don't care." She gave the person on the other end the name and address of the hospital, as well as Rivers's room. "Get over here now."

She disconnected before any more excuses could be made, then turned to Rivers. "Okay, Riley, showtime. Spill."

41

"*Inside an hour,*" Alli had said, but more than ninety minutes passed without the promised return call. Limas was awake. Evan watched him rise, walk on stiff legs to the toilet. When he emerged, he stretched, crossed to the galley, had the attendant pour two mugs of coffee. Bringing them back, he handed one to Evan before he plopped himself into the adjoining seat.

"What happened back there at airport security?" he said as he sipped his coffee.

"We were made," Evan said. "Somehow the GRU found out our whereabouts."

"That's worrying, isn't it?"

Evan looked hard at Limas. "I wonder who could have told them?"

Limas had the mug almost to his lips. Now he lowered it. "You don't think it was me, do you?"

"You're my prime driver."

When Evan put her coffee aside without tasting it, Limas grunted, picked up Evan's mug, and very deliberately took a couple of generous sips. "Satisfied?"

Evan took the offered mug and drank.

"I didn't call or in any other manner contact anyone, let alone someone from the Russian side. Besides, according to you, I'm mates with Anton Gorgonov. And even if that was the case—which it's not—and I told him, how would it get to the GRU?"

In a way he was right, Evan knew. On the other hand, and given the heightened enmity between Gorgonov and General Boyko, penetration by moles on either side was a fait accompli. She decided to go in an altogether different direction. "Have you forgotten *you're* the Russian side, Peter?"

"Did you consider Aunt Lyudmila to be on the Russian side?" When Evan made no reply, Limas went on. "I know I'm not Aunt Lyudmila, but honestly, I'm the next best thing. Anyway, I'm all you have."

"Maybe." Evan drank more coffee, which was dark and rich, the way she liked it. "But I can't help wondering who has who."

"The eternal conundrum between lovers and friends."

"Since we're neither, that has no bearing here."

"Well, we certainly are *something* to each other." With that pronouncement, Limas drained his mug, settled back in his seat, and closed his eyes.

Then Evan's mobile began to vibrate. She rose and went down the aisle to a secluded spot where she could have this conversation in private.

"Charles was supposed to deliver this in person, but now I will do it myself," Alli said without preamble. "We have rock-solid intel that the most notorious DOD black site has returned to operation."

"What? The black site program has been dead and buried for years."

"Resurrected, my friend."

"Which black site?" Evan had no good memories of DOD personnel. None at all.

"We don't know for sure. If we ever had records of DOD's black sites they've been lost in a fire we had several years ago. But like all of DOD's past sites this one is in a location one would never expect. By piecing together an incomplete jigsaw from far-flung sources, we've narrowed it down to somewhere in Germany."

42

When Roger Hollis entered Riley Rivers's hospital room, he found only one occupant. Isobel was lounging on the bed, legs crossed at the ankles.

"You know, that old guy out there has—as the docs say—expired," he said, hooking his thumb over his shoulder. "What's he still doing in the corridor?"

"Who am I, Dr. House?" Swinging her legs around, Isobel bounced out of bed, stood facing him.

Hollis frowned. "Where's the fire?"

"The fire," she said, swinging past him to shut the door, "is wherever you are, dear Roger."

Hollis's frown deepened. "Meaning what, exactly?"

"Well, that's what you're going to tell me."

"What?" Hollis rubbed the blue stubble on his square jaw. It was clear he'd been burning the midnight oil, had pushed sleep far away from himself. "Have you lost— You know, I think that encounter with Peter and his friend Louise Steadman has had a long-term effect on you." He shook his head. "Clearly, you're not yourself."

"Well, I could say the same about you, because someone in this room's not himself, but it's definitely not me." She came right up to him, stared him in the face. Her eyes gleamed like bear traps about to spring shut. "No, you see, Roger, today, right this minute, I'm more myself than I ever have been."

"Isobel, you're not making sense."

"Why did you try to run Riley Rivers down?"

"Say what now?"

He took a step back, but she just advanced on him, keeping the same distance between them.

"Why did you use a vehicle identical to mine? Why did you want to make him think that I was out to kill him?"

Hollis retreated another step and again she followed him. Now his back was against the side wall. His head hit a cheap print, skewed it off its axis. He opened his mouth, closed it again without uttering a sound, let alone a word.

"But I already know, Roger. You're an adder at my breast, a fly in my ointment, a spanner—as the Brits say—in the works."

"What in the world—?"

She poked his chest with a stiff forefinger. "I get it now. You don't want me getting my intel from anyone else. You're jealous. But why? Do you have a thing for me? Or are you afraid of what someone else might dig up on you?"

"Now wait a fucking minute—!"

"How many entities are paying you for your data-mining software? Limas helped you build a company to do good, and what do you do with it behind his back? So Nemesis, and the Russians? But which Russians? Not the SVR, not the FSB. That only leaves one corpus: GRU."

"Hey, I thought we were in this together? Who cares which Russians we're working for? Aren't we together?"

"We're not in anything together, Roger. We never have been."

After a stunned second, he said, "So you're, what, a double agent?"

"This isn't about me." Isobel kept staring at Hollis. He was one of her targets. She knew a lot about him, but not all. Now was the time to peel back the last layers.

At that moment, the door to the bathroom opened and Rivers emerged, dressed in his street clothes. He paused for a moment, his eyes narrowed. He'd seen this guy before—he was sure of it—but where? Then his memory snapped into place. He was the person Isobel had been looking at during Yana Bardina's funeral. Rivers stepped forward to stand at Isobel's side, his face drained of color. "How does this shithead know anything about me?"

"I saw you leaving Isobel's house," Hollis said matter-of-factly. "I got your car tag number. That's all I needed to data-mine you, though your connection to Isobel is still—Agh!"

Another poke from Isobel, harder this time, caused Hollis to make a grab for her finger, intending to bend it, break it, send her down to her knees where, no doubt, he felt she belonged. But she anticipated his physical attack, and so buried a knee deep in his groin. A whoosh like a balloon deflating came from the agonized depths of his abdominal cavity. With great alacrity, she stepped away as he doubled over.

"A goddamned mole," she said.

"I heard," Rivers breathed. "For the GRU. For Boyko."

"So it would seem." Isobel pulled Hollis's head up by his thinning, sweat-slick hair, stared into a face twisted by pain. "Right, Roger?"

"Go fuck yourself," he growled in a watery voice.

"I'd say you've done a pretty good job of that." Her balled fist collided with the hinge of his jaw, dislocating it.

"Ow!" One of the hands protecting his bruised genitals flew to his cheek. He made the same sound, only more pitiable, when he touched the dislocation.

Isobel squatted down in front of him. "Now here's

what we know. For two months now the GRU has been using a new ultra-sophisticated netbot called Soul Searcher. I doubt they could have done that without your help. Am I right, Roger?"

She hit him again. "How about you tell me why you would align yourself with General Boyko." She half-turned toward Rivers. "What was it you discovered about Soul Searcher, Riley?"

"That it's far more sophisticated than either APT 28 or Fancy Bear."

"So here's our proof, Roger," Isobel said. "The GRU made a quantum jump in their tech." She cocked her head. "How much did GRU pay you for your services, Roger?"

Hollis tried one more time, but his attempt to say "Who?" came out as "Ooo?" He couldn't purse his lips.

"The GRU." Isobel could afford to be patient now. "Fucking Boyko, whose ass you wipe." She tut-tutted. "But what was I thinking? I'm so sorry, Roger. I should never have dislocated your jaw." So saying, she took his jaw between her hands. Ignoring the terror on his face, she braced herself. A violent motion of her hands caused him to cry out like a wounded bear. "There, there," she said softly. "Better now?" His red-rimmed eyes stared at her pleadingly. She took a breath, let it out slowly. "You know, Roger, it occurs to me—belatedly, I admit—that you weren't cut out for this sort of life. Yana got you into it, but it was a Venus flytrap. Now she's been murdered and you're in way over your head."

"You're right. Of course you're right. But, dammit, I loved her. I was so blinded I did what she asked." His voice was muddled, his words garbled as he struggled with the pain in the aftermath of the dislocation and relocation of his jaw.

"How's that?" Isobel sat back on her haunches, listening carefully.

"The software we came up with got the attention of GRU. Someone from Boyko's personal staff contacted me, told me who and what Yana was. At first I didn't believe him, but then I saw pictures of her with other men—and some of them were . . ." He made a face. "You wouldn't believe what she had these guys doing."

"I think you mean that you thought you were the only one doing those things with her."

"I'd never heard of half of them before I met her," Roger wailed. "They were so . . . satisfying. They turned my legs to jelly."

"I know exactly how the Russians work, Roger."

Hollis's jaw dropped open. "Oh, God, what have I done?"

"Over and over again." She grinned down at Hollis, baring her teeth.

Hollis gave out with an animal moan, began rocking, a mournful keening coming from deep inside him.

Her rage was nearer the surface again, and she struggled to control it. "So Boyko is your controller."

Hollis seemed to have clammed up. She made a sudden move at him and he flinched. "Yes and no," he said thickly. "He was, but then he handed me off to someone else. A man named Alice."

"Alice," Isobel said, as if tasting the name on her tongue. *Who the fuck was Alice?* she wondered. The Russians were notoriously tight-lipped about their personnel; most controllers didn't know who the others were handling. It was a way to keep things compartmentalized, to limit the damage if an asset got blown and gave up his or her controller's operational name under duress. Even so, with her intelligence information access from her Mossad days largely intact, she should at least have heard of Alice, but she hadn't. "Tell me more, Roger, before I dislocate your jaw again."

Hollis closed his eyes for a moment. When he opened them, Isobel was grinning at him.

"I'm still here," she said. "Who is Alice?"

"Other than the fact that I surmise he works for GRU,

for Boyko, I have no idea, I swear it." Hollis took a shuddering breath, let it out slowly. "Boyko pays me more for providing him with intel he uses mostly for personal gain. At least that's what I gather."

"I don't think you gather very much at all," Isobel said with such a sharp edge he winced. "You are one crap-eating dick. What else do you have for our ears only?"

"I can tell you more about Boyko," Hollis said, desperate now to save his own skin. "It seems that everything Boyko is up to these days is personal."

"How so?" Isobel asked.

"That I don't know."

"Hmm," Isobel reached out, softly patted the side of Hollis's face. The corners of her mouth turned up as he flinched. "I don't believe you, Roger." With her hand still on his jaw, she added: "Please don't disappoint me."

Hollis was making little grunts of pain. He heaved a sigh of capitulation. "You know that Boyko and Gorgonov were schoolmates, they go back a long way. Well, they're now in the midst of a bitter feud."

"Origin?" Isobel asked.

"Unknown," Hollis replied.

"Really?" Her eyes narrowed. "We need you to get to the bottom of it."

Hollis, staring into her unrelenting gaze, realized that he was finally and completely undone. He understood that there was only one way he was going to get out of this alive. "I think it might possibly have to do with their respective mistresses."

Isobel was excitedly aware that her mining expedition was about to strike gold. "What exactly d'you mean?"

"Now that both their mistresses are dead—I think each one killed the other's—their war seems to have escalated."

Rivers had been bending over her, straining to hear what was coming next. "Christ," he exclaimed, "this has all the hallmarks of a blood feud. It's like the Clantons and the Earps. I wonder whether it will lead to a modern-day shootout in Tombstone."

"But how did it start?" Isobel said. "That's what I'd like to know."

"Maybe it's like this," Rivers said, straightening up and taking a deep breath. "Okay. So. Thompson was an SVR asset, and now he's someone else's asset. Why? My best guess now, hearing about this feud, is he was poached by the GRU. By General Boyko, specifically. Maybe that's what started the whole thing. And he'd be the only one with enough power to pull off something like that. Now consider the nature of the asset. Thompson is the Secretary of Defense. A bigger fish I cannot imagine."

"Unless it's the president of the United States," Isobel added archly.

Rivers's laugh when it came was a bit uncertain. "Right. Of course. But that's . . ."

"The stuff of films?" Isobel finished for him.

"Yeah, yeah," Rivers said. "What was the name of that film, Hollis? You remember it, of course you do."

Hollis looked from one of his interrogators to the other. "*The Manchurian Candidate*?"

Isobel nodded distractedly. She was ready to get into the meat of the matter. Hollis hadn't so much as said "boo" at the mention of Thompson. He knew. She stared at Hollis fixedly. "So what d'you think of Rivers's theory?"

Hollis said, "I want something in return."

"You might get to live," Isobel told him. "How's that."

Hollis nodded sullenly. "Poached," he acknowledged. "In the tumult following the disappearance of Lyudmila Shokova. Gorgonov was focused on finding out what happened to her, at the Sovereign's order. He took his eye off the ball, Boyko moved in."

"Huh." Isobel sat back. "I do believe you're right, Riley. That's got to be the origin of their blood feud."

"What would that mean for us?"

Isobel gave a grunt. "Either the general will consolidate his power or Gorgonov will kill him."

Something leapt within Rivers's breast. "If Boyko poaching Thompson *is* what started the feud, maybe we can use that knowledge in some way."

"I have something else," Hollis said, abandoning his humble posture and sitting up straight. "And this tidbit is worth a lot more than the last one."

Isobel crouched down beside him again. "Speak, Roger, or forever hold your peace."

"I trolled the dark web for Boyko." His speech was returning to normal as he became used to the pain in his jaw. "I found something very interesting. More than interesting, actually. Much more. It's a game changer."

"Really?" Isobel's eyebrow arched upward. "Continue. The suspense is killing me."

"As a young man Gorgonov had an affair with another man in St. Petersburg."

Isobel's eyes opened wide. "You have proof?"

"Chapter and verse."

"And how is it that you've held on to this bombshell?"

"I hate Boyko, to tell you the truth. I hate myself for allowing him to coerce me into giving him intel. I was going to use it as leverage to sever my ties. My golden parachute."

"But you're going to let me have it, yes?"

"I can show you all of it. Every last word and photo."

A sly smile broke out across Isobel's face. "What d'you want?"

"My life. My company. Everything stays the way it was before I walked into this fucking trap."

"That's not possible. You know how this works."

"I want—"

"We don't always get what we want, Hollis, but sometimes we get what we need. What you need is your company back. That I can do. But from this moment forward you belong to me. Is that clear?"

He nodded.

"Say it, shitbird."

"It's clear, Isobel."

"Now show me the goods."

He nodded, groaned. "I will. And to prove my good intentions I'm going to throw in yet another bit of goods that should interest you greatly, to say the very least. Proof about Thompson."

Hollis licked his dry lips. "I swear, Isobel, you'll see just how valuable I can be to you."

"You should have been this helpful to me all along. When you thought we were in this *together,*" she said mockingly, but then helped him up. "You would have saved yourself a lot of pain." She turned to Rivers. "Time's up on this venue. Riley, let's get you signed out. My car's waiting downstairs for us."

■ ■ ■

On the way to her townhouse, she produced the mobile she used only occasionally, pressed a speed-dial key. When she heard the familiar voice at the other end, she said: "I have the answer." Listening attentively, she tried to keep her impatience in check. "I understand. Come over to my place as soon as you can break away."

43

From the outside, Marlowe's Bar & Grill wasn't much to look at, but inside it was a cozy nest of richly shining wood panels and bar, square columns painted black, and blue backlighting that should have been garish but somehow wasn't. The place was smoky and convivial, packed with red-faced Austrians. The burgers and thick-cut steak fries were good and the Bavarian beer excellent.

Evan and Limas sat across from each other in a darkened booth along the wall at right angles to the bar. They were in the middle of Salzburg. Obersalzberg lay eighteen and a half miles to the south in the Bavarian Alps. They would have been in Obersalzberg by now but for the two-hour delay getting out of the airport in Tbilisi, and almost getting caught there by the GRU.

"Wild Thoughts" by DJ Khaled was emanating from speakers high up in the four corners of the room, but no one seemed to be listening.

"I wish they'd cut that out," Limas said testily.

Evan watched him without expression.

"The music, I mean," Limas went on. "There's more than enough noise in here as it is. I can barely hear you without leaning over the table." Which was exactly what he was doing.

This wasn't the first time it occurred to Evan that

Peter Limas possessed no tradecraft. If indeed he was a spy, he was a very poor one. Hadn't Lyudmila arranged for him to have training? Or perhaps her true intention had been to get him out from under that whole side of life. In fact, that chimed with the Lyudmila she knew. Still, it was inconceivable that Gorgonov or, for that matter, any of his controls, would send a sleeper out without the proper training in tradecraft, let alone for wet work. Unless, clever fellow that Gorgonov was, he chose Peter precisely because he wasn't an agent, someone she could smell out.

The proprietor wandered the room, shaking hands, exchanging bon mots with locals and regulars. Every once in a while, he'd throw a sidelong glance their way when he thought they weren't looking, but Evan saw him every time, and marked his suspicion. It might be the famed Austrian suspicion of foreigners, or it might be something more specific and, therefore, sinister.

And yet when he reached their table, he extended a meaty hand, introduced himself as Herr Hennig, and spoke to them affably in the typical overly polite manner of the region. He bought them a round of beer, and an after-dinner drink of his finest brandy, all the while trying to weasel out of them where they were from, where they were staying, and, most insistently of all, where they were headed.

"My brother runs a travel service," he told them, smiling through his walrus mustache. "I can give you the best places to stay, the best restaurants to eat at, all at very fine prices because I know everyone in the area."

Evan thanked him in the same overly polite manner, while informing him that they were in Salzburg on business, and magnificent as the surrounding countryside looked, they had little time to enjoy it.

"What a pity," Herr Hennig said. "And what business is it that brings you to Salzburg?"

"We're exporters," Evan said.

Herr Hennig swept two snifters of amber brandy from the waiter's tray and set them in front of them. "Exporters of what, may I be so bold as to inquire?"

"Anything and everything, my dear sir," Evan replied, and tipped her snifter to her lips.

Herr Hennig nodded, smiling like their long-lost uncle. "Yet still, perhaps you would have time to tour the former salt mine in Hallein, which is now a wonderful tourist attraction. 'Salzwelten Hallein,' it is called now. 'The Hallein World of Salt.'"

"What a delightful suggestion! But ah, well, if only we had the time," Evan said in a mournful tone. "But work is work, as I am certain you understand all too well, Herr Hennig. The hard work you do around here is quite apparent and much appreciated."

Herr Hennig beamed. "You are too kind, *gnädige* Fraulein." He gestured with a theatrical sweep of his arm. "Please savor my brandy." He gave a little bow, but stopped short of clicking his heels.

"There's a decent fellow," Limas said when they were once again alone.

Evan emitted a short laugh. "Don't be fooled, Peter. Herr Hennig was mining for information." Evan took another sip of the brandy, which was indeed quite fine. "The first thing you need to learn about the Austrians is they're hypocrites. They come at you with a smile while holding a knife behind their back."

"Aren't all people hypocrites? It's more or less part of the human condition."

"True enough." Limas may not have made a decent spy, but he was far from stupid, Evan thought. "But in the case of the Austrians they have a head start, not to mention that they run faster."

The skin at the outside of Limas's eyes crinkled as he laughed. "The next time I speak with an Austrian I'll keep that in mind." At once, he sobered up. "But what kind of information was he mining for?"

"Our destination," Evan said. "You heard him mention Hallein."

Limas nodded. "Yes. 'The Hallein World of Salt.'"

"Well, it just so happens that the area around Obersalzberg is known for its salt mines." Evan set aside her snifter. "I don't think it was a coincidence that Herr Hennig mentioned 'Salzwelten Hallein.'"

Limas's brows knit together. "Do you think he knows that's where we're headed?"

Evan shook her head. "He was fishing, that's all. But I do think that if we'd been stupid enough to tell him where we were going, a number of people—some of whom would no doubt like nothing better than to stop us—would be made aware of our destination."

"You mean the Russians who tried to hold us over in Tbilisi, or Nemesis, both of whom are trying to kill us both."

Evan shot Limas a look. No matter how much she tried to disbelieve his story about being Lyudmila's nephew, the coin kept coming up on the opposite face. She would have liked to explore this anomaly further, but the truth was she was exhausted, as she was sure Limas was. What they both needed most now was a good night's sleep so they would be rested for tomorrow's journey across the border into the Bavarian Alps, and for whatever they were going to find there.

■ ■ ■

But sleep was not Evan's willing partner. She stood by the window in her small but immaculate hotel room, staring out at the sepia-colored night, scanning the street for loitering figures or inhabited vehicles parked in a stakeout. That she saw neither did little to reassure her. First of all, she wasn't convinced that they had not been followed here from Georgia. She was more concerned by the attempted Russian military intervention at the

Tbilisi airport than she had let on to Limas. Questions kept bedeviling her: the first was Peter Limas himself; the second was her thoroughly unpleasant conversation with Alli regarding the possible resurrection of a DOD black site; third, she still had no clear idea of how large or powerful a network Nemesis commanded. How many countries were its acolytes in? Did it have local and/or regional police and politicians in its pocket? And, speaking of pockets, how deep were Nemesis's? Who or what was behind the neo-Nazis? Who or what was funding Nemesis? The Russians? It seemed highly unlikely that it was self-funded, not something on this international scale.

Restless, she dressed, went downstairs. Outside, the sky was cloudless, but a reddish haze from the city's light pollution made stargazing a thing of the distant past. She wasn't concentrating on the sky, anyway, but rather quartering the immediate area as she walked. Shadows lay strewn across her path like chess pieces in a broken game. She was surrounded by Gothic architecture, a remnant of the country's ignominious past.

Forty minutes later, she returned to her room, having found no sign of human surveillance; she had checked her room—and Limas's for that matter—for any form of electronic surveillance, finding nothing. All was quiet, all was still, as if a thick blanket of snow covered the entire world.

She undressed, and finally, reluctantly, drew the eiderdown over her. She stared at the ceiling for some time before her eyes closed in a troubled sleep. As she tossed and turned she was again assailed by images, strange and yet at the same time familiar, snippets like lightning flashes illuminating for seconds at a time in the moonless, starless night of her unconscious mind.

The red-brick mansion loomed large in these tableaux, and always the ravens circling pitch-black against the piercing blue sky—a sky she now very much suspected was Alpine. She felt the nearness of the mansion, as if it had a magnetic hold on her, as if the closer she got, the stronger that pull became until it became irresistible. Deep down in her subconscious she was aware of the danger—one greater than any she had encountered before. But what she didn't know, what eluded her no matter how hard she set her mind to it, was what the danger entailed. And she knew—though maddeningly she didn't know how she knew—that she would only understand the nature of this danger when she came face-to-face with it.

And by then it might be too late.

▪ ▪ ▪

Brenda had chosen the nonstop eight-hour flight to Munich and a minimum two-hour drive to Obersalzberg rather than a long multi-leg flight into Salzburg. She was traveling as Amy Kendall, vice president of a computer sales company domiciled in Grand Cayman. Should anyone call to check her out they'd get an apologetic voicemail requesting the caller leave a message for the unavailable Ms. Kendall.

The most direct route from Munich to Obersalzberg, Google Maps informed her, was via the high-speed A8 motorway. She planned to rent a car at the airport, paying in cash, and drive like a demon, maybe making it in under the two-hour barrier, but as so often happens in life, her plans did not work out.

While she was waiting in line at the rental car agency, two suits came up on either side of her, and asked her quietly and politely to get out of the line. They spoke English with a distinct Bavarian accent. When she refused, they told her in no uncertain terms what would happen to her if she did not comply. At the same time, she felt the muzzle of a pistol pressing into the small of her back.

"All right," she replied. "Let's all calm down."

"We're calm," the one on her left said softly. He

smelled of camphor and something acrid she couldn't quite place. "And we will remain so only if you come with us." The other man jabbed her with the pistol's muzzle. "Now."

The man on her left took possession of her overnight bag while the other steered her through the ultra-modern terminal with the pistol's muzzle. Strange faces were coming at her from all directions. Odors of draft beer, sauerkraut, and boiled sausages assailed her in such strength she almost gagged. Being frog-marched by a pair of Bavarian apes to God alone knew where might have had something to do with the sick feeling in the pit of her stomach.

Outside, under a buttermilk sky pierced by needlelike steeples and square brick bell towers, the stench that had nauseated her dissipated quickly, smothered by clouds of exhaust and diesel fumes.

A large black BMW was idling at the curb, awaiting her appearance. The man on the left opened the rear door, put his hand on the top of her head, all but shoved her onto the backseat. Then he climbed in beside her and closed the door. As soon as the man holding the pistol took his position next to the driver, the BMW took off. Fritz gave her a pat down, relieved her of her mobile phone and her watch.

"Where are you taking me?" Brenda said.

"Relax," the man she had dubbed Fritz replied in a voice that sounded as if he had a mouth full of razor blades. "We have a long way to go." His lips reminded her of slices of raw liver.

The man who rode shotgun—whom she had dubbed Hans—half-turned in his seat, leered at her with avid eyes and a set of alarmingly large teeth yellowed like the fingers of his right hand by nicotine. "Some looker you are, *schatzi*."

"Shut up," Fritz said.

Hans shrugged, turned back around, staring out the

windshield. But it wasn't long before he was humming the "Horst Wessel Lied," the old Nazi rallying song.

"Shut the fuck up," Fritz said, and Hans did. Clearly, Fritz was the senior of the two. He was also beefier, ruddier, and, it seemed to her, a bit older. He had a face like a slab of uncooked mutton, with little black eyes like the buttons sewn onto rag dolls. Bulldog jowls and a cauliflower nose completed the unwholesome picture. By contrast, Hans was as thin as a pencil, with the high, domed forehead of a professor. Balding prematurely, his thin golden hair waved like chaff in the wind. A scar ran down the left side of his narrow jaw. His blue eyes were as milky as a day-old corpse. From what Brenda could see, the driver looked like someone out of central casting for a Nazi feature film.

They entered a motorway on-ramp, and the BMW accelerated. Glancing at the speedometer, she calculated they were traveling at around 100 mph. It wasn't long before she realized that they were barreling along the A8, heading southwest toward the vicinity of Obersalzberg. *First-class transport,* she said to herself, the wry comment helping to fight off the anxiety that threatened to overwhelm her cool decision-making process. Above all, she knew, it was imperative to keep her wits about her every second. She could not afford to give in to anxiety, fear, or despair. These were the true enemy. As long as she remained focused there was always a chance to get out of almost any situation—another one of Evan's invaluable teachings from their time in Berlin.

With that in mind, she settled back in the seat, closed her eyes to slits, so that Fritz might believe that she was so relaxed she was taking a nap. Meanwhile, she was taking note of all the road signs and kilometer markings in order to keep herself oriented should she have the chance to escape and call for help. She must not, under any circumstances, give up hope. Occasionally, Fritz and Hans spoke to each other, and Brenda cursed herself for not having the facility with languages Evan had. She spoke passable Russian, Arabic, and Farsi, but her knowledge of German was rudimentary at best.

The only word that was recognizable to her was "*Watzmannhaus,*" which both men repeated several times. She was well aware that Watzmann was the third-highest mountain in Germany, and was often associated with Berchtesgaden, once the summer home of Adolf Hitler and later, as war approached, the heart of the Nazi Third Reich. She also recognized "*haus*" as meaning "house." Wasn't the German name for Hitler's Eagle's Nest *Kehlsteinhaus*? A deep shudder ran through her. What had she gotten herself into? And, just as importantly, *how*? How had she been made at the airport? No one—not even Butler—knew she had even left the States, no less where she was going, and under what legend name. No matter how she looked at the question, no reasonable answer seemed possible. Was there yet another enemy in the field, one who had been hidden from her and from Butler? Or was Peter somehow involved? Had he betrayed her once again? Right at this moment she could not imagine how. She felt blind, as if she was standing so close to a single tree she couldn't see the forest that had arisen all around her.

But in a strictly practical sense all of this ideating was academic, really. The one thing she had been deliberately—almost desperately—ignoring was her compromised physical condition. The truth was, even after the restless sleep she'd had aboard the flight, she felt like yesterday's rubbish. Her head throbbed as if it was being assaulted by a pile driver, every muscle in her body ached to some degree. Dr. Selsby had been right. She needed rest—a long one. She couldn't help thinking of the genuine concern on the doctor's face, of how he had ordered her to bed for at least a week, otherwise she ran the risk of doing herself permanent harm. At the time, it had been a given that Brenda would ignore that order—she had entertained no other alternative. But now that she was well and truly in the soup, she could not help but think that she simply wasn't up to another prolonged physical battle. And what did that say about her chances for survival?

44

Isobel's townhouse was unnaturally still when Butler arrived via the back door. It had been a number of long, difficult hours before he was able to break away from the action intel briefs and the strategy meetings with his lawyers on how to handle his appearance before Brady Thompson's congressional committee, which, he was certain, was set up to discredit him and dismantle MI7. He knew that he was at the precipice, that this was likely his last fight. The committee would either break him, casting him out as a pariah in the intelligence community to which he had dedicated most of his adult life, or damage his reputation so badly that he would no longer be trusted by both his colleagues and his own people. He already knew that General Aristides had side-stepped this process and was now out of the picture so far as he was concerned. So much for powerful rabbis!

He saw no possible positive end to his predicament, and if he had not been made of such stern stuff, if his personality had not been forged in the crucible of fieldwork, he might have packed up and returned to Berlin, where both he and Zoe had left a full life and friends who loved them. It was times like these when he questioned why he continually took the hard, dark road, when other, easier, sunnier forks had been presented to him.

It was in this anxiety-ridden frame of mind that he knocked on the door to Isobel's mansion. It was opened almost immediately, as if the man who let him in had been waiting for him. He passed through the kitchen and warren of back rooms, mounting the curling staircase that always reminded him of a pale-as-a-ghost boa constrictor he had once stumbled across in Nicaragua, emerging from a moss-covered hollow log like toothpaste from a tube. As he reached the second floor he wished Izzy had at least given him a hint, other than saying the enigmatic "*I have the answer.*"

Nothing, however, could have prepared him for the sight awaiting him in Izzy's private study. Two men he had heard of but never seen were with her. One, Roger Hollis, was curled on the floor, hands pressed against a lower jaw so swollen he looked like an Orc. He was staring at the floor in front of him, so lost and in pain he didn't bother to raise his eyes to see who had entered.

The other man, the one standing by Izzy's side, watched him approach with a wide-eyed stare of astonishment. He was not, however, as astonished as Butler was.

Halted in mid-stride, he looked from Riley Rivers to Izzy, who was unaccountably smiling as if everything was hunky-dory, which it most assuredly was not.

"Izzy," he said sharply, "what the hell is this?" He pointed at Rivers. "This is the prick who's been sending out the poisonous fake news items about me."

Rivers goggled. "What's *he* doing here?"

"Right," Isobel acknowledged, ignoring Rivers's outburst. "That's because he's Moscow-controlled."

"Hey!" Rivers, startled, twitched as if he had just been tasered. "What the fuck—!"

"Shut up, Riley," Isobel snapped. "Keep still."

But Rivers was far too incensed to stay quiet. "Are you fucking out of your mind?"

Turning on him, Isobel said in a low voice so filled with menace that Rivers froze, "Do as I say, Riley. Believe me when I tell you that your life depends on it."

Turning back to Butler, she said, "Here's the deal. This little shit, Riley Rivers, is an SVR asset. This other little shit"—here she pointed to Hollis—"has been pimping Rubicon Solutions out to the GRU—or more specifically pimping out Soul Searcher, the netbot that has targeted you, to General Boyko."

"Soul Searcher," Butler said.

"Right. Soul Searcher was built with Rubicon Solutions's help."

"What is going on here?" Rivers seemed greatly diminished, and why not, the ground had opened up beneath him.

"Everything's changed, Riley," Isobel said.

"But I've been helping you!"

"You're venal, Riley. This makes you vulnerable. Even worse, it makes you stupid." She tapped his flaming cheek, and he winced. "I gave you your chance, Riley. When I took you to Yana Bardina's funeral that was a warning. But you didn't heed it. You were too busy filling your pockets with the money Moscow was adding to your offshore bank account." She smiled, not unkindly. "You see now how your venality blinded you, made you stupid."

Rivers was so bewildered he blurted out: "So you have no loyalty to anyone or anything, then?"

"My loyalty is to my family," Isobel said. "It always was and always will be."

Unexpectedly, save possibly to him, Rivers began to cry. Silent tears magnified his eyes, spilling down his cheeks, plopped onto the floor like the unwanted largess of a leaky faucet.

Isobel turned her attention to Butler. "Look at these men. What are they made of anyway? Piss and shit and everything nasty."

Rivers was dumbfounded, but neither Butler nor Isobel paid him the slightest attention.

"It might seem odd that Boyko and Gorgonov have gotten themselves directly involved in field missions," Isobel went on, ignoring the two broken men, "until you discover that the two of them are locked in a mortal struggle for control of the Russian intelligence orgs."

"I know that much," Butler said. "But there's an animosity between them that seems entirely personal."

Isobel nodded. "I couldn't agree more."

"But how is this relevant to Hollis being here, and in this condition?" Butler cocked his head. "And why do you look like the proverbial cat that swallowed the canary?"

Isobel couldn't help chuckling. "Yes, indeed. It's all about the Boyko-Gorgonov steel cage death match, as will become clear in a minute." She handed him a folder. "Hollis did a little data mining for Boyko and now we have this." She indicated the file. "Hold onto your hat. As I told you over the phone, I have the answer."

That smile of hers could melt a thousand hearts, Butler thought, as he read through the contents of the folder.

"You're never going to go before that committee, Ben. Or any other."

"Ben?" Rivers croaked. He was done weeping, but more confused than ever.

Again, he was ignored.

"It's *Manchurian Candidate* time," Isobel continued. "Your personal nemesis, Secretary of Defense Brady Thompson, is a pawn of a foreign power, as they say."

Butler read over the file. "Our old friend General Boyko pops up again."

Isobel nodded. "Like a bad penny. Gorgonov went after Thompson when he was most vulnerable and caged him. And then Boyko stole him from Gorgonov."

Butler looked up at Isobel. "It's no wonder POTUS has been cozying up to the Sovereign. He listens to everything Thompson tells him." He considered for a moment. "But now another layer of intrigue has been added. Boyko has started going off-campus, guiding missions without anyone inside or outside the GRU knowing about them."

"Like Nemesis?" Isobel asked.

Butler nodded. "I'm thinking Boyko is secretly funding Nemesis as yet another forum for destabilizing the United States."

He had finished reading the intel that would, when he released it, damn Brady Thompson, all his statements, pronouncements, and positions, while at the same time exonerating himself of the hateful lies and innuendos, guided by Moscow and, by extension, Rivers himself. Then another thought hit him. Was there another path? A better path?

He slapped the file against his open palm. "Izzy, I can't thank you enough for this."

"Wait." Isobel grinned. "There's more."

"How much more?"

Isobel laughed as she handed over the second file Hollis had printed out for her. "This shows that Gorgonov made a slight misstep while he was in college in St. Petersburg. Well, more than a slight misstep. His male lover put his diary from that time online—buried over the years in the dark web—along with those compromising photos."

Butler studied the photos carefully. "This will mean the end of him."

"If we do the right thing," Isobel said.

Butler turned to Hollis. "Hey, you, get this stuff on Gorgonov to Boyko, Eyes Only, Extremely Urgent."

"I told you I'd be helpful," Hollis said in such a pathetic tone of voice Isobel almost felt something for him.

Almost, but not quite. "And then it will be time to raise the ante."

Hollis fidgeted. "What d'you mean?"

"You're going to contact Alice, and we're going to trace the call."

▪ ▪ ▪

All the leaves were gone and the sky was gray. Thunder rolled through the high Alps and, occasionally, a serpent's tongue of lightning flicked downward to the earth.

"Where are we going?" Peter Limas said as Evan drove hard and fast. "You seem to have a specific destination in mind."

"I do." Evan flicked her high-beams, maneuvered the rental car around a lumbering semi. "Berchtesgaden."

"How do you know that's where Nemesis is?"

"You told me, Peter."

"I did? How? When?"

"Remember when you told me that your aunt Lyudmila showed you two or three photos of her brother, your father?"

Limas's brows knit together. "Sure. But I thought you didn't believe me."

"I have an eidetic memory," Evan said, "and this is what you told me, verbatim: 'But he was much younger then, before he was stationed in Parechgadem, a place I never heard of and couldn't find on any map.'" Evan glanced at Limas. "You remember saying that as well?"

"Of course I do. But—"

"I wasn't paying close enough attention to you at the time . . . honestly, I was so concentrated on whether or not to believe you were Lyudmila's nephew. You calling her 'Aunt Lyudmila,' it threw me."

The day had grown dark, as if with an eclipse, and a wind had got up. It was as if the violent storm that had delayed them in Tbilisi had followed them here into the Bavarian Alps. But here snow, not rain, was coming.

"You also said that she had told you where that place was, where she had rescued me. And last night, I couldn't sleep, I kept running our conversations back through my mind, thinking it all through. *Parechgadem.* It's the Old High German name of Berchtesgaden, which, ironically, means 'hay shed' or 'one-room hut.'"

Limas shook his head. "I'm still not getting it. What does that have to do with—"

"Berchtesgaden was Hitler's summer home and home base of the Third Reich."

"I thought that was Berlin."

"A common misconception," Evan told him. "In fact, Berliners hated Hitler and the Nazis in general. The Third Reich's high command trusted only Bavarians, who embraced Hitler and his fascist policies wholeheartedly, never Berliners."

Again, she glanced at Limas. "Do you see the other piece of irony here, Peter?"

Limas thought a moment. "The parallels to America now?"

"Exactly. Fascism is embraced in the countryside, where wealth and education are in short supply. It's always the big cities that fight the hardest against any form of extremism. Germany then, America now."

"So, your thought is where better for Nemesis to have its headquarters than in the Bavarian Alps."

Evan nodded. "And somewhere in Berchtesgaden, the better to absorb his dark power."

"Christ," Limas breathed.

"That's one way of putting it," Evan said dryly.

Snow started falling, a silent curtain, muffling even the smallest sounds of the world around them.

45

Snow muffled everything but their voices.

"Almost there," Hans said in heavily accented English, so Brenda knew he wanted her to understand what he was saying.

Fritz chuckled evilly. "Surprises galore, for this one here."

"Surprises are hardly the word for them," Hans said, peering ahead into the snowy road. They had turned off the A8 some twenty-five minutes ago, by Brenda's inexact count, and had been snaking steadily up the mountain on a secondary road.

"What would you call them, then?" Fritz asked, though it seemed to her that he was only marginally interested in the answer.

"Terrors," Hans said definitively. "I would call them terrors."

Fritz looked over at their prisoner, chuckled again. It was definitely an evil sound, she decided, and sent a ripple of apprehension through her. "I suppose you could call separating body from mind a form of terror." He made another sound, like an animal lowing. "But then there's Major to think of."

"Speak of terrors." Hans made a show of shuddering.

"I don't like even being in the same room as Major. He gives me the creeps."

Fritz nodded. "He is the stuff of *alpträume*—how do you say in English?" He clicked his fingers.

"Nightmares," the driver said.

"Nightmares. Ah, yes." Fritz leered at her. "Major is a fucking nightmare come to life."

After this, what seemed to her staged back-and-forth, Fritz and Hans lapsed back into silence, punctuated, at intervals, with brief bursts of Bavarian German directed at one another.

She knew they had meant to frighten her, to soften her up, to force her mind to anticipate the hateful things that were sure to come. It was a common enough tactic used on prisoners. Nevertheless, the phrase "almost there" was the one that reverberated most forcefully in her head, mostly because it was the one real thing they said she could be sure of.

Twenty or so minutes more brought them to another turnoff. They were quite high up now; she'd had to clear her ears three times since they left the A8.

The snow had abated enough so that she could see the Watzmann's signature double peak, as if through her grandmother's lace curtains. The road was snow-covered, and the BMW's tires made a sound like a sleigh rushing over a hill.

As the way steepened, the weather changed again, sleet hammered the BMW's top and hood, sounding to her like the warning of a rattlesnake about to strike.

Out of the corner of her eye Brenda noticed Fritz fiddling with a square package. "What is that," she said, more to keep up her nerve than for information, "a schnitzel sandwich?"

The acrid odor hit her just before Fritz pressed the anesthetic-soaked cloth over her nose and mouth. She struggled, her legs flailing, but he was straddling her, pinioning her arms. Her eyes grew round, and just before a velvet darkness overtook her, she saw looming up ahead what looked like a huge castle out of a child's picture book. *The evil wizard's lair,* a voice echoed inside her.

Then, like the dead of winter, all was still.

■ ■ ■

"Berchtesgaden," Limas said, shaking his head. "It was there in front of me all along."

"The best place to hide anything," Evan said as she maneuvered their rental car through the old town's streets, "is in plain sight." The cobbled streets were home to stone and half-timbered buildings straight out of *The Sound of Music*. It seemed as if at any moment men and women in lederhosen might appear, their voices raised in song. "Deutschland Uber Alles," perhaps. But maybe those were simply echoes.

She pulled into a parking spot, and they got out into a mixed swirl of snow and sleet. The air was sharp and icy; their exhalations preceded them as Evan led them along the sidewalk past a haberdasher's, a tobacconist with its wire rack of the day's snow-specked papers, and a cabinetmaker's shop.

"Well, we're in the vicinity," Limas said. "But how on earth are we going to find Nemesis's actual headquarters?"

"Ask someone," Evan said.

Which elicited a laugh out of Limas. "You're joking."

Evan smiled, opened the door into a pub. "Fancy a bite to eat, Peter?" she said in a perfect upper-class British accent. "I do."

The pub was dark, beery, and cozy, insofar as anything on Hitler's mountain could be termed cozy. It was that hour between lunchtime and after work, and the place was all but deserted. Only a sprinkling of inveterate drinkers and a couple of tourists seeking shelter from the snowstorm inhabited the place.

Evan chose a table against the wall opposite the front door, ordered two beers and cheese-and-sausage rolls from the buxom waitress who sauntered over. They were silent while the beer was brought over in large metal tankards. The food came soon thereafter.

"But really," Limas said as they ate and drank, "how are we to proceed?"

"I already told you."

Limas shook his head. "I don't understand."

"You aren't meant to," Evan said sharply. She had already drained her beer. "Need a refill?"

"What? No. Thanks. I've half yet to drink."

Instead of calling over the waitress, Evan rose and, tankard in hand, crossed to the gleaming hardwood bar. Leaning her hip against the bar's edge, she smiled at the bartender and began talking to him. Limas wondered what they were saying. It had taken all of thirty seconds for the bartender to refill Evan's tankard, but they were still engaged in conversation. Surely Evan wasn't asking him the way to the Nemesis headquarters. That was absurd.

When she returned, Limas said, "What was that all about?"

She didn't bother to sit again, just put several bills on the table and said, "No joy, I'm afraid. Finish your roll, we're leaving."

Outside, Limas felt an immediate chill after the damp heat of the pub. The sleet was ending, replaced with a weird form of fog that clung to them like the tendrils of some sea beast. He shivered inside his thick coat, stuffed his hands in his pockets.

"Where to now?"

"Aren't you still thirsty? I know I am," Evan said jovially, as they entered the main square of the old town with its non-working central well and fountain. She selected a biergarten across the square, seemingly at random. Its outdoor seating area was closed for the winter, looking abandoned and forlorn.

Though the biergarten was cavernous, in all other ways it was virtually indistinguishable from the pub they had just left, and Evan played out basically the same sequence of events—the only difference being that she ordered sausage and sauerkraut to go along with their draft beers. After draining her glass, she excused herself to use the facilities, then swept up her empty stein, sauntered to the bar, and engaged the bartender in conversation. This time, however, the back-and-forth was briefer and ended with the bartender's face going red and shouting his disapproval of whatever Evan had said to him. She peeled off some euros onto the bar top. Limas was already moving, and they hurried out into the foggy late afternoon.

"Information gathering not going so well?" Limas said through a hearty burp. "What did you say to piss off the bartender?"

"That was him," Evan said as they turned onto a side street, and ran almost headlong into another pub. "Not me."

Limas shook his head. "What do you expect anyone here to tell you? I'm totally at sea."

Evan shot him a look. "And so far inland." She gestured as they entered. "Take a table and order whatever you want."

"I couldn't possibly eat or drink another thing."

"Then just take a pew near the door and say you're waiting for a friend."

Limas nodded. "Will do."

This pub was smaller than either of the previous ones. There was something of the hunting lodge about it, with its bare wooden beams, its huge stone hearth in which a fire crackled and flickered, and a rack of antique rifles over the center of the bar. One of them was a Mauser 98. Evan smiled to herself as she approached the bar. The bartender was a big, beefy fellow with the bloated cheeks and red-veined nose of the inveterate drinker. Evan ordered a draft beer in Bavarian German and when she tasted it, said, "Ah, this reminds me of home."

"You're from here, Fraulein von Feuer?" the bartender said, after Evan introduced herself. He raised one of his caterpillar eyebrows. "A noble name." His head was otherwise entirely free of hair, skull shining in the dull light.

"Thank you, but, no. However, my father was born and raised on the mountain." No one from here ever referred to it by its name.

"What was he in the war?"

There was only one war these people spoke of. World War I was far beyond their collective memories.

"A sniper on the Eastern Front." Evan indicated the rack with a nod of her head. "I recognize that Mauser 98. My father used one of those."

The bartender half-turned. "That one still works. I tend to it every month like clockwork."

Evan sipped more of her beer. "You wouldn't by any chance be interested in selling it, would you? It would have sentimental value, you understand."

The bartender shook his head. "Sorry, no."

"He made it back, one of the very few," Evan said. "Lost four fingers and both feet to frostbite."

"A true hero, I understand." The bartender nodded sagely. "But there's nothing I can do." He spread his spatulate hands as he leaned across the bar, lowering his voice. "You see, it has the Death's Head engraved on it." The feared Death's Head was the symbol of Heinrich Himmler's Totenkopfverbände, the section of the SS responsible for running the death camps as well as overseeing Nazi-occupied Europe. "It's against the law to sell or trade in Nazi paraphernalia."

It interested Evan that he used this word, not *memorabilia*. It meant that for him, there was no nostalgia involved in these items. They were still of use to a Nazi like him.

"Even to use the swastika." The bartender shrugged. "I mean, what can you do?"

"I understand completely," Evan said in a mournful tone of voice. "Nevertheless, I'm thinking that my journey back to the roots of my Fatherland will be sadly lacking without my being able to take back with me some token of that period when my father was a hero."

Now both caterpillars climbed above the bartender's eyes. "You mean to tell me that you don't have any of his medals, Fraulein von Feuer?"

"All was lost in the Allied bombings, I'm afraid," Evan said with just the slightest touch of malice.

"So much was," the bartender lamented.

"The real German way of life."

The bartender hammered his fist onto the zinc bar top hard enough that Evan's stein did a little jig. "Exactly so," he agreed.

A customer at the other end of the bar summoned him and he excused himself to tend to the order. Evan stayed just where she was, part of her figuratively holding its breath. She did not look at the bartender, but rather at the Mauser 98 with a clear longing.

When the bartender returned, he resumed his low tone. "Your pain is a shared one, *gnädige* Fraulein. I cannot help you, but—" Reaching down under the bar he drew out a scratch pad and the stub of a pencil that looked like a squirrel had had its way with it. "Perhaps a mate of mine can." He scribbled a name, Joachim Wenzel, an address, and mobile number. As he tore the sheet off, slid it across to her, he added, "Tell him Markus sent you. I'll phone him in advance."

Evan bowed her head. "I am much obliged." She

pulled out some bills, but Markus waved the money away.

"The proud daughter of the war hero von Feuer doesn't pay here." He smiled, showing a pair of gold teeth. "This much I can do for a comrade in arms."

46

The Danilov Monastery, in the Danilovsky district south of central Moscow, was built in the late thirteenth century by Daniil, the first Prince of Moscow. Its white fortress-like appearance was no coincidence, as Daniil originally built it as a redoubt to defend the outskirts of the city. Nowadays it served as the headquarters for the Russian Orthodox Church.

At precisely twelve minutes to 9 A.M., General Boyko strode beneath the pink St. Simeon Stylite Gate-Church on the north wall. He entered the Church of the Holy Fathers of the Seven Ecumenical Councils. His footsteps echoed hollowly off the walls, every square inch of them covered in ornate frescoes of the Holy Fathers and of the historic Ecumenical Councils. There was still a bit over an hour until worship started. Once begun, it ran continuously every day until 5 P.M.

Crossing to the small main chapel dedicated to the Protecting Veil, he stood staring at the ornate iconostasis for a moment, contemplating the foolishness of all belief in God, as opposed to the necessity of religion to keep the populace docile and under control. He opened the battered soft-sided leather attaché case he had brought with him, took out a brown bag from which he extracted a chocolate brioche, and began to eat, slowly and with great relish.

As he ate he thought of how well he had positioned himself, even up to this moment. He thought of his mistress, dead by Gorgonov's hands. He thought of his darling daughter, terrified by Gorgonov's hands. He thought about how delightful it was going to be to end his enemy's life today, this very morning. In a matter of moments. And then he would be truly free to pursue his desire to see the governing of Mother Russia turned over to the methodical, almost scientific organ based on the Third Reich's reign in Germany. Then the real rise of the Russian Federation as a major global power could begin.

When he was finished with his breakfast he licked his fingertips one by one and returned the bag to the attaché case, which he kept open beside him.

He had no need of glancing at his watch. He knew it was nine o'clock by the sound of footsteps behind him. He turned to see his hated and feared enemy coming toward him.

"Enough of this shit," Gorgonov said in a hushed but tense tone of voice. "You crossed the fucking line with the assassination attempt. And mere blocks from the Kremlin, no less."

Boyko raised his hands, palms out. "I know nothing about that."

Gorgonov's eyes narrowed. "What d'you take me for? The attempt had your fingerprints all over it."

"You've got this all wrong. I didn't—"

"One of my men was killed by that fucking poison meant for me."

"Better him than you." Boyko took the brown bag from his case again, drew out another chocolate brioche. "I brought you breakfast. I ate one just before you arrived. I swear they're the best in all of Moscow."

Gorgonov eyed the general without so much as a glance at the pastry. "You must be joking."

"No? Sure?" Boyko shrugged. "Well, all right then. I'll have it myself."

Gorgonov waited until he'd consumed the whole thing. "Your jovial demeanor ill suits the occasion. This feud must end here, now, at once before one or both of us is killed."

"I couldn't agree more," Boyko said, wiping his fingers on his military greatcoat.

"You started this," Gorgonov said, looking on with distaste, "by poaching Brady Thompson, the SVR's best American asset."

Boyko shrugged his great shoulders. "Ah, you were so busy trying to find Shokova, I thought I'd take him off your plate," he said smugly, sucking a flake of crust from between his teeth. Then his tone turned ugly. "Now it is what it is, Anton Recidivich. Thompson is mine."

Gorgonov's fingers curled at his sides. "You stealing from me, killing my people, attempting to assassinate me . . . it's at an end. I want Thompson back."

Boyko laughed. "I don't think so. Here's what's going to happen." He balled up the paper bag, dropped it into his attaché case, then took out a black manila folder. It had two diagonal red stripes across the upper right corner. He held it out to Gorgonov.

"What's that?" Gorgonov said, eyeing it suspiciously.

"The end," Boyko said, "of all things." He smiled like a crocodile approaching his dinner. "For you, anyway."

"I don't want to see it."

"No?" The general opened the folder. "Well, then, I'll read it to you."

He had only begun when Gorgonov snatched it out of his hands. The file contained a transcript of the diary of a male student Gorgonov had known in college, a day-by-day history of this student seducing the young Gorgonov, of their eventual trysts together in a flyblown room of a cheap hotel in the so-called gray belt section of St. Petersburg, crammed with old abandoned factories and "commieblocks," crumbling high-rises of communal apartments where three and four families festered cheek by jowl.

The diary spared no detail of the trysts—the murmured terms of endearment, the lovemaking, the sweat-soaked aftermath where the young Gorgonov spoke to his lover of everything he was doing or hoped to do.

Then there were the photos of the two of them, naked, entwined, the entering and the entered, like Greek wrestlers with oiled bodies and avid eyes. Taken how? With a system the lover had set up beforehand, or by some third party, hidden in a closet or behind curtains? It didn't matter; the photos were real, and that was enough.

"All this was pulled off the dark web, Gorgonov, where your lover had stashed it because, I assume, he couldn't bear to part with it. Cherished memories, and all that." Boyko took the file out of Gorgonov's limp grip. "This will ruin you, you know." He was openly gloating now. "Once the Sovereign sees what's in here it's off to Siberia with you. Not even a show trial or a firing squad for you. You will be lost to your wife, your daughter, your entire family. It will be as if you never existed."

The general cocked his head. "Or. I could simply hold onto this and you could tender your resignation. Go into the private sector, become a businessman, do whatever you want. Just as long as you don't bother me. I never want to see or hear from you again."

He slapped the file against his open palm, grinning. "The choice is up to you."

"Good morning, gentlemen."

Boyko turned at the sound of the all-too-familiar voice.

"Sovereign," he said, nearly choking on the word.

"I love coming here, General," the Sovereign said. He was wearing a vaguely military leisure suit over a shirt with an open collar. The gold cross lay conspicuously between his pectorals. His mink-colored cashmere overcoat was slung across his shoulders. "It's so peaceful early in the morning, don't you agree."

"Indeed it is, Sovereign," Gorgonov said.

"What, may I ask, are the two of you doing here?" the Sovereign said with a bland look on his face. "Not attending services, surely."

Boyko was too stunned to utter a word.

"We're trying to iron out an ongoing dispute, sir," Gorgonov said.

"I detest disputes among my high-ranking people. Whatever the dispute is must be settled immediately." The Sovereign moved closer to the two men, into the light. Behind him, a rising tide of overlapping echoes as the faithful filed in to begin the first of the day's services. The worshipful and the profane in such close proximity without either one paying the slightest attention to the other.

When he was close enough, the Sovereign said, "What have we here?" and took the file from Boyko.

"A very serious situation, Sovereign," the general said. "I have discovered that Anton Recidivich Gorgonov is not fit to command the SVR. In fact, as you can see, as a closet homosexual he isn't fit to command anything."

The Sovereign raised his eyes, his heavy, penetrating gaze falling squarely on General Boyko. "What is this I hear concerning an assassination attempt on Anton Recidivich?"

"What?" Boyko, caught off-guard, took an involuntary step back. "I don't know anything about—" He stopped abruptly as the Sovereign fanned out photos for him to see.

"Who is that you're talking with, General," the Sovereign said. It wasn't a question. "I do believe that is Vilen Vladimirovich Aliyev. Correct me if I'm wrong, Anton Recidivich."

"You're never wrong, Sovereign."

What a fucking suck-up, Boyko thought bitterly. He knew he was rapidly losing ground. Still, as any human being would, he held out a modicum of hope. "But that information on Gorgonov's past is indisputably damning, sir."

"No, General, it's not. Unlike these photos of you and the head of our far-right movement, who you hired to assassinate Anton Recidivich, the information you have here is false. You see, I've seen it before. When, you might ask? Well, it was when my people created it and planted it in a very dark corner of one of the sectors of the dark web the GRU routinely monitors."

It was at this moment that Boyko felt the trap snap shut on his leg. He felt all the air go out of the morning. Silently, he cursed himself for being led like a lamb to the slaughter.

"For you to find," Gorgonov added. "Which you did." Twisting the knife in the wound.

The Sovereign nodded. "That is entirely correct, Anton Recidivich."

Behind him appeared two men from his Federal Guards Service. Between them was the sniper the general had handpicked. One of the bodyguards was holding the long gun at his side, barrel pointing down.

"Who is this man, General?" the Sovereign asked in a tone of voice that made it clear he already knew. "One of your men?"

The taste of defeat was like ashes in Boyko's mouth. "Yes," he said so softly that the Sovereign barked at him, making him flinch. "Yes," he repeated more loudly.

"And what directorate is this person in, General?"

The floor was tilting under Boyko's feet. "He's *spetsnaz.*"

"Special Forces, I see." The Sovereign eyed Boyko. "And what is his specialty, General?"

You know, you know! Boyko wanted to yell. It was torture drawing this out. "Corporal Levrov is a sniper, sir."

"And you brought him here to, what, finish off the assassination Aliyev's people botched?"

Boyko's tongue seemed to have swollen in his mouth.

"When Anton Recidivich came here alone in good faith."

Boyko felt his breakfast starting to rebel.

The Sovereign nodded to one of his bodyguards, who held out an SPS handgun to Levrov. It was one of the finest pistols in the world, loaded with armor-piercing 9mm bullets. All of the Sovereign's bodyguards carried one. This one was fitted with a silencer.

"Take it, Corporal Levrov," the Sovereign ordered. When Levrov had done so, he turned back to Boyko. "I told you that I detest disputes."

The chanting coming from the first of the morning's services caused the air to vibrate as if they were at the base of a waterfall.

"Corporal Levrov, General Yuri Fyodorovich Boyko is a traitor to his Sovereign and to the Motherland," the Sovereign intoned. "Do your duty."

Without hesitation, Corporal Levrov raised the SPS and, wisely waiting until the liturgy reached a crescendo, fired one shot into Boyko's heart, completely obliterating it.

Afterward, Levrov did the donkey's work in dragging Boyko's body out, using a preplanned route that would keep his death a secret. Two more men arrived to scrub the magnificent tiled floor clean of blood and gore.

When they were alone, the Sovereign looked with disgust at the photos in the black file. "That was a close call, Anton Recidivich."

"Yes, sir."

"Boyko almost succeeded in taking the same path as the Traitor." He meant the unmentionable Lyudmila Shokova. The Sovereign's gaze seemed to penetrate all the way to the back of Gorgonov's brain. "That, Anton Recidivich, is the only close call you get."

"Understood, sir."

"Then it's done." The Sovereign placed an arm across Gorgonov's shoulders. He smiled, taking a deep breath of the stone and incense. "Now let's join the service and give thanks for the dawning of this glorious day."

47

Brenda awoke staring into the eyes of a demon, yellow as citrine. Which was decidedly odd, since she found herself in a beautifully appointed room, full of bright chintz, oversized furniture, paintings of pastoral scenes of the Germany that once was, a Germany that had been obliterated in two world wars.

She was reclining on an old-fashioned European chaise longue with scrolled wooden arms and fringed in earth-toned moiré fabric. In fact, almost everything in the room, which was of generous proportions, was earth-toned, except for the vase of fresh violets on the bureau against a side wall. But maybe, she thought, that sepia glow was due to the strong rays of the setting sun streaming through the west-facing windows. Clearly, the snowstorm had exhausted itself while she was unconscious.

But then there were the yellow eyes that seemed to pierce her to the core. The eyes were embedded in a huge furred head with a long muzzle. The moment she had opened her eyes, the black lips had drawn back from black gums to reveal a set of long yellow teeth, as sharply pointed as the Alps outside the windows. The dog—she thought it must be a dog; she recalled reading somewhere that wolves were not tamable—was massive, black as pitch. Its ears were flattened against the fur of its elongated skull. Not a good sign. Nor was the low menacing growl coming from deep in its throat.

"Good boy," she said automatically, stupidly. "Be a good boy and please stay where you are."

"He will," came a voice that startled her. "As long as you stay where you are."

She turned her head to see a slim-hipped wisp of a man, with an aristocratic mustache to go with his aristocratic bearing, his spine so straight he might have been ex-military.

"Who are you?" she said in a thick voice.

The man slipped into a plush chair across from her that seemed more feminine than masculine. He wore a fitted three-piece suit complete with gold watch chain. There was a flower in his right lapel, as if he had stopped off on his way to a wedding or a funeral. In his left lapel was a silver pin of two ravens beak to beak.

"Nemesis," she said. "Well, at least I know *what* you are."

He crossed one leg over the other at the knee, revealing silk socks. "How are you feeling?"

Brenda studied him while she tried desperately to clear her head of the last tendrils of anesthetic. His skull was narrow, his forehead high, his nose sharp, his lips thin. He had a widow's peak which, along with his jet-black hair, lent him a saturnine aspect. "I very much doubt that you really care," she said in measured tones. "But if you must know, I'll answer your question if you answer mine."

He clasped his hands atop his knee, like a bishop readying a sermon. "Fair enough, I suppose."

"I'm feeling just dandy," Brenda said archly.

He gave her a pained smile. "By 'dandy' I'm assuming you mean 'fine.'"

"Answer my question." Brenda was so aware of the black beast's proximity she had to hold herself together.

She was far more afraid of the dog than she was of the man.

Another pained smile that seemed more like a grimace this time. "I'm afraid not." He rose. "Your faith in human nature is misplaced, I'm afraid." He crossed to the door. With his hand on the knob, he said, "You're not in a friendly place. Nothing good will come of you here. Better you learn that now rather than later."

As he was opening the door, she said, "What about this . . . this *animal*?"

"Oh, you mean Major. He is the scion of a long line of dogs specially bred by the Herr Meister."

"The Master?" she said. "What is this, medieval Germany?"

"Here at Watzmannhaus that is a close enough approximation," the man said with an almost formal nod.

"Don't leave me here with—" But he had already exited, locking the door behind him.

Major's citrine eyes examined her with an inhuman fanaticism that dizzied her. She was barely able to breathe. Her skin crawled.

■ ■ ■

The storm had abated, cleansing the Alpine sky of clouds. The air was washed clean, perfumed now by pine boughs and woodsmoke.

Joachim Wenzel, a retired locksmith, lived in a small, neat half-timbered cottage a half-mile above Berchtesgaden. The opened door revealed a blacksmith of a man with arms like Popeye, a crafty smile, and a glass eye that stared at Evan without blinking. He wore an oil-stained leather apron over a denim work shirt the sleeves of which were rolled up to his elbows. He still smelled of metal shavings and oil.

"*Gnädige* Fraulein, *mein* Herr, good afternoon, and how may I be of assistance?" he said in a soft voice completely at odds with his physical appearance. He sounded as if he still sang in the church choir.

Evan introduced herself. She decided that, for this purpose, Limas would be her personal assistant.

"Ah, yes, Fraulein von Feuer. Please come in." Wenzel stood back to allow them entrance. They stood in a small foyer, off which a steep wooden staircase rose to the second floor. Wenzel led them into a living room with comfortable furniture, a couple of Durer prints, and a stone hearth in which a cheery fire blazed. An intricate cuckoo clock took pride of place on the center of the rough-hewn mantelpiece.

"Markus informed me you might stop by for a chat." He extended a thick callused hand. As Evan took it, his eyes opened slightly in surprise. "I know a workman's hand when I feel it, Fraulein von Feuer. What is your profession, if I may be so bold?"

"I make custom-built sailboats," Evan replied without missing a beat. "Small ones, no more than twenty or so feet in length."

"An old-world profession, Fraulein von Feuer. And a noble one." Wenzel's smile revealed several gaps in his teeth. "I commend you."

Evan thanked him.

"And your father. A hero of the war." His head bobbed. "Markus told me. I trust you don't mind."

"Certainly not."

Wenzel pressed his palms together as if in prayer. "May I offer you a drink? Beer? Schnapps, perhaps? No?" He gestured. "Please make yourselves comfortable."

Evan and Limas chose the sofa, while Wenzel sat in a chair facing them. Between them was the fire.

"Now what would be your pleasure?" Wenzel said. "A memento of the Berchtesgaden your father knew, is that it?"

"Exactly," Evan said.

"Understood."

Wenzel rose, crossed to a magnificently carved Biedermeier highboy cabinet, pulled open the curved doors to reveal an opening where the back panel once was. A safe had been set into the wall, accessible through the open cabinet. Keeping his body between Evan and the safe, Wenzel spun the dial right-left-right, then pulled a lever, which opened the thick steel door. Inside was a cache of Nazi memorabilia the likes of which Evan had never before seen.

Stepping back, Wenzel gestured. "Take your pick, Fraulein von Feuer. These items are not relics. I keep them fastidiously clean; they are all in perfect working order. Even so, I think you'll find my prices more than fair."

Evan stepped up to the open safe to better survey the stockpile of handguns, Hauptsturmführer's caps, medals, SS and Kripo warrant discs, ammo, knives, sheaths, bayonets, belts, even some new packs of RDX C-4, along with timers and the lot, used by Nazi sappers near the end of World War II. Improbably, there was even a pair of officer's boots, as highly polished as the day they were tugged off a dead Obergruppenführer's feet. She ran her fingertips lightly over the items as if to make sure of their authenticity, but kept her eyes on the officer's boots.

"What size are you, Fraulein von Feuer?" Wenzel asked, seeing the object of Evan's gaze. "Perhaps you would like to try them on?"

Evan shook her head. "They're far too large, Herr Wenzel." The thought of stepping into them made Evan's stomach churn. "What I'm looking for in particular is something with the Death's Head sigil on it."

"You have a particular interest in the Totenkopfverbände?"

"My father's interest, really," Evan said.

"Ah, well, in this I must disappoint you, I'm afraid. Every piece of the Death's Head paraphernalia has been purchased by a certain party higher up on the mountain."

"And who might he be?" Evan asked.

She turned around to face Herr Wenzel, the muzzle of whose modern-day Mauser pistol was pressed against the side of Limas's head.

48

The last day of the year, and, oh, wouldn't it be lovely if it was snowing, Butler thought as he drove across the Key Bridge into Virginia, heading north on US-29. Instead, it was in the forties, the sun was shining out of a whitened sky, and birds were flying overhead.

Brady Thompson's country house—estate was more like it, Butler observed as he arrived—was a stately Colonial a bit south of Wolf Trap with a four-column porte cochere out front that could not have looked more like Tara. The Secretary of Defense had finally decided to take a day or two off, he had learned, upon arriving at his office, before he returned in the new year to skin Butler alive.

The five-acre estate was girdled by a high stone wall. Black iron gates, as formidable as any he had ever seen, would have barred the way had they been closed. A large holly wreath hung on each of the gates. He drove through, but almost immediately was stopped by two Secret Service suits with dark glasses and earwigs. *Straight out of central casting,* he thought as he zipped down his window.

One of the suits peered at him, then checked out the entire interior as if he suspected Butler of smuggling something nasty into the Thompsons' compound.

"You've made a wrong turn, sir," he said. "Please back up and turn around."

Butler flashed his ID. "I'm here to see Secretary Thompson."

The suit grunted, turned away, and spoke into his wireless mic. He listened for a moment, then said, "Got it," and turned back to Butler.

"I'm afraid the Secretary is otherwise engaged," he said with no inflection at all. "You can make an appointment to see him after January second. Just call his office."

Butler smiled sweetly. "I'll see him now, if you don't mind."

The suit's face hardened like baked clay. "Sir, this is the last time I'll tell you. Back up and turn around. You have no business here."

He turned up the wattage on his smile. "Ah, but I do. Please inform the Secretary that Benjamin Butler is here—"

"I did that already, sir, and was told—"

"Tell him that I'm here with General Boyko."

The suit peered into the interior of his vehicle again. "You're alone, sir."

In an instant, Butler's smile vanished behind gathering clouds. He had no more patience with this clown. "I'd hate to be in your shoes if the Secretary fails to hear what I have to tell him."

The suit seemed about to reply, then thought better of it. Shrugging, he contacted his base again. There was a longer wait this time, presumably because whoever he had communicated with had set off to find Thompson and give him the news directly.

At length, the suit gave the impression of listening to the voice coming through his earwig. "Right," he said. Addressing Butler, he said, "Go on through, sir. The Secretary will see you in the Blue Room."

The Blue Room, Butler thought. *This man has the same delusions of grandeur as the Sovereign.*

He drove on, parked in the front court between a Porsche Panamera and a Ford Expedition. The interior of Thompson's country house was as grand as the exterior, filled with crystal chandeliers, rosewood side tables, expensive furniture, and, most amusingly to Butler, portraits of several presidents, including Ronald Reagan and Bush Sr. Everything was perfectly symmetrical: two of everything, as if the place had been decorated by Noah.

A young man dressed from head to toe in Ralph Lauren met him at the front door and led him down wood-paneled hallways to the Blue Room, whose walls were, unsurprisingly, painted a robin's-egg blue. The sofas and chairs were upholstered in sapphire leather. Even the carpets had blue backgrounds. Two cherrywood sideboards took up one wall, a trio of windows overlooking a lawn down to a pool, covered now, made up another. Opposite the windows was a massive oak desk, to one side of which was an American flag on a gilded flagpole.

Butler was staring out the middle window when he heard a rustle behind him, causing his skin to raise in goose bumps. It was like being back in the field. He did not turn around, even when Thompson said: "You have one helluva nerve, Butler. You know that?"

When he turned into the room to face Thompson the same high-wattage smile he'd fed to the guard at the gate wreathed his face.

"Good to see you too, Brady."

Frowning, Thompson took a step toward Butler. "Why you insolent—"

"Shut up and listen to me." He slipped out the folder he'd kept hidden under his long overcoat. "What I have here is chapter and verse on your recruitment by the Kremlin."

Thompson's upper lip curled. "You're insane."

"First by the SVR, then the GRU," he continued relentlessly. "Specifically General Yuri Fyodorovich Boyko, head of the GRU, who somehow poached you from the SVR."

He shrugged, ignoring Thompson's goggle-eyed glare. "No matter which way you slice or dice it you're the Kremlin's top asset inside my federal government." He raised the file, waving it at him as if it were a miniature of the flag hanging limply beside his desk. "I've got hold of it all, Brady, every stupid, venal misstep you made on your road to perdition."

"Give me that." Thompson snatched the folder from Butler's outstretched hand. As he leafed through it beads of sweat stood out on his forehead and upper lip. Sweat ran down from his receding hairline, stung his eyes, making him blink rapidly. "Lies," he said. "All lies. And I can prove it."

Butler studied him without an iota of pity. "I'm afraid you can't, Brady. Everything in there has been verified, including the encoded communiqués between Boyko and you." He shook his head. "There's nowhere to run, nowhere to hide."

Thompson wiped the sweat out of his eyes. "Okay, well, I suppose you want me to squash the hearing in exchange for this. I can do that. I'll call Willis off."

Butler gave him a pitying look. "My dear Brady, you're thinking way too small."

Thompson blanched. "You're not going to go public with this. I'll be ruined. Think of my family, for the love of God."

"You should have thought of them before you became a traitor."

"I was already in too deep. I had sunk so much money into Moscow properties. They dazzled me with their plans and designs. It looked like a slam dunk."

"They made it look like a slam dunk."

"Hindsight is twenty-twenty," Thompson said bitterly, unwilling or unable to take responsibility. A typical narcissistic trait. "And, Jesus Christ, I knew what would happen to me if I tried to back out. I'd seen the stories of the deaths of certain federal employees in and around DC. Hit-and-run accidents, food poisoning, one a suicide. Accidents, they were called, but I know better. No, my control gave me no choice."

"There's always a choice."

Shoulders sagging, he shook his head. "Not for a man in my position." He looked suddenly too small for his impeccably tailored suit.

"Then there's really no choice for you now, either, is there."

An odd pleading note came into his voice. "You're going to ruin me, aren't you?" Clearly, he was very frightened.

"On the contrary, Brady, I'm going to give you back your life—almost. I have another role for you to play."

Thompson stared at Butler, dumbstruck. He wanted to say something, but the words seemed stuck in his throat.

"I'm going to keep you in place," Butler said. "Everything will remain as it was—except for the cancellation of the hearing. Oh, and walking back your previous statements and giving me your full support, of course. You'll proceed as if nothing untoward has happened. Your communiqués with Boyko will continue, with this one exception: you'll pass on to me every instruction you're given. And when you, yourself, contact Boyko it will be with intel that I personally give you." His gaze skewered Thompson. "Is all this clear?"

Thompson backed up, half-fell clumsily into a chair. His hands were so limp that the damning file fell to the carpet.

"Brady," Butler snapped.

"Yes." His head came up. "Yes, you've made yourself perfectly clear."

"Good." Butler smiled at him. "How do you contact Boyko?"

Thompson sighed. "A private encrypted mobile phone is sent to a PO box every two weeks."

"The PO box is in your name?"

He shook his head; he already looked defeated. "A cut-out. I don't know who it is. He—or maybe she, who knows—leaves the mobile for me in a specific spot at a specific time."

"Where's the current phone?"

"Right here." Thompson reached inside the breast pocket of his suit. "I keep it with me at all times."

"Okay, then." Butler held out a hand. "Give it here."

"What, now?"

"No time like the present."

Without another word, Thompson handed over the mobile.

"I'm going to have this device cloned. Whenever you use it I'll be able to hear or see the entire conversation. Every time you're given a new mobile you'll contact me via a system I will give you verbally. You'll memorize it."

"And then what?"

"Then we'll clone that one. And on and on."

Thompson gave him a quizzical look. "You mean you're not going to take me into custody?"

"Oh, no." Butler grinned. "You're much too valuable an asset to roll up. Besides, if I burn you, the Russians will just find someone else to take your place. No, everything will stay just as it is. With the exception that everything the Russians ask you to do I'll know about it. And, from time to time, I'll be asking you to give your control bits of intel."

"*Dezinformatsiya,*" Thompson said woefully.

"Welcome to the wonderful world of the double agent, Brady." Butler's grin widened. "Now how about inviting me to lunch? I'd so love to meet your family."

49

They came for Brenda before the light had completely fallen from the sky, two brawny men with military crew cuts, blond, blue-eyed. Aryan through and through. They said not a word as they stepped smartly into the room in which she was incarcerated. Taking up places on either side of the open door, they stood still as statues. Brenda saw a shadow moving in the hallway beyond, then a sharp whistle, high-low-high, and Major turned tail, trotting out of the room. His departure left a distinct absence, as if a black hole had been erased from this sector of space. Without any conscious volition she gasped, sucked in a breath, let it go, feeling a sense of relief so profound tears sprang to her eyes.

By that time, the two men had crossed to her, lifted her by her arms and marched her out. They stood guard outside the small toilet while she urinated. It took a while, so overfilled was her bladder; much of her time near the end of her stay had been spent in blocking out the building pain.

Afterward, she splashed water on her face, the back of her neck, luxuriating in the feel of the cool water running down her back and chest. She wished she could take a shower; she smelled like roadkill. The stink of fear was worse than anything; it shamed her.

Back outside, she was led along the hallway, down a gilt and marble staircase that looked as if it belonged in Versailles. On the main floor, they went through several rooms, including a sumptuously furnished library that would have done any men's club in London proud.

Through the enormous kitchens, out the back, past what appeared to be herb and vegetable gardens, now slumbering peacefully beneath a half-melted blanket of slush.

Ahead of her she could see an open space perhaps half the size of a parade ground. On the near side a wooden chair had been placed. She was pushed down onto it. Her two guards stood on either side of her.

The moments ticked by. With each one she grew more apprehensive. Even though she knew at their base all the things to which she was being subjected were straight out of the interrogator's handbook, she had to admit they were starting to get to her. And when Major appeared from behind her, his approach muffled by the snow cover, her heart fairly skipped a beat. Something she had seen in his eyes, as if he were the embodiment of pure evil, plucked the strings of atavistic terrors in the most primitive part of her brain.

Someone brought a large wire cage, set it down on the opposite side from where Major sat unnaturally still, unnaturally patient. Then she saw a hand stroke the fur of Major's back. She tried to turn, anxious to identify its master, but one of the guards gripped her shoulder so hard she winced. The person behind her, one hand still on Major, slapped her cheek hard. The wordless admonition was clear: eyes front.

One of her guards left her side for a moment, knelt beside the cage, and released whatever was inside. In a flash, she saw the fox, its thick ruddy tail bobbing as it sprinted across the open space. Moments later, Major's master took his hand off the dog's back, and the beast leaped after his prey as if shot from a cannon.

It took little time for Major to overtake the speedy fox. Grabbing it by the scruff of its neck, Major tossed it into the air. The instant it landed, Major was on it. His great head bent and, in the peculiar stillness of the onset of evening, Brenda could hear the crunch his great jaws made as he ripped out the fox's throat.

"There," the voice came from the man standing behind her, "that's how it's done."

And Brenda knew that she was looking at her own end.

■ ■ ■

"Be so kind as to tell me your real name, Fraulein." Wenzel gouged the muzzle of the Mauser so hard into the side of Limas's head that Limas gave a tiny gasp. "Or I shall be forced to blow your personal assistant's brains out."

"Go ahead," Evan said brightly. "He's pretty, but he's lousy at his job. I was going to fire him when we got home, but you can save me the trouble."

"What?" Limas almost yelped.

He started so violently that Wenzel, surprised as well, glanced at him. In that instant, Evan threw the SS knife she had plucked from the safe before she'd turned around. It buried itself to the hilt in Wenzel's side, and the German collapsed, his mouth agape.

Limas's face was white and drawn. "Were you really going to let him shoot me?"

"What d'you think?" Stepping forward, Evan pushed Limas away, crouched down beside Wenzel.

"Who bought up all the Totenkopfverbände memorabilia?"

Wenzel was in shock. His mouth worked but nothing emerged except a sound akin to someone gargling. Both hands were pressing against the sides of the wound.

There was a minimum amount of blood seeping out of him.

Evan slapped his cheek hard to focus him. "Herr Wenzel, be so kind as to tell me who is hoarding the Death's Heads." When no reply was forthcoming Evan slowly curled her fingers around the hilt of the blade. "Herr Wenzel, you're an old hand at war, I can see that. A veteran of the Fatherland like my imaginary father. You know what will happen if I pull this knife. You'll bleed out in a matter of minutes. There won't be anything I or anyone else can do to save you."

Wenzel looked at her. His upper lip curled in a snarl, but he said: "The place you want is Watzmannhaus."

"The headquarters of Nemesis."

Wenzel squeezed his eyes shut and nodded. His breathing had become labored, his breath stentorian, like a longcase clock whose works were rusting away.

"And who—?"

"Herr Doktor Cuervos," Wenzel managed to get out. "Or should I say Señor Doctor Allis Cuervos. Returned from Argentina. But originally from fine Nazi stock. Bavarian through and through. His real name is Allis Riefenstahl." His livid lips curved upward into a ghastly parody of a smile. "Yes, his grandmother was Leni, the genius filmmaker, favorite of Herr Joseph Goebbels." He paused to see the effect his reveal had on the two imposters. Evan showed nothing, but Limas raised his brows, either in disbelief or amazement. Apparently choosing to believe it was the latter, Wenzel went on. "Nowadays, the good Herr Doktor lives in a red-brick mansion a quarter mile farther on, then turn left. For all the good it'll do you."

The room spun in front of Evan's eyes. Suddenly, all she could see was that red-brick mansion; all she could smell was the stench of blood, guts, and fecal matter overlaid by the acrid odor of carbolic and bleach; all she could hear was a man's voice intoning, "*Get up, get up, get up,*" as if it were a mesmerist's spiel rather than an order. Evan—*that* Evan—could only think *Get up,* and keep on doing what she had been doing, using every muscle in her body, every fiber, every cell of her being to continue the task that had been set before her . . .

"Then you don't know." Wenzel was speaking, but it sounded as if he were coming from a long way off.

She heard someone else, Limas most likely, saying, "Know what?"

"That's not why you're in such a rush?" Wenzel answering, like a bell tolling in a distant valley. "They have the woman."

Limas moved, brushed against Evan's shoulder. "What woman?"

Evan, coming slowly back to herself, to the present, saw Wenzel staring at Limas. "What was her name now? Oh, I don't know . . . maybe . . . No, that's not it." The malicious expression on his face was proof, if any more was needed, that he was deliberately drawing out this last bit of knowledge he held over them. He tried to move, groaned as he lapsed back against the sofa leg. "And then again, you may not know her, or even care what they're doing to her, let alone whether she lives or dies." He shrugged, and winced in pain, breathing hard through his half-open mouth. "So then possibly I shouldn't even bother to speak her name."

"No!" Limas crouched down. "You'll tell us her name."

Wenzel was laughing silently, his eyes alight with a fanatic's pale fire. "Oh, yes. *He* wants to know. Your shitty assistant. But I forget, he's not really your assistant, though I am becoming convinced that he's as shitty as you said."

Limas made a lunge at Wenzel, but Evan held him back.

"Poor boy," Wenzel said. "He so wants to know." His

gaze shifted. "And do you, as well, Fraulein Whatever-your name-is?"

But Evan heard the voice commanding her, "*Get up, get up, get up* . . ." Her stare was so implacable that Wenzel blinked, swallowing hard. "He's not like you, *gnädige* Fraulein, is he? No. Sad for one of you, but which one, I wonder?" That silent laugh again. "But now I remember her name, so why delay any further?" He looked directly at Limas. "Myers, isn't it? Brenda Myers."

At the mention of Brenda's name Limas leapt at him, outstretched hands like claws, but Evan again held him back.

"Hold on, Peter. He's wrong." Part of her knew she wasn't thinking clearly.

"Mm, but I'm not," Wenzel said thickly. "Not by a long shot." With great difficulty he clucked his swollen tongue. "And what they're doing to her, well . . . you can't even imagine."

But Evan could. She thought of the four agents strung up by their ankles, their throats ripped out. By what? She could feel Limas shaking like a leaf in a gale, and knew he was thinking the same thing. Evan let go of the knife handle. She'd gotten more than she'd expected out of the German. Time to head up the mountain to the red-brick mansion, to Watzmannhaus.

But Wenzel wasn't finished. A defiant look distorted his face. He puckered his lips and spat at Evan. "Heil Hitler!" he cried.

With an animal cry, Limas reached around Evan and pulled out the blade.

50

Brenda was taken inside, but the image of Major returning to his master, the bloody pulp of the fox's throat in its mouth, remained, as if seared on the backs of her retinas. She was deposited in the plush library and told by one of her guards, "Sit anywhere you like."

She chose the high-backed chair closest to the hearth, where a fire snapped and crackled. She leaned forward, warming her palms. The heat was a balm on her cheeks and forehead. A tray was brought. Despite her desperate situation, her determination to survive was unabated, and her body needed fuel. The food and drink on the tray made her mouth water. With the first bite into the cabbage leaf stuffed with venison she nearly groaned in ecstasy. There were thick slabs of coarse black bread and deep-yellow butter, bratwurst and sauerkraut, all washed down with rich black coffee laced with schnapps.

When she was finished, had wiped her lips with the cloth napkin provided, the tray was whisked away. A second pot of coffee, an enormous mug, and a small glass beaker of cream was set on the small round table at her right hand. Then she was left alone, but not for long—certainly not long enough for her to explore the room, let alone find a way out of the house.

Major was the first into the library. She was half out

of her chair, on her way to one of the draped windows, and she froze in the glare of those wicked eyes. The creature stood in the doorway, poised, she was certain, to attack, until she relapsed back into the chair. Then he padded across the jewel-toned rug to crouch by the side of the chair, the twin of the one she sat in, which was set on the opposite side of the fireplace.

Again, she was hyperaware of the moments ticking by. She felt her heart throbbing in her chest, felt the delicious food she had just eaten start to rise up from her stomach as her belly clenched tight. All of a sudden, the room felt overheated. She could scarcely breathe.

Then, all at once, like a wraith appearing out of thin air, Major's master sat down beside the dog.

▪ ▪ ▪

Perhaps Evan could have stopped Limas from letting Wenzel bleed out; perhaps she should have, but she didn't.

Get up, get up, get up . . .

Retribution? She didn't know. She wouldn't know until she was once again inside Watzmannhaus.

"That fucking Nazi might well have shot me!" Limas was still clearly shaken up by his latest brush with death.

"There was no chance of that." Evan was making another inventory of Wenzel's weapons cache. She needed to keep her head clear. She needed to barricade her mind against the waves of revulsion that beat against her consciousness with escalating insistence. "He wanted something from me." She grabbed a bunch of items she felt it prudent to take. "As long as I didn't give it to him you were safe as houses. That's how you Brits say it anyway."

Evan searched around, found the battered leather satchel Wenzel used to carry his tools to and from his shop. It smelled of oil and cold metal. Dumping out the tools, Evan shoved the items inside, turned back to Limas. "If I was going to sacrifice you, Peter, I'd let you walk out the front door right now."

Limas peered into the small foyer. "Why? What d'you mean?"

"The moment Wenzel told me that Cuervos had bought up all the Death's Head paraphernalia I knew that bartender Markus was a member of Nemesis. He was displaying a Mauser 98 sniper rifle on the rack behind the bar. He said it had a Death's Head insignia on it."

"So this prick here was Nemesis as well."

Evan nodded. "And since he knew about Brenda, he had obviously contacted someone at Watzmannhaus. I have little doubt that Cuervos sent a couple of his agents down the mountain and that they're out front right now."

"Do you think he was telling the truth?"

"About Brenda? It's certainly possible."

Limas grabbed his hair with both hands. "How did I get here?" he cried. "How has all this happened?" He shook his head. "Was this all set up by Aunt Lyudmila? She showed me your photo, told me to find you if something happened to her. It did, and I found you. And now I'm here on this dreadful mountain with its hideous history." He stared at Evan. "Part of me feels like a chess piece being moved around a board by an unseen hand—my aunt's hand."

He sat down on a chair, his foot struck part of the corpse, and he recoiled. "Evan, Evan, what are we going to do? If Nemesis really has captured Brenda, there's no time to waste."

"On the other hand, it might be part of a trap."

Peter jumped up and strode rapidly around the room. "Well, which is it?" He sounded distraught. "You always know what to do! What do we do now?"

"Keep away from the windows," Evan ordered. "Whoever is out there is most likely waiting for a prearranged signal from Wenzel."

Limas stopped pacing and glared at her. "So, what,

we just sit here while Brenda is—I mean, God alone knows what they'll do to her."

"Calm down, Peter." Evan, who was having more and more difficulty holding herself together as she contemplated revisiting a long-forgotten nightmare from her past, focused on the immediate situation. "We'll walk out of this house."

"Really?" Limas's attempt at a laugh turned into a sob. "I don't see how."

"Neither do they. And that's our edge." Evan was loading a Mauser from the wall safe. "Do you know how to use one of these?"

"More or less."

"Let's hope it's more." Evan handed over the weapon.

"Now what?" Limas asked. "We make like Butch Cassidy and the Sundance Kid?"

"Now we call the mobile number we got from Amiran's phone."

"What the hell?" Limas said when Evan held out her mobile.

"Take it."

"Why?"

"You're going to speak with Cuervos."

"Me?"

"I told you, Peter, you're now part of the solution. Punch in the number."

"And then what?"

"When Cuervos asks who you are tell him you're Peter Myers, Brenda's brother."

"What? No. He'll check."

"He won't," Evan assured him, although she wasn't at all sure that Cuervos wouldn't, but right now she didn't have a better idea. She gave the ploy better than even odds. "The only thing that will catch his attention is your keen interest in Brenda. He'll want to use that interest. I'm betting he'll be curious enough to invite you up to Watzmannhaus."

"Assuming he does," Limas said, "where does that leave you?"

"I'll be going with you."

"I doubt the good Herr Doktor will appreciate that," Limas said, appropriating Wenzel's phraseology.

"Oh, he won't," Evan said. "Of that I have no doubt at all."

Just then Evan's mobile vibrated. Limas stared at it, then handed it over to Evan. When Evan took it, she saw a brief text message from Butler: THE ATTACHED TWO PHOTOS BELONGED TO VORON. BRENDA FOUND THEM IN THE BOMB-MAKER'S WORKSPACE. Evan, looking first at the one of the young man in uniform, recognized the Bavarian Alps in the background to be the very area where they now were. Zooming in on the young man's face, she thought she caught a hint of someone familiar but then the sensation slipped away, and the face looked like many others she'd seen before. As for the big black wolflike dog who dominated the second photo she had no clue. Did it belong to the young man? Had it belonged to Voron before she'd come to America? Impossible to say. When were these photos taken? At the same time or . . . It was only when she zoomed in that she saw the wide leather collar. It was half-hidden in the beast's thick fur, but wasn't that—?

She tilted the mobile, then zoomed in on the collar further. Which was when she saw the glimmer of the two embossed silver ravens, the sigil of Nemesis.

■ ■ ■

"My name is Dr. Cuervos," he said in an accent so odd Brenda couldn't place its origin. "And you are Brenda Myers."

"How do you know that name?" she queried him.

"But since we're destined to be intimates, you must call me Allis, Brenda."

"I'm not Brenda Myers, whoever that is."

"Feeling better, are we?" Dr. Cuervos possessed a most disconcerting smile. It made him seem like the friendliest person in the world.

"I'll feel better," Brenda said, "the moment I walk out of here."

He was a slender man who had clearly once been athletic. He had close-cut steel-gray hair, wide-apart eyes, clever and curious. He wore jeans, a starched white shirt, and black boots, polished to a high sheen. Affixed to one collar was the now familiar pin of the two silver ravens, beak to beak. He sat at ease, one leg crossed over the other at the knees. His hands lay on the armrests. Their backs were black with hair almost as wiry as Major's coat.

"I'm afraid that isn't going to happen, Brenda. At least, not anytime soon, and certainly not in the condition you're in now."

He gave her a hard look, a deep chill racked her, and it was at that precise moment she realized something quite important. "I've seen you before."

"I rather doubt that."

"But I have. A photo of you. As a young man." She paused, thinking. "And come to that, I've seen Major before, also in a photo."

Dr. Cuervos cocked his head, still watching her . . . like a raven.

"Yes, they were on a wall in a barn. I took photos of them just before I killed her."

"Killed who?"

Those two words seemed forced out of him, which gave Brenda, at least, some small measure of satisfaction. Until, that is, she said, "Voron."

The moment she named her victim she knew it was a mistake from which she might never recover. Allis Cuervos's face grew red. An odd kind of ugliness invaded it, as if something from another world or another part of his brain had taken hold of him, turning him into a completely different creature altogether. As if he had taken on the aspect—no, even more—the personality of Major. When he opened his mouth Brenda could imagine the fox's bloody throat caught between his teeth.

■ ■ ■

Evan handed her mobile back to Limas. "Okay. Make the call to Cuervos now."

Limas, seeing that he had little choice but to acquiesce, activated the mobile's screen. Up came the photo of the young uniformed man with the Bavarian Alps behind him.

"Is this what you were just sent?" he asked.

"Yes. It's a photo Brenda found. It belonged to the woman who made the car bomb. Why?"

Limas's brows knit together in concentration. "I've seen this photo before—or at least one like it."

"How is that possible?" Evan asked.

"It was one of a handful Aunt Lyudmila showed me when I was in London." He looked up at Evan, his face ashen. "Jesus Christ, Evan, this is my father."

51

As Cuervos rose from his chair Major emitted an unearthly growl aimed directly at Brenda. Cuervos bent from the waist, gripped the arms of her chair as if he were about to rip them off, and loomed over her. Face-to-face, he smelled of cigarettes and woodsmoke and a kind of animus as corrosive as battery acid. His lips pulled back from his teeth in the same malicious rictus as that of Major. *Maybe,* Brenda thought to help keep herself sane, *this was as close as he could come to smiling.*

"We suppose you're wondering how it became known that you were coming, *when* you were coming, *where* you would cross into Bavaria. And, we suppose, *how* you could possibly be found out, since you were traveling under legend." He watched Brenda carefully, gauging her reactions. "Yes, one can see that you're curious to know the answers to these questions; how could you not be?" The tip of his tongue emerged from between his teeth, wet his lips as if he were about to dig into a long-awaited plate of food.

"You were under surveillance, Brenda. You remember Dr. Selsby, don't you? The doctor who treated you, yes? So kind he was, so understanding that you told him everything that happened to you down on the farm, yes? And he counseled you, didn't he?"

"He told me to stay home." Brenda, regaining her voice, found it thick and uncertain, a consequence of the mounting shock adding now to the multiple traumas she had recently suffered. "He said I needed bed rest."

"He wasn't lying. You did. You do. But did you listen to him? Of course you didn't. You did the opposite. But, this is your personality, is it not?" His intense scrutiny of her face was making her heart flutter in her chest. Or maybe it was what he was telling her, that Dr. Selsby, the doctor she had, at low ebb, confided in was Nemesis. *Likely both,* she thought with an internal gasp.

"In the parlance of the hunt, Dr. Selsby is what is known as a beater. He beat the bush in a way certain to drive you here, toward this very confrontation."

"Why?" Brenda's throat was very dry, but she was damned if she was going to ask him for water—for anything, come to that. "What am I to you? I'm just a cog in a machine. A very specialized machine that has you in its sights."

Now a smile broke across his lips, like an invader storming a castle. "A cog you may be, Brenda. But, oh, what a *special* cog you are." He was gripping the arms of her chair so hard his knuckles turned bone white. "You want to know what makes you special. Of course you do." His head extended on its neck so that their noses were almost touching. "What happened down on the farm, Brenda? You encountered someone. You killed that someone."

"Voron."

"Her operational name."

"She made a bomb that almost killed me. She killed my partner."

"Your *partner.*" Cuervos nearly laughed. "She ended the swinish life of another *Jew.* A *heroic* act to be celebrated."

Brenda looked at him as she would a poisonous wolf spider. "She was a murderer."

"Trained by us. One of our specialties is death."

"Who are you, really?"

"Dr. Allis Cuervos."

Brenda laughed. "Ah, no. You have the Slavic eyes and cheekbones—"

"Since it no longer matters, the name we were born with is Arkady Illyich Shokov."

Brenda's heart skipped a beat. "Wait. What? Shokov? As in Lyudmila Shokova?"

"Ah, yes. My most likely late unlamented sister. Dr. Allis Cuervos is our *operational* name, just another part of the legend of a scion of the hidden Fourth Reich out of Argentina." His head moved again, and she flinched as his lips grazed her ear. "You murdered our daughter, Brenda. And for that you must pay most dearly."

Brenda gasped. "Your daughter? But I don't know your daughter!"

Arkady Shokov hissed. His expression turned bitter. "Voron was her operational name. It was Illyena Shokova you murdered."

The sudden chaos of Brenda's life threatened to overwhelm her. She felt panic and terror lapping at her thighs. If they rose any higher she would be lost, truly lost. Into her mind came images of her father. That was inevitable, of course. Coming home from a high school date that had gone wrong—the soft kisses turned suddenly into grasping, then groping. Her breasts squeezed, nipples pulled, a hand snaking up her thigh, pushing aside her underwear. All the while saying, *No, no, no!* And Alan, like a wild beast, grinning, saying, *You want it, I know you do. You think you're the first girl I've been with?* Then she had bitten down on the fleshy part of his hand between thumb and forefinger so hard blood gushed up and he wailed. She had fled the overheated car, crying and gasping. Running, running all the way home. Only to find her father on the living room sofa with a topless woman astride him, while her mother was in Maine, visiting her sister and nephews.

Focus, she ordered herself sternly, pushing down on the nausea that threatened to undo her completely. Focus on getting intel from him. "If you wanted me dead, why didn't you instruct Dr. Selsby to do it in the hospital? It was the perfect place."

"Perfect? Ah, no. A public place like that was so far from perfect it was untenable. Your death would have triggered an immediate investigation, one in which Dr. Selsby certainly would have been ensnared and quite possibly caught. I need him in place, undiscovered. One of our ravens that bring us useful information periodically.

"Far more important is that when we said you must pay most dearly we meant at our hands. Consider the person dropping bombs from an airplane or the operator directing a drone strike: death can be either anonymous or personal. Allow me to assure you that there will be nothing anonymous about your death." He reached down to stroke the raised hackles of Major's neck. "It will be very, very personal, indeed."

■ ■ ■

"I don't understand this photo," Limas said. "What was that bomb-maker doing with it? I mean, both my parents died when my sister and I were young."

"Voron had two photos," Evan said. "You need to look closely at the shot of the dog." She showed Limas the photo, zoomed in on the dog's collar. "What do you see there?"

Limas's eyes opened wide. "Nemesis's sigil."

"Right," Evan said. Ever since she'd noticed the Nemesis sigil on the dog her mind had been furiously at work, making all the possible connections, correcting, then working out more. Voron. Russia. Bavaria. Berchtesgaden. A young soldier. Lyudmila's brother's posting. The dog with the sigil. Now was the time to take the plunge into the deep water and see what floated and what drowned. "So tell me, Peter, what if the dog belongs to your father?"

"What?" Limas's eyebrows shot up. "That would mean . . ."

"That your father didn't die as you believed. It would mean that he's still alive."

"But why would Aunt Lyudmila tell me—"

"Lyudmila was a complicated woman, with complicated motives. She was divided between the East and the West, with one foot in each place. As I've said, she loved Mother Russia, but she hated how it was being governed. This put her in an extremely perilous situation."

Limas shook his head. "What does that have to do with my father?"

"It's becoming increasingly clear that your father was the polar opposite of everything Lyudmila stood for. In that sense, he was Lyudmila's greatest nemesis. I believe your father's intractable nature is what motivated Lyudmila to spirit you away to England."

"But what about Illyena? What about my sister? Why did she return to Russia, when Aunt Lyudmila made sure we were safe in England?"

"That remains a mystery. I'm guessing only your father knows the answer, and I think Watzmannhaus is where we'll find him. He's hidden himself well. It looks like he's the head of Nemesis."

▪ ▪ ▪

"Drink this," Arkady Shokov said.

Brenda twisted her head away from the cup of what looked and smelled like Russian Caravan tea.

"It will make this next part easier," he said, "though God knows you don't deserve it."

Still, Brenda refused to drink the laced tea, pressing her lips firmly together.

"No?" Arkady Shokov shrugged. "No matter." He

stood up in front of her. "Well, you can't say you weren't warned." The punch he delivered to the side of her head came so fast that she had no time to try to duck. She felt a blinding pain as she pitched into a vast hall full of echoes . . .

. . . And then nothing at all until she regained consciousness some unknown time later. Except that nothing looked right. She had the mother of all headaches, blood pounded in her temples, and she felt as if her eyeballs were going to explode. Her shoulders burned; her ankles were on fire, bone grinding against bone.

Whatever she looked at was upside down, and for several long and terrifying moments she was so disoriented that she couldn't even put two coherent thoughts together. She tried to calm herself by looking carefully at her surroundings, which consisted of gray cement block walls, a polished cement floor with a drain in the center. So far as she could tell it was windowless; light came downward from a ceiling she could not see. The space had the stench of old meat and bleach about it.

She closed her eyes, which, oddly, only increased her sense of vertigo. After taking several deep breaths she opened her eyes again, trying now to focus on the bigger picture. And then, through her pain and mounting fear she realized that she was hanging upside down by her ankles. Just like the four agents. The meat stench seemed to rise off the polished floor, which was, she saw now, stained with the residue of human blood that had resisted even the most vigorous scrubbing. All at once, whatever was in her stomach rebelled, came flying upward—or downward—erupting out of her mouth as she retched and retched until her abdominal muscles ached.

Just then, while she was trying to regain her breath, she heard the click-click-click of animal nails on concrete. She smelled Major's muskiness before she saw him, the enormous creature coming into her angle of view. He went right to her vomit, lowered his head, and licked the floor clean.

His head came up and those lambent citrine eyes glared at her. He licked his slick black lips, opened his jaws, the foul stink invading her nostrils as he raised his head to look her in the eye.

52

They burst through the front door firing their weapons. Evan hurled a burning log into the face of the one in the lead. He screamed, dropped his weapon as, hands to his face, he crashed to his knees, whereupon Limas kicked him in the solar plexus, and he did a nosedive onto the rough wooden floor.

It was the second man through the door that Evan was focused on. He was nimble, leaping over his fallen comrade as if he had been expecting serious resistance. His target was Limas, but Evan was already behind him, chopping down on the crease of his neck, paralyzing the main nerve running down his arm. The gun clattered to the floor as he lost his grip on it. He pivoted toward Evan, who struck him again. He staggered back a pace, then came at Evan once more, now swinging a knife in his good hand, the wicked serrated blade glimmering in the firelight. Evan dodged the thrust and buried her fist in the man's throat, cracking through cartilage. The tip of the knife made a second rip in Evan's coat, missing her ribs by a fraction of an inch. Evan grabbed the wrist, twisted it, distracting the agent long enough for her to deliver a debilitating blow to the soft area just below the sternum.

The agent went down and stayed down. His head

swung back and forth as he fought to catch his breath. At least until Evan stood him up. As Limas held a gun on him, Evan ordered him to strip, which he did, all the while begging her not to kill him. She said nothing, let him ramble on, focusing on his voice as she dressed herself in the agent's clothes. The fit wasn't great, but it was good enough, at least in a pinch—and this was a pinch if ever there was one. She looked in the man's wallet for his name: Dieter Paull. Ordering Paull to climb into her own clothes, Evan flipped on Paull's mobile, touched the speed-dial buttons until she found the only one that had been set.

When she heard the voice on the other end of the line, she said, pitching her voice low, in an uncanny imitation of Paull's, "I have the man calling himself Peter Limas." Evan was thinking clearly again; this was the better way to go.

"What about Evan Ryder, Dieter?"

"Dead, sir. I shot her three times through the heart. Even for her that was more than enough."

"Bring the body, along with Limas."

"One more thing," Evan said. "Limas claims his real name is Vasily Shokov."

"And you believe this nonsense, Dieter?"

"Limas says your real name is also Shokov, sir. Arkady Illyich Shokov. But you're Bavarian German just like the rest of us, is that not correct, sir?"

Silence on the line, just a slow, meditative breathing. Then: "Bring him now."

The call was over.

■ ■ ■

"You are going to kill me, aren't you?" Dieter Paull asked in a voice that sounded as if it were filtered through ground glass.

Evan bundled him into the shotgun seat of the

BMW—Bavarian Motors Works, what else?—he and his pal had used to drive down the mountain. His wrists were bound with cord she'd found in Wenzel's kitchen. Now Evan tied his ankles and swung his legs into the car. Limas was positioned in the backseat, gun to the back of Paull's head.

Throwing the satchel into the well of the passenger seat, Evan slid behind the wheel, depressed the brake, and pressed the ignition button. The engine purred like a tame tiger. It had begun to snow again, icy crystals that fluttered down, clinging to the car's hood and windshield. Evan set the wipers to work.

"To answer your question, you won't die," Evan said. "As long as you don't fuck around, as long as you direct us to Watzmannhaus."

"You think Wenzel lied to us?" Limas said.

Evan put the car in gear and made a broken U-turn. "I think if we followed Wenzel's directions we would have had a good chance of running off the mountain."

They joined the main road and drove upward.

"You're on, Dieter," Evan said. "Don't disappoint me."

"Half a mile," Dieter said in a thin, hoarse voice.

Evan followed his directions. The farther they climbed the more difficult it was to see. She drove slowly, though thoughts of Brenda made her want to race upward. No point in getting killed in the process of trying to save her—if, in fact, she really was at Watzmannhaus. It seemed to her that virtually everything Wenzel had told them was a lie.

"When you see the stone and half-timber house on your left—there! Go another two hundred yards and turn right."

"Where does that turnoff to the left take us?"

"The road is very bad there, rutted and extremely dangerous," Paull rasped. "A vehicle went down the mountainside there the night of the first snowstorm of winter.

The weather has been so bad they haven't had a chance to mend the guardrail."

Evan glanced at Limas in the rearview mirror; Limas nodded. It was as Evan surmised: the lie Wenzel had told them was meant to kill them.

The side road to the right came up so quickly in the snow Evan almost missed it. As she made the sharp turn the BMW slewed a bit before the snow tires bit in. This road was a white road—as the Italians call them—paved in gravel, rather than tarmac. A private road. The tires gripped better here. They crunched through the newly fallen icy layer. The road was narrow, certainly not wide enough for two cars to pass each other. Periodic turnouts had been hacked out of the fir trees on either side. The road wound its way a surprisingly long distance, its S-curves making it impossible to see what lay farther ahead than the next bend.

Evan was aware of Paull in the periphery of her vision. The Nemesis agent was sitting up straighter, had set his shoulders. Staring through the windshield, his eyes were flicking back and forth. Several moments later, two members of Die Raben, the First Tribe, in full black leather motorcycle gear appeared out of the firs, trailing snow behind them like fairy dust. Except that fairies didn't carry semi-automatic pistols.

One stepped in front of the BMW, his weapon pointed squarely at Evan, forcing Evan to roll to a halt. The second Die Raben tapped on Evan's window, and she slid it down.

"ID."

"Here's my ID." Evan grabbed his head, slammed it down onto the sill of the open window. As blood spurted, she drove the man's head into the side mirror with such force the skull and the mirror both shattered.

"*Nicht schiessen!*" *Don't shoot!* Evan shouted as she opened the door. The second guard was already moving, tracking Evan with his weapon as Evan took several steps toward him.

"Das ist weit genug!" That's far enough! the Die Raben said, confusion in his voice, clearly straining to recognize this unfamiliar person dressed in familiar clothing.

"Sorry," Evan said, keeping to Bavarian German. "That shitstick called me a fucking Berliner. I don't take that from anyone." Bavarians hated Berliners, thinking them elitists. Berliners considered Bavarians hicks.

The guard's second of hesitation while she spoke was all the time she needed to throw one of the knives she'd pulled from Wenzel's safe. It lodged in the man's throat. His hands flew to his neck, but his breathing had been disrupted and soon enough he was kneeling on the ground beside his fallen weapon. As Evan approached he scrabbled in the snow for the semi-automatic. Squatting down, Evan pulled the knife out and slit the man's throat. Then she dragged him by his feet into the snow-covered underbrush between two firs.

Returning to the BMW, she resumed their slow drive on the winding road. "Feeling better now, Dieter?" she said.

Paull's head sunk down onto his shoulders as if he were a frightened turtle.

At length the road, like all roads, came to its inevitable end. Evan saw the structure looming up in front her—the enormous red-brick mansion. It looked more like the castle of a madman, who had, during its construction, used one architect after another. The result was a jumble of styles: Gothic, Roman, Neo-Classical.

"Christ, the original owner made a right hash of it," Limas said, staring out the window. "What a compete horror show."

In that he was right in more ways than he could possibly know, Evan thought, as she slowed the BMW to a stop. She sat staring at the place—the place out of her past. She wondered, oddly, where the ravens were. Now that she was here, really and truly here, she recalled there was something about the ravens, a sense of soaring, of freedom. Two things she did not have while she was trapped here.

Trapped. Yes, trapped.

She had been trapped here—by whom? Her handlers at the DOD? Why would she have been brought to a DOD black site used to interrogate defectors, exposed moles, and enemy agents? And why didn't she remember the incident except in jagged flashes? Had something been done to her to ensure she forgot the interrogation?

It made no sense. And yet here she was, back at the place that in some way she had yet to remember or understand. She felt rooted to the spot, as if she had been frozen in this position behind the BMW's wheel.

"Evan, what is it?" Limas said.

"Look at her; she's finished," Paull said with a smirk. "It's over for both of you."

That's when Evan turned and hit him so hard his head bounced off the side window. Blood ran from his cracked skull, and his expression went slack.

Limas recoiled into the backseat. "Evan, what's he talking about?"

They entered the parking area in front of the building. Evan pulled in where three other BMWs—all four-wheel drives—stood cold and idle. They were slowly being buried in snow. Maybe the ravens were buried too, Evan thought. She hoped not.

"Keep your gun hidden before you leave the car," she said over her shoulder as she dipped both hands into Wenzel's satchel. "And whatever happens, play along."

Limas craned his neck, peering at Evan, who was now under the dashboard, working away like a sapper herself.

"What are you doing?"

Evan ignored the question. Moments later, she stepped out of the BMW, opened the rear door, grabbed

Limas by the front of his coat so that he stumbled as he emerged. Evan, playing the part of Dieter Paull, kept hold of Limas as they mounted the wide stairs between stout, ugly Corinthian columns that had no business being a part of this monstrosity.

"Are you crazy?" Limas hissed under his breath. "This will never work."

"Luckily, Herr Paull was none too tall," Evan replied sotto voce. "And it doesn't have to work for long."

She held Limas in front of her, obscuring her stature, kept her head down, the brim of her cap obscuring her face.

The oversized iron-bound oak door opened onto a shadowed interior before Evan was even close enough to knock. Pushing Limas ahead of her, she crossed over the threshold.

53

Brenda must have passed out because all of a sudden she twitched, which started her on a short pendulum swing. At the same time, she became aware of a conversation—or, at least half of a conversation. Arkady Shokov was speaking into his mobile phone.

"—believe this nonsense, Dieter?" he said in a tone so sharp she felt the stab of consternation he was able to hide from whomever was on the other end of the call, but not from her.

And then he said, "Bring him now."

Him? Who? she wondered. *Who was Dieter bringing here? Could it be Evan?* Her heart lifted, but only momentarily. He'd said *him*.

And then she felt something cold and wet, and there was Major, so close to her she almost had to cross her eyes to see him. His black snout extended and he sniffed the tender skin of her throat.

She screamed, and was once again pitched into the black pit of unconsciousness.

▪ ▪ ▪

An enormous crystal chandelier lit up the circular foyer. To the left was the library, to the right what everyone who worked in Watzmannhaus called the grand salon, and straight ahead was a sinuous staircase up to the second floor. It was on the third floor, where the ceilings were low and the windows narrow as castle slits that the real work of Watzmannhaus occurred.

The floor of the foyer was imported white Carrara marble—its color signifying the area's salt mines, connected by a vast network of tunnels, most now long abandoned—with the single exception of a large rectangle of local stone set into the center of the floor, fiery with the chandelier's light. Engraved into this block were the words "RAVEN'S NEST," the real name of the place, the one by which someone at DOD had christened it when it had been chosen as one of the organization's black sites.

The sight of the engraving caused a spasm in Evan. A trapdoor opened and she fell through into the past. She fell to her knees, head swinging back and forth as if she had lost control of it.

"Evan, what is it?" Limas crouched beside her, tried to bring her to her feet. "Was Paull right? Is this the end for us?"

And then it was too late. There were too many Die Raben, too many weapons, too much animus, and, when Limas fired off a shot, vicious beatings for both of them.

▪ ▪ ▪

Brenda, roused by the sharp report of a pistol, looked around as best she could. It wasn't a vehicle backfiring, surely. Her shoulders and arms were on fire, and her feet were numb. Her head throbbed as if she were at a death-metal concert.

As best as she could determine she was alone. No guard, no Arkady Shokov taunting her. Not even the feared Major was to be scented, heard, or seen. Something new had been added to the house while she had been unconscious—a sense, a vibration. The taste of salvation maybe. Or was that simply wishful thinking? Either way, she knew she had to find a way out of this situation before Arkady gave the signal for Major to tear out her throat, before he greedily watched her bleed out like a pig at slaughter.

She wondered if Evan was coming for her, and with her, Peter. She wondered if they knew she had followed their path, that she was here. She wondered if they had even made it here yet, if they were on the mountain, if they were close. She didn't want to think about Peter; she thought about Peter. She remembered being in his arms, the ecstasy he had brought her. The darkness that was enfolding them even then.

She shuddered.

She had never thought of herself as a damsel in distress, even in her worst moment in the field when her life was in the balance, and even now, hanging upside down, parched, frightened of the death that had been promised her, she refused to give in to helplessness, the male view of the female condition. For some time she had been husbanding her resources, preparing herself. And maybe being scared out of her wits had added to her strength, rather than draining it.

She was alone and this was the time. Taking several deep, meditative breaths she tried to jackknife her torso upward. She missed on the first swing, came closer on the second, then ran out of steam on the third, getting barely halfway up.

Tears stung her eyes and she cursed herself softly because she was running out of time. The invasive vibrations in the house were building, and because there had been only one shot fired she had to conclude that the intruder—surely Evan—had been unsuccessful, and if that was indeed the case, then Arkady and Major and at least one guard would logically be bringing her to this interrogation abattoir.

Closing her eyes, she gathered herself, breathing slowly and deeply down to her pubic bone, oxygenating her muscles. She steeled her nerve and then one, two, three swung herself upward, this time grabbing onto her calves, holding herself in that position while she swung back and forth, propelled by her effort. Now she walked her hands, one, then the other, up toward her ankles, finally grasping them. Pausing to catch her breath, feeling her heart pound as if it were about to burst through her chest.

She surveyed her new perspective, and her heart sank. There was no way she could see to unknot the cord that bound her ankles. This cord led up to a thick metal hook affixed to the ceiling, one of a line of hooks, identical in size and shape. The one on her right looked loose. Holding on to one ankle she reached out to the next hook in the line with her right hand. Just missed. She began to rock herself as a mother would rock her baby in its cradle. This made holding onto her ankle more difficult than it already was, but on the third swing she gathered enough momentum to hook two fingers, then all of them around the bottom curve of the hook. Her weight caused the hook to dislodge, and on her second yank it came loose.

She was about to try and use the sharp end on her cord when she heard the sound of footfalls in the hallway outside the door. Quickly, she stowed the hook down her trousers. She could hear voices now. With a whoosh of breath she let go with her left hand, and she was upside down again.

Facing the floor once more, she saw the bits of painted ceiling plaster that had fallen when she had dislodged the hook. She set herself to swinging again. The key was turning in the lock. She bit her tongue, hard, steeling herself not to cry out as she opened her mouth, let the blood drop down onto the tiny pile of plaster, covering it. She held her arms outward, using them to balance herself, to kill the swing she had set up.

The door opened.

Major rushed in, his claws clicking on the floor, and before anyone could say a word the animal licked up her blood, the ceiling debris with it. She saw all this in a hallucinatory flash. Split seconds later the room and everyone in it grayed out. The effort she had expended short-circuited her already overtaxed system and once again her world went from everything to nothing.

▪ ▪ ▪

"I can see the resemblance," Evan said.

Arkady Shokov sniffed. "I look nothing like my sister. She's the spitting image of our mother. I, on the other hand, take after our father."

Evan stared at him implacably. "You and Lyudmila have the same eyes."

Two Die Raben had bound Evan to a wooden chair before transporting her like a sultan on a palanquin into the windowless room on the third floor, where Brenda hung like a side of unflayed beef. As for Peter Limas, he had been placed in a corner, bound hand and foot, kept absolutely immobile by Major who sniffed his crotch inquisitively.

Arkady had dismissed his men, who locked the door behind them when they left.

"You did a remarkable job of faking your death."

"Car accidents," Arkady huffed. "Burning, burning bright like a tiger in the night. So bright, so hot that even the teeth melted."

"And what about your wife?"

Arkady's face drifted into a distant smile. He was a darkly handsome man, his looks and manner seductive, whereas Lyudmila's beauty, paired with her obvious and shockingly "unfeminine" ambition, had been intimidating. And yet, they were both charismatic, born leaders.

"How does it feel to be back here, Evan?" Arkady

asking a question that negated Evan's own. "Quite disorienting, I imagine, judging from your extreme reaction downstairs."

"What would you know about that?" Evan said.

"For the love of God," Limas interjected, "cut her down."

Evan winced. That was precisely the wrong tack to take with someone in power. Your anxiety let them know that you were vulnerable to the kind of persuasion Evan did not want Brenda subjected to. She already looked like she had had more than enough to endure. Her immediate goal was to get Brenda down and out of here, but exactly how she was going to do that was a mystery, and one she needed to solve in the next couple of minutes.

And now Arkady turned his attention to Limas, which was another thorny issue. Evan wished Peter would just keep his mouth shut, but truly, how could he? He had come face-to-face with the father he thought he had lost forever when he was young. What must that be like? Evan wondered. How would she feel if her own father suddenly surfaced, came back into her life? As a monster? An impossible question to answer, of course.

She watched Arkady with one eye, while she monitored Brenda's condition with the other. As Arkady stalked across the room to stand behind his animal, Evan noticed a minute flick of Brenda's head. She was staring fixedly at her. Something was up. She was trying to tell her something.

"And you," Arkady's buzz-saw tone cut across Evan's thoughts. His eyes were so wide apart they were unnerving. His head was tilted slightly to one side, as if an operation long ago had tightened the tendons on that side of his neck. His hair was pomaded, as shiny as his highly polished boots, which were of the sort Evan had fingered in Joachim Wenzel's hidden safe. Nazi officer's boots—what had once been known as jackboots. And like a Nazi officer, his field gray trousers were tucked into their tops. The cuffs of his heavy black flannel shirt were open, the sleeves rolled up to his elbows. His forearms were surprisingly muscular and covered with the same wiry black hair that covered the backs of his hands. Lyudmila's brother's face gleamed like a well-tended work of art.

Arkady, leaning forward over his animal: "What the hell are you, anyway?"

"I'm your son, Vasily, Father. Vasily Shokov."

"No, you're not," Arkady snapped. "You're the SVR's lackey. Gorgonov's tool. That's what and who you are."

"You're wrong, Father."

"You're nothing to me. Something that has soiled the sole of my boot." When Arkady slapped Limas across the face, the animal bared its yellow teeth and growled deep in its throat. Evan had heard such growls before a hunting animal was about to spring on its prey.

"You're right," Evan said. "He's nothing. It's me you want, Arkady."

Arkady turned on his heel. "And why would I want you, Evan?"

"You were about to tell me."

One of Arkady's carefully groomed eyebrows lifted. "Was I?" His heels clip-clopped as he recrossed the room to where Evan sat. "I don't recall."

"Of course you do," Evan told him. "You opened the door. You asked me how it feels to be back here."

"I did, didn't I?" Arkady turned around so that with his back to Evan he was facing Brenda. "You know, I haven't decided yet whether to kill her." He spoke to Evan as if Brenda wasn't in the room. "Do you know why, Evan?"

"I can guess."

"Really?" Arkady slid a knife out of its sheath, placed the flat of the blade between Brenda's inner thighs. "Go ahead. You have one guess and one only. If you guess wrong, I'll turn this blade on its edge and begin to cut."

"Evan!"

"Shut up, Peter," Evan snapped.

"That's right, Evan. Peter. Not Vasily. My son died the moment he became Lyudmila's bitch, then went running into Gorgonov's arms like a frightened child."

So Peter had been telling the truth, Evan thought, with an unexpected jolt of something like happiness. She had wanted to believe him, she realized. He really was Lyudmila's nephew. Something stirred inside her at the knowledge.

Brenda's eyes were closed. Evan couldn't tell if she was conscious or not, nor had she any idea how long Brenda had been hanging upside down, or how much longer she could tolerate it. She needed to know that.

"She looks good upside down," Evan said now. "How long has she been strung up?"

"Ah, well . . ." Arkady stroked the blade against Brenda's thigh. "How about this? If you guess right I'll tell you."

"Fair enough."

"'Fair?'" Limas shouted. "How is any of this fair?"

"Evan told you to shut up, Peter." Arkady tapped the knife against Brenda's flesh. "My advice is to listen to her."

"Your advice!" Limas's voice dripped contempt. Nevertheless, he kept quiet after that.

Arkady nodded, as if in response to an inner voice. "Go on, Evan. What possible reason could I have to spare this *espion*'s life?"

"Her name," Evan said. "Brenda is powerful. A name out of Arthurian mythology. Brenna le Fay came before Morgan le Fay, the accomplished sorceress—a match even for Merlin, so it has been written."

"And why should that mean anything to me?"

"The leader of the Third Reich was bewitched by the legends of the ancient Germans, the Celts, who crossed over into the British Isles many times. He believed in magic, Arkady, and so do you. Brenda or Brenna, is the Celtic name for 'raven.' A great misfortune will befall you if you kill Brenda."

Evan still could not see Arkady's face, but Arkady said, "She'd been hanging for thirty-six minutes before you arrived, although I daresay it seems like thirty-six hours to the young *espion*."

"Your Russian slip is showing, Arkady."

With that, Arkady turned around to face Evan. "Russian, German, Bavarian, Argentinian, it's all the same."

"Not to your followers, it isn't. Not to Die Raben, who are Bavarian to the roots of their hair."

Arkady took a threatening step toward Evan. He still held the knife in his fist. "Do you know how I know you were here before?"

"I do."

Arkady looked at her skeptically. "You're bluffing."

"Let's say I am," Evan said. "Then you have nothing to lose by making another wager. If I can't tell you how you know I was here before you can cut me with that knife. But if I can, you'll cut Brenda down."

"Hast du nicht mehr alle Tassen im Schrank?" Have you lost your mind? "Why would I agree to that?"

"Actually, I'm doing you a favor," Evan said. And when Arkady laughed, a bark not unlike the animal's bark, Evan went on: "You must follow the Uthark runic order, Arkady." When Arkady made no comment, Evan said, "It was posited in the 1930s—a theory Hitler picked up on and subscribed to—that the Uthark runic order, a modern interpretation of the ancient Futhark alphabet—creates cyphers, but I'm betting you knew that already."

"What has this to do with—?"

"Everything, Arkady. The Dark Mother, the bringer of necessary but painful change. She's known in India as Kali, Malka-ha-Shadim in proto-Jewish culture, and Maha-Kali in Indo-Germanic tradition. The cypher in the

Uthark runic order, however, reveals that her name is Mórrigan, later corrupted to Morgan. Brenna, the Raven, taught Morgan le Fay all she knew of magic."

She nodded her head toward Brenda. "You also might remember the story of Merlin hanging Brenna le Fay upside down for defying him. An hour after that, King Arthur Pendragon, the man Merlin was sworn to protect, was killed."

Evan's eyes glittered. She held Arkady's gaze as a hypnotist would, praying that this confabulation of myth and fabrication she had made up on the spot would entrap him. "From what you've told me it's getting on forty-five or fifty minutes since you hung her up there, Arkady. You have very little time left."

Arkady's ruddy face had gone bone white. He brandished his knife as he came toward Evan. "Speak, Evan. How is it I know you were here before? Where did that information come from, hmm? Who told me?"

"No one told you, Arkady." In her mind's eye was the photo of the young Arkady Shokov in this very area. She heard again Limas telling her what Lyudmila had said: that his father had been stationed in *Parechgadem,* the old form of Berchtesgaden. "You were here at the time."

Blood flushed Arkady's face again. "If you know all the answers why are you still asking questions?"

"Cut her down, Arkady. Brenna is a human hourglass."

With a snarl, Arkady turned and sawed through the cord that bound Brenda to the hook. She collapsed, and Limas cried out wordlessly. She lay on the floor like a puddle of rainwater, still as death. Evan hoped that she was still alive; she had something important to tell her.

But she needed Arkady distracted for just a few moments more. "Your wife, Arkady. What happened to her?" Evan asked. She almost added that Limas had a right to know, but that would only infuriate the man.

"She went the way of all flesh. Dust to dust." Arkady

had his back to Brenda, but at her fall, his animal had turned, and now, nostrils flaring, he trotted over to investigate. It was clear the beast was already familiar with her scent, and now he had clear access to her.

"That's not an answer," Evan said.

"That's all the answer you or the traitor here will get." His hand came down on the scruff of the animal's neck and immediately he sat, tongue hanging out, pulsing with each panting breath. "The rest you will just have to imagine."

"My imagination is not what it used to be," Evan said, counting down the seconds.

"Ah, yes, the lost piece of your memory. All this—the Raven's Nest—is coming back to you in fragments now though, isn't it." That barking laugh again, like a sea lion. "But I'm betting that you still don't remember what happened to you here. Not really." He stepped closer, leaned in. "Why were you here, Evan? What were you doing?" His eyes glimmered, his lips glistened just like his animal's. "Pissing everyone off, I should think. *Du musst immer aus der Reihe tanzen. You always have to get out of line*. That's your specialty, isn't it?"

There was to be no answer to that question. At that moment, the bomb Evan had rigged under the dashboard of the BMW, made with the three packs of C-4 she had taken from Wenzel's safe, exploded, shaking Watzmannhaus's stone walls as it obliterated the BMW and the ones on either side. As for the third, it was rocked on its heavy-duty shocks, its windows blasted out, its alarm shrieking, and, not more than seventy seconds later, it was engulfed by fire.

54

Arkady lunged at Evan. "What did you do?" But it was only a feint. Turning on his heel, he crossed to the door, knocked in a pattern and, when the door opened, he whistled for the dog, and together they went out to investigate. The door was locked behind them.

"Brenda!" Limas called to her. When she began to move, he said, "Are you all right?"

But she didn't answer; she didn't even glance in his direction. Looking up at Evan, she crawled on elbows to where Evan sat bound to her chair.

When she was near enough, she stuck her hand into her waistband, drew out the hook. With fierce determination she set about shredding the cord attaching Evan's ankles to the chair legs. It parted like the Red Sea, bringing Evan the freedom to rock the chair back and forth, using her feet to generate enough force that when she jammed the chair back against the stone wall it splintered. After that, it was easy enough to free her wrists.

Kneeling down, she untied Brenda's ankles and helped her stand, supported her while she wobbled slightly as the blood flowed back into her blue-white feet. She started to stamp them to counter the surge of pins and needles created by the normalizing circulation.

"I shouldn't have come," she whispered hoarsely. "I was in no shape to take this on."

"Rearview mirror," Evan said, but when she tried to move away to untie Limas, Brenda grabbed on to her.

"If you leave me now, I'll simply fall down again."

So with one arm wrapped around her waist Evan walked her over to Limas's corner. At this point Evan had to let her go in order to work on the cords around Limas's ankles.

Brenda grabbed hold of Limas's shirtfront.

"I'm so happy to see you," he said. "So happy you're alive."

"Are you?" she said as she buried the hook into his abdomen.

"Ak, ak, ak," Limas gaped.

"You betrayed me."

"Ak, ak, ak . . ."

"Your orders from Gorgonov were to get close to Evan so you could kill her."

"Ak, ak, ak . . ."

Evan had jumped up, now gripped both of Brenda's wrists, squeezed one hard enough to force her to let go of the hook. "What are you doing?" she yelled. She pulled Brenda away from Limas, who had collapsed onto his knees like a penitent on the dusty road to Calgary. He was bent over the hook, which protruded from his abdomen like a broken question mark.

When Evan let go of Brenda, she sank down to the floor. Her face was flushed and there was a mad glint in her eye.

"Ak, ak, ohhh . . ."

"I had to do that, Evan." Her voice was a watery trill. "He violated me; he was sent to kill you. I did it for both of us. The exigencies of fieldwork. You must see that."

Evan didn't bother answering her. She was too busy catching Limas before he fell on his face.

"Peter," she said. "Peter . . ."

"Call me Vasily, Evan." His upper lip was peeled back in agony, revealing gums running with blood. "I was Gorgonov's errand boy. My father was right about that." He tried to give Evan a smile, nearly made it. "But I was never meant to kill you. Gorgonov wanted me to be the new Lyudmila for you. He wanted me to become your friend—and I did, Evan, didn't I?"

"Yes, Vasily, you did."

"But that's where it would have ended. I didn't . . ." He looked down at the back end of the hook. "Oooh. Oh, God. I didn't know—I . . . I couldn't know—what it would mean to have you as a friend."

"Stay calm, Vasily. Conserve your energy."

But Vasily was listening only to the voice inside his head now. "Evan, I know I can't touch this hook. I know what will happen if it gets pulled out. I saw it happen, yes, I did."

He looked up at Evan again. His face was deathly pale and there was a terrible sound emanating from his chest, as if he had swallowed a rattlesnake. "I wonder . . ." His eyes were losing focus. "I wonder . . ." The sounds of voices outside the door startled them all, as if they had been inside their own private faraway world since Arkady and the dog had rushed out.

Now they were coming back.

"I wonder." Limas sounded like he was underwater, which, in a way, he was, drowning in his own blood. "I wonder what happened to my mother. Evan, can you please find out?"

Then the grate of the key in the lock, the dog barking continually as it scented fresh blood. These sounds brought Limas back to himself for just a moment, long enough to wrap both hands around the protruding half of the hook and pull it out with a scream and a rending of flesh.

55

Major bounded in first, took one look at all the blood running over Limas, and fixed his lambent gaze on Evan. He launched himself at Evan, fast as an indrawn breath. Evan snatched up one of the shattered chair's legs. She was holding it perpendicular to her chest when Major landed on her. The leg acted like a stake through the heart of a vampire, piercing all the way through the enormous animal's body. Still his huge claws tried to rake Evan, his bared teeth snapped again and again, trying to take off a chunk of her face. She might have bisected his heart but it beat on, black as his fur. Black as his soul.

He was fighting for his life when he had no life. But he was a beast and didn't know that. All he knew was that his prey had hurt him and he had to kill. He tried. He did his best, and there was Evan's blood flowing, coating his claws, dribbling into his mouth, which he sucked up with his tongue. A tongue that went flaccid as the beast shuddered and spasmed. In his citrine eyes, fixed on Evan, was a hatred that went beyond mere malice. There was something inside this animal, something ancient and dreadful. And then it was gone, like a puff of smoke or a spurt of ink, dispersed into the air around it.

He was dead. Finally dead.

Arkady was in the room by this time, and he hurled

himself at Evan, teeth bared, knife blade point first. Waiting until the last instant, Evan heaved the canine corpse up and away, so that it took the stab of Arkady's knife.

Evan took advantage of Arkady being off balance and slammed him nose first against the big black dog's spine. Then she had Arkady in her grip, because the fight with Major, the precipice of death so close, had energized her, the razor's edge between life and death never more vivid and close. She drew the knife out of the beast and held the blade, runneled with blood and gore, against Arkady's throat.

The two guards had stepped into the room, their weapons raised.

"It's not possible." A sere wind in a dying field. "You killed Major." Arkady was almost in tears. "You fucker, Major was magic. Major was invincible."

The guards looked from their leader to his slain familiar. They couldn't care less about two bloody humans; they'd seen too much of human blood and entrails here.

Evan paid Arkady no mind, held him in front as a shield. "Now you're going to help us get out of here," Evan said to Arkady, loud enough for the guards to hear.

Still, Arkady was unresponsive. "Major," he whispered. "Major was magic. Protected by our runic spells."

"Arkady." Evan slapped him hard on the back of the head. "Pay attention, Arkady."

"The car bomb," Arkady said, recovering a semblance of himself. "How did you know to time—?"

"I'm carrying a wireless detonator," Evan told him.

"Impossible. You were searched thoroughly."

Evan spat out a small plastic disc she'd secreted between gum and cheek. "Not thoroughly enough."

"Clever. As clever as you killing Dieter and wearing his clothes." He shook his head. "But all your vaunted cleverness won't do you any good, Evan. Where will you go? We own the whole mountain and everyone on it. Our people are everywhere, armed to the teeth. No one will lift a finger to help you."

Evan pushed Arkady forward. "Help Brenda to her feet. Maybe being kind to her now will keep you from dying today."

Arkady did as Evan ordered, bringing Brenda slowly to her feet. But his muscles were tense and straining. He was readying himself. For fight or for flight? For Evan it didn't matter; she needed to keep her senses alert for either one.

Brenda's head hung down, her hair across her eyes, obscuring her expression. Her breathing was unnatural, and Evan didn't like it. There was no time to waste. She needed to get her out of here as soon as humanly possible.

"*Jetzt sichern!*" *Back up now!* Evan told the guards, who looked to their leader. He gave them a curt nod, and they stepped out of the room.

The three of them moved out. In the corridor, just past the threshold, Brenda grabbed the semi-automatic out of one of the guard's hands. This was Evan's first clue that she had been playing possum, that her powers of recovery were greater than any of them gave her credit for.

Breaking away from Arkady's grip, she turned her back, facing the way they had come. She walked backward, covering their rear.

Down below, the foyer was filled with armed Die Raben.

"Now what are you going to do?" Arkady said. "You can't go down there; they'll overpower you long before we bleed out."

But Evan had no intention of descending into the maelstrom of the Fourth Reich the new Führer was seeking to create. The moment she had awakened in the interrogation room the memory flashes had come fast and furious. She knew that room, had been in there during a time she could not remember.

"Why were you here, Evan? What were you doing?"

Arkady asked rhetorically; clearly he knew: "*Pissing everyone off, we should think. Du musst immer aus der Reihe tanzen. You always have to get out of line. That's your specialty, isn't it?*"

Heading down the corridor, toward the west wing of the Raven's Nest, Evan saw again the two ravens. They flew in front of her, as if leading her on, flickering in and out of the shadows, in and out of focus. She felt a pain she could not name, felt a weight she could not see. Phantoms were all around her. She heard shouting, the sound of pounding feet. Shots, now, and more shouting.

Watzmannhaus was unnaturally still and silent. It was as if the entire structure were holding its breath. And yet Evan's broken memory caused her to hear, see, and feel shards of the past she could not fit together, though she was becoming more and more certain that they were all, in their own ways, vital to her.

How? *How?* If only she could decode the cyphers her brain was receiving.

Something inside her—some knowledge with which she was now intermittently in touch—drove her forward, holding onto the scruff of Arkady's sweat-soaked collar. They passed the top of the staircase down to the second-floor landing. More armed Die Raben started to mount the stairs, staring up at her with implacable hate-filled eyes. She ignored them, pushed on toward the far end of the corridor.

Behind her, Brenda said, "They're close, very close," in a low, rough voice, as if she had been shouting for hours, and perhaps she had, silently, in the depths of her throat.

"Keep them back," Evan said, and immediately Brenda shot two of them in the chest. They went down with a sound like someone dropping a bureau out of a second-story window.

"I told you only to keep them back," Evan said.

"And now they have fallen back," she told her. "They

didn't think much of me, didn't think I had balls. Now they see that I'll shoot them; they're afraid to come closer."

Evan couldn't fault her logic, but it seemed far too easy for Brenda to shoot to kill for her taste.

They had almost reached the corridor's end when Evan stopped them. "Right-hand door."

"It's a guest room," Arkady told her. "There's nothing in there. It's a dead end unless you're considering climbing out the window, in which case you'll be shot the moment you fling one leg out."

"Open the door," Evan ordered. "Now!"

It took a hard shove between the shoulder blades before Arkady complied. They crossed the threshold.

"Brenda, stay in the doorway," Evan said. "Shoot anyone who makes a step toward us."

"It will be my pleasure," she said, in that same low, guttural tone Evan found somehow disturbing. And then she pulled the trigger one more time; more bodies fell. This seemed to energize her. Evan had hardly forgotten that she had so quickly jammed a hook into Limas, but now was not the time to contemplate the ramifications of the murder.

Arkady hadn't lied—the room was a guest bedroom of medium size. It contained a bed, dresser, mirror, a writing desk and chair, and little else beside the door to a closet. There were a pair of small leaded-glass windows. Outside, darkness had fallen and a northerly wind was scraping the bare branches of a sturdy oak against the wall, as if the tree wanted to get in. Evan couldn't think why.

Evan approached the closet. Twisting Arkady around, she opened the door.

"What d'you expect to do?" Arkady's voice had a sharp edge. "Hang us up to dry?"

Ignoring him, Evan pushed away the array of wooden hangers with her free hand. And there they were on the back wall: the two ravens, joined at the beak. At some time in the dim past they had been carved into a panel in the wall.

Reaching in, Evan pressed the carving and the panel swung open. Arkady was so surprised nothing came out of his mouth. Evan pushed him through, into the darkness beyond. Then she called to Brenda.

Brenda squeezed off one more shot, then ducked through the guest-room door, locking it behind her.

"Hurry," Evan said, holding out an arm, guiding her into the closet and through the open panel. Then she closed the closet door and shut out what light remained in the room. In pitch blackness, she moved the hangers back into place, led the three of them through the opening, and swung the panel shut behind her.

56

Evan flipped a wall switch and light flared—a bare bulb hanging from a length of flex—revealing the small semi-circular landing on which they stood. Below them: a circular metal staircase whose flaring treads wound around a central pole.

Arkady looked as if he were about to have a stroke. "How did you know about this place?"

Evan took a long flashlight from a niche in the wall. "Down," she ordered. "You first, Arkady. Brenda, guard our rear."

"On your six, Evan," she said, using the military term.

"Are you steady, Brenda? Are you able to go on?"

"Quite steady, Evan. Trust me."

Evan had no choice but to trust her.

They descended in silence, Evan keeping an eagle eye on Arkady, Brenda on the lookout for anyone clever enough to have worked out where they had gone. They kept going down, farther than the ground floor of Watzmannhaus, lower even than its basement. And still the staircase wound down into what seemed the bowels of the mountain.

"This is how you helped Lyudmila escape!" Arkady stopped, turned back to Evan. "You sonuvabitch. The two of you vanished right in front of our eyes, and this is how you did it."

Evan poked him hard in the small of the back. "Keep going, Arkady."

Arkady turned and continued downward, with Evan and Brenda following. "No one knew it was you, of course. You were disguised as one of Shokova's men; no one knew it was you."

Evan pushed him harder, and Arkady stumbled forward. He wasn't even looking where he was going; he was too enthralled by these revelations.

"But how did you manage it?" His voice was plaintive. "No DOD recruit trained here."

Evan said nothing. Peter Limas had never lied to her; it was Lyudmila who had lied to Peter, turning the real events on their head, saying she had infiltrated this place, rescued Evan. In fact, it was the other way around: Evan had rescued Lyudmila. She was hit so hard with this revelation that she stumbled, and Arkady laughed, believing that her strength was waning. For a moment, Evan lost track of where she was—or, more accurately, *when* she was. In a flash she was beside Lyudmila again, as Lyudmila led her through the tunnels. And with this image—so strong Evan could smell their sweat, hear the drip of water through the mineral—the entire episode came flooding back to her, and she remembered everything. Her heart was beating hard against her rib cage, she heard the blood roaring through her ears. For an instant the world turned upside down. Then, just as abruptly, it was returned to her, like an offering or a gift.

"And yet you knew about this secret," Arkady was saying, "about the way into the salt mines. How? How did you know?"

Of course she now knew: it was Lyudmila who had guided her, Lyudmila her Virgil, holding her metaphorical lamp high through the darkness. Lyudmila who had meticulously done her research, who had told her that the Nazis, über-practical, not to say paranoid, had built escape tunnels into all their houses on this mountain, using the salt mines, so that if they were attacked by Allied bombing raids, they could hide there, safe within the mountain, and, if the worst came to the worst, they could disperse through those tunnels, escaping the invading enemy.

But she wouldn't tell Arkady any of this; let him keep wondering. Like all magic tricks, this one had a simple answer. Instead, this rejoinder: "And you, Arkady. You had already defected by the time you were assigned here, hadn't you?" She had learned that he loved nothing better than to talk about himself. "You were recruited by us—by elements of the DOD."

"They had good use for our expertise," Arkady said, by way of acknowledgment. "We became a room with a unique view into Russian intelligence."

"But you didn't stay long, did you?"

His face screwed up in a sneer. "You fucking Americans. You think you own the world. You think you're better than anyone else when what you do best is export your shit all over the world, dumping your teeth- and mind-rotting products all over us. Your ghastly materialism, your prejudices. Every fucking day you send cluster bombs assaulting us with your rampant consumerism. You shove it down our throats as if we were ducks with fattened livers. What a hateful act." Arkady's face was filled with blood and bile. "The fact is you hate everyone but Americans—white Americans, at that. And to top it off you want our thanks! You want us to bow down to you as our saviors! Christ, you're all insufferable!"

Spittle flecked his lips, turned his chin shiny. "Well, we're the ones with brass balls. We're cracking open American arrogance. We're bringing out your own worst instincts. We're helping to instigate a second Civil War that will tear the country apart. And after that happens, we'll be able to do what the Third Reich failed at. Our army will rise up and destroy whatever's left of you."

"Right now you don't look like you're going to be doing much of anything," Evan said, "unless it's what I tell you."

"You fool! You don't understand anything, so now we will spell it out for you, give you the ABC's as if we were in kindergarten. Nemesis is financed by a cabal of American billionaires, men of an ultra-conservative nature."

Evan was rocked to her core. Could it be true? It certainly was plausible. Also horrifying. Treason at the very heart of America. "Are you telling me that Russia isn't involved?"

Arkady threw her a pitying look. "Of course they're involved. But, by God, they aren't financing us. How could they? The RNU has hardly enough money to hold itself together, and as for the GRU, General Boyko is as abstemious as Scrooge.

"No, it's the America for Americans, the robber baron billionaires that fund us. They are out to emulate the original robber barons like John Jacob Astor, Cornelius Vanderbilt, John D. Rockefeller, Andrew Carnegie, Jay Gould, J. P. Morgan. The men who controlled land speculation, the railroads, shipping, lumber and tobacco, financial institutions, oil, coal.

"Coal!" Arkady laughed so hard tears stood out in the corners of his eyes. "Can you believe it? Coal has been dead and buried for decades. Even the Sovereign knows that." He shook his head. "But not for these American billionaires."

"And the goal of Nemesis?" Evan wanted to keep Arkady talking, telling her more about what she needed to know regarding Nemesis. "Besides thrusting America back into the Middle Ages, I mean."

"What a magnificent goal!" Arkady crowed. "But not all the way back to the Middle Ages, Evan, no, no. Just back to the 1930s. And just like then these modern-day robber barons wish to maximize their profits. To do this, they are manipulating the American political system in order to shield their corporations from federal and state regulations, exempt them from taxes. So they funnel tens of millions of dollars into the campaigns of candidates they control. Spend hundreds of millions to buy up local and regional media—newspapers, radio, television stations—and stock them with personnel to whom they dictate their agenda. And a dull-witted, poor, and poorly educated slice of the country, easily led and manipulated, eats up what they're selling—the resurgence of white America.

"And, of course, that's not all. They're being aided wittingly or unwittingly by evangelical Christians, as fanatic in their own way as the Muslim jihadists." The sardonic laughter ramped up. "Such fools! You see what slaves religion makes of people?

"Ultra-conservative billionaires, powerful evangelicals. They've had enough of liberal America. They're dedicated to a country led by a charismatic tyrant they can control. And we have been in the midst of it."

During this hair-raising colloquy, they had reached the bottom of the staircase. Evan flicked on another switch and they saw the two ravens etched into the floor at their feet.

"What is this place?" Brenda, in a slight daze, was still trying to get her head around the scope and reach of Nemesis, which went far deeper than either she or Butler had ever imagined. Nemesis was not just another terrorist group, not just a German neo-Nazi uprising. It was a full-blown revolution of catastrophic proportions.

"It's part of the salt mines interlaced throughout the mountain," Evan said.

"It looks like a labyrinth." She stared into the hazy distance, where branches led off in at least six directions.

"For anyone not knowing their way, it is," Evan answered. "I don't like the way you're walking, you're wobbling badly. Your ankles are almost frayed raw. Tell me if you can't—"

"What are you going to do, carry me?" Bending down, Brenda unlaced her boots, kicked them off, then shed her socks. She sighed. "Ahh, that's better."

Again, Evan had no choice but to trust her. She didn't see how she could control Arkady and at the same time keep Brenda upright. She indicated which way they should go and they headed out of the landing into the second tunnel on their left. Evan switched on the flashlight. There was another silence for a time. The mineral odors became more and more intense along with a mounting chill and the unmistakable clamminess of the deepest days of winter. Occasionally, they passed thick wooden trestles nailed across pillars that helped hold up the tunnels.

"These must have made good hiding places in the end times of the war," Brenda said.

Evan nodded. "For the Nazis and for the resistance. On their way out, German sappers left booby traps to slow down the Allied infiltration."

When he next spoke, it was clear that Arkady was still on the same track he'd been on since they went through the raven panel. "So this is how you got her away from us."

"From you?" Evan grabbed Arkady's shoulder, whirled him around. "From you, personally? Or the DOD?"

"Why, yes, from us. From us both, you could say." Seeing the surprised look on Evan's face, Arkady laughed. "Ah, you still don't remember, do you? All right, then, we will fill in the gaps in your memory. Lyudmila was captured by DOD agents, brought here for interrogation. We were to be the lead interrogator."

"Your own sister." Evan was aghast. "How could you?"

"*Yebat-kopat,* that's like asking the moon why the sun takes away its darkness." Arkady turned his head and spat. "Lyudmila got the best of everything. She was better than us in school, in sports, in the arts. And with the boys! *Yoptel-mopsel!* They all wanted that bitch. Every one of them. She was like a fuck-magnet. She got the best of us at every turn. Every time I made headway, there was our bitch-goddess, Lyudmila, there ahead of us. Bad enough we were beaten, but by a girl yet! Our sister! *Mein Gott,* what a humiliation. We're so very happy she's out of the picture for good, swallowed up by the world, I expect."

He lifted a forefinger. "Oh, we know what you're thinking, but no one at DOD knew who we really were. Our legend was lock-tight, unassailable." He shrugged. "In any event, we were so looking forward to the interrogation. We had already been witness to the kinds of atrocities DOD perpetrated in their black sites—and this place, the Raven's Nest—was the black site to end all black sites. Even most people inside DOD itself had no idea of its existence, let alone what went on there in the name of American world supremacy."

His smile turned into a grimace. "But you showed up before we could get going. Who knew you and Lyudmila were friends? Who would even have imagined it? But you came and even after we worked you over for going off piste, for unauthorized access to a restricted facility, you managed to spring her."

"What was Lyudmila doing here?"

"What d'you think? Spying. You let her get away with a head full of secrets. *Our* secrets. She knew who we were; she recognized me on sight. We got to her before she could give us away. Then you showed up. By what sorcery you freed her and escaped with her into these tunnels is a complete mystery."

"I'll tell you if you tell me how you managed to make me forget what happened here."

Arkady grinned. "I don't mind telling you. In fact, it's a pleasure. Psychotropics, my dear Evan. Experimental drugs we were testing for your own DOD." His grin widened. "Now how did you effect your es—"

Evan struck him full on the nose with the heel of her hand. His head snapped back, and Brenda laughed as blood spurted from the center of his face.

"*Ach, scheisse!*" Arkady's voice was thick, his forearm covering his broken nose. "*Du Schwanzlutscher!*"

"What did he say?" Brenda asked.

"You don't want to know," Evan replied.

57

Arkady's revelations—about who was funding Nemesis, the truth about why Lyudmila and Evan had been at Raven's Nest, what had happened to them both there—momentarily clogged Evan's head. Her thoughts strayed, to Lyudmila, and then to her short-lived but intense relationship with Peter Limas, what they had been through together, and Peter's shocking, ignominious death at the hands of the lover he'd betrayed.

In that moment of introspection, Arkady broke away, sprinted down the salt mine tunnel. Brenda squeezed off a shot just before he vanished into the Stygian darkness, and then he was gone. The percussion startled Evan back to the present and she rushed forward, following after Arkady. But Brenda, gathering strength from her determination to punish this man, yet another who had breached her defenses, violated her mind and her person, brushed by her, running on bare feet, and was soon swallowed up by the darkness as well.

"Brenda, wait!"

Evan hurried on, swinging the flashlight's powerful beam from side to side. She did not go full tilt the way Arkady and his desperate pursuer had; she was on the lookout for trip wire and pressure-sensitive plates wired to buried bombs. Plenty had been cleaned out since the end of the war, but others remained in the abandoned sections of the mines. There were good reasons to keep miners and tourists out of these areas: detonations had been known to cause massive cave-ins and tragic loss of life.

But a growing concern for Brenda urged her forward, and if it wasn't for the beam of light she would have missed the trip wire, a shimmering thread of death. The beam moved beyond the trip wire but she saw no sign of footprints on the ground.

Backtracking, she went to her right, and there she spotted two sets of footprints—boots and bare feet—and she hurled herself down the tunnel.

She saw Brenda limned in her beam of light. "Over here, Evan!" Her face looked beatific. The way the beam of light caught her, her head seemed wreathed in a halo. "Over here, I have him cornered!"

"Brenda!" she called. "Brenda, be careful! Don't move! There are—!"

But the rest of the sentence was lost in the explosion that threw Evan off her feet. She fetched up flat on her back. The tunnel had vanished in the dense fog of powdered rock and debris. Jumping up, mouth and nose in the crook of her left arm, she pressed forward. The flashlight was of minimal use, the beam of light reflected back by the floating debris. She coughed, despite the protection her elbow offered.

The salt fog grew denser the farther she went. It became harder to breathe. Her eyes burned; they started tearing in order to protect themselves. It felt like daggers had lodged themselves in her eyes every time she blinked. Salt coated her hair, the tops of her shoulders, the backs of her hands, turning them white.

She saw Brenda then—or at least her hand. It was sticking out of a rock pile. Evan ran to her and, on her knees, cleared away the debris, revealing her wrist, then her forearm. But it was no use. Brenda's fingers were stiff and unmoving. They looked like they were made of bone, as if all the skin and flesh had been stripped off them.

Still, bent over her, Evan worked frantically to free her from her prison of salt. But like Lot's wife she had been turned into a pillar of salt. She had run too quickly after the human equivalent of Sodom. She had been unable to turn her back on evil, and for that she must be remembered.

While Evan bent over Brenda, the ghost from the depths of the salt mine came for her, leaping over the top of the mound the explosion had made. He caught Evan unprepared, and was on her before Evan had a chance to defend herself.

Arkady's hands grasped the sides of Evan's head in a viselike grip. He slammed her head against the ground, again and again. His mouth hung open, his eyes blazed out of a salt-caked face more animal than human. And once again Evan was reminded of Major, how connected the dog and the man were.

Arkady's open mouth loomed above her, teeth bared. He was snarling as he kept slamming Evan's head into the ground. Evan's vision was doubled, the edges gone black, as if she could see only what was directly in front of her.

Evan thought of Lyudmila and Bobbi, and she thought of Brenda, and of Peter Limas, who was Vasily Shokov. Vasily, who truly had no reality—nothing about him was what it had seemed to be. Evan was losing her train of thought, she was forgetting where she was, what was happening to her. She was lost in the forest of those lost to her.

And then the two ravens flew across her mind's eye. The ravens who had guided her when she saved Lyudmila, when their friendship was finally forged for eternity. And it was the ravens who saved her now. She fumbled in her pocket for the necklace she had taken off Marina Mevedeva's corpse. Reaching blindly up, she somehow succeeded in jamming those two silver ravens into Arkady's left eye. Using her thumb, she pressed them through the bursting eyeball, shredding the retina.

Arkady's scream echoed through the salt mines. His hands flew to his ruined eye. As he reared up, Evan smashed her fist into his ear, twisted her hips, throwing off Arkady's weight. Evan's head hung down, swinging back and forth like that of a wounded animal. They were both animals now, shedding whatever veneer civilization had provided.

It was only the two of them, wounded and in pain, sorrowful and vengeful in equal measure. Just the two of them, and Arkady, for all his wily feints and single-mindedness, was no match for Evan, though he tried his best, you had to give him that much, at least, but nothing else. Nothing at all. He was the cause of all this death and destruction. He was a one-man death camp in which humans were incinerated, body and soul.

And, in the end, there he was spitting blood, death close, creeping closer on little cat feet. He looked up at Evan with a single red-veined eye, and said in a thin, reedy voice that seemed to come from the place he was about to fall into, "Our only regret is Vasily is already dead. We would have wished him to know how we killed his mother, that bitch who betrayed us by fucking our best friend, and how much we loved doing it. We strung her up—"

"Stop," Evan said, crouched over him.

"Oh, no. We strung her up by her ankles and we koshered her. We ripped out her throat and bled her until there was no life in her. No life at all." He stared up at Evan, so close to death, unable to reflect a human expression. "How we wish we could have watched his face when we . . ."

And then he was gone, his eye staring into the infinite mystery.

Evan tossed Arkady away as if he were a rag doll. She was bleeding in several places, not the least of which was the back of her head, which hurt like hell. Nevertheless, she spent the next twenty minutes trying to free Brenda from her tomb, at the end of which time her nails were ragged, her fingers bleeding. There was too much on Brenda; she would need a bulldozer to free her. So Evan buried her carefully and fully, and tried not to think of what she had done to Vasily Shokov.

Afterward, she pulled the bloody ravens out of Arkady's eye, wiped them off until the silver shone up at her through the beam of light. Pocketing the pendant, she left that place of horror and death and, using signposts from her fully cleared memory, made her way through the labyrinth. But at some point her extreme exhaustion overcame the last of her adrenaline. She slid down, her back against the salt rock of the tunnel.

She tried to understand how Brenda could have killed Peter, Vasily, why her response to what he had done was so violent, but she failed. On the other hand maybe the answer was all too apparent. Living in the shadows, in the margins of society, changed you. How could it not? For some people—and it seemed increasingly clear Brenda was one—the sanctioned killing of another human being made the deed all too easy. And if you weren't careful, killing became something that you needed, something that you *wanted.* Without it, life was dull and uninteresting. You were lumped in with all the drones walking the streets, working from nine to five at jobs they hated, dieting and bingeing, watching the Kardashians or the Real Housewives of wherever, buying clothes they didn't need, squandering friendships, fucking people they hardly knew or cared to know. Who wanted that? Surely not Brenda. For her, the killing had already become addictive, and like a drug she had come to crave it more and more, to find reasons to keep killing. This was a truth of Evan's profession, but it was so disturbing, so enervating to confront, she turned her thoughts to another truth.

She missed Vasily, the name by which she chose to think of him now. His true name. What a strange life he must have lived, lied to about his father, moving from one country to another, from one identity to another, to another. How could he ever know who he really was? And that was the problem, Evan realized. If you don't know who you are it's impossible to form an allegiance, and for Vasily his only possible allegiance was to his beloved Aunt Lyudmila. Why hadn't Lyudmila told him the truth? Perhaps, with what she knew had become of her brother, Lyudmila believed Vasily wouldn't be safe if he knew the truth about his father, nor have any chance at all for a normal life.

Evan turned off the flashlight and rested then. She felt as close to death as she ever had.

At some point, she heard voices, sharply raised, calling to one another in Bavarian-accented German, and knew Die Raben were in the mines, searching for their leader and for her. She listened to them for some time with no thought of changing position in the slightest, and eventually they moved away, farther and farther, until their voices were lost in the echoes of the past.

The darkness closed in. Apart from her slow breathing and her steadfast heartbeat, silence.

EPILOGUE

SUMATRA
FEBRUARY

Lyudmila Alexeyevna was watching an orangutan when Evan came up beside her. The orangutan was female, her body half-hidden by enormous leaves of the rain forest, shining with moisture, and she was watching Lyudmila right back. In fact, it was impossible to tell who was checking out whom. There was about the orangutan a sense of welcome, of belonging from which Evan could not look away. Her eyes seemed wise as an owl's, as if behind them lived a very old soul that knew secrets humans would never know.

"Her name is Marie, after the little heroine of 'The Nutcracker,' who stood her ground against that gigantic mouse," Lyudmila said without taking her eyes off the orangutan. "That's the name I gave her, anyway. She seems okay with it. She comes every day at this time and I fancy we speak to each other with our eyes. Like old friends."

She turned to Evan, at last, touched the healing scar on Evan's cheek. "You found me."

Evan drew out the tiny wooden carving of a Sumatran naga morsarang. "This was unmistakable."

"Only to you."

Evan nodded. "Only to me." She fingered the carving.

"It's the twin of the one I have from the sweet sixteen trip I took Bobbi on."

"Indeed. You showed it to me once we got to know each other." She took a breath. "You once told me those were the happiest weeks of your life."

"I did?"

Lyudmila nodded.

Tears came to Evan's eyes. "Well, I suppose they were. London, Paris, Amsterdam, Copenhagen, and then all the way down here to Sumatra."

But still she was holding herself back, and Lyudmila, knowing her so well, recognized this.

"What's troubling you? There's something—"

"Why did you lie to Peter? I don't understand. Why would you tell him that you came to save me when it was the other way around?"

"Ah, that."

"Yes, that," Evan said firmly. "Your seemingly inexplicable action requires an answer."

"It does, indeed." Lyudmila hesitated. "Listen, Evan, you got to know Peter, you knew what he was like. He never would have been cut out for a field agent's life. That's why I spirited him away. But he got sucked in anyway, despite my best efforts.

"The truth is . . ." She sighed deeply. "I wanted Peter always to think of his aunt as invincible, to never doubt her." She looked at Evan imploringly. "You must see I had to keep that fiction alive for his sake, for my beautiful Peter."

She was weeping openly now, and Evan, her heart melting, drew her into her arms. They embraced then, holding each other close, kissing each other's cheeks. Lyudmila was careful of Evan's scar.

"You are forgiven," Evan whispered. "Peter was a special boy."

"Thinking what you thought, I'm so glad you came."

Lyudmila's ice-blue eyes were shining. Her blond hair was pulled back from her sharp-featured face. Her eyes drank Evan in in the way a thirsty woman drains a glass of water and asks for more. To Evan, she seemed even more beautiful than she remembered.

"I would never not come," Evan said. "And you are invincible, Lyudmila—or nearly so."

Lyudmila smiled through her tears. "You have a lot to tell me, I expect."

"Sadly, I do."

Lyudmila wiped her eyes with the back of her hand. "Everything is tinged with sorrow these days," she said. "Except here, where humans don't exist. Just the animals. A pure and simple life."

"Everyone is hoping you're dead." Evan very much hoped that Lyudmila would tell her how she managed the trick of vanishing so completely even the SVR and GRU couldn't find her. In time, she had faith she would.

"In a way, I am." Lyudmila turned back to Marie, smiled without showing her teeth. Marie responded in her own way, and Evan was entranced. "But I'm not the only one who has died with a secret," Lyudmila said.

Evan turned, her pulse ringing in her ears. "What's that supposed to mean?"

She saw now that Lyudmila had been holding a manila folder close to her side. She'd been so elated to see her friend, she hadn't noticed it until this moment when Lyudmila handed it to her.

"You need to read this." There was a look on Lyudmila's face she had never seen before, a curious mixture of determination and sorrow.

Evan found herself reluctant to open the folder. "What is it?"

"Just . . . go ahead."

The envelope contained a file with a black jacket. A crimson ribbon ran diagonally across the upper right-hand corner. Evan recognized the jacket. Of course she did. She'd been privy to a number of these. But, as it turned out, none like this one.

Evan's heart felt dipped in ice as she opened the file and saw an all too familiar face. Her head came up quickly, and she fixed Lyudmila with a basilisk stare. "This is a fake. It has to be."

But Lyudmila was shaking her head. "It isn't." She gave Evan a rueful smile. "For a dead person I've been quite busy setting up a clandestine network of people I can trust absolutely. One of them gave me this. I'm afraid it's straight from the SVR central server."

"But my sister . . ."

Evan couldn't find it in herself to finish, so Lyudmila did it for her.

"Your sister was a sleeper agent."

Evan felt the earth beneath her feet drop out from under her; the world tilted on end. Nothing made sense anymore. "I don't . . . I can't fathom how that's possible."

"That's what we're going to find out."

Evan was momentarily bewildered. "We?"

Lyudmila stepped close enough to grip Evan's arm. "You're going to need my help." When Evan shook her head, she said, "There's more." She nodded at the file. "Keep reading."

Evan closed her eyes for a moment. "For the love of God, just tell me."

"It will be better if you read it for yourself."

"Later," Evan said. "For now, I want to hear it from you."

Lyudmila sighed. "All right then. Your sister was part of Directorate 52123, we think within the SVR."

"But there is no Directorate 52123 within either the SVR or the FSB, so far as I know," Evan said. "The number doesn't even conform to the Russian directorate standard *nomenklatura*."

Lyudmila nodded. "True, which is why we're not

sure Directorate 52123 is part of SVR." She reached out, tapped the open page. "In fact, it's so secretive no one I've contacted is aware of its existence, or can find any trace of it. The sole evidence of Directorate 52123 is in this file."

"Which was in the SVR central server."

"Very, very deep within it."

Now Evan did scan the first three pages, saw everything Lyudmila had just told her, and more. Bobbi had been recruited at the age of sixteen, in Copenhagen. It was Bobbi's choice to go to Copenhagen. She said she'd held a childhood dream of falling in love with a tall, handsome Nordic man, and wanted to give it a chance to come true. Instead, inexplicably, she fell in love with Russia. How? A tall, blond Russian? Evan felt on the verge of weeping with despair and rage. The best weeks of her life, and Bobbi was being seduced into being a traitor to her country, her very way of life.

"I can't go on not knowing how she was recruited." Evan's voice was clotted with emotion. "And why."

Lyudmila nodded. "As you say, I say."

Evan's eyes grew large, and now at last the tears fell. She pulled her friend into her embrace. "Thank you," she whispered. "Thank you."

"Revenge has become our way of life," Lyudmila whispered. "Now we enter the darkness."

ACKNOWLEDGMENTS

Certain facts within this novel require acknowledgment, for they come from proper sources—sources who cannot be named, let alone written about. Nevertheless, I want to once again thank those sources for their help and advice. Of course, by definition, this being a work of fiction, facts are only a basis for extrapolation. So any inaccuracies are my responsibility, not theirs.

I wish to thank my agent, Mitch Hoffman, for his patience and many kindnesses, as well as for his sage advice. Thank you to Linda Quinton, my publisher and friend, for her ongoing belief in me. Thank you to my publisher and friend, the one-of-a-kind Tom Doherty, for making me feel like a member of the Tor/Forge family.

Thank you to my editor and wife, the author Victoria Lustbader, for her love and support, and for her keen and expert care and feeding of my manuscripts. Without you, well, I just don't know. . . .

Read on for a preview of

THE KOBALT DOSSIER

ERIC VAN LUSTBADER

Available in spring/summer 2021
from Tom Doherty Associates

A FORGE HARDCOVER

PROLOGUE

THREE AND A HALF YEARS AGO

"The obliteration of the face," Anouk said, "is essential." She regarded Bobbi Fisher with her gray-flannel eyes. "This point cannot be stressed enough. Without complete obliteration it may be possible to forensically retrieve the teeth." She lifted a long forefinger. "Even one tooth can be enough for identification, and you will be undone. Exfiltration cannot be accomplished."

She paused, a broad-shouldered woman with muscular arms, thick legs, and features as blunt as a weapon. Bobbi had turned her head to check the closed door to the square room—a kitchen that had been turned into an ad hoc classroom. Bobbi sat on a high stool at the central polished concrete island. By her right hand was a pitcher of ice water and a glass tumbler. Fists of rain beat against the streaked windows, blurring the restless trees that separated this two-story house from the identical ones around it. The rain-swept streets were as clean and clear as one would expect in a new development in Virginia, suburban sprawl of DC.

"Bobbi." Anouk's voice was as sharp as a knife blade. "What are you looking at? You are required to pay strict attention."

"Where is Leda?" Bobbi said without looking back.

"I am here now, Bobbi." Anouk, standing beside the

refrigerator, arms at her side, hands half-curled, stood as straight as a sentry. "It is to me that you report."

Bobbi's head snapped around. "My condition when I was recruited was that Leda—and only Leda—would be my handler."

Anouk's smile bared her small white teeth. "That was some years ago," she said. "Leda has moved on."

"Then I should have moved on with her."

Anouk pursed her lips in distaste. "You had an affair with Leda, didn't you?"

"That's none of your business."

"Everything about you is my business, Bobbi. You should know that." When no reply was forthcoming, Anouk went on: "It was quite torrid, from the reports I've read."

"Damn you."

"Ah." Anouk grinned like a crocodile. "At last I have your undivided attention."

"Indeed, you do."

"Well, then, you should know that Leda is dead."

"Dead? No."

"Purged." Anouk sneered. "And I can easily arrange for you to follow her."

Bobbi rose from the stool. "Is that a threat?"

Anouk shrugged. "You'd better get used to it; it's my method."

Grasping the tumbler Bobbi drained it of water. "I want something else," she said. "Something sweeter." She walked the length of the counter, to where Anouk stood. "Excuse me." Anouk moved just enough so Bobbi could reach down for the handle of the half refrigerator tucked beneath the counter.

As she opened the refrigerator door, she smashed the tumbler against the edge of the counter. Anouk's arm was coming but, anticipating, Bobbi grabbed her wrist, controlling it. Anouk was stronger than Bobbi, but Bobbi had the leverage, and, in any case, she only needed a split second to drive a knifelike shard into Anouk's left eye. Anouk jumped as if electrified. Bobbi kept tight hold of the bottom of the tumbler, ground it farther and farther, until the tip of the shard pierced Anouk's brain.

She stepped smartly back, avoiding both the corpse's collapse and the last spurts of blood. The kitchen's door opened. She turned to see Leda step smartly inside, close the door behind her.

Leda smiled. Everything about her was medium: height, weight, features, and yet there was something about her, something magnetic that was almost a physical thing. You might not recall her if she passed you on the street, but if you sat down opposite her in a bar or restaurant for drinks, you'd be hard-pressed to pull away.

She didn't even bother checking out the sprawled body, merely stepped over it as she crossed the large square room. "You haven't lost your reflexes, I see," she said.

"Or my rage."

The two women embraced.

"Fisher. I never could get used to your married name."

Bobbi shrugged. "What's in a name?"

Leda chuckled. "It's been a long time since we've seen each other."

Bobbi nodded, a smile wreathing her face. "Too long. Texts are no substitute for the real thing."

They kissed, then broke away. Though it was a businesslike kiss, their eyes were shining, a remnant of what once was.

A man and a woman in boilersuits and latex gloves entered, but Leda bade them wait with a commanding wave of her hand. Now she crouched down, examining Anouk's corpse with the thoroughness of a forensic pathologist. When she rose, she said, "*Idem.*" *Come on.*

Leda led her through the sparsely furnished living

room and into a space that would someday be a den or a media room, leaving the suited and gloved pair to clean up the blood and get rid of the remains.

Bobbi's eyes narrowed. "She knew about our affair."

"Did she?"

"She said she read about it in reports."

"That was an out-and-out lie."

"Really?" Bobbi cocked her head. "But isn't that your job: to recruit through seduction?"

"Seduction is only part of my job description. A small part—or, more accurately, a *selective* part. I'm much more elevated than a sparrow, else I wouldn't be here now, with you. I am your handler."

"But you have seduced others."

Leda's expression turned enigmatic, as if two or more thoughts had occurred to her at once. "You're jealous."

"Of your time, not of your charms."

"Perhaps," Leda said. "Listen to me, Bobbi. I did seduce you. Yes, I did. Without question. But let's not mince words: you wanted to be seduced."

Bobbi thought about this, thought about how right Leda was. She *did* want to be seduced. Badly. Perhaps desperately. Was that need a weakness in her? If so, she would do well to eradicate it. On the other hand, she was where she wanted to be, so why should she care about the rest? And yet, she did. She had an innate abhorrence of weakness in any form. With an almost physical wrench, she returned her thoughts to the present. "You didn't answer my question: how did Anouk know about our affair?"

"Well, now," Leda said with a twinkle in her eye, "that's an excellent question."

A silence yawned between them. Behind the kitchen door scuffling, muted sounds of the cleanup in progress. Otherwise the house, being new, was very still.

Then Bobbi had it. "*You* told her."

Leda laughed softly. "It did get your blood up, her knowing, didn't it?"

All at once, it seemed obvious. "So this was a test." It wasn't a question.

"Oh, it was more than that."

"Seriously?"

"You were always meant for greater things, Bobbi. I hand chose you. I didn't seduce you on a whim or because I detected a weakness. You did not hold a position advantageous to us."

"No." A slow smile. "Evan is like an impenetrable vault."

"Well," Leda said, "we'll see about that."

Bobbi frowned. "Meaning?'

"You will see." Leda went to the kitchen and returned with an ice-rimed bottle of vodka, two spotted water glasses, and a manila envelope, also ice-rimed, tucked firmly under her arm. She poured triple shots into both water glasses and handed one to Bobbi. Leda lifted her glass high and Bobbi followed suit. They drank in the Russian fashion, all in one. They were clearly toasting something, Bobbi's graduation? Anouk's death? Bobbi had no idea what.

Leda set aside her glass. "Anouk was your final exam," she said as if reading Bobbi's mind. "Your schooling has been long, I know. And now you have graduated summa cum laude. As a consequence, two weeks from now Bobbi Ryder Fisher will cease to exist. She will die. And from then on you will be known only by a new operational name I will give you when you leave here."

"A new life." Her eyes flicked to the envelope, but she said nothing. She knew to wait.

Leda nodded. "It's what we promised you. It's what you wanted above all else. Is that still true?"

Bobbi was incredulous. "Of course!" She had married

knowing what would happen someday. Paul had insisted on kids and, frankly, when consulted Leda was all for it, wisely saying that it would only deepen Bobbi's cover. "*But there's a risk,*" she had warned. "*A mother's love can—*" "*I have no trace of a maternal instinct,*" Bobbi had interrupted. "*I don't see the point of children, not in this day and age.*" And Leda had been satisfied.

"Nothing whatsoever has changed since I was read the terms of my recruitment."

"Then to your first—and last—assignment in DC." Leda returned to the refrigerator, removed a five-by-seven photo, which she handed to Bobbi. It was a head-and-shoulders shot, the image lacking vivid color, flattened due to the long-lens surveillance camera with which it had been taken. "You know this woman, yes?"

"Of course," Bobbi said. "It's Benjamin Butler's wife, Lila."

"She's a friend of yours," Leda said, "yes?"

"You want me to go to Berlin?"

"Mrs. Butler arrived here this morning," Leda said. "Her father isn't well."

Bobbi considered this for a moment. "It was you who made him unwell, wasn't it?"

"Well, not me personally," Leda said, half-offended. "But, yes, it was achieved on my order."

"So the end could come here, where I am."

Leda's smile spread slowly, like butter in sunlight. "You are my best pupil, Bobbi. I knew it the first time I laid eyes on you, in Copenhagen when you were seventeen. We're like family now."

"How?" Bobbi said. "How could you know I'd be your best pupil?"

"Between you and your sister you were the one having fun."

"I was enjoying life."

"No," Leda said. "You were devouring it."

▪ ▪ ▪

Forty-eight hours later and after a brief respite the rain had persevered, though reduced to a drizzle. The residents inside the Beltway, umbrellas unfurled, hurried along slick sidewalks. Those bravely, or foolishly, without sprinted toward crowded doorways or shimmering awnings.

Bobbi saw Lila Butler before Lila saw her. She had texted Lila the day before, made a date for a shopping expedition and lunch, "to take your mind off your father," she'd said. Lila had been openly grateful for both the break and the company of an old friend, giving Bobbi the sense that living in Berlin was starting to grate on Lila. Bobbi had a remedy for that.

She looked both ways, waited several moments, checking her wristwatch for the time. Her heart rate picked up as she crossed the street against the light to intercept Lila before she turned in to the department store where they'd arranged to meet.

Beneath Lila's umbrella, they embraced. Lila had always been birdlike, but now she was thinner, paler, and the wetness on her cheeks was tears, not raindrops. Bobbi's hunch had been right: Berlin did not agree with her.

Bobbi first asked after Lila's father's health. It was failing, quickly. Bobbi wondered what Leda's people had given him. Only then did she ask about Berlin.

Lila sighed deeply. "Berlin is so gray," she said. "And the people . . ." Lila shivered. "They're friendly on the surface. Maybe too friendly. Underneath there seems a darkness—the river Styx running through them. And now the immigrant issue has given a fervent raison d'etre to the neo-Nazi movement."

They were standing at the curb in order to avoid the crowds of foot traffic along the sidewalk, shoulders touching beneath Lila's umbrella. Bobbi placed a gentle hand on Lila's arm, bony as a sparrow's wing.

"I'm sorry you're unhappy," Bobbi said with one eye on the oncoming traffic. "How about Zoe. How's she doing?"

"Unlike me, Zoe loves it over there. But then again she's four so her world is as small as any four-year-old's."

"Be sure to give her my love, though I doubt she remembers me."

"Of course she remembers you," Lila exclaimed. "She remembers everything and everyone."

Bobbi smiled. She saw the SUV. Its rain-streaked tinted windows reflected the buildings and the low sky as if in a fun house mirror. "When do you think you might all come home?"

Lila shrugged. "I don't know. Ben's still got business over there."

"Of course. So, how long will you be in DC now?"

"That will depend on my father's condition. But I already miss Zoe."

"Your father's health aside, and even missing Zoe," Bobbi said, "I think the trip back here will be good for you, even if it's only for a few days. Berlin is so gloomy, isn't it?"

"*So* gloomy." Lila smiled. Bobbi had forgotten how the space around her lit up when she smiled. "I'm so glad you contacted me." Lila gave Bobbi's arm a brief squeeze. "I can't tell you how good it feels to see a friendly face. Things are pretty grim at my parents' place." And she leaned in to give Bobbi a peck on the cheek.

Which was when Bobbi appeared to stumble off the curb. She swung Lila around. Off-balance, Lila's umbrella tilted, shielding them from the eyes of the bustling crowd on the sidewalk. Bobbi let go of her elbow and hip-bumped her, hard, directly into the path of the SUV, now speeding toward them.

Bobbi had started moving away even before the sound

reached her ears, the *thunk,* heavy, wet, ominous. She eeled her way through the crowd at precisely the same pace as those around her. Behind her came the squeal of tires, screams, shouts, and the crowd began to press toward the curb, attracted to the scene like mice to cheese. The approaching wail of sirens found her on the fourth floor of the department store, shielded by a forest of expensive designer dresses, heading toward the escalator down to the entrance on the far side of the store.

www.ingramcontent.com/pod-product-compliance
Lightning Source LLC
LaVergne TN
LVHW050912080826
845145LV00001B/64

* 9 7 8 1 2 5 0 3 5 6 7 4 1 *